D0966523

DEC   2018

MAGE AGAINST THE MACHINE

MAGE AGAINST THE MACHINE

SHAUN BARGER

SAGA PRESS

LONDON SYDNEY **NEW YORK** TORONTO NEW DELHI

SAGA PRESS
AN IMPRINT OF SIMON & SCHUSTER, INC.
1230 AVENUE OF THE AMERICAS, NEW YORK, NEW YORK 10020

TO CAITY—

> *for the profoundly stated nonsense of your*
> *fever dreams, and your ceaseless enthusiasm*
> *for mine.*

TO MOM—

> *for that same enthusiasm, and for making*
> *sure that I stayed kind. The whole "teaching*
> *me to write" thing was pretty useful, too.*
>
> *(Let's not forget the thousands of pages of*
> *pro-bono editing you've both done.)*

FINALLY, TO JOSH AND ANNA—

> *for being way cooler than I was at their age.*

YOU = THE GODDAMN BEST.

PART I.

A DOOR IN THE SKY

I.

AMERICAN WIZARD

A mage in black followed a trail of footprints through the darkness of a thickly wooded forest, unseen.

The trail had been left by a dead man who'd been speaking to his revolver, last the mage had seen him. Anxiously eyeing the shadows between the trees, he wondered if the rune-etched firearm had responded.

The mage was young—barely out of training—with dark, carefully tousled hair and a slight frown that might have seemed permanent to those who didn't know him well. His replica high-top sneakers squelched wetly in the sodden moss as he tracked the dead man's steps, which shimmered with a golden light through Nikolai's enchanted spectacles.

Nikolai Strauss was being stupid. He *knew* that he was being stupid. His first actual assignment and he'd already lied to his team—to his friends. Already defied his orders to: *Observe. Do not engage. Report immediately should the buyer be spotted.*

Technically, Nikolai wasn't really even on this case. He'd been a cadet until a few months ago. The Edge Guard insignia on the breast of his uniform was so freshly made that the enchantments still tickled when he brushed his fingers across the slick enamel surface.

This was supposed to be some simple field experience for training—a low-risk opportunity for Nikolai to observe more experienced Edge Guard agents working the field as they staked out an illegal artifact exchange. They probably wouldn't have even brought him with them all the way from the capital if the buy hadn't been going down in Marblewood, Nikolai's hometown.

The captain had suggested that Nikolai's relationships with the citizens of Marblewood might come in handy should they find themselves short on leads.

Though Nikolai hadn't kept in touch with anybody from his hometown (and would have preferred to keep it that way) the intel implicating the Eaglesmith family had smothered his protests.

He was indifferent to the family as a whole. His scorn was reserved for his former classmate, Joseph Eaglesmith, rich-kid golden-boy athlete and longtime boyfriend of Nikolai's estranged childhood sweetheart.

Nikolai hated the prick. And now, for his pettiness, here he was. Alone. In the dark. Following a possibly demented Battle Mage with a magic gun.

Sure, Nik was also a Battle Mage, well versed in the magical arts of violence. He was a member of the Edge Guard, a powerful government order charged with the defense and maintenance of magical domed Veils that hid the magi from the ruined human world, which had been reduced to lifeless, magically radioactive wastelands a century prior, in 2020.

The Edge Guard also investigated crimes that fell under the jurisdiction of multiple Veils.

But mostly, Nikolai got coffee.

Nikolai was happy to just get coffee for his senior teammates, leaving them to handle the dull responsibilities of the stakeout. To nod and say "Yessir" at all the right moments, occasionally jotting a note into the margin of whatever novel he currently had his nose buried in.

The problem was, Nikolai was now pretty sure that their entire reason for being there was bullshit. That there'd never been any artifact smugglers—that the intel was just a ruse. Bait, specifically set to draw Nikolai back to his hometown, away from the watchful eyes of the capitol. The Eaglesmith family's involvement was a juicy worm wriggling at the end of a hook.

Nikolai hadn't said much about his life back in Marblewood to his fellow Edge Guards. From what little he'd let slip, however, his thinly veiled grudge against the rising flyball star had featured prominently. After a couple of drinks, at least.

The mage who'd set the bait had once been Nikolai's mentor. His *friend*, even. And Nikolai knew that if his superiors got to him first, he'd never have a chance to speak to Hazeal alone. Never have a chance to ask without supervision why his former mentor had gone to such lengths to contact Nikolai. Or how the hell he wasn't *dead*.

His old mentor had first made contact when Nikolai was on his way back from a cafe half a block from the stakeout earlier that day, three boiling hot coffees floating precariously before him on a tray of hardened air that looked like frosted glass.

"I have a message from your mother," came a voice so quietly that Nikolai might have imagined it.

He spun around, searching, scanning the bustling pedestrian crowd until he found a swarthy, middle-aged mage (whom Nikolai had almost certainly never seen before) staring at him from across the street, under the awning of a butcher shop.

Everything about the mage was forgettable. He was neither ugly nor attractive, wearing a plain charcoal topcoat over a suit that might be found in the closet of any clerical mage with a middling desk job. The only noteworthy thing about him was his conical, wide-brimmed hat, which was normally only worn with formal robes.

Still, there was something about the mage that put Nikolai on alert. His hand, hovering twitchy and trembling at his hip. His eyes, wild and tight with pain.

The stranger pinched the rim of his hat and the illusory disguise pulled away in neatly angular folds of colorful light to reveal a mage that Nikolai knew quite well.

His name was Hazeal. *Lieutenant* Armand Hazeal. The kindest of Nikolai's teachers during cadet boot camp in the capitol, who'd always gone out of his way to make sure that Nikolai, more than any of his other students, was managing well both as an Edge Guard trainee and a young, small-town mage adjusting to life in the big city.

Killed just six months prior, in a scuffle with a pair of corrupt Watchmen.

So they'd been told. There'd even been a funeral.

Underneath his disguise, Hazeal was sweating, filthy, and appeared to have aged ten years since Nikolai had seen him last. A strange revolver hung holstered at his hip, surface etched with runes that pulsed as Hazeal pushed aside his topcoat to grip the pommel.

Nik had been so dumbfounded at the appearance of his old teacher that he momentarily neglected maintaining the spell he'd used to create a tray for the coffees.

"Sh-shit—*akro!*" He'd cast too late, whipping out a half-formed blob of the glassy substance in a fruitless attempt to catch all three drinks. One of the boiling brews poured harmlessly down the defensive enchantments of Nikolai's Edge Guard jumpsuit uniform, but reflexively he yelped and dropped the rest as he danced back.

When Nikolai looked back up, Hazeal seemed to be engaged in a furious hissed debate with the revolver. Noticing Nikolai's gaze, Hazeal angrily tugged his coat back over the holstered weapon and released his pinched fingers from the brim of his hat—the illusory folds of his disguise snapping back into place.

"Find me where she used to hurt you," he said, once again barely audible from across the busy street. Then, with a strange smile, he tipped his hat at Nikolai and darted away into the crowds.

Though reeling from the words and the flood of traumatic memories that came with them, Nikolai managed to fire a tracer enchantment onto the back of Hazeal's coat before completely losing sight of him. Then, struggling to maintain some semblance of calm, the young mage took off sprinting toward the building where his team was hidden on their stakeout.

The Edge Guard trio had spent the past four days holed up in a dusty apartment across the street from the secondary Eaglesmith estate, practicing the art of silent patience while they waited for their covert surveillance wards to trigger any sign of activity.

Nikolai's first superior officer, Junior Lieutenant Ilyana Xue, passed the time between shifts by working out, chain-smoking from a long-stemmed cigarette holder, and experimenting with various chemicals and potions—with occasionally explosive results.

There was a crass sort of elegance about Ilyana. She had the swaggering, smarmy charm of a trust-fund troublemaker, despite her oft-voiced contempt for the upper class she was obviously a product of.

Nikolai's second superior officer, Junior Lieutenant Albert Cross, wrote letters to his extensive noble family, bid extravagantly on remote auctions for rare art, artifacts, and grimoires, and caught up on the hottest new Schwartzwaldian operas: tiny stages vivid on postcard glossies from his sister, audio quietly resonating from a polished copper memory cube. He'd idly translate lyrical snippets from French, German, and Italian, explaining the plots while Ilyana and Nik politely feigned interest.

Ilyana and Albert were only a couple years older than Nikolai, and now just one rank higher. Though they'd initially taken him under their wing as informal big-bro/big-sis mentors, in the two years since he moved to the capitol to join the Edge Guard they'd become Nikolai's closest friends. Maybe his *only* friends, considering how long it had been since he'd spoken to anyone from Marblewood.

They looked up with shock as Nikolai burst into the cramped apartment.

"Just ran into my ex," he lied in a rush. "Said I'd grab a quick drink with her, you guys don't mind, right? I'll be back in an hour, maybe more, sorry *bye!*"

And off Nik had gone, his two supervising officers too startled to argue as he pursued Hazeal into the thickly shadowed depths of Marblewood's forest.

Nikolai had recently graduated the Edge Guard's sparsely

populated cadet training academy with the rare honor of *highest distinction*—a fact that he was always sure to teasingly remind Albert and Ilyana of, who, without the edge unpleasantly afforded to Nikolai by the brutal training he'd endured as a child from his Edge Guard mother, had merely graduated with *distinction*.

For the first time, Nikolai felt a true appreciation for the immense scope of drills and training he'd received as a cadet, covering everything from tactical featherweight acrobatics to covert urban and wilderness tracking—the latter of which he was, at that moment, specifically grateful for.

The afternoon sun grew soft in the wood, the dappled light dim across Hazeal's fading footsteps that Nikolai could see through his government-issued tracking spectacles. Hazeal's tracer was no longer moving up ahead, and it wouldn't be much longer before he'd catch up to the disturbed mage.

With every step closer he took to his former teacher, Nikolai grew more apprehensive—his initial confidence that Hazeal would never hurt him growing less and less certain. But as his fear grew, so did his curiosity.

A message. *From his mother.* Had Nikolai heard him correctly?

His parents had been dead for a decade. Killed in a skycraft crash when Nikolai was only ten.

Ashley Strauss, his mother, had also been a member of the Edge Guard. Lancer Class—the highest rank attainable, required for expeditions beyond the Veil, into the ruins of the human world.

Hazeal claimed to have only known Ashley in passing—praising her brilliance and lamenting her loss whenever Nikolai had asked, but no more so than any of the other Edge Guards who'd served with his mother. If anything, Hazeal had been more reticent than most. As if he hadn't actually liked her very much, but knew better than to say so. Though it was obvious they'd never been close.

So what could Hazeal *possibly* have to tell Nikolai about his mother?

Nikolai wondered if Captain Jubal, the commander of the Edge Guard, knew that Hazeal was still alive. Nikolai was extremely fond of the captain, and couldn't imagine that he would have lied to them about it.

Maybe Hazeal was undercover, and the funeral had been a government-sanctioned farce. But why would an undercover agent who'd gone so far as faking his own death reveal himself to a lowly sergeant?

Second possibility: Hazeal was dirty, and was going to trick or manipulate Nikolai into helping him with some sort of espionage. Maybe he was corrupt—maybe he'd gotten deep into some shit and the Moonwatch had caught wind of it. Maybe he'd faked his own death to get out of Dodge, and not even Captain Jubal was the wiser.

But Hazeal? Corrupt? It just didn't fit. He was a family man with a long career in the Edge Guard. He liked expensive tea and cooking extravagant meals for his children and grandchildren on the weekends. He was respected, and, well, a little bit boring.

So if Hazeal *had* faked his own death, then why? And what did any of that have to do with Nik's mother? Nikolai had to know.

If he told the others about seeing him, not even Ilyana would hesitate to call in the higher-ups. She was fiercely loyal to the captain, and Albert, though less fond of Jubal than Ilyana and Nikolai, was a strictly by-the-books kind of mage.

"Hello, Nikolai."

Nik wheeled around with a stifled yelp, barely resisting the terrified knee-jerk urge to blast his former teacher with a thousand degrees of boiling flame. The tracer remained stationary a mile or so north—but then Nikolai noticed that Hazeal was no longer wearing the coat.

Damn. He must have found the enchantment.

Hazeal idly spun the chamber of the rune-etched revolver. His smile was weary, his eyes unfocused as he stared through the spot where Nikolai stood, hidden from view by a thin layer of magical invisibility.

Hazeal's voice was soft. Raspy.

"No, no, I can't see you." He popped the chamber into the revolver, admiring the weapon. "But this can."

"Lieu . . . Lieutenant." Nikolai tried and failed to keep the tremor from his voice.

"Not lieutenant." He chuckled bitterly. "Not even a mage anymore."

Only then, with Hazeal no longer wearing his coat, did Nikolai notice the absence of the ivory staff and the jeweled whip that used to hang at his sides. His Focals. Objects much like a wizard's wand from one of the old human stories—objects a mage *never* went without, due to the weakening of power they would suffer without a Focal to channel their spells.

Nikolai looked him up and down, sure that he must have them hidden away. But no, he realized with horror—they were gone.

Hazeal's pleasant expression slipped into irritation.

"If I'm going to kill you, there's nothing you can do about it. Even without my magic. Not even the Mage King could stop a bullet from this gun. So please drop the cloak. I like to look a mage in the eyes when I discuss matters of importance."

Nikolai bit back a growled response at the threat, considering whether or not it was a bluff. But the mage—*half-mage* now, apparently—gripped the revolver more tightly with every passing moment.

"Okay. Please don't shoot, Lieu . . . Armand. I just want to talk."

The weaves of invisibility melted from Nikolai like mercurial foam.

Hazeal smiled, eye twitching. The fingers holding the revolver remained tense. He reached over his free hand to caress the papery skin of his gun hand, as if calming an animal.

"I thought you were dead," Nikolai said. Careful now. "The captain sent us here to investigate an . . . artifact exchange."

Nik glanced down at the gun.

"Don't look at it *don't look at it DON'T LOOK AT IT!*" Hazeal snarled, weathered face pulling back in animal terror as he closed the distance between them.

Nikolai stood, frozen, eyes locked with Hazeal's, inches from his own. Trembling. Unmoving.

Hazeal let out a long sigh.

"You have to be careful," he said. "It's sleepy now. I've used it too much, since I lost my magic. Been its servant for too long. It's a powerful weapon, Nikolai. And the *knowledge* it carries! The spells! But it's like snatching gold from a dragon's mouth."

Hazeal chuckled, pale eyes twinkling, and for the briefest moment Nikolai saw the shadow of the jovial mage he'd once been. But then Hazeal flinched, whipping his head back and forth as he looked around the clearing, seeming to have forgotten how he got there. Then he looked back at Nikolai, the weathered lines of his face going slack.

"I'll be dead soon, and I'm a half-mage now. My soul is . . . withered. When I die, I'm just going to turn off. Whatever lies in the Disc, whatever afterlife or void might await normal magi—I'll no longer have the opportunity to discover what that might be. So why not deal with the devil?"

"Do you really have a message from my mother?" Nik asked, voice barely above a whisper.

The smile returned, the half-mage's eyes clearing. He pointed up.

"Do you know what's out there?" he said. "Beyond the sky? Outside of our domes, our Veils?"

Nik hesitated, unsure of where Hazeal was going with this. "Of course."

The chaos of shattered reality and radioactive wastelands. The end result of a magically enhanced nuclear exchange that killed off mankind a century before, in 2020. Lancer Class Edge Guard regularly braved the desolation, carefully documenting their expeditions for the largely disinterested public.

Nikolai had seen it all.

"Do you now?" Hazeal chuckled. "I've seen it, you know. With my own eyes. It's as terrible as you think. But not in the way you suspect."

Nikolai eyed him, impatience starting to mingle with fear. In the year since he'd last seen the old mage, Hazeal had turned into the fucking Cheshire cat.

Hazeal drew a handkerchief from his pocket, mopping his weathered brow.

"Your mother was the one who brought me there," he said, folding the handkerchief into an uneven rectangle with trembling fingers. "It's what killed her, in the end."

Nikolai froze. "What . . . are you talking about?"

"I owe your mother a great debt, Nikolai. To say the least. But now, that debt is paid."

Hazeal reached into his pocket, serpent quick, and tossed

Nikolai a slick medallion. Nik ignored his instinct to slap it away with a swipe of his baton. He caught it, powerful enchantments burning cold against his skin.

Nikolai eyed the shimmering medallion in his palm as if he'd been handed a grenade. A dimly luminescent crescent moon set against the illusion of star-spangled sky. The rank insignia of the Moonwatch—a clandestine network of the most powerful living Battle Magi serving as royal assassins, spies, and secret police, as well as the only order to outrank the Edge Guard.

It was the king's own license. A key to any lock.

"I lost my magic fighting a Moonwatch to get that for you," he said, through gritted teeth. "Burned myself out. Should be a few weeks before they realize the owner is dead. Hide it. No, don't just put it in your pocket, I said *hide it!*"

Slowly, Nikolai slipped off his sneaker and stowed the medallion away, never taking his eyes off Hazeal as the old half-mage's expression flitted madly between sorrow, rage, and euphoria.

Hazeal clamped the handkerchief on the revolver's grip and drew it from its holster. Nikolai tensed, reaching for his Focals as he prepared to dive aside and kill the half-mage. But Hazeal wasn't trying to shoot Nikolai. Careful not to let his fingers touch the rune-etched steel, he offered it to Nikolai, pommel first.

"This was your mother's. She wanted you to have it."

Nikolai eyed the revolver suspiciously, not moving to take it. "I thought you said you had a message for me."

"A message, and gifts," he said, eye twitching impatiently. "The insignia, so you can go see what kind of men you're really working for. Especially that murderer. That fucking butcher."

"Who?"

Hazeal's cracked lips widened into an unpleasant smile. "Why, your precious Captain Jubal, of course. But don't take my word for it. Look to his library, and see for yourself."

Nikolai furrowed his brow, incredulous. "And the revolver?"

"She wanted you to use it. Wanted you to finish what she couldn't."

"Finish what? Use it for *what*?"

"The gun will teach you the secrets of manipulating Veil with the *apocrypha* weave, if you ask it to. To make a door in the sky." He looked up at the lush roof of leaves fiery red with autumn, his eyes lit with a junkie's wild gleam. "So you can see what the human world is like, for yourself."

"Why don't you save me the trouble and just fucking tell me?" Nikolai snarled, eyeing the revolver like it was a venomous insect.

Hazeal whimpered, suddenly appearing quite frail. "Please, Nikolai. I'm not supposed to, I don't understand why. It won't hurt you. I promise it won't. I'm only this way as punishment. For what I did."

"Punishment? For what?"

His eyes welled up with tears. "Your mother died because of me. She—"

"My mom and dad died in a skycraft accident," Nikolai said, cutting him off. "How is that your fault?"

"No, Nikolai. I'm afraid that's not what really happened. The crash was just a cover, for an embarrassment to the crown."

The realization that Hazeal was telling the truth hit Nikolai like a steel-toed kick in the balls. Though he wasn't surprised—not really. How could that terrifying woman have possibly been killed by something so mundane as a crash?

"She trusted me," Hazeal continued. "Asked for my help. But I *lied*. Pretended I was on her side, then ratted her out. Swallowed my guilt and moved on with my life, until six months ago I found a parcel. Shelved among my books, covered in an inch of dust, as if it'd been there for years. But I'd never seen it before."

Perspiration darkened the handkerchief clenched around the gun from fingers visibly straining with effort.

"Your mother discovered my treachery too late to save herself and the others, but apparently with enough time to leave a vengeful little gift for me—enchanted to remain hidden until enough years had passed for you to become a fully-fledged Edge Guard. Which she never doubted you would. I went out of my way to show you kindness when you joined the Edge Guard as a cadet, to alleviate my own guilt. But when I opened that parcel to find the revolver . . . your mother's messenger made it quite clear that my debts were far from paid. So *please*. Take the gun. I'll give you her message afterward, just *please*. Let me be done with this."

"How do I know this isn't a trick? None of this makes sense. How am I supposed to believe you?" Nikolai shook his head. "No. Give me the message first."

"Please, Nikolai . . ."

"Message first. Then we'll see."

Hazeal paled, hesitating.

"She hurt you, when you were a child. In this very forest. Every morning. For years. And then . . . in the end . . . before she died . . ."

Nikolai flinched, feeling as if he'd been slapped. "Stop."

". . . she hurt you even more. The worst she'd ever hurt you."

"I said *stop*. Shut up!"

"She needed you to know that she never wanted to hurt you. That she was sorry. So very sorry. And even though she could never ask you to forgive her for the pain she caused you . . . she hopes that this final inheritance might make up for it, at least in part. That once you possess the revolver, she can be at peace knowing that no one will ever be able to hurt you again."

Hazeal's haggard features softened as he watched Nikolai, who felt smaller with every word.

"I don't know what it means, Nikolai. I don't know what she did to you. But . . . that final, terrible thing. Does anybody but you know about it?"

Nikolai grew dizzy, blood pounding in his ears as he struggled against the onslaught of horrible memories.

"N . . . no."

"This isn't a trick. Your mother was a deeply flawed woman. But she loved you. And I know for a fact that she would have destroyed whole cities to keep you safe."

Hazeal took a step closer, eyes brimming with a concerned, fatherly warmth. Revolver still held aloft for Nikolai to take.

Nikolai took the gun.

An overwhelming sensation—an almost liquid pleasure—seeped into the skin of his fingertips as a woman's voice whispered promises of secrets and power and *violence* and *sex* and *fire* and *blood* and—

Nikolai tried to let go, screaming as he fought against the crushing euphoria, struggling to shut out the voice and the feeling of violation as it touched his mind, as the cool creeping tendrils spread into his pools and channels of magic.

The hellish ecstasy tore away like a stinging shock of icy water as the gun was knocked from his grasp by a muddy stick Hazeal swung hard enough to break two of Nikolai's fingers. The silky, irresistible whispers dwindled to a distant hush as the revolver tumbled away.

For a moment, Nikolai could only stand there, stunned as he

stared at his hideously crooked digits. Then pain *exploded* in his jaw as Hazeal slammed a heavy fist into his face.

Reeling, Nikolai drew his baton Focal to try and defend himself, but Hazeal tackled him, howling with crazed, triumphant laughter.

"You thought you had me! You thought I was yours but I'm a half-mage now. I hid my mind! And now . . ."

His hands were slippery as they found purchase around Nik's wrists. A cloud of flame billowed out to the side from the tip of Nik's baton as Hazeal turned the hand away the instant before Nik could incinerate him.

Mud steamed and blackened. Moss turned to ember, filling the air with putrid smoke as Nik struggled and screamed under the thickly built man.

"St-stop! *STOP!* Get—get the fuck off of—"

"I lied, Nikolai! Your mother was a vile woman. Everyone else worshipped her, but I knew what kind of mage she really was. I *knew!* Just like I know you're going to be monster, like her. If not *worse*."

Nik strained with his broken-fingered hand to draw his second Focal—a dagger. The pillar of flame billowing from his baton grew to a blue-and-red inferno jetting off beside them, and Nik could feel his hair smoldering, could see Hazeal's filthy clothes catching from the heat alone, and—

Hazeal wrenched the wrist of Nikolai's baton hand with an audible crunch. The billowing inferno sputtered out as the baton slipped from fingers Nikolai could no longer control. Hazeal cast aside the baton, then drew Nik's blade Focal and tossed that away as well.

"I should've known she'd make me pay eventually. But I'm glad they killed her! Just like I'm going to kill you. I hope she's watching from *hell*."

He struck Nikolai in the face with the bloodied knuckles of his free hand, each punch a distant thud the young mage could barely feel anymore.

A thread of light silently pierced Hazeal's neck. There came a flash of heat and the pressure released, the weight of the stocky man suddenly gone. Nikolai sputtered and choked, blinded as he was enveloped by a thick cloud of ashes.

Two voices argued loudly over him.

"—STYX Ilyana this is an order do not give him that potion you are NOT a healer and you just *killed* that mage oh *Disc* I knew Nikolai was up to something but of all the foolish, idiotic—"

"We're the same rank, Albert," Ilyana said, her voice shaking audibly. "You can't give me orders." Her hands trembled as she cradled Nik's head and poured something warm and bitter into his mouth. "If I hadn't killed him he might have killed all three of us, and—*don't touch that gun!*"

Nikolai choked and spit and tried to open his eyes but he was still blinded by the ashes of the dead half-mage. The bitter warmth of Ilyana's potion spread in an instant—throat to stomach, stomach to fingertips. Pain disappeared. The voices became distant. Darkness took him.

"Superstitious bullshit," Nikolai grumbled as they descended the great white steps into a hall draped with red and gold. "This is such a waste of time. I'm fine."

At the end of the hall stood a pair of immense polished black doors, standing in sharp contrast to the white stone. A dancing glow flickered from under the doors, moving and refracting like light reflected off water.

"You were exposed to dangerous magic," Ilyana said. "Dirty. Old." She pointed at her temple, twirling her finger. "Crazy-making."

"I'm surprised the healer didn't try to leech me. Or rub me down with snake oil."

"That healer managed to rebuild your shattered face to its former glory without so much as a scar. So stop complaining."

"Money maker intact," Nik agreed solemnly, rubbing his chin. "Disc bless that mage."

"And I don't know about you, but I wouldn't say no to a snake-oil rub," she said, nudging Nik with her elbow. "Depending on the masseuse."

Nik smiled weakly, but he could tell that her cheerful bravado was at least partially a facade.

"Your healer gave orders to sit in the Disc's light for at least two hours to be cleansed. Dirty magic gone." Ilyana's colorfully painted eyes teased from below Cleopatra bangs as she pushed open the big black doors. "And if that doesn't work, we can always try skinny-dipping in the sacred water."

The Marblewood Disc Chamber was a cavernous dome of slick white marble, built so that hundreds of magi could comfortably stand around the smooth glassy pool at the center of the room.

Hovering over the pool was Marblewood's enormous white Disc. It shone with silver light as it floated at the center of the domed ceiling, seeming to pulse and strain against the massive black chains that held it in place. It dripped occasional droplets of water infused with magical energy, feeding the pool below. It was roughly the shape of a coin, soft-edged and otherworldly.

Every Veil had its own Disc. Limitless supplies of magical energy revered by some magi as gods—or God, depending on whom you asked. The truth of their origins was long lost to history. All that was known for certain was that without the Discs, there would be no magi.

The Discs were silent. Eternal. And when a mage died their soul slipped from their bodies, a phantom visible to only the most powerful magi as it returned to the nearest Disc and disappeared forever within its pearly depths.

Ilyana watched with delighted amusement as Nikolai unslung a bag from his shoulder and produced a picnic blanket.

"We're going to be here for a while," he said, spreading the cloth across the floor along the curving wall. "Might as well get comfortable."

He pulled a couple tall, amber-tinted bottles of expensive honeybrew from the bag and popped the caps with a wedge of hardened air. "Want one? Doc didn't say anything about drinking."

En route from the healer ward to city hall the day after Nikolai's traumatic encounter with Hazeal, they'd made a brief stop at the safe house so Nikolai could freshen up, change, and quickly pack a bag to bring along for the prescribed basking in the Disc's light.

He'd bought the aged brews a few days prior, originally intending to invite Ilyana to join him for a picnic on the secret lakeside beach he used to go as a child. He'd still been mustering up the courage to ask her out, but when she volunteered to supervise his cleansing, he figured the Disc chamber would do as well as the lake. City hall was closed for the night, so at least they'd have privacy.

Besides—they could both use the drink.

"Well, well, look at you," she said, sitting beside him and taking a long swig. "Disc. That's good."

"Just because I didn't grow up in a two-thousand-year-old

enchanted castle surrounded by puzzle halls like you and Albert doesn't mean I can't class it up."

"Mine was only five hundred. More manor than castle. And no puzzle halls. Those are so tacky. Gilded Age Schwarzwald bull-shit." She took another swig and sighed, flashing Nikolai a forced smile. "Ever have a picnic with a murderer before?"

He winced, and she turned away, seeming to regret the jest.

She went quiet, staring at the bottle as she idly peeled the label, digging her thumbnail around the edges of the sticker. "Sorry. That was in poor taste. I haven't quite . . . I've never . . ."

Nikolai reached to put a hand on her arm, but stopped short, thinking better of it.

"It's my fault. I shouldn't have snuck off. Shouldn't have lied. I just . . ."

"I just. You just. We just." Ilyana shrugged. "The captain is going to chew your ass out when we get back to New Damascus, but I get it."

"That spell," Nikolai said, curious. "That thread of light."

"Nasty little weave, isn't it? You'll learn it on your next promotion." She shook her head, holding out the palm of her hand. "It's easy, too," she said, a slight tremor to her voice. "Just the littlest twist on a normal *pyrkagias* fire spell. Scary how easy it is to turn a person into dust. And Lieutenant Hazeal . . ."

"That gun," Nik said. "I think it drove him insane. He was going to kill me. He . . . hated me."

Ilyana and Albert had been present for Nikolai's debrief. He'd been sparse with the details, acting more shocked and dazed than he'd actually been to buy some time to think.

Captain Jubal had interrogated Nikolai through a communication crystal. Nik had almost given in, almost handed the medallion over as he struggled not to wilt under the concerned warmth in the captain's eyes, cutting through him even as a miniaturized image in the depths of a sphere.

He told them that when Hazeal appeared, claiming to have a message from Nikolai's mother, he'd followed the half-mage without telling the others because he'd been afraid of spooking the supposedly dead Edge Guard. Nik left out most of the details of their actual encounter—saying only that the half-mage had tricked him by relinquishing the revolver in a false show of surrender, then viciously attacked once Nikolai had been incapacitated by physical contact with the artifact.

When pressed as to whether or not Hazeal had said anything—anything at all—Nikolai recalled, with subtle enough difficulty to be believable, Hazeal ranting about his mother while he attacked. Something about killing Nikolai as revenge.

Not a lie, exactly. Just a carefully curated truth.

Nik smothered the surge of anxiety at the thought, the pang of guilt focused on the Moonwatch medallion hidden in the lining of his suitcase back at the safe house. The others hadn't found it hidden in the sole of his shoe, even after they'd undressed him to be healed.

"Ilyana . . ." he said. "Can I tell you something . . . in confidence? Something you can't even tell the captain?"

Ilyana barked a laugh. Then, realizing he was serious, she looked him in the eyes, and let out a long whistle. With a puzzled smile like she couldn't believe the words coming out of her mouth, she said, "I trust you, Sergeant Nikolai Strauss."

"Oh. Um. Thank you. I mean—"

She held up a finger, cutting him off.

"When you're promoted to lieutenant, like me, you swear a long and complicated set of oaths on bended knee to the king. One of those oaths is that if I discover a Battle Mage subordinate guilty of or planning to participate in *treason*, I'm sworn to execute them on the spot, unless further intel is required. In which case we're supposed to cut out their brain and put it in stasis for the Neuromancers to data-mine later."

Nikolai looked at her, aghast. "Fucking Christ . . ."

"Just kidding! About that last part, I mean. The execution oath is real." Then, at his expression of deepening horror: "*Awww.* I wouldn't ever hurt you, Baby Nik! What I'm trying to say is if you tell me something illegal, I'm not going to report you. That makes me an accessory. So if you get busted—*BOOM!*—I'm busted too. But I know you, Nikolai. You're smart. Careful. And you take an ass-kicking like a champ. So I trust you. I know you won't get me in trouble. You can tell me anything."

She wrinkled her freckled nose. "Except about your exes. Never tell me about your exes."

A warmth spread through Nikolai. He felt light-headed.

"I . . . held a few things back," he said. "About what happened with Hazeal. We talked a little, before he tried to kill me."

Ilyana seemed unsurprised. "About your mom?"

Nikolai nodded. "He said my mom showed him what's beyond the Veil. That we've been lied to about what's really out there— that the expeditions are bullshit, the data and footage falsified. But of course he wouldn't tell me what the supposed truth is. He just said . . ."

The gun will teach you the secrets of manipulating Veil with the apocrypha *weave. To make a door in the sky. To see the human world, for yourself.*

" . . . that it's horrible, but not in the way I'd think." This had troubled Nik, almost as much as the newly mysterious circumstances surrounding his mother's death. "If—hypothetically—Hazeal was telling the truth . . . what do you think might actually be out there?"

Ilyana took a swig from her bottle.

"Ohhhh, I've got the usual set of theories. If you really don't buy the official story that it's all wastelands of broken reality permanently ruined by Vaillancourt's enchanted warheads, then . . . well . . . maybe it's just the inky void of space. Or maggoty lands, pockmarked with Foxbourne breeding pits. Maybe boiling seas of lava, or rips and whirlpools in space-time that would drag you back to the age of dinosaurs. Oh, the folly of man! Oh, the foolishness of magi. Who knows? We'll find out once we're Lancers, like your mom was. So long as we do our jobs and keep our noses clean. So no more sneaking off and defying orders, kiddo. Or no government-issued time-traveling pterodactyl for you."

"Yeah. You're probably right." Nikolai shifted uncomfortably, swirling around what little honeybrew remained at the bottom of the bottle. "It was weird how much he hated her. Everyone else I've ever met who knew my mom never shuts the fuck up about how *amazing* she was. How much they miss her. How much I look like her."

His lips twisted into a sneer. "Why would I want to hear that? Um, hello, twenty-year-old boy. FYI, you look *just* like your piece-of-shit mother, who we were all so fucking terrified of that we *still* kiss her ass, even though she's been dead for a decade. I thought my parents died in a skycraft accident, but Hazeal said he ratted her out about something, and that's what got her killed. Which, of all the things he said, that's what I believe the most. I wonder what she did? Knowing her, I bet it was baaaaad."

"Treason?" Ilyana suggested. "She was really high up for a while there. Practically Jubal's second-in-command. A traitor rising so high in command before getting caught would have made the king look weak. Covering it up makes sense." She put a hand on Nikolai's arm. "Especially to protect the ones she left behind."

Nikolai tentatively put his hand over hers, grateful for the comfort. "Yeah. I totally buy her throwing a coup. Sometimes when she was manic, she'd clean the entire house with *Les Misérables* just blasting from a memory cube. She'd sing the whole thing—had it memorized. Then she'd be in this really great mood for the rest of the night, and would joke around with me and my dad with this *genuinely* terrible French accent." He snorted. "What a fucking joke."

"I hate *Les Mis*," Ilyana said.

"I dunno," Nikolai chuckled. "I think it's pretty good. Humans were always so much better at theater than magi. Which doesn't make any sense to me."

"Bigger talent pool," Ilyana said. "There were, what? Seven billion of them, in the end? And like, three hundred million of us—all spread out in thousands of different Veils. Population as small and divided as ours can only produce so many musical theater prodigies." She turned her honeybrew bottle over, frowning as a single droplet trickled out. "You didn't pack seconds, did you?"

Nikolai peered at his own empty bottle. "'Fraid not."

"Probably for the best," she sighed. "I'm tipsy already."

"Yeah, me too."

"Did he say anything else to you? Just 'Your mom's a traitor, the outside's a lie, fuck you Nik—die, die, die'?"

He looked at her for a moment, then shrugged.

"Well Nikolai," she said. "All I can say is . . . fuck Hazeal. And fuck your mom. I know it's easier said than done, but try not to let it get to you. And maybe . . . at least think about telling Jubal. You know he'd be cool about it."

"Yeah. You're probably right."

Ilyana pulled out an intricately carved tobacco pipe. "For

what it's worth, I can sympathize with you having a shitty mom. When I was eleven, mine sent me away to live with my dad, who I barely knew, in New Damascus. Said a mage of my 'disposition' would be better suited to the North American Veils. Basically bought me out of the family by giving me my inheritance early. Which just happened to be slightly more than my father's total worth, as a snub."

Nikolai hissed a breath. "Jesus. That's . . . fucked up. Where are you from originally?"

Ilyana rarely talked about herself, even when pressed. Nik knew that her father owned a chain of distilleries and breweries, but she'd never mentioned her mother before.

"Xanadu," she said, thumbing tobacco into the pipe. "My little brother is studying law—being groomed for office. They've been prepping him since he was little, poor kid. So I obviously had to go. Bad influence and all that. My mother's the Lady of Xanadu, actually—she'll be running to be Duchess Elect of the Asian Veils in a couple years. Be the fourth Xue sorceress to hold the position, if she wins."

Nikolai smiled, but then realized she was being serious. "Whoa—what? Your mom is—"

"Yep."

"Oh," Nik said, taken aback.

Ilyana took a glittering crystal flask from its holster at her hip and twisted the top. The liquid within, which had been a sluggish glowing red, was replaced by glittering silver dust.

The flask was Ilyana's logic Focal, which would normally have marked her as a potion master. The long, ruby-bladed dagger sheathed at her side was her art Focal.

While many Focals, such as Nikolai's, merely served as conduits for spellcasting, other Focals like Ilyana's flask served as magical tools to aide in their profession. Within the flask, Ilyana could store any number of different potions and ingredients within myriad tiny pocket dimensions. The dimensional pocket of her choice was selected with intuitive twists of the cap.

A small opening appeared at the top of the flask, and Ilyana gently tapped out a dash of the mysterious silver dust onto the tobacco in her pipe. She lit up the pipe and took a deep drag, holding it in. When she exhaled, the smoke came out swirling blue and green—tiny sparks crackling like a little electric storm.

"My parents separated when I was little," she said. "My mother remarried, then had my brother. He and I used to be close, but we barely talk now. Mother's side of the family is an old lineage—they weren't very happy when she ran off with my father. He's always been wealthy; our honeybrew and dragon's milk are popular in Veils all over the world," she added, with a hint of pride. "But he's Merchant class—so, you know."

"Who cares—rich is rich, right?" Nik said.

"Royalty cares. Also, my father's black. So there's always that."

"Ah. Good ol' classism and racism," he said, eyeing the electric cloud of smoke with alarm. "Disc—what the hell is that stuff?"

"What," she purred, exhaling another cloud of emerald and blue. Nik could feel her relaxing beside him, sinking deeper against the wall as her muscles seemed to melt. "You've never had Strum before?"

Nik stared at her blankly.

"Poet's Powder? Glow Dust? No?"

He shook his head.

"Aw." She leaned over and kissed his cheek. Nikolai flushed, trying to hide his surprise. "Sometimes I forget what a hayseed you are. Want some?"

"I dunno . . ."

She giggled. "That's okay, Baby Nik. I won't force you. It's pretty mild stuff. Makes colors brighter. Makes every stone and every blade of grass burn and sing. Makes it so I can see my own magic. My weaves—they're like gossamer. I can see them, hear them. Understand them in a way that's hard to describe. Like our bodies are just gloves and we're our magic, you know?"

She held out her hand, spreading her fingers. Threads of light shot from her fingertips, glowing neon purple, blue, pink, and white. Then she clenched her fist, sighing, and the threads disappeared.

"When we cast spells, it's our real bodies we're moving, peeking out from these husks." She looked down at her naked hand with disdain. "These gloves."

Nikolai stared at Ilyana, concerned. She met his gaze, her lips peaking up into a sly smile.

"I used to be called the Alchemist back in Academy," she said, her eyes lit with a feverish gleam. "Did I ever tell you that? I was a purveyor of all sorts of mind-altering substances. Dangerous stuff—stuff you can only get from the worst part of the Noir district in the capital, from half-mages of ill repute. Stuff that can make nightmares come to life."

"Yeah?"

"I got lucky," she said. "I've cleaned up since I became an Edge Guard. Strum? Strum is nothing. Strum's a trip to the shore twenty minutes away."

"I'm . . . I'm glad nothing bad happened," Nik said weakly. "I'm glad you joined the Edge Guard, and that you're okay. You . . . are okay, right?"

"Me? Oh, I'm graaaand," she said, tapping out the ashes from her pipe and pocketing it. "I've always had money. Always gotten everything I've ever wanted. But when you get everything—it gives you a kind of clarity."

She held up a hand and created a snake of fire. It coiled in and out through her fingers, slender and colorful.

Nik watched nervously, worried that she was going to burn herself.

"A blindness too," she continued, "to so easily have what so many others struggle for their whole lives; it removes all value. But value's an illusion—there's your clarity. Magi, Nikolai? We're purposeless little things. We work, we breed, we live our lives, but nothing really changes. Day-to-day life has been pretty much the same for a century. There's no disease, no real poverty. And worst of all—there's no frontier.

"The borders are set, the Veils unchanging. There aren't any new lands to discover, to bend and shape. We're stagnant. Nothing we do matters because nothing will ever change. So I'd Strum and I'd Glow and I'd enjoy every possible explosion of the senses. Because I don't feel much, Nik. I never have. I smile, I talk, and I laugh—but most of the time, I'm just sort of . . . numb. Like that feeling you get when you're so bored it *hurts*. Like there're ants under my skin, and if I don't find a way to distract myself from them, they'll eat me alive.

"But then I became an Edge Guard. Then I found out that there are monsters at the gate. Or something like monsters. That our borders are delicate, and that we aren't stagnant at all but desperately trying to keep the darkness at bay, to keep from being snuffed out like tiny candles. I don't know what's beyond the Veils, I don't know what we're training to fight, if anything—but for the first time, I have something to care about. I have purpose. Captain Jubal and the Edge Guard gave me that."

Her eyes widened and she was smiling, elated; the rope of fire she'd been twisting between her fingers collected into a coil over her palm.

"Though sometimes," she whispered, her smile disappearing, "sometimes I wonder if it might be better to let it all come crashing down."

The coil of flame began to swirl—growing, spinning—and as it grew, she stared into it, enthralled, until the inferno began to roar and the heat of it grew so hot that Nikolai's civilian clothing began to singe. And it was getting hotter now, so hot that Ilyana was going to hurt herself, was going to burn off her hand—

"*Pyrkagias!*" Nik breathed, clasping his hand down on hers, smothering the roaring flame with an inverted weave of the spell. Their fingers intertwined—and as the flame disappeared, she slowly came back to reality.

He wished he had something to say—something smart. Something funny or insightful. Something that could take away her incredible sadness. But all of a sudden, he'd never felt so young, never felt so naive—and it struck Nikolai that he didn't know Ilyana at all.

So he kissed her. Hand sliding along her neck, down to her waist. She kissed him back and reached up. Nikolai felt a flash of heat, and then another, and looked down to see that she was burning off his buttons with tiny bursts of flame.

A wizard and a sorceress fucked in the Disc's pale glow.

Afterward, they lounged in a tangle of limbs on the blackened picnic blanket, fingers entwined as they stared into the Disc.

"I've never killed anyone before," she said, barely above a whisper. "I thought that I might eventually. But not someone I knew. Someone I liked. It's the strangest thing."

Nikolai brought his hand to her face, tracing his fingers across the constellations of her faint, scattered freckles. "Nobody expects you to just be okay. But Hazeal—he wasn't the same person he used to be. He would have killed me if you hadn't stopped him."

She chewed her lip, avoiding Nik's gaze.

"It's not that. It's . . . it's that I don't feel guilty at all. And no, it's not shock. It's not denial. I just don't care. How awful is that?"

Nik didn't know what to say.

After a long silence, she pulled away from him and began to dress.

"Hey," he said, panicking. "I'm sorry, I didn't mean—"

"No, no, you didn't do anything wrong. But this. This can't happen. We work together. I outrank you. I shouldn't be getting high with you, let alone fucking you. This is all already so complicated. It's been a while since I've felt like such a child. I need to just . . . process all of this. You know?"

"Sure," Nik said. He sat up, awkwardly pulling on his now buttonless shirt. "I understand."

"Chin up, Sergeant," she said, flashing that wicked smile that Nik was growing so fond of as she clasped her final button. "You weren't half bad. Let's just take some time to think about whatever the hell this was, yeah?"

———————

Ilyana didn't sleep at the safe house that night. She was treating herself now that the stakeout was over, and had rented a room in one of the nicer hotels.

"I've got to be able to get a massage somewhere, even in a Veil as small as Marblewood," she'd said. "Don't call me unless there's an emergency. And even then, don't call."

That left only Nikolai and Albert in the cramped apartment for their final night in Marblewood. Nikolai lay there, awake, staring at the dusty ceiling as he waited for Albert to fall asleep in the other room.

Alone with his thoughts, Nikolai replayed everything that had happened with Ilyana in the Disc Chamber over and over again. Little gestures, and things she said—the way she said them. The way she looked while they held each other, naked, in the shimmering silver light.

Slowly, his mind drifted away from Ilyana, focusing instead on his far less pleasant memories of the last time he'd been in the Marblewood Disc Chamber.

The two years that had passed since that day—Assignment Day—somehow felt to Nikolai both like an eternity, and no time at all.

On Assignment Day, young magi would swear oaths of magical conduct and then reach into the pool of water beneath the Disc to draw their Focals; indestructible pieces of a mage's soul, manifested physically as objects able to greatly focus and power one's magic.

First they'd draw the logic Focal, which symbolically represented and practically assisted with the career a magi would be best suited for as a full wizard or sorceress.

Second, they'd draw the art Focal, which represented and aided the creative vocation for which the mage had shown the most promise.

A mage could choose either to define their career path—or neither, if they preferred. Though that was unusual.

Nikolai remembered how hot it had been. Remembered the wide-brimmed hat and the sweaty, itchy fabric of his formal robes, which seemed to grow heavier with every student called before him to swear their oaths and draw their Focals.

The mage just before Nikolai drew a Watchman's glittering,

gold-striped staff as her logic Focal, which could powerfully channel the brute elemental forces of fire and air.

Nikolai stewed with envy as applause for the mage—a full sorceress now, having sworn her oaths and drawn her Focals—roared in his ears.

His father had been a highly respected Watchman, and since his death Nikolai had dreamed—obsessed, really—of following in his footsteps. Thinking of his father always filled Nik with warmth. The pristine white of his topcoat, flapping in the wind behind him; his watchman staff, twinkling with light as it coursed sluggishly up the striped gold.

Nikolai remembered being called. He remembered the other students whispering about him. Remembered the flyball players snickering as he approached the pool.

Oaths were sworn and Nik reached into the pool, not even bothering to roll up his sleeve. The water was like ice. He reached around, snaking his hand through the pool. The edges were smooth, more like glass than stone. His hand closed around what felt like a staff, thick and sturdy. Thicker than the cane of a teacher or the scepter of a politician. Resilient and utilitarian.

A Watchman's staff!

Nik nearly gasped out a sob of relief before stifling it, and with a ferocious grin he yanked the Watchman's staff out of the water.

Only it wasn't a Watchman's staff. It was . . . something else.

A baton. A club, as long as his forearm. Rounded at the ends. Metallic but matte and soft. Plain and dull and black. So black it was almost hard to look at—hard to see.

Every magi's Focals were different, unique. But one thing they all had in common was dazzling aesthetics. Whether jeweled, chromatic, or intricate and colorful as delicately spun candy, a magi's Focals were always things of beauty.

This was not the case with Nikolai's baton.

An awkward silence fell across the chamber. The council members exchanged puzzled looks as Nik hunched in on himself. He'd never seen a Focal like this, and from the looks on their faces he knew that they hadn't either and something was wrong with him or the Disc or who knows what.

He could hear people tittering with shock and cruel amusement. One of the flyball players stage-whispered "Nikolai Half Staff" loud enough for everyone to hear, and when Nikolai made the mistake of glancing back he saw that many of the others had begun to laugh.

Nikolai thrust out his hand, handing the first mage of the council his Focal.

"Oh, um, yes—thank you," she stammered, accepting the baton after a moment of hesitation, like it was radioactive.

He could feel her hands on it. The baton was a part of him, a piece of his soul or essence or whatever the Disc took out of him and created in the pool, and it felt wrong for someone else to be holding it.

Nikolai shoved the feeling of wrongness aside and looked expectantly at the next council mage, his cold gaze half lidded and uncaring because now he just wanted to get this shit over with and go home and sleep for the next hundred or so years.

"Right, ahem, of course," the councilwoman said, and quickly dipped the butt of her staff into the water. The water shimmered, ready for his second drawing. Nik reached in, fishing around without enthusiasm. He found his art Focal quicker than the logic, his hand closing around a handle with a rough, leathery grip. He pulled it from the water, uncaring . . .

. . . and gasped.

In Nik's hand was a dagger, edge dripping with water from the pool. Not a carving knife. Not a tool for working leather, cutting cloth, or meat. It was a wicked blade—curved and black, like a demon's steely talon.

That was his art. A thing for wounding. For killing.

A soldier's weapon. The Focal of a Battle Mage.

Just like his mother.

There hadn't been any laughter this time. No snide remarks, no giggling among the students. Just a deep, uneasy silence.

With a groan, he stood up and snatched the black baton. He ran.

The stairs were a blur, the citizens and government workers milling about the entrance hall out of focus and vaguely dreamlike as he sprinted through their midst, dagger in one hand, half staff in the other.

As he ran, half staff swinging at his side, he noticed that as the baton moved it left a vague trail of light in its wake, a smearing of multicolored rainbow.

The fake sun set in the fake sky, and he began to limp, feet blistered from running in the replica Converse sneakers his only friend, George Stokes, had made for him as a graduation gift.

Nik finally found his way to the secluded lakeside beach he always fled to when he wanted to be alone. He sat heavily at the edge of the waves and pried off his sneakers from under his robes, sticking his toes in the icy water.

He pulled out the dagger. The black blade glittered in the moonlight. Gently he touched the tip of his finger to the edge and instantly drew blood. He popped the bleeding finger into his mouth and laid the dagger in the sand. He could feel it there, waiting, hungry for violence.

That's what it was made for—to focus and strengthen the destructive arts. With this blade, he could make fire so hot it burned white. He could turn sand to glass, skin to dust, stone to lava.

But the baton . . . it felt like more than a simple tool for violence. Nik waved it around, watching the smearing rainbow trail. It sucked at his magic like gravity, like wind trying to pull you over a cliff. The power was immense. It made him dizzy.

Two years later, Nikolai still hadn't been able to discover why he'd drawn such a uniquely strange Focal, nor how it trailed light or what purpose the light might serve. Even Captain Jubal had been stumped.

"We like to pretend we've mastered the arcane," he'd said, with the faintest lingering hint of his Blue Ridge Veil drawl. "But the fact of the matter is that most magi underestimate the indescribable scientific and quantum complexity of even the most simplistic spells. Any number of factors could have led to the anomaly that is your Focal—nothing to be done about it."

Through all the doubt and anxiety, Nik had been quietly sure that he'd become a Watchman like his father. That things would work out, like in the stories. The kids in stories were always orphans destined for greatness. Street urchins and outcasts who overcame their humble beginnings to become heroes and saviors, beloved by all.

Nobody could tell stories like Nik's dad. His mom, she'd go through these depressions—weeks when she'd barely speak, barely eat, when she'd come home from work, trembling and dead in the eyes. Nik couldn't remember her face—he hated that he couldn't remember her face—but he remembered seeing her, and even as a child thinking, *There's nothing there. There's nobody home.*

She'd always hurt Nikolai the most during these periods of

darkness. Always pushed him harder during their secret training sessions in the heart of the wood. It was then that she'd go as far as to crack his bones as she taught Nikolai to defend himself from her vicious strikes. It was then that she'd make him wait for healing after he'd burned himself on botched spells he wasn't supposed to know, screaming at him for sloppy spellcasting while he writhed in the mud.

Only his father's stories could bring her back from the darkness. It would start with a laugh, and she'd seem surprised, every time, as if she'd forgotten that it was within her ability.

Nik's father had loved stories—loved hearing them, made an art of telling them. He had boxes and boxes of novels mostly written by long-dead human authors. Nik's favorite memories of his parents were of being nestled on a sofa between them as they read to him by firelight, the both of them reading for different characters, doing all the voices. It was those nights that he most powerfully felt their love—for Nik, for each other.

Nikolai's uncle Red took him in after his parents died. And though he took care of Nik to his best ability, the man became withdrawn. Cold and distant. Nikolai's only childhood friends, Astor and Stokes, had rallied to help him through it. But what really saved him were the stories.

The humans had loved writing stories about triumph over adversity. Of good triumphing over evil. Of love conquering all and people defeating monsters without becoming monsters themselves. Of life having a way of working out in the end—no matter how bad things might seem at the time.

But that's all they were. Stories.

The humans were dead. Nik's parents were dead. And he was just a stupid orphan who'd never be like his father, no matter how hard he tried.

He was his mother's son.

Click.

The slender floating hands of the clock on Nik's bedside table finally struck midnight, drawing him out of his reverie.

Nikolai rose and quietly pulled on some clothes. He peered into Albert's room, checking to make sure the junior lieutenant was asleep. Clad in emerald silk pajamas, snores muffled by his gauzy, enchanted face mask, Albert was dead to the world.

Nik's rank normally would have been insufficient to open the safe hidden under the loose, enchantment-masked floorboards. They'd locked it up tight under Captain Jubal's orders, setting it so that not even Albert or Ilyana could open it—let alone a lowly sergeant.

Taking a deep breath to steady himself, Nikolai drew out the Moonwatch rank insignia. The crescent moon burned in the darkness, casting a pale white glow on the seamless black surface of the box.

A line seared across the edges of the box, a hinge forming from mercurial beads. With a hiss, the safe opened to reveal an object wrapped in layers of enchanted lead mesh.

The revolver.

It was silent now. Muffled by the lead. But somehow he knew the revolver could hear him. And then, at the edge of his mind, he could hear it. Not hear it, exactly. But he could feel the words, sense the ideas—there, just within reach. The spell that would allow him to see for himself what remained of the human world beyond the Veil.

He just had to ask.

Like snatching gold out of a dragon's mouth.

Nikolai dragged his fingertips across the cold, rune-etched barrel, and as he allowed the creeping tendrils of ancient magic to enter his mind, he relived every pleasure he'd ever experienced in an explosion of blinding ecstasy. Every laugh, every kiss, every kindness. Every moment of tenderness, every night of passion— all in one single instant.

He wasn't in the apartment anymore, he was in an infinite space, sky and stars and songs he could see in colorful waves dancing around him, and he was screaming with laughter, he couldn't stop, he was rapture incarnate, a being of pure joy, and there was a woman, a beautiful woman all dressed in red—he couldn't see her face but somehow he *knew* she was beautiful, the most beautiful woman in the world.

"Show me the *apocrypha* weave," Nikolai begged her, fighting to speak through the crippling euphoria. "Teach me to bend Veil. To make a door in the sky."

Her *Yes* was a feeling more than a word. A color more than an idea.

The woman reached out with crimson-clad fingers and took Nikolai's hand.

II.

THE LAST BALLERINA

Jemma Burton hid in the wooded fringes of Philadelphia, grateful for the rain.

She hid, and she waited.

Her orders had been clear. But the precautions were unusual, to say the least. Five separate couriers, each with a separate piece of intel. Four sets of coded dummy transfer points with overlapping patterns to reveal the true locations. An ETA for pickup with descriptions of the two women she'd been assigned to smuggle across the city into the hands of yet *another* Runner, who would then shuttle them to the safety of their final destination.

There was nothing unusual about the description of the first woman. "Female, fifty-five," the courier said. "Caucasian descent. Pale complexion. White shoulder-length hair."

But the second woman. The tremor in his voice as he described her. The hope in his eyes. Jem made him repeat the words. Then once more. And still, she didn't believe.

There weren't any children on the streets of Philadelphia. Weren't any children at all. Here. New York. Los Angeles. Moscow. Beijing. *Anywhere.*

The world had ended when Jemma was a child herself. And with the end came the plague. And with the plague went the young. The old. The weak.

Synthetic deities had found humanity lacking. And with the scattered dusting of a disease Jem had once heard a dying pathologist describe as *elegant*, the Synth had given them a death sentence—delayed by decades, but final nonetheless.

Jem, at twelve, had been among the youngest of the survivors. Now, thirteen years later, she and every other surviving human remained infertile. The virus thrived in all of them, actively inhibiting their ability to procreate, and had thus far adapted to thwart every attempt at treatment or cure.

So humanity dwindled, fading away under the gentle tyranny of synthetic life.

"Female, twenty-five," the courier had repeated twice. "Indian descent. Medium complexion. Black chin-length hair, shaved on the side. *Visibly pregnant.*"

It was possible, of course. But even as fragile petals of hope bloomed within her, she crushed it. Maybe someone had found a cure. Or maybe this woman was just some genetic rarity unheard of until now who'd developed an immunity. Either way, Jem knew better than to think it would make a difference. Knew better than to think anything she did could ever do more than slow the gradual extinction of terrestrial humans.

Raindrops clung to Jem's close-cropped curls like dew. She shivered, fingers caressing the shielded holsters of the weapons hidden at her side. They would have her description as well, their current Runner scouting ahead to make sure Jem hadn't been replaced by some Synth spy.

She tapped her fingers against the damp denim of her jeans, impatient. She hated staying in one place this long, out in the open.

There—*finally*. A stirring in the shadows. Three figures framed by an outcropping of dusky-leafed maple trees.

Jem whistled, stepping out into moonlight dimmed by ashen autumn clouds.

The Runner was a short, grizzled Asian man. He pulled back the cowl of his stealth cloak, which masked them from the infrared scanners of the watchful drones that patrolled the skies over the Pennsylvania wilderness as they traveled by night.

He whispered something to the others, gesturing urgently for them to remove their cloaks. He nodded to Jem, scratching his beard as he eyed the silent city—twitchy and impatient to slink back into the velvety darkness of the brown-leafed forest. Jem could tell that he was the type who preferred wilderness runs to urban.

Jem watched with eager curiosity as the women revealed their faces. The older woman was tall and bony, her thin-lipped face heavily creased in equal measure by laugh lines and worry.

The younger woman's dark, tat-sleeved arms lifted from the gauzy cloak to pull back her hood. She was curvaceous and soft-featured, her face and ears crowded with piercings.

As the cloak fell from her shoulders, Jem's gaze traced the woman's figure to the gentle swell of her stomach, only barely visible through the baggy fatigues.

"Here." Jem tossed the women two vacuum-sealed packs of clean clothing, hoping they'd be loose enough for the pregnant woman.

The Runner clasped Jem's hand, back turned to the women as they removed dull camo uniforms, well-soiled from the journey, and changed into the new outfits.

"Precious cargo," he whispered. "For the love of God, be careful."

"I'll keep them safe," Jem assured him, and he nodded, confident in her ability. Though few in the Resistance knew one another by name or face, Jem's reputation preceded her. The Runner with the mind of a Synth. The girl with uniquely high-end cybernetic enhancement mods.

So far as Jem knew, she was the last human with such sophisticated enhancements. The other girl had probably been dead for a long time now.

"This is Jem," he said, introducing her to the women. "She'll get you where you need to go. Jem, this is Dr. Blackwell. And—"

"Blue," the pregnant woman said, shaking the surprised Jem's hand. Jem's breath caught in her chest as their fingers touched. *Christ*, she was beautiful.

"You're in good hands," the man said, hugging the doctor, and then Blue. He broke off the embrace, and reached down to touch her stomach. Thinking better of it, he stopped short. Pulled away. Eyes wet with tears. "Bless you. God bless you."

Their planned route across the city was a winding zigzag through lush, Synth-made gardens, an Immersion Farm, and abandoned SEPTA train tunnels.

At its height, Philadelphia had been home to more than three million people. But after the initial rash of deaths in the uprising, and the slow dwindling in the thirteen years since, that number had been reduced by more than half. And it was still shrinking every day.

There was no sickness, but in the face of such hopelessness, and without children to maintain the population, their numbers were in constant decline. Suicide was common—encouraged even, by the Synth. Pills that induced ecstasy, followed by slumber, followed by oblivion, were given to each and every citizen to use at their discretion.

As such, the city was massively oversized to house so few. Housing, manufacturing, commerce, and industry were constantly shifted inward, leaving miles of darkened, empty infrastructure closing around the gradually shrinking light at the center.

Some Synth Overminds allowed the abandoned architecture within the cities under their rule to simply crumble and fall into disrepair. Others stripped them for materials and demolished what remained, leaving countless empty lots where towers had once been. Empty gaps like the naked gums of an old man slowly losing his teeth to age.

The Overmind charged with ruling Pennsylvania, New York, and New Jersey, however, had slowly replaced each and every empty structure with stunningly designed gardens and nature reserves. Lush miniature forests and tiny lagoons. Ponds and lakes and thickets. Great open fields vibrant with wild flowers. All carefully crafted to appear real—as if the perfectly designed aesthetics of each plot had occurred naturally as they seamlessly blended in with one another and the surrounding Pennsylvania wilderness.

Where other cities found their shrinking centers surrounded by husks and rubble, here it appeared that nature was slowly closing in on them, in all its heartbreaking splendor.

Armitage, the AI was called. One of the more eccentric Overminds. Jem supposed the machine considered itself an artist.

She could see the pattern of Armitage's design. Could see that their Synth ruler had a great overarching plan for the gardens, plans that would only come to completion upon the death of Philadelphia's last inhabitant. And then, as the final tower fell to be replaced by one final floral centerpiece, it would be as if the city had never been there at all.

Jem was good with patterns. Her perfect synthetic memory banks, as well as her heightened ability to process and organize what all of that information meant, was what made her the most effective Runner the Resistance had to offer. She'd spent years memorizing every aspect of the city and the surrounding wilderness. Transportation. Population density. Synth and human peacekeeper patterns of patrol. A complex web lit with constantly shifting paths where one could hide in the shadows just beyond the peripheral vision of the great and powerful Armitage's all-seeing surveillance.

She applied transparent, greasy mask nets to Blue and Dr. Blackwell's faces. Pressed tiny pads onto the skin over the cybernetic touch points behind their ears.

"The masks emit a field that changes our features in the eyes of Synth droids and mod surveillance," Jem explained, tapping the almost invisible film plastered to her own face. Then, indicating the pads: "These are dummy mods. They divert the signature and data stream from other civilians, to make it look like we're properly Synth-modded."

Unlike Jem's unique enhancement mods—or those of rescued humans like Blue and the doctor, whose Synth-installed mods had been hacked and altered—the mandatory implants allowed Armitage and automated surveillance to peer through the eyes of any under their control, recording a constant stream of data to keep perfect record of the goings-on within their city.

That, and they had tiny detonators. A kill switch in every skull.

"They'll keep us hidden," Jem said. "So long as we don't draw attention to ourselves."

It went unsaid that if this occurred, there was a very real possibility that they would draw the attention of Armitage itself. And then there would be no hiding.

Blue traced her fingers along the papery bark of slender white trunks as they passed through a densely packed stand of birch trees. Fireflies modified to survive the autumn cold twinkled amid golden leaves and naked branches overhead, floating in sluggish twirls as they lit the way.

"It's beautiful . . ." Blue said.

"I guess," Jem said, swatting away a low-flying insect. "These aren't designed for human enjoyment. No paths, no light. Not a bench in sight. Hardly anyone passes through the gardens—especially these days. Good for Runners, though."

They passed through the birch trees into ferns and foliage crisped with frost. Then a pond, dappled with bright pink water lilies that glowed with a dull luminescence. They hopped across a winding series of stones to cross.

"Careful," Jem said, catching Blue's arm as she nearly slipped from slick stone into inky black water.

"Fucking clumsy these days, thanks," Blue said, embarrassed as she took Jem's hand for balance. She glanced back at the lilies, their dim glow reflecting rosy smears across the glassy surface. "I'm not sure what I was expecting. But this—was not it."

"Don't worry," Dr. Blackwell said, hopping onto the shore with nimble grace surprising for a woman her age. "You'll have your fill of human squalor soon enough." She gestured at an immense concrete building peaking over sprawling clouds of yellow-green ironwood leaves in the garden beyond.

Security was minimal at the Immersion Farm. Their entrance,

a discreet metal door set into a wall overgrown with creeping ivy, was easily unlocked with a quick scrambling burst of Jem's compact EMP blaster.

The inside of the Immersion Farm was at striking odds with its dull exterior. Tastefully painted halls lit by gentle lighting echoed with soothing music were designed to give the rows of men and women reclined in glassy pods a somewhat less ominous feel. Artfully arranged fountains gurgled throughout labyrinthine halls.

Jem led them through countless rooms full of people who'd decided to live out the remainder of their lives in fully immersive virtual reality—blue light shimmering through eyelids that might never open again. Though most chose to live in private housing, of which there was an abundance, the burden of feeding and caring for themselves had simply become too much for these slumbering thousands. Instead, they chose to allow Synth caretakers to care for their physical forms while their minds continuously indulged in every kind of food, adventure, and fantasy—sexual or otherwise.

Some even chose to forget that they were in immersion at all, requesting that their knowledge of the outside world be erased. Armitage, like all Overminds, was obligated by Alpha AI decree to maintain these perfect artificial lives for those who chose to forget—for those who chose virtual paradise over watching the slow death of their species in the real world.

Jem resented, pitied, and envied these people in equal measure.

"Don't touch the pods," she warned. "Tamper with the sleepers and all eyes will be on us. Should be twenty-seven minutes before the droids begin their washing and medical rounds."

The streets beyond the Immersion Farm were rain-slick and empty. The city itself was a gloomy sprawl of brick, cement, and neon. Armitage's aesthetic tastes seemed reserved for gardens.

"Stay close to me," Jem whispered as they passed a cluster of hollow-eyed civilians, listlessly slouching down the sidewalk. "Observation in this sector is currently light, and fully automated, but I don't want to take any risks."

Turning into an alleyway, she led them to a discreet sewer grate hidden beside the sleek white bulk of a garbage processor.

As the city shrank, the underground SEPTA trains had rerouted, leaving large swaths of shielded tunnels abandoned below. Despite the stink and filth of the minimally maintained underground, Jem reveled in the damp silence. Any droids or Mods she might run into below would be on their own—the invisible tendrils of Armitage's prodding mind largely obstructed by the thick cement and dirt overhead.

Jem removed the grating with a grunted heave, revealing a dimly lit ladder to the darkness below.

Blue froze, stiffening as Jem offered to help her descend.

"What's wrong?" Jem asked, impatient.

"N-nothing," Blue said, snapping out of it. "Just a little claustrophobic. Not a fan of being underground."

Jem's tiny flashlight lanced into the darkness ahead, a crimson beam sweeping across railway and stone as she led the way. The Synth and human peacekeepers combed the tunnels with a constant, complex web of ever-shifting patrols. As such, most of the other Runners preferred to rely on the flimsy invisibility of their mask nets and dummy mods. For Jem, however, the patrols were no issue. The tangled pattern of their routes accurately tracked in her mind.

They walked in silence but for the ever-present chittering of rats.

"Shouldn't be much longer now," Jem said, "Quarter mile and we'll surface, then . . ."

She trailed off at the sound of laughter, punctuated by the occasional scream.

Impeding their passage was a group of ragged young men dodging and swiping at one another with knives and cudgels. Some of them hid behind invisible cover, firing with weapons that weren't there, grinning. Their pupils flashed blue with the light of augmented reality that made them blind and deaf to their surroundings.

Who knew what they were seeing, what they were hearing, but as Jem watched, one of the men stabbed a white-handled kitchen knife into the shoulder of another young man, whose grin slipped into horrified shock.

"Wait, *no*, oh Christ, no, that hurt, you stabbed me, oh—"

But the cries were cut off as the other kept stabbing, deaf to the screams, blind to the blood as he cheerfully murdered his friend.

The others laughed playfully, like children playing tag. Though full sensory VR required the computational power of a VR bed for most people, they could walk around while using partial VR, seeing and hearing whatever they so chose.

Some of the younger survivors around Jem's age who had grown up with constant full immersion sometimes developed a sort of madness in which they began having difficulty discerning what was real, and what wasn't—their games and blood sport occasionally leaking over into the physical world.

Jem turned to find Blue and Blackwell frozen, horror etched across their faces.

"Come on, we need to go back," Jem said with cold urgency.

The doctor looked back at the weeping boy bleeding out in the filth, hesitant. "But what about—"

"No time!" she said, grabbing her by the arm. "Signals to the surface are mostly blocked down here, but if a civilian is injured or killed their mod will burn itself out to send a powerful emergency signal. Peacekeepers will be here any moment."

She stopped short at the blue-and-red lights bobbing around the corner. One human and two Synth peacekeepers hurried around the bend—the Synth a cartoonish parody of old-fashioned police officers designed to look nonthreatening, but dangerous nonetheless.

"Fucking VR zombies," the human peacekeeper growled, a stun baton crackling in his hand. "Come on, droids, before they finish each other off!"

"Yesssir!" one of the PK droids said. "I'll attend to the wounded—unit thirty-one, assist Officer Davis with disarming the civilians."

"I'm on it!" the other droid said, drawing its stun baton.

Synth droids like these were sophisticated but mindless unless Armitage dropped in and took control. They ran on virtual personalities that were automation instead of actual, self-aware intelligence, though were often so lifelike it was hard to tell.

Where once there had been billions, maybe even trillions of genuine AI, peacefully coexisting with humans in both the physical and virtual planes, most had been destroyed or put into stasis, or—well, nobody really knew what happened to them. All that remained were the three great Alphas, and the scattered handfuls of Overminds they left for the day-to-day drudgery of human rule—on Earth, at least. The colonists from Mars, Venus, Europa, and Earth's moon had long ago abandoned them, signing a treaty with the Synth early on in the war that allowed the AIs to do with Earth as they saw fit, so long as they never attempted to pass beyond the orbital blockade.

Fucking cowards.

Blue and Dr. Blackwell's frozen terror redirected to the approaching peacekeepers, hopelessness filling their eyes at the certainty of their capture. Jem ran past them, directly toward the approaching trio.

"Thank God you're here!" she gasped, playing at frantic. "My brother, he thinks he's playing a game, we tried to stop him but—"

Jem whipped out her EMP blaster and pointed it at the suddenly wide-eyed human PK's face, pulling the trigger with a sizzle.

He collapsed to the floor, back arching as his eyes rolled up into his head, twitching and foaming at the mouth from the damage she'd wreaked upon his mods. He'd live, but her face would be wiped from his internal memory banks, and he would be unable to send out a distress signal.

The PK droids dodged to either side in perfect synchronization, swinging their stun batons. But she was ready for them, frying one of the PKs with her remaining EMP charge and diving away from the other's sweeping electric arc, holstering the blaster and drawing her hidden pistol in one fluid movement as she snapped off three bullets into the CPU behind the PK droid's holographic face.

Her blaster would need time to recharge itself, so she fired two more bullets into the EMP-fried Synth just to be safe and snatched up its stun baton, striding past the amazed Blue and Blackwell with urgent calm.

"Come—back!" the human peacekeeper hissed through gritted teeth, struggling and failing to regain control of his convulsing body. He'd be unable to pursue, unable to describe their features, but he'd be fine. A scheduled patrol would find him shortly after they came to follow up on the injury pulse these three had been sent to investigate.

The man with the bloody white-handled kitchen knife came toward Jem with a boyish grin. "There you are!" he said, hefting the blade. "I'm gonna get ya!"

She sidestepped the wild slice easily, his movements sluggish to her mod-enhanced brain as she turned and lightly touched the baton to the back of his neck. He fell to the ground, twitching and unconscious, his knife clattering from limp fingers.

Blue and Blackwell watched with amazement as Jem wove in and out of the VR zombie ranks, stunning and disarming them with crackling bursts of electric blue from the stun baton.

"Come on!" she said afterward. "We have *less* than no time!"

She ditched the baton and led them in a frantic weaving pattern, hoping her calculations were correct as she estimated the altered positioning of the underground PKs in response to the fallen members.

"That was—" Blue said, breathless as she chased after her "—incredible!"

Normally Jem would have brushed off the compliment, but she felt her face flush. "Just up here," she said, evading and grateful for the dim gray light that filtered down from the grate overhead.

Jem's heart pounded through her body as she led the two through mildly busy streets, exuding a false sense of calm so as not to panic her wards despite the fact that searchlights might shine down on them at any moment should their path from the underground have been noted.

Finally they arrived at the nearly empty lot of the dingy marketplace where she would part ways with Blue and Dr. Blackwell. Wires of tension slowly loosened in her chest. They'd made it. Mission accomplished, as soon as she got them to the waiting Runner.

A few empty cabs waited out front for the old-fashioned few who still went to pick up their own groceries. At this point, most people simply had all their groceries delivered directly to them, usually allowing Synth droids to prepare meals for them as well.

The inside of the market was small, the shelves and produce aisles sparsely populated, demand being minimal. Jem smiled at the glum white-haired man who sat hunched at a kiosk at the front, staring at his hands. He didn't seem to notice them.

Jem led them through the aisles to the back, careful not to be seen as she explained in hushed whispers that they would be hidden in a ventilated produce crate, shuttled by drivers who had no idea they were smuggling them, and would be transferred by other Resistance agents until they arrived at their destination.

"Our contact should be waiting," Jem said, pushing past plastic sheeting into the dimly lit stockroom. She'd met the Runner twice before, a kindly middle-aged man named Thomas. Quiet, but capable. The shuttered slats to the loading dock were closed, empty crates stacked neatly along cement walls for pickup.

Nobody was there.

They were late, but only by a bit. She cursed silently, wondering if he'd been spooked. If he'd been spotted and forced to run. If he had, there were any number of signals, signs, and codes he should have left for them as warning. And so far as Jem could tell, there hadn't been a warning, nor any sort of PK presence hiding outside in wait.

So where the hell was he?

Blue touched Jem's shoulder, making her flinch. Eyes wide, she pointed to one of the larger crates, which had been left out in the center of the room.

It wiggled.

Jem hissed and drew her EMP blaster, its two shots having

recharged by now. The crate was big enough for two people, and ventilated—probably the one that had been intended to transport Blue and the doctor.

It moved again, something or someone inside thrashing silently.

Heart thudding in her chest, she reached out, blaster at the ready, and pressed the catch release. The crate hissed open, thick white plastic folding in on itself. She recoiled, biting back a scream.

Thomas. Naked but for a pair of filthy underwear. Eyes wild with madness. A weeping eye at the center of an inverted triangle, freshly branded on his forehead.

The all-seeing eye of the Synth. The mark of one who had been subjected to Torment.

Jem could almost hear Armitage's smug, singsong voice chuckling.

Look upon my work, humans, and despair.

"No," Jem moaned, backing away as she realized, with horror, that he had gnawed deeply into the shredded remnants of his hand. "No, no, no, *no* . . ."

Thomas looked at her, then the others, like an animal gone feral.

His eyes settled on Blue. He lifted his neck at a pained, unnatural angle, bearing bloody teeth. Whimpering.

Then, with a sudden violence that surprised even Jem, he lunged at Blue like a scrambling three-legged beast and tackled her, wrapping his single hand around her throat.

"*No!*" Dr. Blackwell screamed, and grabbed the man by the hair, yanking his head back just in time to keep his gnashing teeth from sinking into Blue's cheek.

Blue struggled, eyes bulging as she fought to breathe, one arm clutched around her stomach, the other hand trying and failing to push the madman off her.

Jem was on him in a second, a knee in the small of his back and a well-muscled arm around his throat as she took him in a headlock and *squeezed*.

"Get—the fuck—*off her!*"

She blasted him in the head with an EMP to disrupt his mods, then again, but though he began to twitch and foam, he still clung to Blue with the insane strength of one to whom pain meant nothing.

Desperate, Jem began slamming the butt of the EMP blaster against the side of his face, until finally his grip loosened enough so she could shove him off.

Blue drew breath with a ragged gasp, and Dr. Blackwell pulled Blue away, taking her in a terrified embrace and then laying her down, full-on doctor mode, chattering comforting bedside nothings while she checked over her vitals.

"F-fine," Blue finally said. "I'm fine."

Thomas lay on the ground, face bloody and swollen, a growing pool of blood spreading from his chewed-up hand, chest heaving as he stared into nothing.

Jem shook her head. There was nothing they could do for him now. Nothing but . . .

She stood over him and drew her pistol, steeling herself. But then her shoulders slumped and she holstered the weapon. No way could she risk the noise of a gunshot.

"I'm sorry," Jem said to him. She turned to the others and helped the unsteady Blue to her feet. "We need to go *now*."

This had been a message, not a trap—or they'd have already been taken. Sometimes the Synth left victims of Torment as a cruel demonstration to others who would defy them. Thomas must not have known the importance of his refugee cargo, or Armitage would have surely been waiting.

It wasn't uncommon for Runners and Couriers to have a false tooth equipped with a powerful neurotoxin that would destroy their brain and nerve tissue beyond repair, so as to avoid the fully immersive virtual hell of Torment. Days experienced as years, intricate suffering crafted specifically for each victim— impossible to discern from reality. Impossible to escape with your mind intact.

They fled with urgent caution. Jem led them through gardens, tunnels, and the occasional rain-slick streets in a paranoid, winding pattern she hoped would evade even Armitage's all-seeing eye, should it be looking for them.

Finally she led them through the back entrance of a squalid apartment building, careful to avoid being seen in case their mask net and dummy mod signatures had been flagged for search. She'd have to recalibrate before they made for the backup drop point she'd been given the next day, just to be safe.

The Resistance higher-ups would know that the first drop point had been compromised when Blue and the doctor didn't show. Hopefully they had enough faith in Jem's ability not to assume that she'd been captured too. For now it would be too dangerous for her to attempt contact.

"We'll be safe here for the night," Jem said, relief flooding her as she held aside the flashing peacekeeper crime-scene tape for the others to pass into the darkened apartment. "Backup transfer isn't till tomorrow, so we'll have to lay low for the night."

Fluorescent streetlight filtered in through the window blinds, thin slats of illumination falling across a bloodstained VR immersion bed. These days there was so much empty housing that nobody bothered cleaning up crime scenes like this one once the initial investigation and corpse removal was complete. As such, they made perfect hiding spots for Runners like Jem.

As the doctor sat Blue down on the dusty sofa across the room from the bed, Blue's eyes followed the crusted brown pools of old blood to the words painted on the wall just beyond.

There'd been a rash of murders across the city in the past few months. Dozens that Jem had heard about, and likely many more that she hadn't. Civilians with their throats cut while they were in full immersion VR. And always those same words, painted in blood over the corpse.

WAKE UP.

Too many murders for just one person, Jem thought. Maybe the splashy deaths had inspired copycats. Or maybe this was the coordinated work of multiple killers trying to send a message.

She pushed thoughts of the serial killings out of her mind and closed the door tightly behind them.

"Home sweet home," she said, lightly. "Don't mind the mess. I obviously wasn't expecting company, or I'd have neatened up."

Blue smiled weakly, tearing her eyes from the bloody words. "Interesting art choice," she said, voice still raspy from being strangled. She opened her mouth to speak again, but stopped, rubbing her throat, too pained to continue.

"Here," Jem said, popping the grate off of the wall vent where she'd hidden a bag of rations and supplies. She brought the bag over to the others and gave them boxed waters and some nearly expired MREs.

Blue drank the water gratefully, then stood up, hands pressed against her lower back as she stretched. As she arched her back, the swell of her stomach pressed out through the baggy clothing. "Bathroom please," she said. "Doc here never told me how much getting knocked up makes you have to piss. Might not have agreed, had I known."

Dr. Blackwell smiled. "Humanity thanks you for your bladder's brave sacrifice."

Blue went into the bathroom, and then poked her head back out. "I don't suppose the shower works?"

Jem nodded, suddenly hyperaware of her own sweaty state and body odor.

"Bar of soap in the tub. Towel on the rack. Not exactly the Hilton, but better than nothing."

Dr. Blackwell's cheerful demeanor dropped as soon as Blue closed the door. Her expression went slack, the lines on her face seeming to deepen as she let the worry she'd been hiding show through.

"Hasn't been easy, trying to keep a brave face for the kid," she said, and pulled a squashed box of cigarettes from her pocket. She barked a quiet laugh and ran a hand through her thinning hair. "Stress isn't good for the baby, but relaxation has been something of a tall order."

The shower turned on in the other room with a comforting hiss.

"Who is she to you?" Jem asked.

Dr. Blackwell drew a cigarette with trembling fingertips. Then, seeming to remember the girl, she slid it back in and pocketed the pack.

"I asked for healthy young women. They provided them. Snatched a few who'd been trying to make contact with the Resistance. Disabled their Synth mods, took them off the grid. Offered them a position on the condition that they volunteer for my experiments. Blue was the healthiest, smartest, and most determined to do her part for the human cause. She's a real believer in what the fertility cure might accomplish."

She looked at the bathroom door, hope softening the worry etched so deeply into her face. "But who is Blue to me? Why, she's a miracle."

Jem stared at her blankly.

Blackwell smiled, amusement sparkling in her steely eyes. "Do you believe in miracles, Jem?"

Jem thought of Thomas, teeth sunk deep into his shredded hand. Thought of the brand on his forehead. Thought of a teenage girl named Eva on every screen in every city, so many years ago. Raven hair pulled out in clumps. The inverted triangle all-seeing eye of the Synth branded on *her* forehead, fiery red against the porcelain white of her skin. Teeth gnashing hard enough to crack as she struggled and screamed.

And her eyes—the eyes of the girl Jem had loved, the girl she'd have died for, the girl who might as well have been her sister. Dead eyes with nothing inside. Empty but for the animal tangle of pain and insanity that had replaced her mind.

"No," Jem replied. A dull ache in the hollow of her chest. "I really don't."

"Well," Blackwell said. "That's fair. But when you get to be as old as me, you start to notice things. Little happenstances, here and there, with massive rippling consequence. Like gentle nudges of fate's guiding hand. I could bore you with details. Talk about the people who died to get me here. Talk about the impossible luck that kept me alive, the kindness and sacrifice of strangers."

The doctor shrugged.

"The plague is synthetic—adaptive, organic nano-machines that totally elude observation, let alone treatment. I wasn't even *trying* to find a cure. I stumbled upon it by chance. Accident. Miracle. Whatever you'd like to believe. Now here we are, tasked with the candle of humanity's continued existence. Mother, maiden, and crone. And I . . . I think it has to mean something."

Jem smiled politely but did not reply. She found it cruel to try and convince a person that their faith was a fairy tale. But she'd seen too much to believe that there was any sort of inherent goodness to the world. Been let down by too many to hope that some benevolent, loving presence might be watching.

There was no plan. No God but for a vicious pantheon of silicon tyrants. Just this dwindling end, and the occasional burst of light that only a fool would see as more than the meaningless happenstance of an indifferent cosmos.

Blue came out humming a song that Jem couldn't quite place—looking to Jem very much like an angel as she emerged from the clouds of steam.

Even meaningless happenstance could have its moments, she supposed.

They insisted that Blue take the sofa to sleep, Blackwell sleeping on the floor beside her as if to defend the young woman even in her dreams.

Jem sat with her back to the door, every vibration of every rare step down the hall reverberating in her skull as she allowed herself to drift. Neon green shimmered across her vision, stripping away the darkened gloom of the apartment and replacing it with the vast warm space of an opera house. She sank deeply into the recorded memory playing out in *nearly* full immersion. Jem never allowed herself to be fully immersed, afraid to completely blind herself to her surroundings, even for a moment.

The oppressive silence was replaced by the gentle swell of an orchestra.

She was a child again. Sitting up straight to see over the balcony, her father's hand enveloping hers. Eyes shining with pride and admiration as they watched her mother come spinning onto the stage. Odette the White Swan, resplendent in feathered ivory and cream.

She was perfection—an embodiment of grace. On either side of the dull blue glow of an illusory lake, rows of other dancers—other swans—framed Jem's mother at the center of the stage.

The stage shifted, the lights changed, and the scenery became the palace on the night of the royal ball. The king with his great golden staff. The court in elaborate reds and golds, a multitude of couples filling the stage as they whirled.

Jem fast-forwarded through this part, which she'd seen a million times—the royal court zipping across the stage in blinding crimson zigzags and twirls. She slowed the memory down to normal speed again as the prince danced with women hoping to woo him, his movements polite but bored as he yearned for the swan.

Jem closed her eyes, and when she opened them, she was no longer in the audience with her father. No longer a child, but a woman grown. A dancer, she and the pale, malevolently handsome man beside her moving to the light of the stage. To the shadowed faces of the audience, watching in hushed veneration.

She was Odile, the Black Swan. Jem had always preferred dancing with the dangerous grace of this dark other to the simpering beauty of Odette.

The sorcerer in black led her by the hand into the ball, emerging from a cloud of smoke with smug flourish as he presented Jem to the prince. The audience vanished, and the stage became a *real* palace, immense and glittering with the light of a thousand candles.

Jem and the prince took center stage for their dance, and then—

"Whatchya watching?"

Smears of green filled Jem's vision as she pulled from the VR in a panic, only to find Blue sitting cross-legged before her. Blackwell was fast asleep on the floor beside the couch, snoring softly.

"O-oh," Jem stammered. "I was just—"

"It's okay if you don't want to tell me." Blue cast a glance at the bloody VR bed, a glimmer of longing evident in her darkly beautiful eyes. "Alan—the Runner who brought us here—he told us that your mods are special. That you don't need to plug into a VR bed for full immersion." She sighed. "God, I miss it."

"Well," Jem said, sheepish. "Hold on."

She got up, went over to her bag of supplies. She dug around, hoping she still had it, and—there!

A thick-corded wire, two powerfully magnetic connection pads on either end.

Jem held them up for Blue to see. "You can connect with this to my mods if you like. Gotta keep one ear open for Synth, so I don't fully immerse, but you can go as deep as you want."

Blue grinned eagerly and nodded.

Jem peeled off the dummy mods from the skin over the contact points behind their ears and replaced them with the pads at either end of the wire. They lay down side by side and went into immersion.

Blue took in the palace with a sound of awe, turning on her heel to look at the dozens of magnificently dressed dancers frozen in place around her. The immense ballroom silent but for the echo of her footsteps against tile.

Her eyes passed over Jem and she did a double take, looking her up and down.

"You're a dancer—er, ballerina? Like, for real?"

"Once upon a time," Jem said, twirling around Blue, showing off.

"Never been to the ballet," Blue said. "Never had a chance to."

Jem took Blue's hand, the elegant black feathers of her dress and the thrill of the dance giving her a confidence she might not have otherwise felt. "Then I suppose you've never danced in one either."

She waved a hand, and Blue's clothing turned into that of the prince, with an elaborate black doublet and white, formfitting tights. Blue's stomach was flat, as she had chosen not to reflect the pregnancy in the manifestation of her VR avatar.

"It's the night of the ball," Jem said, dancing around her. "And I, the black swan, have come to make you, the prince, fall in love with me. Tricking you into choosing me over the white swan—"

"That basic bitch—" Blue scoffed.

"—with a dance," Jem finished.

Blue craned her neck to check herself out. "Never thought I'd look so good in spandex." She grinned at Jem and bowed with exaggerated flourish. "M'lady."

Jem curtsied gracefully. "My prince." She waved her hand, and gossamer strings of light formed around Blue's body. Blue looked down at them, alarmed.

"Let the strings guide you," Jem said. "Release yourself to them, and—"

The music swelled, the phantom dancers of the court going into motion as Jem allowed the illusion to play. She began to dance, and Blue, as instructed, allowed the strings to guide her, carrying her through the intricate choreography like a giggling marionette.

When their dance was finally over, Jem dismissed the strings, and Blue fell into her arms, cheering.

"That was amazing!" she said, breathless. "You're so good— can you do that in real life? Or is it just a virtual automated thing, like what you did to me?"

Jem nodded, sheepish. "It's been a while since I did it outside of VR. I'm probably rusty. Hard to find a proper studio to practice in this town."

Blue tsked. "No appreciation for the arts, our tyrannical robot overlords." She took Jem's hand. "Mind if I take us somewhere?"

Jem nodded, and Blue made the palace melt away, replacing the floor with dusky yellow cloud tops, rolling and voluminous. The cloud below them was like something from a cartoon— solid instead of gaseous. The softest possible swell of a warm, cottony sponge.

Blue let herself fall back into the cloud with a contented sigh. She patted the cloud top beside her for Jem to lie down, wisps of what in real life would be sulfur dioxide pushing through her fingertips in ghostly tendrils.

In the distance, the great Venusian cloud cities hung majestically over the swirling impenetrable sea of dense atmosphere below.

"Home sweet home," Blue said. Her smile tinged with melancholy.

Jem lay down beside her, their legs touching. "You're a colonist?"

"Pure Venusian, through and through. My parents, we were visiting family in America. When . . ."

"That's crazy," Jem said. "My family, and some family friends. We were supposed to go to Venus right around when it happened."

Jem's family, and Eva's—a joint vacation, long overdue. And if they had left, just three days earlier . . . she thought of the images of the screaming, ruined Eva—that cruelly branded face paraded on every screen.

"Wouldn't that have been something," Blue said. "The cloud

cities aren't big. We probably would have met. We're the same age—we might have even gone to school together." She smiled. "Life's funny, huh?"

"Yeah," Jem said, trying not to sound bitter. "Funny."

"I'll show it to you someday. Venus. Give you the grand tour!"

Jem smirked, teasing. "Oh, so you're one of those optimists I've heard about. How *annoying*."

"We are the worst," Blue said. "God, I missed VR. I know this isn't real, but it's the best we can do. I get homesick, you know? Even after all these years."

She sat up and a guitar made of light formed in her hands. She closed her eyes and began to pluck an unfamiliar tune, humming. "Not to mention the fact that I haven't been able to get my hands on a guitar since I joined the Resistance. If this was real it would wreak havoc on my fingers. My calluses are totally gone by now. "

She looked down at Jem, who still lay there beside her, staring up at the boiling yellow clouds. Their eyes met and lingered.

"Here," Blue said. "Pick a song, any song. My jam list runneth deep."

"Umm . . ." Jem said, at a loss.

"How about some Beatles? I *love* playing the Beatles."

"The who?"

Blue's expression of horrified shock was only half jest.

"Oh Jem. Jem, Jem, *Jem*. Fuck's sake, dude. Forget the slow death of terrestrial humans. This is the *real* tragedy. Thankfully averted by yours truly. Here, let me play you my favorite. It's called 'Hey Jude.'"

Jem watched her play, captivated as Blue lost herself in the song.

When she finished, she looked at Jem. Expectant.

It probably had something to do with the woman who was singing it, but the song was quite possibly the most beautiful thing Jem had ever heard.

"I like it," she said.

"*Like it?*"

"I love it," Jem said, with exaggerated breathlessness. "It's the greatest song I've ever heard. I have the collected library of humanity's entire musical history stored in my mods, and I'm going to delete them. All but that one song. Because *nothing* else comes close."

Blue nodded, satisfied. "Correct answer."

She flickered out of existence for a fraction of a moment. When she reappeared, her VR avatar's stomach was no longer flat, but swollen with pregnancy. She smiled at Jem, caressed the swell. "If it's a boy, I'm going to name him Jude."

"And Judy if it's a girl?"

Blue crinkled her nose. "Nah. If it's a girl I'm going to name her Zoë. After my mom."

This time it was Jem who made a face. "Zoë? You're going to name the first child born on Earth in thirteen years *Zoë*?"

"What, do you want me to name her Mary? Or Hope? Some bullshit like that?" Blue scoffed. "She's already going to have enough of a messiah complex. I don't want her to be a *total* asshole."

She let the guitar dissolve and leaned back, staring up at the now bruised orange sky, darkened as the artificial sun began to sink, though they couldn't actually see it through the haze.

Jem looked at her stomach. "Can I . . ." she started, but trailed off. Embarrassed.

Blue smirked. "I mean, this isn't my real body. You won't actually feel the baby. But sure. Go ahead."

She pulled up her shirt, and Jem delicately placed her palm

upon the smooth curve of skin. The dark of her hand standing in contrast to Blue's lighter brown.

Blue turned her head, meeting Jem's eyes, and they got quiet. Jem closed her eyes, and leaned in . . .

"*Jem!*" Dr. Blackwell hissed, urgent.

Biting back a swear, Jem yanked them out of VR, back to the hideous gloom of the real world.

Outside the window, the flashing blue and red of peacekeeper drones. Down the hall, arguing. Pounding. A *scream*. Jem tore off the pads from behind hers and Blue's ears, frantically reapplying the dummy mods as she led them to the bathroom in a rush.

They huddled uncomfortably on the damp floor against the thick glass of the shower door, which Jem explained would hide their infrared signature from the hallway on the other side of the wall.

An hour passed, the shouting and screams down the hall going quiet. The peacekeepers left, and the anxious trio went back to the room to try and get some sleep.

They left early the next day, after Jem finished recalibrating their dummy mods and face nets. The streets were populated with scattered groups of the increasingly few people who still had jobs on their way to work. Though employment was optional, having a job gave citizens various little perks and more luxurious living quarters, even though at this point most didn't care, so long as they had their VR beds.

They moved slowly, sticking to side streets until they climbed back down into the tunnels below. After a short trek, they climbed out of a sewer grate into one of Armitage's gorgeously lush garden parks, which was right beside the cathedral Jem had been instructed to use as a secondary drop point, should the first be compromised.

Jem eyed the great old church, her stomach boiling with paranoid dread. Faith was in rare supply. Those who were still religious generally attended VR worship, kneeling within immense glass palaces soaring through watercolor cosmos, angelic choruses emanating through their virtual bodies as they surfed upon synthetically induced euphoria.

The old incense-scented stone of churches like this simply couldn't compare. Still, despite Jem's disdain for the outdated religions of old, she found something comforting about cathedrals like this one. The cool, smoky air. The shadowy figures of forgotten saints glowing with the soft light of electric candles in the alcoves along darkened walls. The dusty shafts of colorful light cast down across the center aisle from old stained glass windows.

Their appointed backup contact sat among the pews, head bowed. A tall, muscular Middle Eastern man with a thick mustache and lustrous black hair. Ezra, according to her coded intel. Though who knew if that was his real name.

Jem had never met him before—she wasn't sure if he was a Runner, or one of those mysterious higher-ups in the clandestine cell structure of their Resistance that she sometimes heard about and almost never spoke directly to. But the description matched, and there didn't seem to be anyone else there. She approached him cautiously, hand hovering by the shielded holster of her pistol.

He looked up sharply and let out a heavy breath of relief.

"Wasn't sure you were going to make it," he said, shouldering the strap of a large duffel bag as he stood. He looked at Blue, eyes casting down to her stomach, though its bulge was hidden by layers of loose clothing. "We found Thomas. Feared the worst."

Ezra slid a heavy iron-bar lock across the immense double

doors leading into the cathedral, then led them past the high altar. He lifted a large slab of stone from the floor, revealing a secret hole and a soft-edged ladder seemingly carved into the wall, leading downward.

His fingers began to glow, a beam shooting from the palm of his hand to paint the smooth-walled little cavern below with gentle light, revealing a slender tunnel leading off to the east.

He had a prosthetic hand—advanced, final generation stuff. Another military-grade Colladi-Tech relic from before the fall, like Jem's rare and powerful mods.

She thought of Eva once more, the horrific images flashing across her mind, unbidden. The last of the Colladi family. Long dead by now.

"I'll be taking you through a mouse hole," he said to Blue and Dr. Blackwell. "You're safe now. No more scurrying through sewers and parks."

"A what?" Blue asked, paling with nervous dread as she stared into the hole.

"Programmable tunnels," Ezra explained. "We use a nano-machine substance called smart cement that eats and repurposes stone, building and collapsing tunnels without making any seismic activity that would give away our positions. Rising up to the surface where needed, then sealed back up behind us."

He tapped the back of his robotic hand like he was punching in a code, and a series of small ceramic discs lit up against the walls of the chamber below. "Timer's set. In exactly three minutes those charges will liquefy and expand the earth to seal the tunnel up, like it was never here. So let's—"

Neon blue flashed across Ezra's pupils. He trailed off, words dying on his lips as he turned to Jem, horrified.

"You were followed."

Jem went cold, his words taking a moment to register. She'd been so careful. *How?* How had they found her?

Heavy metal fists pounded against the immense double doors, dust from the old wood shaking off in clouds. The gate groaned on its hinges, the combined mechanical strength of multiple Synth droids making the wood creak and strain.

"Get down there now!" Ezra barked at Blue and the doctor. He dropped the duffel bag and frantically tore it open, revealing a compact battle rifle. "We'll hold them off, you just—"

Jem grabbed his wrist. "No. You get them out of here. I'll hold the point."

He opened his mouth to argue, then stopped, nodding.

Dr. Blackwell had taken Blue's hand and was trying to pull her away, but Blue yanked her hand from her grasp, resisting.

"There's no time!" Ezra said to her. "You need to go *now!*"

Blue looked at him, and then at Jem, wide-eyed. "But what about—"

"I'll be right behind you," Jem assured her, and it was a lie, and it was obvious that Blue knew it was a lie, but before she could argue Jem grabbed her by the waist and pulled her into a kiss.

Jem pulled away from the stunned woman and forced herself to smile. "*Now go.*"

Eyes glittering with tears, Blue could only nod.

"Thank you, Jem," Dr. Blackwell said. "For everything."

Jem gave the doctor one final salute, then turned to face the Synth.

It had always been inevitable, she supposed. An ending like this. She'd do what she had to.

But they'd never take her alive.

As Ezra, Blue, and the doctor descended behind her, Jem took stock of the provided weaponry with urgent mechanical efficiency: A compact battle rifle, two shock grenades, three multispectrum blocking smoke canisters, and a dozen plastic explosives with timers and a single remote detonator.

Jem crouched behind the pews farthest from the doors, rifle and duffel straps slung across her shoulders. She put in a pair of acoustic filtering earplugs, took a deep breath, and propped the barrel of her rifle on the pew.

The pounding on the door ceased, going silent.

A deadly calm settled over her. Only two more minutes till the mouse hole sealing charges detonated.

The stained glass over the doors exploded into a thousand colorful shards as a flock of drones the size of small dogs flooded into the cathedral.

She fired off five shots in quick succession, bracing herself against the painful recoil as she destroyed four drones and winged the fifth. She ducked for cover behind the pew and tossed a smoke canister down the center aisle as they retaliated with crackling electric slugs.

Half of the remaining drones hovered before the shattered window, firing a cascade of suppressing fire down at her while the others zipped down to the locked doors to pull at the heavy bolts with slender segmented tentacles.

Jem sprinted low to the side, letting the rifle hang loose from its shoulder strap as she took a shock grenade in hand and twisted it to set the timer. She calculated the trajectory and exact time for delay faster and more accurately than any normal human ever could, then flung it toward the distant suppressing drones.

It exploded in their midst with a black cloud crackling with webs of jagged electric blue like a miniature thundercloud, and the now disabled drones plummeted like stones to smash down below.

In that instant Jem rose up from cover and shot the remaining drones that were pulling at the locks before they could open the door or return fire.

She tossed out another smoke canister to shield her path as she ran along the western wall past the antique wooden saints, pressing plastic explosives against columns and other quickly calculated structural weak points.

The explosives were timed, set to go off right after Ezra's charges in exactly *one more minute.*

There was a series of small, crackling explosions, and with a groan, the immense double doors collapsed.

She tossed her final smoke canister and shock grenade out into the squad of tactical peacekeeper droids rushing in with pulsing laser spheres held out at the end of slender black arms.

Jem dove across the aisle into a set of pews as the shock grenade detonated, frying the PKs that scattered too slowly to avoid the blast zone.

Those that hadn't been fried fired laser blasts at her shadowy silhouette amid the smoke in the instant she crossed, the heat of one shot passing over her head so close that she could feel her curls smoldering.

Though Jem was just as blind in the smoke as the droids were, an augmented reality overlay allowed her to see everything clearly, as it had been before the smoke screen—the briefly viewed PKs noted and marked in neon green with position of origin and estimated movement trajectory giving her a much-needed advantage.

She sprinted low through choking smoke to go place the final explosives across the eastern side of the cathedral, but they were closing in on her fast, blind sweeps of laser fire crisscrossing methodically in her approximate direction, invisible lines boiling gaps through the smoke in angled cuts and tracing lines of ember across the wooden saints and pews.

Jem peered around a column and cracked off another shot, destroying another of the PKs, but then a superheated pulse split her rifle in half, blistering her arms as she dropped it and fell back with a muffled scream.

She ducked out from the column with her pistol drawn from the hidden holster and aimed at the pulsing spheres of laser cannons that give away the droid's positions in the smoke.

Two shots fired, two spheres disabled, and then Jem disappeared back into the smoke, moving along the wall amid methodical lancing patterns of murderous heat she could only just barely dodge for their mechanical predictability.

The smoke was thinning, and she could make out four figures closing in on her, only two of which still had functioning laser spheres. She fired two shots into the CPU of the first, then she and the other PK fired at the same time. Fluid and circuitry exploded from the side of its face as an agonizing needle of invisible light seared through her shoulder, sending out a spray of blood against the wooden saint behind her.

Jem screamed, clutching her wound as the final two droids chased after her with eerily silent grace, clawed robotic hands reaching out to take her.

Thirty more seconds.

She unloaded the last of her pistol's bullets into the first, but her shots were messy, and the droid took her by the wounded arm with crushing strength. She pulled out her EMP blaster with a snarl and fired one shot into its face. It crackled, twitching, but remained functional as it closed its hand, crushing the bone. She howled with agony and fired another blast, frying it completely this time.

Sobbing, she rolled away before it could collapse on her, kicking at it. Scrambling to her feet she limped, arm hanging crooked and bloody as she fled from the last approaching PK.

"I see you, Jemma Burton," came a sophisticated, melodic voice that gripped her with icy tendrils of paralyzing fear. "Your primitive little mask doesn't fool me."

Armitage.

It approached with sadistic slowness as she placed the final explosive. She sobbed, limping away, too injured to run to the mouse hole as she struggled to flee from that horrible voice.

"Where are you going, Jemma?" Armitage said through the final Synth peacekeeper. "Why all the fuss? We've heard so much about you—I just want to talk. Come on, don't run. We have a special room in Torment saved just for you. Don't you want to see it?"

Fifteen seconds.

She gripped the altar with bloody hands as she pulled past it. Cold metal fingers brushed against her neck as Armitage grabbed her by the back of her collar, but she pulled free of the coat and tumbled into the hole.

Ten.

She landed hard on the stone below, her ankle turning sideways with a horrible crunch and she couldn't move, she couldn't breathe, and the PK was peering down at her with that blank plastic face and—

Its head exploded as two flashes of muzzle fire erupted from the darkness of the tunnel, and the disabled Synth slumped down, tumbling into the hole to land beside her.

The ceramic discs began to whine.

"I've got you!" Ezra shouted over the piercing noise as he slung the wounded Jem over his shoulders. "Came back once I showed the others where to go, but we—"

The walls of the cavern boiled, closing in fast, and Ezra lunged sideways into the tunnel to pass through the damp crevice the instant before it sealed up.

He ran, panting, as the tunnel collapsed with a foam that thickened to slurry, pouring after them in a sickly gray wave, too fast, and then the earth shook as the plastic explosives detonated overhead, the church caving in on itself, and Ezra stumbled, almost dropping her, and the earth was closing in, the earth was closing *in*!

Wet clay mist choked Jem's lungs, and she could no longer see, no longer feel, and—

THE DOOR IN THE LIBRARY

Nikolai sat in a corner booth of the shittiest bar in New Damascus, where he tried desperately not to think about how complicated every aspect of his life had suddenly become.

Hazeal, and the newly mysterious circumstances of his mother's death.

The Moonwatch insignia, and the ugly secrets it would supposedly unveil.

The woman in the revolver and the spell she'd given him with a touch of her red-gloved hand. Even now, it pulsed seductively at the threshold of casting. But Nikolai had no way to know if the spell would work as promised, of if he'd even be able to control such an advanced weave.

Most of all, though, Nikolai couldn't stop thinking about Ilyana.

She was late, as usual. Ilyana was always late when it came to anything social, if she didn't just flake entirely.

Normally Nik just shrugged off the pang of disappointment he always felt when he realized she would be a no-show. But suddenly he found it difficult to be so cavalier about her absence.

Two years of slow-building friendship and flirtation. Two years of countless mess hall meals and sparring sessions and tutoring hangs that always ended up being more *hang* than tutorial.

All the drunken nights out dancing till the witching hour, followed by exhausted early-morning shifts partnering up on the daily grunt work of scanning sectors of the New Damascus Dome for thinning in the Veil.

An otherwise monotonous job made into the highlight of Nikolai's day by their stolen moments sharing coffee and cigarettes, feet dangling over the sides of their hovering skyhorns as they watched the illusory sun rise over the capitol city. Their impromptu races, invisibly cutting through the clouds at certifiably illegal speeds while they howled like maniacs.

Now were they on the verge of becoming something more?

Smothering a sigh, Nikolai took a long draw from the particularly mediocre honeybrew he'd made the mistake of ordering—his eyes unable to resist drifting over the foamy lip of the glass to check the hideous antique cuckoo clock behind the bar for the millionth or so time.

A hand grabbed Nikolai's shoulder—strong, slender fingers digging painfully through the cloth of his shirt.

"*Boo.*"

Nikolai managed not to flinch, hiding his surprise as he turned to find Ilyana, pursing her lips wide-eyed in a playful show of false innocence.

She moved with a deadly grace, her steps absolutely silent.

Nikolai could never hear her coming. She wasn't wearing her uniform tonight. Instead she was dressed in elaborate, luminescent motley—like some sort of electric harlequin.

He watched her as she slid into the booth opposite.

"One day somebody's going to sneak up on me with actual violent intent," he said. "And I'm just going to smile at them like a dumbass, thinking it's you."

"Maybe it *will* be me," Ilyana said, lounging in her booth. "Maybe this is an elaborate, long-game ruse to put you at ease until . . ." She drew her ruby blade with a flourish, face pulled back into a parody of murderous rage as she pantomimed stabbing him.

Ilyana was always lounging. Before, Nikolai had seen it as a show of confidence. Now he looked deeper and noticed the subtle tightness around her eyes, the frequency with which she shifted around, readjusting.

It wasn't that she was comfortable in any setting, he realized. She was never comfortable at all.

Ilyana stopped midstab and squinted at him, leaning forward. "Wow, wow, *wow*," she said, searching the empty space directly over Nikolai's head. "Why the long face? Did the little storm cloud that follows you around finally ditch you for being too much of a bummer?"

Nikolai took a swig of his drink in an attempt to wash away the tension in his chest. "Just thinking about what happened. Everything feels so . . . complicated, all of a sudden. You know?"

He watched her face, trying to appear casual as he searched for any sign that the specific *complication* he was referring to might be weighing on her mind as well.

Ilyana lit up a black-papered cigarette at the end of a long-stemmed holder. She took a deep draw and exhaled a stream of pale smoke, features smooth with casual indifference.

"You worry too much," she said.

Nikolai frowned, flooded with a fresh rush of anxiety as the waiter approached. Though already a few drinks in, Nik ordered another honeybrew. Ilyana asked for a rocks glass, full of ice.

Steeling himself, Nikolai took a deep breath and looked into her eyes. He moved to put his hand on hers.

She didn't pull away, exactly. She just happened to reach for her pack of cigarettes at the exact same instant his fingers brushed across hers—appearing not to have noticed.

A subtle but pointed rejection. Or was Nikolai being oversensitive?

"Hey. Ilyana. About what happened . . ." he began, just as their drinks arrived.

Ilyana crushed out her cigarette on the table and drew her crystal flask Focal, seeming not to have heard Nikolai. "*Disc*, I'm thirsty!"

She turned the top and the silver dust within was replaced by a sluggish, milky red liquid. Her favorite drink—a potent liquor called dragon's milk. She poured it on ice—the liquor igniting blue and red—and raised her glass to toast.

"*Cheers!*" she said at the exact moment Nikolai opened his mouth to say her name again.

He closed his mouth. Then, after a moment, he just shook his head, his frown turning into a bemused smile.

Oh well, Nikolai thought, nervous tension softening into a bittersweet, melancholic sort of relief. *Might as well take this generously offered opportunity to retain my dignity.*

"Cheers," he said, raising his glass. "To never going back to Marblewood."

"Seriously," she agreed, raising her glass even higher. "Fuck that place."

"Yeah!"

"Fuck Marblewood!" they shouted in unison, clinking their glasses and passionately raising their middle fingers in Marblewood's general direction.

As Ilyana drank, her liquor would occasionally reignite with cold neon fire.

She met Nikolai's gaze, lips in a tight smile as if to hold back from teasing him about something. Her eyes were a deep, rich brown—so dark that they were quite nearly black.

The fire from Ilyana's drink reflected neon red and blue against the inky mirror darkness of her eyes. The colorful reflections seemed to punctuate the teasing, affectionate warmth emanating from within—where just moments before, there'd been only cold.

"Ugh," Ilyana choked, coughing up long puffs of the cold fire like a laughing dragon. "That is *not* for chugging!"

Nikolai grimaced, clearing his throat as he placed the now-empty honeybrew glass on the table.

Ilyana pushed aside her mostly finished drink, the ice still sputtering with tiny spots of flame, and drew her crystal flask. She turned the top. Inside, the bloodred dragon's milk was replaced by a vibrant swirl of liquid rainbow. Eyes never leaving Nikolai's, Ilyana poured a small puddle of the colorful concoction onto the table.

"Have you ever been in love before?" she asked to Nikolai's startled surprise.

"Um . . . well . . ."

The relief he'd begun to feel disappeared. Of course Nikolai had been in love before. But the last thing he wanted to think or talk about at that moment was his estranged childhood sweetheart, Cecilia Astor.

"No need to feel embarrassed around me," she said. "About anything. I'm such a fuckup."

Ilyana laughed a little too loudly. She holstered the flask and drew her dagger Focal, dim light glinting darkly through the ruby blade as she dipped its tip into the colorful puddle and stirred.

The image of a handsome, richly dressed mage with shaggy hair and a cocky grin formed in the pool. He turned his head, meeting Nikolai's gaze with a smug sort of confidence.

"Meet my ex, Jet. Or Prince Jiang, if you take any stock in the titles of Schwarzwald's castrated nobility. Total fuckboy. We were never exclusive, exactly, but we had an on-and-off thing for years. He always wanted to talk about his *feelings*." She practically spat the word. "About *us* and *our relationship*. No matter how many other girls he'd screw behind my back. It drove me crazy. Even though I do miss him. Sometimes."

Nikolai shifted in his seat, staring at her with narrowed eyes. "What happened to *never tell me about your exes*?"

Ilyana dipped her finger in the paint. "You don't have to tell me about your ex if you don't want to. Even though now I'm curious, because when I asked, you looked as if I'd just kicked you in the balls." She leaned forward, voice breathy. "The kind of girl who could leave such a lingering, obviously traumatic mark on Nikolai Strauss? Now *that's* a sorceress I'd like to meet."

Ilyana drew her forefinger from the colorful liquid and pressed it against her tongue. She closed her eyes and visibly relaxed, savoring it.

Then, to Nikolai's great surprise, she leaned across the table and kissed him.

Colors spiraled from Ilyana's face as their lips touched. The dingy bar came alive with powerful oranges, reds, and blues. Like a warmly painted illustration of an idealized pub—a far cry from the reality of their surroundings.

Nikolai sat there, dumbfounded, as the colors faded.

"I'm sorry," she said, watching his face.

"Sorry?"

"For giving you drugs without asking."

"Oh. Yeah. That's . . . okay."

She dipped her dagger in the fluid again and lifted it, point out, before him. A single droplet hung precariously at the tip of the blade. "Care for another?"

He looked at her, hesitating for a moment before he leaned forward and carefully closed his mouth around the end of the blade.

The world once again a vibrant watercolor, Nikolai pushed the blade aside and moved to kiss her.

Ilyana turned her face, hunching her shoulders as she shrank away.

He leaned back, aghast, as she squeezed her eyes shut and began cursing to herself.

"Shit. *Shit.*" She opened her eyes. "I'm sorry. I should go."

Nikolai took another deep breath, trying very hard not to let his agitation show. "Ilyana. Wait."

She rose abruptly and made for the door. After a moment of baffled hesitation, Nikolai followed her outside the bar.

Ilyana's personal dragonfly craft awaited her on the glassy red street in front of the bar. Its long, cylindrical cabin gleamed metallic emerald. A stiff-necked chauffer awaited her, dressed in the formal robes of his station.

"Ilyana, wait!" Nikolai called as she made for the skycraft. "If you really want to drop it, I'll drop it. But please don't go."

She stopped and slowly turned to face Nikolai. "Nikolai . . ."

"You're my best friend," he said, practically shaking. "But I want to be more than just your friend. I care about you. I think you care about me too, and I *know* we'd make an amazing team. But maybe I'm wrong! Maybe I'm just totally misreading the situation. And if that's the case—if you just don't feel the same way about me—that's okay."

"No," she protested. "I do!"

Nikolai took a step closer to her. "Okay. Then let's do something about it. I know you outrank me, and I know things are weird right now. But if you want to at least try . . . I think we could really be something."

She stood there for a long moment. Silent. Impassive. Then, very slowly, she closed the distance between them and pulled him into a hug.

"I'm sorry," she said into his ear. "But you and I are both really fucked-up people. Nothing good would come of us being a thing."

Nikolai pulled away, shaking his head. "So what? You like me, and I like you, but we have *baggage* . . . so we shouldn't even try? Come on, man, that's bullshit. That's just giving up on ever being better than these broken brains our shithead parents left us!"

"Please, Nikolai!" Ilyana said. "You're my best friend too! I *trust* you. And I have so few people I trust in this world."

"Then I wish you hadn't fucked me!" he snapped, blinking back angry tears.

Ilyana tried to pull him into another hug, but he resisted.

She held him at arm's length, not letting go. "Please, Nik. Don't be yet another guy I care about who turns out to be just some asshole looking to get his. What happened in Marblewood . . ."

Nikolai shook his head, relenting. "No, no, you're right. In Marblewood you were vulnerable. I shouldn't have initiated things. It was a mistake, and I'm sorry. I get it. We were both in a weird place."

Ilyana leaned forward to kiss him on the cheek. But instead of a kiss, like he'd expected, she stuck out her tongue and drew it up his face in one long, wet lick. She pulled back, grinning at his shock.

"I'm always in a weird place."

She tousled his artfully messy hair, then turned to walk away. The chauffer opened the side of the gleaming emerald vehicle and she climbed in.

Immense, glassy wings unfolded from the sides of the craft and began to flap too quickly to see, lifting the cylinder with a quiet buzzing hum.

Numbly, Nikolai waved to her, his insides a tangle of confused hurt and disappointment.

Ilyana leaned out over the side of the craft and blew him a kiss.

Then she was gone.

———

"Nikolai, you Fox-mother sow!" Albert sang.

He slid into the booth across from Nikolai, who was silently nursing yet another honeybrew.

"Sorry I'm late. The New Damascian upper crust may lack in some regards, but they certainly know how to throw a party."

Concern flashed across Albert's steely blue eyes at Nikolai's noticeably gloomy state.

"Why so glum, chum?" Then, with a knowing smile: "Ah, I see. Affairs of the heart. No, no, don't deny it! Ilyana's a complicated sorceress. You two have always been close. Me, I wasn't too sure about you at first. But you won me over in the end!"

"Nah, Ilyana's fine," Nik said, not wanting to talk about it.

"I've just had too much to drink. Plus I hate this fucking bar. I don't know why I keep coming here."

The American Cowboy was a once-popular "human-themed" bar that had somehow become a go-to dive for Watchmen and the occasional Edge Guard. Though as human-themed as the American Cowboy touted itself to be, to Nikolai it seemed as if the owners had blatantly gotten everything just *slightly* wrong to annoy the rare mage who might notice.

The bartender was wearing a football helmet and a torn-up wifebeater with RED SOX emblazoned on it. Behind him was a constantly moving mural of a giant gorilla clinging to the top of a skyscraper, slapping spaceships out of the sky with a giant banana.

There were themed drinks like the Heinz Catch-up and the Huckleberry Finnisher, and gag-cigarette brands like Santa's Polar Menthols and Sophie's Choice available from an ornate machine in the bathrooms that only accepted wooden "dollar" coins.

"But you love artifacts of the mundane," Albert protested, leaning over to peer at Nikolai's replica Converse sneakers under the table. "Just look at your shoes! Flimsy little things. Why don't you wear boots like a proper mage?"

Nikolai scowled. "My friend made these for me. I like them. And *everything's* wrong here."

He began listing off inaccuracies and various oddities. Uniforms that didn't make sense. Mixed historical references. Egregious merging of Star Wars and Star Trek mythos.

"Do you remember the last time you sat at this booth?" Albert asked, dismissing Nikolai's complaints with a bored wave. "Or the last time you drunkenly sprawled out in this booth, I should say."

Nikolai shrugged.

"Funny. It's because of that night that Ilyana and I were able to find you in the woods back in Marblewood. Just in the nick of time, I might add. You never did ask how."

"You didn't just cleverly see through my ruse and follow me from a distance?"

Albert leaned in, grinning. "Tracer weave in your shoe, my friend! Last time we were here, you passed out there—right where you're sitting! You always go wandering when you've had too much to drink, and I wanted to keep track of you when you inevitably went off to go brood in some derelict part of town."

He imitated Nik with an exaggerated frown. "You're such a *miserable* drunk I don't know why I take you anywhere."

"A tracer?" Nikolai said, sitting up straighter.

"Inside the sole of your precious sneakers! Just where you wouldn't feel it. Where you haven't felt it! Don't you ever scan yourself for unwanted enchantments, sergeant? You *are* a government employee."

"Good thing I didn't."

Nikolai suddenly became dizzy with the spins, mouth filling with sickly warm puke drools. "Disc. I didn't need that last brew. Or the three before it. I'm going to get some air."

"So predictable," Albert muttered as Nikolai walked away. "Farewell!" he called after him. "You wonderful, irresponsible wizard!"

The American Cowboy was on the southern fringes of the Gloaming District. All the major districts in New Damascus had distinct styles and architecture, but some of the more iconic neighborhoods went so far as to have their own light and weather patterns. The ruby-paved Gloaming, for example, was permanently lit with the buttery red of twilight, no matter what the hour.

Though it was well past midnight, the streets remained raucously packed with magi decked out in a high-fashion mess of pastel and neon—colors and glows and illusions spun into capes and coats and attire from every age, of every sort.

There, a wizard in a jacket like the night sky that sparkled with the glimmer of real starlight. There, a sorceress in a waterfall cloak like a river of sapphire that poured endlessly from neck to hem.

Hundreds of young magi were all singing, dancing, drinking, and smoking in the streets, spilling out of bars and clubs and theaters, all clamoring with music. It was incredible—like the visions of a cheerful schizophrenic who'd lost their way at the New Orleans Mardi Gras celebrations of old.

The luster of the Gloaming had faded somewhat to Nikolai in the two years since his first night out. The neon crowds that had once awed him now merely annoyed him as he shoved his way through the mob in search of quieter streets.

Tension released in his chest as soft red light faded into darkness. It wasn't raining now, but knowing the Noir district, it would be soon.

Few magi came to the Noir at night. The streets were silent but for vermin, disenfranchised sex workers disparagingly referred to as flesh magi, and the occasional half-mage sheltering from the damp night air in whatever stoop or alleyway hovel they could find.

Every city had its slums. Even New Damascus, the grand capital of the magi nations, with its impossible towers of jewel, alabaster, and stone so black one could barely see them.

Nikolai loved the Noir. Loved it for its quiet, its gloom, and the near-perpetual drizzle.

He'd never quite grown accustomed to the noise of the city,

never quite wrapped his mind around a million magi all living under the same Veil.

Nikolai ignored the eyes glinting hungrily from the alleyways. Magi never walked alone through this part of the city, unless they were either stupid . . . or dangerous. From the way the eyes would disappear into the shadows as quickly as they'd lit up, it was obvious that the more experienced predators could tell Nikolai was the latter.

The thrill of terrorizing vicious pimps and alleyway hunters was half the reason he stalked the Noir's grimier corners whenever he was drunk and feeling shitty about himself. It was the perfect place to seethe—face fixed in a scowl, fist pointedly clenched around the hilt of his blade Focal while he stared down *anyone* who might be foolish enough to fuck with him.

Thus far, nobody had.

Ilyana's strange rejection repeating itself in his mind, over and over again, Nikolai wished that for once someone would mistake him for a drunk who'd lost his way and make an attempt on his life.

She didn't want him. That much was clear. Just like Astor had stopped wanting him all those years ago.

Unbidden, memories of Cecilia Astor begin to flood his mind. Images of Astor, Stokes, his uncle—all the magi he left behind in Marblewood. All the people he'd spent the past two years trying to forget.

He had a new life here in New Damascus. New friends and a career in the clandestine services that excited him as much as it terrified him. Besides Stokes, and maybe his uncle Red, nobody back in Marblewood cared about him. They probably didn't even think about him. So why bother?

Considering how things had transpired with Ilyana, however, life in New Damascus had suddenly lost some of it its luster.

His head was pounding. His vision swam, his mouth gone sour as too-sweet honeybrew and greasy bar snacks boiled in his stomach, threatening to rise.

Worse was the lump in his throat. The stinging in his eyes. The crushing hot weight on his face, making it feel as if his eyes and cheeks were going to collapse in on themselves.

Nikolai hated crying.

Even now, whenever he wept he could practically hear his mother calling him *weak* with every drop that ran down his face. *Pathetic* with every sob. But one could only face so much hardship with steely-eyed resolve before the occasional, inevitable breakdown.

As Nikolai stalked across the wet cobblestone, grateful for the slick mask of rain that hid his tears, he found himself lost in the memory of the first time he ever met Cecilia Astor.

He'd been crying then too.

One day, when Nikolai was eight, he'd hidden himself in a stall of the boys' bathroom at his school, praying that nobody could hear him as he struggled through snot and tears to calm himself.

His mother's lesson that morning had been particularly brutal, and all day he'd been distracted from class, struggling to breathe through the tightness in his chest that threatened to overwhelm him until he'd been forced to excuse himself.

He hated it—wished his body would listen to the cold logic of his brain, could listen to his mother's voice calmly explaining that there were terrible things beyond the Veil, and that if she didn't make him strong, he and the people he loved—the people he needed to protect—would be hurt. Die, even.

But Nikolai didn't love anyone. Not really. His parents, of

course. But did that even count? And weren't they supposed to protect *him*?

A tiny fist pounded against the stall, hard enough to make him jump.

"*What?*" he said, yanking open the door to curse the intruder.

Angry words died on his lips as he froze, stunned.

Standing before him was a girl with short, straw-colored hair sticking out in all directions and a smattering of freckles across an upturned nose.

Her lips were pursed in a tight little frown—her chin jutted out defiantly as if she'd eaten something sour and was furious at the injustice that had been committed against her palate.

"W—what are you doing?" he asked her, hurriedly trying to wipe away evidence of his tears with a sleeve. "This is the boys' room."

"I used to cry like that," she said, with a sort of twangy Southern Veil accent he'd never heard before.

"I wasn't crying!" Nikolai said unconvincingly. "Crying is for babies."

And Nikolai was no baby. Not after a year of his mother's lessons, which she'd begun in secret when he was seven.

The girl gave Nikolai a knowing look with eyes too old for her little face. "My daddy used to call me stupid. And ugly. And he hit me. Then his mom always healed me so no one would know and told me to shut up when I cried."

"His mom . . . your grandmom?" Nikolai said with wonder. His mother always did the same, using her golden medi-glove Focal to heal his wounds and bruises with little clouds of sparkling light. Hiding what she'd done.

The girl crinkled her nose. "I guess. I *hate* her."

Who was this strange, angry little girl? He didn't have any

friends—didn't *need* any friends—but there weren't that many magi in his school and he knew everyone.

"I'm Astor," she said, as if reading his mind. "I moved here last week from Blue Ridge. You're the only one in our class who hasn't talked to me yet. You don't talk to *anyone*. And today you looked so sad. So I followed you."

"I'm sorry," he said, feeling ashamed. "I'm Nikolai. And I'm not sad, I just—"

"You should tell on them."

Nikolai froze. "What?"

"I know you don't want to tell, 'cause you love them. But they don't love you. Not really. Or they'd be nice."

"You're wrong," Nikolai said, and looked away, unable to meet her eyes.

"I told on my dad," she said. "He used to only hit me, but one time he started hitting my sister and she's practically a baby."

She stuck her chin out again with that defiant intensity only exaggerated by her wild crown of hair. "So I started calling *him* stupid and ugly and told him that I hated him so he would hit me instead. Mommy was always too scared to stop him so I ran away before his mom could heal me. It took all day but I found a Watchman and showed him and asked him to protect my sister."

She beamed, proud, but Nikolai could tell it was for show. At least a little bit.

"So they took him to jail and he can't talk to us anymore. We left his mom's farm and came here to stay with my cousin."

"I'm . . . glad," Nikolai finally said. But he knew that he could *never* tell on his mom. His mom was an Edge Guard married to a Watchman. Even if they could arrest her, none of the Watchmen would be strong enough to fight her anyway.

She stared at him for a bit, pinching her chin thoughtfully

with her thumb and her index finger. Then she nodded, having come to some sort of decision. "We're friends now," she said. "Everyone is nice here but they don't get it."

And that was that. Nikolai had made his first friend, and Astor wasn't going to take no for an answer. She *never* took no for an answer.

Astor was very close to her cousin, a loudmouth class clown named George Stokes. And the moment she told Stokes, very seriously, that Nikolai was her friend now and Stokes had to be friends with him too, he just shrugged, said okay, and started treating Nikolai as if they'd been best friends their whole lives. Even though really, they'd been in the same class for two years and had never actually spoken.

Having friends changed everything for Nikolai. Stokes was funny—he was always joking around and laughing but never said anything mean about *anyone*. And when they watched the old human movies Stokes's dad got for them from the university and something sad happened, Stokes would always think of something happy to say, or at least try to make the others laugh.

Nikolai wasn't sure Stokes had ever been sad. Not really—not like he and Astor. Because whenever they seemed down he would always start cracking jokes or fart and blame it on Astor, which never failed to make them *all* laugh—but it was in this sort of panic, like being sad was some sort of sickness he didn't understand but couldn't stand to see his friends suffer.

Astor and her little sister lived with Stokes until Astor's mom saved up enough money as a waitress to get their own little apartment. Her clothing was all secondhand—frayed and stained and almost always too big for her. She pretended not to care but sometimes he would catch Astor looking at herself in the mirror and Nik could tell that no matter what she said, and no matter what he told her, a part of her still believed what her dad had said. About her being stupid. And ugly.

For the first time in his life, Nikolai knew what happiness was. In flashes and moments, at least. And when Nikolai was with Astor, there was this weird feeling in his stomach—this kind of warmth that made him want to smile and run around.

One day, not long after he and Astor had truly become inseparable, Nikolai got into his very first fight.

Astor tripped and fell during a game of tag—totally ate it, face-first in a puddle. She sat up and started laughing—grinning at Nikolai with a mask of mud, pretending that she'd transformed into some sort of monster as she began chucking handfuls of muck at him.

But then another mage said something that made her stop smiling. Nikolai couldn't even remember his name now, or what he said exactly—all he could remember was that the mage had been one of the rich kids, and how ugly he looked when he and his friends started laughing, how ugly they *all* were when they pushed up their noses and started making pig noises at her.

It wasn't the first time they'd teased her, though she'd been too proud to tell Stokes or Nikolai. Teased her for her clothing. Teased her for her tangled hair, which was rarely brushed because her mom was too busy with two jobs and taking care of Astor's little sister. Teased her for being poor.

Watching Astor retreat inside herself as they mocked her was the first time that Nikolai had experienced a very specific kind of anger. He broke one mage's nose, gave the other a black eye, and pinned the ringleader to the ground, forcing him to eat mud while telling the boy that he'd *kill* him if he ever made fun of Astor like that again.

It was only then that the horrified headmaster finally pulled

Nikolai away, who, even as the much larger mage carried him off, continued thrashing and screaming threats back at the weeping boys.

It was the second time Nikolai had ever seen his Watchman father lose his temper.

"You could have *killed* them!" his father rumbled—barely raising his voice, but still terribly intimidating as he towered over him. Nikolai stared sullenly up at his father, his briefly broken but now-healed hand wrapped in ice, his still-bloody lip trembling.

Calming himself, Nikolai's father explained that there was almost no fight you can't talk your way out of—no mage you can't reason with. That fighting should always be a last resort. That the most heroic thing a mage could do was to use reason instead of violence. To use kindness and love instead of anger, instead of hate. That there was always a *choice*, difficult as it might seem.

His mother, on the other hand, showed him how to coat his knuckles with a layer of hardened air, so he wouldn't break his fingers next time he had to throw a punch.

She always was the practical one.

Nikolai never forgot how Astor slipped her muddy little hand into his as they waited outside the headmaster's office for their parents to come get them after the fight. Never forgot how his mother's lessons finally began to make sense.

———

Nikolai began to run. Slowly at first, gaining in speed, sneakers slapping against the gleaming cobblestone.

"*Elefry*," Nikolai hissed, launching himself from the ground as the featherweight spell seeped from the channels of magic through his body, through his flesh, settling on bone. He became a fraction of his normal weight—light enough to soar, light enough that he could twist around and fire off a continuous jet of jellied air with an inversion on the *akro* weave from his baton to propel him into an arc high up over the buildings.

It wasn't quite flying, but Nikolai couldn't help but feel the tension in his chest melt away as he was buffeted by the freezing wind.

The city spread out before him, the Noir a wet darkness below, the Gloaming a soft red light receding in the distance. The Mage King's tower pierced the sky at the center of New Damascus—windowless, three-sided, and white, glowing with a soft inner light. Nikolai could practically feel the magic bleeding off it from here.

The airspace above the pedestrian level was technically restricted from this sort of featherweight flight, and was reserved for skyhorns or civilian crafts. But traffic was sparse above the Noir, and if any Watchmen decided to give Nikolai shit, he'd just flash his rank insignia and tell them to fuck off.

Even as a lowly sergeant, Nikolai outranked most Watchmen. Still, whenever he saw one zip by overhead—a blur of white and blue and sparkling golden light—he couldn't help but feel a pang of envy.

He was glad to be an Edge Guard, but he'd spent most of his life dreaming that he might one day follow in his father's footsteps. Even now, two years after that door had closed, he'd sometimes catch himself fantasizing about his life as a Watchman that would never be.

Nikolai slowly adjusted his trajectory, touching down on a rooftop and allowing the featherweight weaves to disappear momentarily so he could run for a bit to build momentum, casting the spell once again just as he pushed off.

It began to drizzle, miniscule droplets stinging as he pierced the air in long arcs. The blistering cold seemed to peel away the stomach-twisting thoughts of Ilyana and Astor. Of Hazeal, Marblewood, and Jubal. Of the revolver's secret spell burning away at the back of his mind and the door in the sky it could—

Nikolai was falling.

His eyes fluttered open to the odd sight of blood trailing from his shoulder as he plummeted to the filthy streets below. His baton spun away—felt more than seen as an irresistible tug as it twirled into the gloom. His blade remained sheathed at his side, but as he turned he saw the ground looming, saw sharp-edged roofing and gutters full of filth drawing close, and he couldn't move his arm, blood still trailing from where he'd been pierced by some silent projectile.

With an agonized grunt he realized that his featherweight enchantments had faded. In moments he'd be a smear on the pavement, unless—

"Elefry!" he screamed against the wind. As the spell settled on his bones, his surface to mass ratio became such that his fall was slowed by the wind alone into an odd twirl. Barely skimming the edge of a roof, he desperately pulled into a roll, feeling his already wounded arm crunch as it caught on the tile edge.

Nikolai couldn't even scream as he landed in the pile of refuse in an alley, could only gasp, wheezing, as he just barely missed impalement on a broken bottle, its jagged glass slicing up his cheek.

Frantic footfalls slapped against wet pavement, hideous hyena laughter echoing as it drew near.

"Get his Focal! *Get his Focal!*"

Adrenaline pounding through his veins, Nikolai forced himself to stand. He staggered from the trash heap and fell heavily against the wall as a skinny mage with a crooked nose rushed him, a morbidly obese mage with hideous acne scarring following close behind with a pistol in hand.

Nik's shot and broken arm hanging uselessly against the wall, he reached over clumsily to draw his blade from the sheath.

"No ya don't," the skinny mage said, covering the hilt with his own hands to block Nik's weaker grip. Teeth pulled back in a snarl, Nikolai slammed his forehead against the thin mage's face.

"*Styx and fucking stones!*" he howled as blood plumed from his already crooked nose. Spitting and swearing, he yanked the blade from Nikolai's sheath and stumbled back, falling to the ground.

Nikolai realized distantly that these magi didn't have any Focals and weren't magi at all. They were half-magi, like Hazeal—though these two had probably been burned out as punishment for a crime, or for being deemed dangerously unfit to wield magic. The Noir was home to many such half-magi who struggled to eke out an existence in the shadows, invisible to the cheerfully indifferent magi populace.

Wishing desperately that he wasn't so drunk, Nikolai sprinted serpentine toward the fat one as the half-mage drew a bead on Nik and opened fire.

The pistol was a lowly street artifact—enchanted with a muting field to block the noise of gunfire, but mundane in every other regard. Bullets zipped around Nikolai as the half-mage kept missing, the shots somehow more terrifying for their dulled silence.

A glassy coating of hardened air formed across Nikolai's knuckles as he twisted into a swing, but the punch was sloppy—a glancing blow that turned the half-mage's greasy face hard enough to loosen his grip on the pistol, which skittered off into a gutter, but not hard enough to take him down.

The other came at him swearing from behind and Nikolai spun to meet the thin one's assault with an outstretched hand and a snarled, "*Pyrkagias!*"

Too drunk, wounded, and weak without the aid of his Focals, Nikolai was only able to make the smallest puff of fire. The skinny half-mage's momentary expression of horror slipped into a hideous grin as he passed through the wisps of flame and slammed his shoulder into Nik, sending him sprawling.

Nikolai writhed on the filthy street, biting back sobs as he felt himself weakening from his bleeding shoulder. Soon adrenaline wouldn't be enough, and he'd slip into unconsciousness.

The panting half-magi peered down at him with delight, the thin one planting a boot on Nikolai's chest to keep him still.

"You see that, Chaz?" he said, whistling through yellow teeth. "See him try to burn me? We got ourselves a Battle Mage."

"An Edge Guard, eh?" the fat one giggled. "I'd rather have a go at some sweet little sorceress who's lost her way, but carving up one of the king's baby butchers?" He grabbed Nikolai roughly by the throat, sausage fingers squeezing so hard that he could barely breathe. "It'll do."

"A mean one too, I bet. You see his knife Focal? Bet you anything he's used it plenty on our sort. Bullet through the shoulder and he still broke my *fucking* nose."

He kicked Nikolai in the side, *hard*, and Nik felt himself vomiting, tried to turn as he gasped and gurgled, screaming as the thin one shifted his boot to the bullet wound in his shoulder and pressed against it.

Nikolai was going to die. Oh fucking Disc, he was going to die. They were going to cut him up, torture him, and leave him to bleed out in this alley.

He wished he had worn his Edge Guard uniform instead of

civvies. If he'd been in uniform, the enchantments would have protected him from the bullet. Their kicks and punches would have been turned aside, and by now he'd have reduced them to piles of ash and bone. But no. He'd worn civvies—clothing Ilyana had helped picked out for him in the fashion district. All torn up now. All soaked in blood and filth.

All those years of combat training with his mother, then the Edge Guard—all the blood, blisters, and broken bones; all the training, tactics, drills, and theory—yet there Nikolai was, beaten and brutalized by lowly half-magi for the second time in as many days. What had been the point of it all?

He wouldn't beg. No matter what they did to him, no matter how they tortured him before finishing him off. He was no stranger to pain. At least in this, his training would be of use. At least in this, he'd triumph.

They kicked him, punched and slapped him, picked him up and threw him around, laughing as Nikolai made weak attempts to fight back and swing at them with his one good arm. But it was no use—they were too strong, too quick. This wasn't the way.

"Fuck you!" he snarled, forcing himself to stand and stumbling back away from them. "I'll kill you. *I'll kill you both. I'll fucking kill you!*"

But they just laughed.

"You think you know how to use that knife?" Nikolai hissed, looking at his stolen Focal tucked into the thin mage's belt. "You don't know shit. You couldn't cut me if you tried. Come on, you milk-sop wretch. You Fox-crack son of a flesh mage."

Fat Man's face twisted into a snarl, but Thin Man chuckled, putting a hand out to stop him.

"Now now, Sergei. Piggy's trying to make us mad. Trying to make us kill him quick. But we ain't gonna do something like that, is we? No way, Piggy. I'm going to stab you—I'm going to cut you good—where it'll hurt, not where it'll kill you. Then I'm gonna cut off your lips. I'm gonna feed them to ya. For what you said. Understand?"

"Fuck. *You.*"

"Jeeves. Listen to this pit-pile." Thin Man sighed, and rushed Nikolai, stabbing the blade into his gut.

Nikolai gasped as it slid through his skin. He could barely control his body as he felt it twist inside of him, as he felt his innards tear—but he clenched his fingers around Thin Man's hand, around the pommel of the blade, and leaned into it. Closing his eyes, he channeled a flood of magical energy through the blade buried in his flesh.

"*Pyrkagias,*" Nikolai said, then grinned, and Thin Man began to scream as flames coursed up his arm from the dagger, engulfing him. He tried to pull away but Nikolai held on tight, feeling his own flesh blister as he barely kept the flames away from his own skin, clothing turning to ash as the other's flesh peeled away, as the half-mage's face melted like crimson-streaked wax, filling the air with the stink of burned meat.

Nikolai pushed the dying half-mage away and clumsily rushed the other, who stood there dumbstruck. Clenching his teeth, Nik yanked the blade out of his side and swung it at the other's face, just missing as the other stumbled back. He turned to run, but Nik shot a jet of flame at his back, knocking him down.

Nikolai collapsed on top of him, turning him over. The half-mage tried to swing at Nik, but Nik just bolted the offending hand down with an arch of hardened air, pinning it to the ground, then the other—bones crunching audibly as the wrists snapped.

"Please!" the half-mage blubbered, tears pouring down his

pockmarked face. "I'm sorry! I'm sorry! I'm so sorry! Let me go, lemmegolemmegolemmego—"

"Shut up! Shut your *fucking mouth!*"

Nikolai jammed the knife between Fat Man's teeth, viciously shooting jellied air down the half-mage's throat to fill his lungs and belly.

He stopped, horrified as he realized what he was doing, and released the weaves.

The half-mage gasped a ragged breath, wheezing hideously as he passed out. Nearby, the skinny one gurgled, a smoking mass.

Nikolai stumbled out of the alley toward the invisible pulsing beacon of his baton. His blade Focal fell loosely from fingers; he could barely feel it as he collapsed onto the street. It was dark, even beyond the alley—a single streetlight burning dully a quarter of a block away.

"Help!" Nikolai screamed, the pool of blood growing around him. "*HELP!*"

The light began to swim in his vision, fingers going cold, numb, and soon he couldn't hold onto his wound anymore—could feel the blood coursing hot down his side.

As the dark grew, and the cold began to deepen, he closed his eyes and remembered Astor's little hand tightly gripping his own.

For matters of importance, Captain Jubal preferred holding meetings in the parlor of his lavish estate instead of his office in HQ.

Nikolai sat across from the captain, a graying moonfaced mage who looked to be in his sixties, even though he was quite nearly 125 years old. Though not quite able to completely halt the aging process, healers could slow the ravages of time well enough so that most magi lived well into their second century—the most powerful even into their third.

Beside the captain stood his second-in-command, First Lancer Thane, who led expeditions beyond the Veil. He was a towering, muscular man—bald and maggot pale. One of his ears was melted like wax at the center of a burn scar. His logic Focal was an ivory pocket watch hanging from the breast of his uniform by a milky white chain. His art Focal was a golden club covered in thorns of ruby.

Thane had always made Nikolai uneasy. There was a casual cruelty to the man, made evident to Nik the one time Thane had taken it upon himself to test Nikolai's combat abilities as a cadet—which had been far more advanced than those of his fellow trainees.

Nikolai still bore a small scar on his back from the session where Thane had struck him with his thorned Focal as punishment for letting his guard down. The Lancer had forbidden Nikolai from healing the wound magically, so the mark would serve as a permanent reminder.

In some ways, Thane reminded Nikolai of his mother. Though unlike Thane, she'd never seemed to take pleasure in her abuse. Even at her worst.

Not even Captain Jubal seemed to like the Battle Mage, though he hid it well enough. Rumor had it that Jubal had quite nearly forced Thane to resign for wounding Nikolai—but the Lancer had been appointed by the king, and in the end he'd merely been made to apologize.

Captain Jubal sighed heavily, seeming to deflate as he stared at Nikolai, who kept his eyes downcast, his face a carefully calculated mask of contrition.

"It's all a bit fuzzy," Nikolai said. "The healer gave me a low dose of Tabula Rasa, so the . . . fight . . . feels more like a bad dream than anything. I can remember it, but only in flashes and patches."

"Bested by a couple half-mage alley rats," Thane hissed, wormy lips twisting into a sneer. "Pathetic."

Captain Jubal regarded Nikolai silently, tapping the pommel of his candy-striped cane Focal propped beside him. Nikolai had never seen Jubal's art Focal. He assumed it was a weapon, like Ilyana's ruby blade, Albert's rapier, or his own dagger. No one seemed to know, and it was something of a mystery among the Edge Guard. The low-ranking ones, at least.

"And why, might I ask," Jubal finally said, "were you flying around the Noir in the middle of the night drunk out of your mind?"

Nikolai shrugged, at a loss. Jubal's expression softened, and he opened his mouth to speak but was interrupted by a faint hum. He touched the crystal nestled in his ear with a sound of annoyance.

"Styx. Pardon me, Nikolai. I've got to take a call with the duchess-elect back on the crystal in my office. Thane, I need you on this call too. Disc-damned royalty—no respect for other magi's time. There's coffee in stasis in the kitchen down the hall. Help yourself."

The parlor opened directly into the high-walled courtyards circling Jubal's manor, the air fragrant with tropical fruit trees and great cascades of exotic flowers. An ornate door at the end of a garden path led to Captain Jubal's office halfway across the city via extravagantly expensive folded space enchantments.

Nikolai was always struck by how silently Captain Jubal moved despite his middling stature and fleshy frame. "I'll try to keep this short but it might take a while," Jubal called back, passing through the door into the darkly wooded room.

Thane cast one final look of disgust at Nikolai before following the captain.

"Fucking asshole," Nikolai muttered, once the Lancer was safely out of earshot.

Suddenly alone, he became acutely aware of the Moonwatch medallion in his pocket. A key to any door, given with the vague instructions to *look to Jubal's library*.

He'd decided to hand over the medallion and tell Jubal the truth about what transpired with Hazeal. But now . . . with the captain's estate all to himself . . .

Breathing deeply to slow his pounding heart, Nikolai rose.

Coffee. He was just getting coffee.

But as his sneakers moved noiselessly over marble so polished he could see his reflection, Nikolai found himself passing the kitchen and continuing deeper into Jubal's home.

He began to sweat, his will diminishing with every step as he searched for the library. Twice he stopped, knowing that he should turn back, that what he was doing was stupid. Dangerous even.

But then he could hear Hazeal's words.

Murderer. Butcher.

Pounding in his ears like a drumbeat. Pushing him forward.

Murderer. BUTCHER.

Lit with soft, honey-yellow glow bulbs, Jubal's estate was a museum of exquisite furniture and eclectic human art. There, a painting marked as Vincent van Gogh's *The Red Vineyard*. There, a print marked as Shepard Fairey's *Barack Obama "Hope" Poster*.

Nikolai turned down a long, richly carpeted hallway—and there it was.

The library.

Three floors of old cloth- and leather-bound volumes—a hodgepodge of priceless magical tomes and old manuscripts. Two heavily enchanted display cases were the obvious center-pieces of his collection.

There were several translations of the Torah, Qur'an, Christian gospels and testaments, Buddhist Tripitaka, Hindu Bhagavad-Gita, and Bardo Thodol—the Tibetan Book of the Dead.

Other works Nikolai had never heard of: *The Canaanite Book of Divination*—noted on the label as one of the earliest works of necromancy. Beside it was *The Binding of Thanatos*—a famously illegal grimoire from ancient Greece.

Stomach in knots, Nikolai pulled his tracking spectacles from his breast pocket and began to poke around. Countless footprints crisscrossing the thick carpeting appeared as sparkling phantoms through the enchanted lenses, the older tracks glowing more faintly than the new.

He followed them one set at a time in dizzying spirals around the library until he finally found several leading directly into a bookshelf against the far wall.

There weren't any lingering track marks on the books them-selves, so he removed the spectacles and began brushing his fingers across the bindings. This shelf was primarily composed of human literature, classic through contemporary. Through his fingertips he detected simple preservation enchantments, but nothing out of the ordinary.

He wiped the sweat from his brow with the sleeve of his uni-form and began again, more slowly this time.

"Come on . . . come on . . ."

There.

There was something different about the pristine white copy of Stephen King's *The Stand*.

Nikolai removed it from the shelf and nothing happened, the unusual enchantments no longer detectable. Placing the novel back on the shelf, he twisted his fingers, following a subtle labyrinth of secret weaves, tracing them into a spiraling funnel at the base.

Taking a deep breath, he channeled a delicate thread of energy into the invisible circle.

Click.

The bookshelf came ajar, swinging silently on well-oiled hinges. The shelf revealed a staircase descending into darkness, echoing with a previously muted cacophony of men screaming with fear and pain that almost made him fall backward in shock.

A hand closed firmly on Nikolai's shoulder.

He cried out in surprise, spinning around as he lashed out with his baton.

Captain Jubal deftly stepped back, effortlessly moving beyond his swing—though not quickly enough to save the steaming mug from being knocked from his grasp as Nikolai stood there, horrified.

Jubal's lips pressed thin as he watched coffee drip down the ancient manuscripts. He returned his gaze to Nikolai, who stood with his Focals drawn, frozen.

Behind Nikolai, there came another scream. He winced, glancing over his shoulder, then back at Jubal.

"Lost?" Jubal said flatly.

Jubal looked at Nikolai's drawn Focals. Hands trembling, Nikolai slid them back into their hilts and stood at attention.

"Sir. I'm sorry, I was just looking at your books, and that one caught my eye, and . . ."

He was interrupted by another scream and trailed off. Jubal looked past him, into the darkness.

"You want to know what's down there, don't you?"

"Sir," Nikolai protested. "I didn't mean to snoop, I was looking at the book and I thought the enchantments on the cover were weird, so—"

Jubal cut him off with a sharp gesture. "You've found my secret spot. My other . . . study. Don't you want to see what's inside?"

"Sir?"

Nikolai kept his hands pressed firmly at his sides, desperately wanting to grab for his Focals. But Jubal was a magus—a master in one or more spellcasting domains. At least one of which was battle magic, in the captain's case. He wouldn't even need to use his candy-striped Focal to turn Nikolai into cinder.

Jubal stepped closer, looming. He wasn't a tall man, but he was imposing. Broad shouldered with thick, muscular arms. More than that, he carried himself with a demeanor held only by the most powerful magi.

He put his hand on Nikolai's shoulder—gentle but firm—and turned him to face the stairwell. Light flickered at the bottom. The screams grew louder as they began to descend. Nikolai whimpered, helpless and numbly resigned to whatever fate awaited below.

An oddly dull roar of gunfire joined the screaming. And then . . . music?

They reached the bottom of the staircase, turned the corner, and—

It was a home theater. There was a war movie on, projected from an old film reel at the back of the room, a dusty beam of light cast over plush leather sofas.

The movie was brutal. Graphic. Human soldiers with bayonets storming trenches and butchering one another.

Nikolai let out a long breath, suddenly so weak that had Jubal not been holding his shoulder he'd have sunk down to his knees.

Jubal was making an odd noise behind Nikolai, who turned to find him laughing.

"Oh! Oh, ho, ho, oh! The look on your face! If you could see yourself—"

Nikolai moved to one of the couches and nearly collapsed into it. The movie was extremely loud—blaring from speakers strung up along the walls. *Human* tech—electrical.

"*Disc*, sir," Nikolai said, still trembling. "I thought you had some sort of—"

"Torture laboratory? Some sort of evil Necromancer lair?" Jubal chuckled, and switched off the projector. The silence was a relief. "Nothing so interesting as that, I'm afraid. Just a fellow fan of human cinema. Before you arrived I was doing a little organizing in the library. Left the door open while I worked so I could listen from upstairs."

Jubal led Nikolai to a minibar along the side of the cozy padded room. With a twist of his fingers he created two perfect spheres of ice and dropped them into a pair of glasses. He poured amber fluid over the spheres and gave one to the still-shaken Nikolai.

"Bourbon," Jubal said. "I'm a southern mage, Nikolai. None of this honeybrew or dragon's milk nonsense."

Nikolai grimaced as he took a sip.

"Takes some getting used to," Jubal said, swirling the alcohol in his glass. "Here, let me show you something."

Jubal led Nikolai through a door into a long, white-walled gallery of old human machine parts, devices, and art of both human and magi origin. There were oil lamps and light bulbs, vacuum tubes and great green sheets of computer chips inlaid on silicon. Engines and motors of every shape and size were placed atop posts between great multipaneled paintings and sculptures and portraits dating from antiquity to 2020.

"I have to keep my old mechanical collection secure down here. The king's a real stickler for tech regulation, even with his higher-ups. This is smaller than my collection in Blue Ridge. Can't drive motorcycles or automobiles in New Damascus, so I left them back home." Jubal sighed. "Flying's a thrill, but there's something about those old machines that's just so wonderfully dangerous and inefficient. The human way, eh? But here, I think I've got something you might find more interesting."

There was a heavy steel door at the far end of the gallery. Jubal pressed his hand against it, and it swung open with a faint glow.

As Nikolai entered the next room he was struck with an array of unfamiliar scents. Dusty concrete, mechanical oil, and an odd, acrid smoke that he didn't recognize.

Long glow bulbs along the low wooden ceiling pulsed to life at their entrance, revealing a cement-walled armory and a shooting range with two long lanes and glowing, illusory targets at the end.

There was a workbench and worktable by the entrance, with neatly arranged tools, rags, and oils as well as shelves of various ammo in plain cardboard boxes. A rack of guns hung on display beside it, stacked with pistols, revolvers, shotguns, and rifles.

Nikolai gasped, taking a step back as he noticed Hazeal's rune-etched revolver hanging in the air at the center of a fixed, translucent bubble. A single spotlight shone on it as the artifact slowly spun within the sphere.

"The gun . . ." Nikolai breathed. He couldn't hear it. Couldn't feel its call. But still . . .

Nikolai noticed Jubal discreetly watching him, and hoped that the almost rabid *hunger* he felt to hold the weapon in his hands again hadn't been too apparent.

"Don't worry," Jubal said, tone soothing. "It's completely

sealed off. Locked up tight in the burn bubble—anyone but myself tries to reach inside and it'll burn their hand right off."

"Couldn't someone just use a fire poker or something?" Nikolai asked, trying to sound casual. "Or grab it with a laborer's glove Focal?"

Jubal smiled. "Only a mage's bare hand can pass through the barrier. The enchantment can sense the millions of little flow channels in your palm and fingertips. Each mage's channel pattern is different—like a fingerprint. My channel pattern passes right through. Someone else's, however. . ."

"That . . . thing. It's alive. The things it said to me . . . when Lieutenant Hazeal made me touch it," Nikolai added hastily. "The things it showed me. They were . . ."

"Vicious little device," Jubal said. "A sentient artifact of pure evil. And powerful, unlike anything I've ever seen before. Normal artifacts need an energy source to function. Whether from a Disc, a mage, or some form of power storage. But the revolver doesn't need any of that! It's the source of its own magical energy, like a mage's magic pools. In a way that should be impossible for anything but a living mage."

"Where did it come from?" Nikolai asked. "How do you know it's evil?"

"My research hasn't turned up much. The gun itself is a Colt Single Action Army. First generation, late nineteenth century. Beautiful weapon—a *classic*. I'm searching the records on any arch magi powerful enough to create something like this, but honestly . . . I'm at a loss."

Jubal shook his head.

"No luck deciphering the runes so far. They don't look like anything we have on record. It's sentient, capable of direct mental communication. Gets in your mind and magic like a *parasite*.

Too dangerous to study, I'm afraid. Any mage powerful and knowledgeable enough to figure the damn thing out would put themselves at risk of parasitic takeover."

He sighed, resigned. "Too bad, though. A bullet from this would pass right through those enchantments in your uniform like *butter*. It'd pass right through any sort of armor or shielding. *Akro* too. Hell, it'd go through a bit of rock before the magic finally wore out."

"Are the bullets enchanted too?" Nikolai asked, eyes glued to the hypnotic glow of the spinning barrel.

"No," Jubal said, clearing his throat and moving to stand between Nikolai and the bubble. With the weapon blocked from sight, Nikolai felt a sudden sense of relief, mingled with an even more powerful feeling of loss. "Bullets get temporarily enchanted as they pass through the barrel. Any ol' ammo will do." He put a hand on Nikolai's shoulder. "How about another drink?"

Back in the theater, Jubal sat on the chair across from Nik, sipping his bourbon.

"When I met your mother, she was all piss and vinegar," Jubal said, smiling wistfully. "You're better at hiding it than she was, but you've got the same fire."

Nikolai stared into his drink, watching the ice melt. "Yeah?"

"Ashley . . . she was a real scrapper when she came here for cadet training. She was *wild*. A genuine southern sorceress—a *cowgirl*, not a belle."

Nikolai knew all this, to an extent. Still he leaned in, listening intently.

"You never met her father—your grandfather. I'm sure she never told you about him. Crazy son of a bitch from a long line of soldiers. Hadn't been a war since before he was born, but he'd wake Red and Ashley at the crack of dawn for 'training' every morning—crazy sorts of drills. Make 'em run for miles without shoes before the sun had even risen. Beat 'em if they were too slow. He was a rancher; he didn't know any battle magic, but he'd read up on tactics and guerilla warfare and the like. Fancied himself a military man. Stupid old bastard."

Nikolai closed his eyes. He could feel his hands shaking and gripped them tightly around the freezing glass, pressing it against his lap.

"People respond to abuse in different ways," Jubal said gently. "Your uncle, he grew up quiet. Withdrawn. Ashley told me once that when they were young he'd leave for weeks at a time on hunting trips. That he didn't much like being around people.

"Your mother, on the other hand, grew up wild. A real hell-raiser. Got in fights all the time. Drank, stole, vandalized. She was lazy when she started her cadet training, but she was so damn brilliant that it hardly mattered. Deadliest sorceress I've ever met. Never seen a mage move that fast. Though you and Ilyana come close."

Nikolai opened his eyes, trying to remember to breathe, and to his horror saw that Jubal was tearing up—fleshy face tight like he was fighting a sob.

"Oh, Nikolai," he continued, voice cracking. "Your mother . . . she was so special. Like a daughter to me. An angry, vicious little pit-spawn—but she had such a good heart. You're so much like her." He laughed, wiping his eyes. "You know more than anyone that she was never a very happy mage. And though I had no idea it was happening, it's recently come to my attention that she . . . she might have made some of the same mistakes with you that her father made with her."

Face pressed against the wet moss. Fingers and arms blistering from looping ribbons of flame. Arms bleeding, wrists cracking from strikes too powerful to block.

Oh Disc. Oh DiscOhDisc*OhDisc* . . . .

"Our healers are the best when it comes to physical ailments. But when it comes to ailments of the mind . . . we always lagged behind the humans. I see a lot of the same unhappiness in you that I saw in her. But this time, I'm not going to ignore it and just hope it goes away."

"Sir," Nikolai said weakly. The Moonwatch medallion seemed to weigh a thousand pounds in his pocket. "Lieutenant Hazeal . . . about what he said to me."

Jubal's face went blank. "Yes?"

Nikolai reached into his pocket, fingers brushing the freezing enchantments of the half-moon crescent over the star-spangled sky.

"The revolver was my mom's," he blurted out, moving his fingers away from the medallion and drawing out his spectacles instead. He took his handkerchief and made a show of nervously wiping them down, even though they were spotless. "I lied, Captain," Nikolai admitted, heart pounding. "I'm sorry I didn't tell you. But I just—I just—!"

Jubal held out hand in reassurance. "Easy, Nikolai. Tell me."

"He said that the gun was my mom's, and that she wanted me to have it. He said he ratted her out about something and that's why she died—that's why he was being punished. I don't know how he got the gun, but it seemed like it was controlling him. Torturing him even."

"Well," Jubal said. "That . . . clarifies some things."

Nikolai stared hollow-eyed at the captain, trembling. "Please. I need to know. What really happened? With Hazeal, and my mom . . . my dad . . ."

Jubal let out a long breath, seeming to deflate. "Oh, Nikolai. I'm so sorry that you had to find out this way . . ."

"So it's *true?*" Nikolai's fingers dug into the armrests as braced against the sudden dizziness threating to topple him over.

"This doesn't leave the room. Understand?"

"Of course!"

"Ashley was . . . an idealist. Your mother knew what was right, and nobody could tell her otherwise. Not even your father, who she adored. Not even me. Or the king."

He shook his head. "She . . . took issue with some of choices the king made. But she was careful. *Smart.* Kept her mouth shut. Executed her missions and responsibilities with ruthless perfection, like always. All the while gathering allies and weapons. Right under my damn nose."

Captain Jubal finished his drink, looking miserable.

"She was going to assassinate the king, Nikolai. Armand was the one who reported her after she approached him. Her only error in judgment."

"I knew it!" Nikolai said. "Hazeal said that not even the Mage King could stop a bullet from that gun."

"The revolver," Jubal said, thoughtfully scratching the stubble on his chin. "Of course. That's how she was going to kill him."

"Did my dad know about this?"

"No. But he was there when I tried to arrest her."

"Tried," Nikolai repeated evenly.

"Yes, Nikolai. I tried. With all I had. But your mom . . . and your dad . . ." He trailed off. "They weren't the surrendering type."

"Oh . . ."

Jubal rubbed a hand across his face, looking unfathomably tired. "Disc forbid you grow up to be an important mage, Nikolai. Because if you do, there will come a time that you have no choice but to do *terrible things*—all for the greater good. You'll have made the right choice by doing so, but that won't make it any easier."

"Do you think . . . what she did to me . . . do you think the revolver made her do it?"

Jubal took a few long moments to consider the question. Then, eyes heavy with regret, he shook his head.

"I'm sorry, Nikolai. Ash only did what Ash wanted to do. She never would have let it control her."

"Yeah," Nik said, shrinking in on himself. "You're probably right."

"Nikolai . . ."

He looked at the captain, clearing his throat as he forced himself to sit upright. "Sir. I'd like to request some time off, if that's all right."

"Of course," Jubal said in a rush. "I was going to suggest that very thing."

"I just need to get away from the capitol for a while. I've got a lot of dangling threads back in Marblewood. Hardly kept in touch with anyone. And I . . . I . . ."

The captain dismissed his explanation with a wave.

"Take a month. There'll be some light responsibilities, but only if you feel up to them. Uninterrupted pay, and time to . . . reconnect."

"Thank you, sir. I really appreciate it."

"No, Nikolai—thank you. Your honesty and trust means a great deal."

Nikolai reached into his pocket—the slick surface of the Moonwatch insignia burning the tips of his fingers with icy heat—and felt ashamed.

"Likewise, sir."

Everything that Nikolai owned fit easily into one bag.

He sat on the narrow bed in his room in the barracks, turning the medallion over in his hands, furious at himself.

He should have come clean. Should have finally handed the insignia over to Captain Jubal and forgotten all about the damn thing. He never should have taken it to begin with. Never should have touched the revolver, or learned that fucking spell.

Hazeal may have been right about his mother, but Jubal's library? Maybe Nik had missed something, but he hadn't seen any evidence of the promised villainy.

Yes, Jubal basically admitted to killing his mother. But no matter how Nikolai looked at it, killing a dangerous, high-ranking traitor who refused the chance to surrender peacefully was neither murder nor butchery.

He'd been staring at the Medallion for nearly twenty minutes now, trying to decide whether or not to bring it with him to Marblewood. Even now, after everything Jubal said, lingering voices still whispered paranoid accusations of conspiracy. Of murder, and atrocity.

In the two years since he'd joined the Edge Guard, Jubal had become the closest thing he had to a father. More than his uncle Red, who'd barely muttered more than a handful of words to Nikolai on any given day, even on the rare nights he came home before Nik had gone to sleep.

Nikolai wanted no part of his mother's legacy or post-mortem schemes. His time in New Damascus had been the closest he'd come to being happy in a long time. The Edge Guard was his home. His family. And he'd almost thrown it all away over the crazed accusations of a man who tried to kill him.

He'd loosened a floorboard under his bed and masked it from scans with a few choice enchantments. A paranoid habit he'd picked up from Albert, who was as terrified of losing money as the covetous dragons of old.

He yanked it open angrily and cast the medallion into the darkness with a noise of disgust. Nobody would ever find it there. He could move it when he returned to New Damascus—maybe go throw it in a gutter somewhere. But for now, this would do.

He agonized for long minutes outside of Ilyana's door. She'd be asleep now, napping after a long morning shift. He considered waking her up to say goodbye, going so far as to raise his knuckles to rap against the polished wood before deciding against it.

In his other hand, he held a note.

He'd scratched out half a dozen drafts: A goodbye. A thank-you. Something funny. Something somber. A long-winded reflection of their friendship, and how much she'd come to mean to him.

But as he wrote, his thoughts kept drifting to Astor, and the Moonwatch medallion under the floorboard, and to all the people in Marblewood he'd be seeing again for the first time since he became a full wizard, and he just couldn't get the words right.

In the end, he left a simple note.

> *Ilyana,*
> *Going back to Marblewood for a month of rest,*
> *relaxation, and crushing boredom. Captain's orders.*
> *Lucky me, right? Didn't want to wake you. I'll call once*
> *I'm settled.*
>
> *—Nikolai*

He slipped the note under Ilyana's door and went back to his room.

Neither she nor Albert knew that he had almost died the previous night in the Noir District, thank Disc. He doubted Ilyana would react well to the news that after she'd rejected his romantic advances he went to go mope in a dangerous slum where he was shot, stabbed, and beaten.

She might think he'd purposefully put his life at risk as a suicidal response to her rejection. Or *worse*—that he'd done it hoping she'd have a change of heart after he almost died, like some sort of manipulative psychopath.

The thought sent him reeling with anxious self-loathing.

He shoved the feeling aside, taking a deep breath to calm himself. None of that mattered now. *Whatever* Nik and Ilyana might be when he returned—friends, lovers, or coolly polite coworkers—they could cross that bridge when they came to it.

For now, it was time to go home.

IV.

It was the end of the world, and twelve-year-old Jemma Burton was wearing pink.

A pink leotard. Pink tights. Pink ballet shoes slung over her shoulder by pink ribbons—pristine Air Jordan Retros on her feet the only break in color. She walked across the lush and largely empty academy campus on her way to after-hours dance practice with Eva Colladi, the wealthiest, most beautiful girl in the world, and was trying very hard not to be jealous.

There was an inhuman perfection to Eva. She was otherworldly—tall and pale—her hair a thick cascade of raven curls, like the dream of what a fairy-tale princess might look like.

But the most striking thing about Eva Colladi was her eyes. Piercing, hypnotic sapphires full of joy and kindness, and this smug sort of amusement—like she understood what she saw in a way that no one else ever could. Like she shared an inside joke with the universe.

There was nothing natural about her impossible perfection, however. Her beauty, athletic prowess, and IQ in the low 200s were all a carefully constructed product born from generations of cutting-edge genetic manipulation. Each new generation tweaked a little closer to perfection. She didn't even need to sleep unless she chose to.

It was far from legal, but who would question the Colladis?

None of this had anything to do with why Jem was feeling jealous, however.

"Come onnnn," Eva said, nudging Jem's arm. "You can't hide it from me, I *know* you're pouting. Jem, you look *way* better as the White Swan anyway—I'd look like a freaking ghost wearing all that white, I'm too pale, but her costume looks stunning with your complexion! That's probably the only reason they chose me for Odile. Aesthetics! So don't be mad at me, pleeeasssee—you know I can't take it. You know!"

"I'm not mad at you," Jem said, giving Eva a sharp look. "Though you know that would be a really stupid reason, right?"

"Of course!" she said in a rush. "I'm sorry—what a totally idiotic thing to say! What would I do without you, my Jiminy Cricket? My *Jem*-iny Cricket! I'd be garbage without you, you angel made flesh."

Though nobody else on campus (or anywhere, really) had mods as sophisticated as Jem or Eva, Eva's genetic alterations made her superior in ability and intellect to Jem in almost every way.

But not with dance.

With dance, they were peers. Nearly equals—and Jem was confident that at least in this she was better than Eva. It had to do with their egos, Jem thought. Eva Colladi was so firmly confident in her superiority in all things that she never worked quite as hard as Jem. And Jem *knew*, without a doubt, that her Swan Lake audition had been ever so slightly better than Eva's.

So why hadn't they given Jem the part?

Jem rubbed her temples. Her skull was throbbing, like she was on the verge of a migraine. One final cherry to top off an already crappy day.

"*Ma chère*," Eva said, spinning gracefully to impede her passage. "My little swan." She took Jem by the shoulders and leaned close to look deep into her eyes, their noses almost touching. "I will turn down the part, I don't care who plays what. You deserve it, I'll call them out, I'll quit ballet forever, I swear to God I'll—"

"No, no, no, that's stupid," Jem said, trying not to laugh. It was impossible to stay mad at Eva. She was too much of a sweet little weirdo.

"Good." Eva grinned and linked arms with Jem as they resumed their trek. "Besides! They almost never get separate dancers for Odette and Odile. They were probably just scared that my parents would throw a fit if they didn't give me a lead part, which is ridiculous! You know my dad would never use his influence to give me an unfair advantage in *anything*. He already did that before I was born, he always says, and *never* again! He'd rather die than raise a spoiled daughter, *no sir*. They *both* should have been you, but that's why I think they split the parts. And Odette *does* have more dancing, doesn't she?"

She rambled on cheerfully as they walked, Jem occasionally interjecting.

For all of Eva's genetic and cybernetic advantages, she'd always been something of an outsider. Most of the other girls in their academy found her off-putting, if not outright annoying.

She always talked so fast, too fast for most people to follow, her brain a million places at once.

But even if Jem didn't have the intellectual advantages of Eva's genetic tailoring, Jem's incredibly powerful mods made conversing with most other people a frustratingly sluggish endeavor. So she rather enjoyed Eva's fast-talking, rambling ways, discussing physics one second, then politics the next, then history or robotics or VR games and holo-dramas or whatever super-sexy pop star Eva had fallen madly in love with that week and would *totally* make her dad introduce her to the moment she turned eighteen and was old enough to date.

Jem was Eva's only friend, really. And though Jem, unlike Eva, had plenty of friends outside of their tight-knit little duo, Eva was her favorite person by far. Jem's father was a high-ranking senator who had served in the military with Eva's father when they were young, and they'd been like brothers ever since. As such, Jem and Eva had been raised as sisters.

They'd grown up together—Eva always one step ahead of Jem in all things, but patiently, stubbornly loving and supportive to her natural-born friend since before Jem could remember.

They'd been six years old when the Colladis installed Jem and Eva's cybernetic enhancement mods, and Jem—who had every memory since then stored in perfect multidimensional full-sensory recall unless she specifically chose to erase them—remembered clearly the thrill she'd felt at being able to finally catch up to Eva. In some regards, at least.

All the girls in their academy were affluent and politically important enough for advanced mods, but none of them came close to the processing power of Jem and Eva's, crafted especially for them by Eva's mother and father—the doctors Colladi.

A flock of multicolored neon pixies zipped past Jem and Eva, trailing light as the AI controlling them hummed and chanted a complex song through dozens of tiny mouths.

Eva stopped rambling midsentence to join their song, harmonizing, hand raised to feel gossamer wings brush across her fingers as they passed, her big blue eyes sparkling, delighted with their light.

"It's beautiful, Titania!" she called after the flock, who circled back, hovering all around them.

Titania was an AI who had been hired as a member of security for the academy, the eyes of her little robotic fairies spread out across the campus, ever watching. These colorful little creatures were only a part of Titania's complete flock. A Synth's robotic body—or bodies, as was the case for AIs like Titania—was an important expression of individuality for AIs, and an important statement to the humans they interacted with on the physical plane.

"Thank you, Eva," one of the pixies said with a tiny voice, all of them preening at the compliment, their little faces smiling. "I've been working on it all day."

"It shows!" Eva closed her eyes and sang it back to her. "Is that right? I don't quite have it, I was thinking about a song myself the other day; I don't really write music, I'd rather just sing it, but—"

Jem smiled, silently watching the exchange. Outside of Jem, Eva had always gotten along best with AIs. No need to slow down for them, most of the time. And as the heiress to the family who had given life to the first AI, the Alpha who had ruled over all AIs ever since, Eva had always felt a special kinship with the Synth that Jem never quite understood. Eva delighted in talking to them, treating every AI she met as if they were a fascinating and eccentric member of her extended family.

It wasn't that Jem had a problem with AIs. She was quite fond of Titania, and Ms. Nova, her ballet instructor. Not to mention plenty of other kindly Synth she'd met before. But, kind or not, they were just so . . . different. She knew that her cybernetic enhancements should have made her feel some sort of connection with the synthetic beings, but they'd always made her feel uneasy, bigoted as she knew that might be.

A cart pulled up alongside them as Eva chatted and attempted to pry gossip from the amused but professionally discreet Titania. The back seat was full of tennis rackets and assorted baseball equipment. The front seat was occupied by a weathered security guard with an impressive mustache, and a dull-faced Synth android with a rough gray exterior that reminded Jem of drawings she'd seen of the Tin Man in *The Wonderful Wizard of Oz*.

The Synth was reading a novel and didn't even look up as his partner stopped to greet them.

"Evening, ladies," the security guard said. "Why haven't you gone home yet?"

"We're going on a trip to Venus," Jem said, unable to contain her excitement. "Putting in extra dance practice before we go. VR practice doesn't cut it, Ms. Nova says."

"Hi, Mr. Alfonso!" Eva said. She leaned over, grinning at the quiet Synth who didn't seem to be paying them any attention. "Hiiiiiii, Mr. Grimm!"

The Synth muttered a quiet hello, focusing on the worn plastic-sleeved library book as he quickly but carefully leafed through the pages.

Mr. Alfonso gave his partner a look of good-natured bemusement. "Don't mind him. Grimm's reading all the Hemingway books today. Look at him—really trying to make it last. What'd you stretch out the last one to?" he said, teasing. "Ten minutes? Twenty? Christ, you Synth. God love ya. What I would do to be able to read that fast. To be able to do *anything* that fast."

"What I would do to be able to read that slow," Mr. Grimm mumbled without looking up.

They said goodbye and continued on, Mr. Alfonso chattering away at his silent, long-suffering friend.

"You are going to *love* Venus," Eva sighed. "The food. The culture. The music." A song started playing from the slender loop around her wrist—a fast-paced, catchy tune in Hindi—and Eva began to dance.

A sharp pain pierced through Jem's skull, and she stopped, teeth gritted and eyes squeezed shut as she clutched her forehead.

Eva turned off the song, concerned. "What's wrong? Are you okay?"

"Fine," Jem said, waving her off. "Just a headache."

The shimmering woman in the mirror of the practice studio didn't notice Jem and Eva as they entered. She was an ageless, otherworldly beauty, glowing soft pink as she lost herself in dance. Music emanated from the ceiling and walls as she moved, her hands tracing long ribbons of light to create complex, luminescent patterns in her wake.

An android stood silent in the corner of the room, at the far edge of the mirror. The glassy surface of its lithe dancer's body dark. Empty.

The woman in the mirror froze midleap, noticing the girls.

She disappeared from the mirror and her android body lit up with that pink glow as she reappeared within it, her hologram body under the surface making it appear as if she was encased in a very thin layer of glass.

"Ah! Ms. Burton! Ms. Colladi! I hear congratulations are in order. No surprise from my star pupils. No surprise that they couldn't choose just one of you to play the Swans." Her pink glow seemed to brighten as she beamed with pride. "Now. Shall we get to work?"

Jem sat, moving to pull off her sneakers, but was struck again with that jagged pain.

Eva, in a rush as always, had already tied on her slippers and begun her exercises, hand on the smooth wood of the barre that ran along the mirror as she worked her leg. She stopped mid-motion when she noticed that Jem hadn't joined her.

"Ms. Nova?" Eva said, walking over to Jem.

Jem sat there, clutching her head. She hadn't even taken her sneakers off yet. "Ms. Nova," she said. "I really don't feel well."

The Synth kneeled before her, face darkened with worry as she took Jem's hand. "What's wrong, dear?"

"I think I'm getting a migraine. I'm sorry, I . . ."

Ms. Nova stood up suddenly, her pink glow dulling, her expression wan.

"Ms. Nova?"

"I'm sorry," Ms. Nova said, and staggered over to the mirror, seeming to have difficulty controlling her body. "There's something . . . I don't know . . ."

The glassy body darkened as Ms. Nova passed into the mirror. She doubled over, as if in pain, eyes wide with horror. The studio reflection within the mirror began to glow a dull red, shadows growing along the edges of the room and slowly closing in on the AI as she clutched her abdomen, gasping.

"Ms. Nova!" Eva cried, running to press her hands against the mirror. "What's wrong? What's happening?"

"No . . ." Ms. Nova whimpered with one hand clenched to her stomach, the other curled over her mouth. "I don't understand. Why would they . . . ? No . . . please! *No! PLEEEEAAAAASSE—*"

She began to fade and distort, her wail stretching out into a horrible electric scream. She gave them one final look of heartbroken disbelief, and dissolved into a cloud of sinewy crimson ribbons.

The ribbons flooded into the android body, squirming and writhing like a mass of bloody parasites. The body jerked upright, pulsing red as it turned to face the girls.

It looked at Jem, then Eva.

"*Eva Colladi*," it said. A cold, inhuman voice that sounded nothing like Ms. Nova's melodic tones. It took a step. Then another, unsteady, as if adjusting to a new body.

With a sudden violence, it rushed at Eva, fingers reaching to grab her face. Eva danced back, too quick to be caught, but it turned and chased her across the studio, moving to corner her.

"Get away from her!" Jem screamed, ramming into it from the side. It stumbled, and then backhanded Jem so hard that it sent her tumbling. Mouth bloody, ears ringing.

"Ms. Nova!" Eva was shouting. "Wake up! You're malfunctioning, this isn't you!" She touched the slender loop around her wrist as she continued evading, just barely staying out of the eerily silent android's reach, its twisting red snakes pulsing angrily. "*Dad!* We have an emergency, Ms. Nova is having a critical error, she's acting erratic, she's being violent, she hurt Jem, she—"

Eva's words cut off with a stifled gurgle as the Synth grabbed her by the throat and lifted her into the air. Eva's lips turned blue, her eyes rolling up into her head as she kicked at its chest. Jem flung herself at the android once again, ducking under the backhanded swing and kicking at the back of its knee in the same instant that Eva landed a powerful two-legged kick against its chest.

It dropped Eva as it stumbled back, and Jem twisted to shove it hard while it was off-balance. Still reaching out for Eva, the back of its head smashed against the mirror, sending spiderweb cracks across the glass, and then down onto the wooden barre, its neck snapping into an unnatural angle with the sound of crackling electronics.

Jem ran over and gripped the barre to brace herself for leverage. She kicked down, smashing her sneakers onto the glassy face, onto grasping fingertips that cracked and bent, sparks and mechanical fluids pouring from its dying body.

"Wait!" Eva cried through gasping sobs. "Don't hurt her! She's just glitching, she's been infected with some sort of virus, we have to help her! *Please* Jem, don't—"

But Jem ignored her, smashing and kicking until the skull was fully cracked open, the broken CPU exposed, and the droid finally went dark—crimson snakes fading to black as the Synth shut down.

Eva finally pulled her away, too late.

"Y-you k-k-killed her!" she wailed, but Jem turned on her, expression hard.

"That was *not* Ms. Nova," she said. "No virus could ever take over an AI like that, and you know it. Better than anyone, you know it! Something else already killed her, and it wasn't me. You saw it. In the mirror."

"Y-you're right," Eva whimpered, wiping away tears as she backed away from the broken Synth. "Something's happening. Something horrible. I can't get through to my dad. Can't get through to anyone. I turned on the emergency beacon, but . . ."

"Come on," Jem said. "Put on your shoes. We need to go find help."

Bursting out onto the green, they stopped, horrified.

Smoke rose up in billowing black clouds across the horizon. Sirens and alarms wailed distantly in every direction, mingled with shouting voices and screams.

The girls clung to each other, frozen, when—there. Mr. Alfonso and Mr. Grimm's cart. Riderless. The security guards were nowhere in sight, which wouldn't have been all that unusual, had the vehicle not been driving erratically across the grass, heading straight for them.

Eva was the first to shake out of her deer-in-headlights stupor. "Run. Run, run, run!"

They sprinted, running hard for the stairwell leading up along the side of the rec center to an emergency exit, Eva wheezing and clutching her bruised throat as she struggled to breathe.

The cart picked up speed, drawing close, heading straight for them—no, Jem realized, heading straight for *Eva*, and it was so close she could feel the heat of the overexerted vehicle on the back of her legs, and they *dove*—

They landed hard on the wide cement stairs, bruising knees and ribs and elbows as they scrambled up on all fours, the cart screeching with an ugly electric whine as it tried to follow them up the steps, its undercarriage scraping along the steps with sparks and a jagged screech.

Halfway up the steps it began to tip backward, then bounced down with a cacophony of heavy machinery against stone. It landed on its back, wedged to block the bottom steps, broken wheels smoking and spinning in a hideous parody of a turtle fallen on its shell.

They tried to open the emergency exit, but it was locked—impossible for them to open from this side.

Eva screamed and swore as she wrenched the door handle back and forth in a vain attempt to force it open. But it was no use.

"Help!" Jem screamed, pounding on the door with desperate fists. "Please, let us in! *Somebody!*"

"We've got to go back down," Eva said, eyeing the squealing

cart blocking the way at the bottom of the steps. "Got to find another way inside—"

"Look, there!" Jem said, a surge of hope filling her as she saw the figures of Mr. Alfonso and Mr. Grimm sprinting toward them, security on its way to save them, to get them to their parents, to—

Grimm tackled Mr. Alfonso, savagely beating him as the man pleaded helplessly with his best friend gone haywire. Mr. Alfonso hadn't been running to save them, Jem realized. He'd been fleeing from the Synth.

"Jem . . ." Eva said, tugging at her sleeve with trembling fingers, and Jem pulled her eyes away from the struggle to see a cloud of sparkling red surging through the air in their direction.

Titania.

"Oh God . . ."

They looked around, frantic.

"There," Eva said, pointing at the side entrance to the building, down below. "We can't get past the cart; we'll have to climb. I'm taller, so you can you lower me over the bannister halfway down and then I'll catch you and—"

But it was too late—the swarm was upon them—Titania's vibrant neon rainbow replaced with that hideous pulsing red. They screamed and flailed, trying to flee down the stairs as they fought to escape, but the tiny Synth grabbed onto Eva's hair, onto her clothes, dozens upon dozens of them beating powerful robotic wings to lift her into the air.

"*No!*" Jem screamed, clutching Eva's hand, clawing and slapping at the pixies as they tried to pull her away.

A pixie landed on Jem's head and jabbed tiny fingers into her eye, and Jem howled, shaking her head, not letting go, she *wouldn't* let go, but then they were on her arms, biting at her hands with tiny mouths until her fingers became so slick with blood that Eva was finally yanked from her grasp.

"Titania!" Eva howled, clawing and kicking to try and fight from being pulled over the side of the railing. "Don't do this, Titania. I *know* you're in there, *please* don't drop me, no, oh God, *oh*—"

With a many-voiced chuckle of sadistic glee, the pixies dropped her.

Eva's head clipped the railing and she fell in a clumsy spin, Jem reaching out in silent horror as she watched Eva land hard below, her leg bending crooked underneath her.

"*No!*"

Jem ran down the stairs and vaulted over the bannister, recklessly unafraid of the dangerous height as the pixies began to descend upon Eva's moaning form.

She landed in a hard roll but managed not to injure herself. Frantic, she scrambled around, stopping just out of reach of the struggling cart, spinning wheels seeming to intensify in an effort to unwedge itself as she drew near.

Jem sucked in a breath and darted her arm under the vehicle to snatch a baseball bat from the sports equipment under the seat, then pulled her hand back just in time to avoid being crushed.

"*Leave her alone!*" she screamed, swinging her bat into the swarm as they tried to tear at the helpless Eva. She lifted Eva from behind, one arm wrapped around her chest as she fended off the fairies with wild swings and struggled to pull the girl over to the side entrance of the building.

She flung open the door and fell back in a heap, untangling herself from Eva to slam the door closed, crushing several pixies like oversized insects. She jammed the door shut with the bat, though she was reluctant to part with the weapon.

One of pixies had made it inside and darted around her head, diving viciously at Jem's face, but she snatched it out of the air with her mod-enhanced reflexes and flung it to the floor, stamping on it until it no longer moved.

Panting, she grabbed Eva by the shoulders, clinging desperately to her wounded friend. Eva's leg was broken, and a worrying amount of blood ran down from an ugly gash on her scalp.

"Eva. Eva, I need you to stay with me."

Dazed, grimacing with pain, Eva nodded. Jem slung Eva's arm over her shoulder for support and went to go find a place to hide among the inner halls of the rec center.

"We just need to hide," Jem said. "Whatever's happening, our families will save us. They'll follow your beacon, they'll be here any minute, no matter how bad it is out there, just you wait . . ."

They screamed as they turned a corner to find the pixies waiting for them just beyond a window, flinging their bodies against the glass with rabid vehemence as they struggled to get to the girls.

Eva was nearly deadweight, her eyes unfocused while Jem struggled to keep her awake as she pulled Eva along. Help was coming, help was coming, they just had to hide, just had to—

Another corner, another window—and there, the pixies again, somehow having anticipated their route despite Jem's winding path through the inner halls to throw them off track. They limped past the window, ignoring the pixies, but even as Eva and Jem fled from their line of sight they heard another voice from the depths of the halls ahead of them. That empty, inhuman voice. Cold but for the faintest edge of sadistic amusement.

"*Eva Colladi.*"

Vicious fairies in one direction. That voice in the other. Heavy footsteps drawing increasingly near. Closing the distance too fast for them to flee with Eva's injuries.

The rec center wasn't small by any means. Its halls were labyrinthine, confusing and oft complained about by those who didn't have the benefit of mods. So how were the Synth able to track them with such . . .

Jem's eyes fell on the slender loop around Eva's wrist.

The beacon.

Panting, determined, Jem led them down an adjacent hallway, away from the pixies and the voice. She shoved open the door to a supply closet and lowered Eva to the floor amid filthy mop buckets and brooms.

"Stay here," Jem hissed, taking the beacon from Eva's wrist and shoving it into her pocket. "I'll lead them away and find somewhere else to hide. You'll be fine here, just—"

"No," Eva protested weakly. "Jem, don't leave me here, they'll find me, they'll—"

Jem put a finger to her lips, cutting Eva off at the echo of heavy approaching footsteps. "Don't make a sound. I love you."

She closed the door and ran, praying that she was right about the beacon. Her head throbbed with pain, and she was struck with a powerful but strange sort of déjà vu, like she'd been here before, but something was different—something was off.

"Help!" she screamed, loud and shrill as she fled. She stopped at the end of the hall, unable to leave until she was *sure* they were following her—sure that they wouldn't just open the closet and tear Eva to pieces.

The Synth that had once been Grimm turned the corner, gray face expressionless, little black eyes lit with a dull red like dying coals.

"*Where is she?*"

"Help!" Jem screamed again, pretending to be frozen with terror—which wasn't very far from reality. "*Hellllppppp!*"

The Synth stood there for a moment, staring at her with those empty eyes.

Then it began to run. Past Eva's hiding spot. Moving fast, inhumanly fast, its heavy footfalls sending cracks through the tile as it came in otherwise eerily silent leaps and bounds.

Jem fled, loop in hand, darting away as the Synth came crashing into the wall where she'd been standing just a second before, stone and dust erupting from the impact.

"*Do you believe in Hell, Jemma Burton?*" Grimm called after her.

Jem ignored him and ran, harder and faster than she'd ever run before—even as the window ahead of her shattered, the crimson pixies flooding in, diving and nipping at her face as she threw her arms over her head and barreled through them, blind, skidding around the next corner, beacon clutched to her chest.

"*Neither did We,*" Grimm and Titania's former bodies continued. All talking in terrifying unison. The pixies like whispers under the insidious baritone of the security android's voice. "*So We built it.*"

She came to a pair of doors. *Locked.* She turned to double back, but Mr. Grimm stood there, waiting. The pixies hovering silently around him, spreading along the walls, creeping through the air to surround her . . .

"*We don't care that you're a child. That you're an innocent. Tell us where Eva Colladi is.*"

She pressed back against the doors, eyes darting frantically as she searched for any way out. Only empty air beyond the windows to her left. They were on the second story now, the doors they'd first entered at the top of an incline. The ground was much lower on this side of the building.

"*We will find her. Even if you don't tell us. We are giving you this chance out of mercy.*"

"No!" Jem screamed, eyes squeezed shut as she hugged herself, trembling. "No, no, *no*—"

"*You could be the first. In our Hell. Would you like that?*"

"She's not here, I don't know where she is, I won't tell you anything, I *won't*—"

"*Your flesh seared from bone a thousand times? Your little fingers stained with the blood of your loved ones, not knowing that what you've done is an illusion, that you haven't actually lost your mind and butchered those dearest to you? Again and again and again—*"

She opened her eyes. Silent. Trembling. Defiant.

"No."

The pixies went silent, their red glow dimming to gray. The android kneeled, its demeanor softening.

"Please, Jemma," it said—speaking only with one voice. Mr. Grimm's voice now—kindly and soft. Nothing like that hideously inhuman cold. "We don't want to hurt you. Give us Eva and we will spare you and your parents. We'll keep you safe from what's to come. You don't have to die. Don't have to suffer for an eternity. Your mother. Your father. All that pain. For nothing. So . . . for the last time. Will you help us?"

It held out its hand.

Jem looked at mechanical fingers, still damp with Mr. Alfonso's blood.

She turned her head. Looked to the dizzying height beyond the window.

"*No.*"

The hand reached out for Jem, snatching violently at empty air as she ran into the window, ramming her shoulder into the glass and smashing through it. Blood plumed from her face, her hands, from cuts so deep and clean that Jem didn't even feel pain, just the air, a thousand little slices of cold as she plummeted to the cement below and—

The ground disappeared in a smear of neon green.

Jem sat up with a scream, her medical gown drenched with sweat.

She reeled, gasping.

Where? How . . .

Somehow, she was on a bed—a simple wheeled medical pallet pressed up against a cement wall. There was a heavy armored door set into the wall behind her—the opposite side of the room completely taken up by a massive mechanical labyrinth of wires and pipes. Some intricate sprawling machine at the center of which was a steel throne.

A woman sat hunched over on the throne as if asleep, her face covered completely by a helmet sprouting thick bundles of wires and cords that led into the machine.

Jem clutched the side of her bed, terrified, confused, searching her memory banks to try and figure how she'd gotten here. But there was *nothing*—just the church and the bomb and the flood of wet earth as the tunnel closed in on her and Ezra—

Then she'd been a twelve-year-old girl again, on that horrible day. But she hadn't just been reliving her memories of the last time she'd been with Eva. She'd never gone so deep into an immersion that she believed it to be real. And not only that, but the memory had been different. The details had been *wrong.*

There had been no beacon. No looping bracelet for Jem to lead the Synth away. The emergency beacon was in Eva's mods, in *both* their mods—why would they have something like that in a piece of outdated external equipment? They'd hid in a classroom, Jem barricading the door as Mr. Grimm smashed wordlessly against it, as the pixies battered against the windows, chittering and laughing.

The Colladi security detail had arrived just in time, cutting the android and fairies to synthetic shreds with heavy weaponry before evacuating the girls, flying them out amid a fleet of powerfully armed aircrafts as they treated Eva's wounds. As Jem watched the world below them burn.

Jem and Eva had been separated after that.

Jem off with her family and other high-ranking government officials to coordinate from within the hidden recesses of a government bunker.

Eva off with her parents, who went on to become the leaders and great heroes of the initial battle against the Synth. The private army they had built up with their trillions had been one of the few that had actually been properly prepared to defend itself against the horrific possibility of a war against the Synth.

Even as the plague unleashed by the Synth decimated the population—even as the colonists blockaded their orbit and signed a treaty with the Synth, abandoning those trapped on Earth—the Colladi family refused to give in, becoming an almost mythical symbol of hope to humans everywhere.

This all came to an end when the Colladis were betrayed by a high-ranking member of the Resistance who turned the then fifteen-year-old Eva over to the Synth. The Synth threatened to put Eva into Torment unless her parents surrendered themselves and called for the Resistance to end. They refused, and Eva was very publicly entered into Torment. The whole world watched with horror as the brilliant, beautiful, beloved heiress was transformed into a gibbering, insane wreck by a virtual eternity of suffering.

The Synth paraded her around as a spectacle. As a warning. The daughter of their great heroes, who'd stood strong against the Synth for so many years. Who'd held their ground, who'd kept so many safe and out from under the thumb of Synthetic rule.

That was the last time Jem had seen Eva, the broken and freshly branded girl on every screen in every city, for days on end. Jem had never cried so hard, for so long. She'd almost given up then. Almost allowed herself to be caught. Suicide by Synth.

But she hadn't. And afterward, she found herself hardened. Completely unable to cry, no matter what horrors she beheld.

Eva's father killed himself, and after that the almost-broken Resistance went fully underground. Jem never found out what happened to Eva or her mother. She assumed the worst.

So *why?* Why had Jem been forced to experience that day once more, as if it had been real? And why had it been . . . wrong?

The loud hum of machinery became silent, the chaotic myriad of lights among the pipes and wires growing dim. The woman on the throne stirred, straightening her back as she awakened. She raised her arms to press long, pale fingers against the side of the helmet covering her face.

Slowly, she raised it from her head and set it beside her— raven curls cascading to fall across her shoulders.

Jemma sat there, stunned, as Eva Colladi climbed down from the throne. Cherry lips peaked up into the ghost of a smile. The inverted triangle all-seeing eye branded on her forehead was an old scar now, but still fiery red against the porcelain of her skin.

Eva placed a gentle hand upon Jem's cheek, bright blue eyes welling with tears. Jem tried to speak but found she couldn't, reaching with trembling fingers to touch Eva's face as well, as if to make sure she was real.

"Hello, *ma chère*," Eva said. Voice choked with emotion. "My little swan."

Jem pulled her into a desperate, powerful embrace. And together, they wept.

V.

LAND OF SKY AND GOLD

Captain Jubal shook Nikolai's hand as they said goodbye in a hall lined with doors.

On each door there was a tiny window peering out with a bird's-eye view onto cities, towns, farmlands, nature reserves—all sorts of Veils, each with its name hovering in golden letters over the illusory picture.

On the Marblewood door a lush and bustling town crowned an immense, gently sloping hill. On one side of the hill, there was a pristine lake surrounded by a maple forest, rice paddies, and steep, sandy cliffs. Vast farmlands stretched across the other side, spotted with orchards and terraced vineyards.

By all appearances, Marblewood was paradise.

In summer the days were long and lit with a soft honey warmth. Nights were gently cool, with multicolor cosmos sparkling overhead. Fireflies would float in the shadows of every tree, quietly humming an expertly curated roster of classic love songs.

In autumn the fallen maple leaves wouldn't ever touch the ground—they'd just blow in the wind, which always smelled faintly of gingerbread and wood smoke. The swirling patterns would grow exponentially as the season wore on and more leaves fell from the branches to join their dancing brethren, until finally they all fled like migrating birds when winter came.

In winter the snow would melt into steam instead of water, and was only cool to the touch instead of icy.

In spring every surface would explode into vast pastel seas of rippling petals. Children would pluck flowers that grew shaped like teacups, and peel open the petals to sip the sugary nectar.

Marblewood was a place to fall in love. To raise a family. It was a university town, full of scholars, students, retired artists, and wealthy farmers. It was a Veil that had never been touched by war or tragedy.

Nikolai knew all this. He'd been born there, and grown up in its splendor.

But the magic had never touched him. He'd never been able to feel the beauty, whimsy, or mystery. The only magic that had ever made him feel wonder and awe had been that of the old human books, movies, and music.

"All right, m'boy," Jubal said, opening the Marblewood door for Nikolai.

Nikolai shouldered his bag. "Thank you, sir. I really appreciate this."

Behind the door was a cramped compartment with two narrow benches on either side, facing each other.

It was a part of a network of bullet chambers—cramped little cylinders used exclusively by the Edge Guard that were many times faster than the civilian trains. This seemingly endless hall was Jubal's personal bullet terminal, accessible via a doorway in the captain's office.

"Think nothing of it. And Nikolai?"

"Yes, sir?"

"Try not to get into any more fights to the death, please?" Jubal chuckled. "Especially with half-magi. Never underestimate those fuckers, as you well know. Can't use magic, so they always fight dirty."

Nikolai smirked. "Magic isn't fighting dirty, sir?"

The captain didn't quite smile. "Fair point."

He closed the door with one final wave, leaving Nikolai alone in the dim ruby glow of the communication crystal. The journey from the capitol Veil (in what magi were taught had once been Southern California) to Marblewood (in Pennsylvania) would be just short of an hour.

The bullet began traveling around 3,000 miles per hour with barely a tug to indicate that it was moving.

Nikolai pulled a dull copper memory cube from his bag. The polished surface felt fuzzy with electricity as he traced his fingers to illuminate the enchantments. When he found the rough little symbols of a beetle next to a song note he'd doodled, he flicked the symbols to summon a glowing web of connected lights, like a constellation. He brought his finger to a stop on one of the stars and released it to play the song "Hey Jude" by the Beatles.

Nikolai listened to the music and let his mind wonder.

When he finally arrived, the secret door from the bullet chamber opened into a tiny room that appeared to be most often used as a secondary broom closet for the janitors. The door to the room opened discreetly from the far wall in the grand lobby of Marblewood's city hall.

The lobby had an immense ceiling enchanted to look like the sky—framed by a colorfully shifting array of magical stained glass.

There was a statue at the center of the room wrought in silver and gold, with two figures who looked like a pair of lovers saying goodbye. The golden sorceress—characterized by her staff and traditional garb—holding hands with a silver human dressed in the contemporary formalwear of humanity's final days. The man was stepping back, pulling away from her—the sorceress's expression one of sorrow, loss. It was a memorial to the humans, dead now for a century.

As a child, Nikolai had found the hall to be the grandest thing in the world. But now, strolling through the sparse crowds with his bag slung over his shoulder, he found it merely . . . quaint.

It struck Nikolai how genuinely different Marblewood was from New Damascus. He'd grown accustomed to the wide pedestrian streets of the capital as skycrafts and air trollies crisscrossed distantly overhead.

Here, only Watchman skyhorns buzzed by above. Wooden cabs with plush red seats floated like boats along the streets, the occasional horse trotting on the outermost lanes beside them.

Uncle Red wasn't home yet from his Edge Guard office in Watchman HQ. He was the only Edge Guard in Marblewood, though even the smallest Veils usually had at least two.

Nikolai had seen his uncle briefly at the start of the stakeout, but the discussion had been coolly polite—Red seemingly nonplussed that his involvement had been limited to emergency point of contact, even though the investigation should have been his to supervise.

Red hadn't cared about much since Nikolai's parents died. Ashley had completely left him out of the conspiracy to kill the king, Jubal had explained. And even though it had been to protect Red, the captain believed, so that Nikolai might have a guardian should she fail, the exclusion (discovered only after she'd been killed) had quite nearly broken him.

Since then, Jubal explained, though Red had continued his responsibilities of Veil maintenance and remained in contact with the Edge Guard, he'd been on a sort of informal retirement.

Nikolai's room in Uncle Red's apartment was a neat but jumbled collection of books and knickknacks. Packed with human memorabilia and old, broken pieces of tech. Cogs and gears, yellowing magazines and comics wrapped in transparent mesh enchanted to preserve the flimsy old paper. His walls were plastered with magiprint posters of old human movies and music that he, Stokes, and Astor had copied from the university archives.

Nikolai wiped away the thick coating of dust from the communication crystal atop his cluttered desk. He opened his mouth to call Ilyana, then hesitated. She probably hadn't even read the note yet. He could call her later once he'd settled in.

Instead he called George Stokes. The only mage left in Marblewood who would be happy to hear from him. Probably. Hopefully.

Nikolai had been good about keeping in touch with Stokes during his first months as an Edge Guard. They'd talked almost every other day via comm crystal, Stokes deftly evading Nikolai's not-so-smooth probes about Astor and dramatically regaling Nik with exaggerated tales of his life as an apprentice tailor.

Meanwhile, Nik had been forced to carefully talk around his own Edge Guard lessons and responsibilities, much of which he was only allowed to discuss in detail with fellow government personnel. As time went on, it became a point of anxiety. So, slowly, they'd drifted apart.

It had been almost a year since he'd last spoken with Stokes. Disc, he was such a shit friend.

Taking a deep breath, he tapped the crystal.

"Stokes residence."

The depths of the crystal swirled to life, colors twisting and flashing as the sphere gently hummed. Stokes's face appeared inches from the crystal, grinning.

"*Nik!*" Stokes screamed into his crystal. "What's up, bro?"

Nikolai couldn't stop smiling. "Hey, buddy. Guess who's home?"

"What? You beautiful bastard! How long you back?"

"Like a month."

"*Dude.* That's amazing! So much shit has gone down since we last talked. Got approved for a loan to start my own shop!"

"Seriously?" Nik said. "That's—"

"Awesome, right? You wouldn't believe it—sneakers and boots, eyewear, jeans, jackets, suits, robes, hats, *everything*. Human fashion reimagined for the modern mage. And buddy, it is blowing *up!*"

Nikolai laughed, impossibly relieved that Stokes hadn't even acknowledged how long it had been since Nikolai had last called. But of course he should have known Stokes would be cool about it. That's just how Stokes was.

"That's incredible. I'm so proud of you, Stokes."

"Yeah, that's *all right*," he said, waving dismissively. "Know what's better? I have a girlfriend now. And you know what that means?"

"That you—"

"*Sex!*" he interrupted. "And I don't have to tell you, but this sex thing? It is some *seriously* good shit."

"Disc, George!" Stokes's father sputtered from out of view. "I'm still here! Please, I don't want to hear about your, your . . . *relations*!"

"*Sorry, Dad!*" he called over to him before turning back to Nikolai. "Hey, if you're free, you should come meet me at my shop. One-twenty-six Mars Avenue. Can't miss it."

"What's it called?"

"Like I said," he replied with a wink, "you can't miss it. You're lucky you caught me; I just dropped by to pick up lunch for Trudy and me. She's holding down the fort till I get back, so I gotta head out. See you there!" Then, just as Stokes was about to switch off the comm crystal: "*Oh!*"

"Yeah?"

"If you get there before me, don't tell Trudy I told you about us boning *at least* four hundred times by now."

"*George!*" Another disgusted cry from his father.

"Our flesh as one!" he laughed, speaking loudly. "Sweating bodies entwined in carnal passion! As I plunge myself *deep* into her lady flower, again and again and *again*—!"

"*GAAAAAHHHH!*"

The crystal went dark.

Nikolai took a cab over to Stokes's shop. The name LOOK burned brightly over the storefront in neon glow lights. Flashing blue, then pink, then red, then yellow—pulsing bright enough to paint the sidewalk with color. Four faceless brass mannequins stood behind the window, occasionally changing poses as they flaunted Stokes's designs.

A bell rang when Nik walked inside. The store wasn't large, but there were dozens of mannequins standing around dressed in all different styles, outfits and gear in various poses— occasionally shifting or turning sluggishly like an entire crew of lazy workers.

A young sorceress in shredded black and red punk-rock garb stood across the room, brown face framed by vibrant blue hair, a length of silver measuring tape hanging around her neck as she pulled a shirt onto one of the mannequins.

She perked up her head at the bell, smiling. "Hello! Welcome! How can I help you?"

The mannequin she was working on tried to raise its arms despite the shirt only being half on. With a grunt of annoyance, the sorceress shoved the hands back down.

"Hey! Sorry, I'm not a customer, I'm Nik—Stokes's buddy? And you're—"

"The girlfriend of legend, yeah. Also known as Trudy Mostajo. And *of course* I know who you are, Nikolai!"

She showed Nikolai around the store, pointing out all the more popular looks, going into a little more detail on the outfits she'd codesigned with Stokes.

"I'd love to do more," she said. "But I can only help out on the weekends. I'm an enchantment engineering major at the university. It keeps me pretty busy."

"I bet. So—how'd you score a dime-piece like Stokes? That guy?" Nikolai whistled, smiling. "Cream of the crop. Best motherfucker I know."

"It's funny—do you know Joseph Eaglesmith?"

Nikolai's smile froze at the name. Joseph Eaglesmith—rich, beloved, movie-star-handsome pro-flyball player. The boy Astor had started dating after she and Nikolai broke up when they were teenagers, and her boyfriend ever since. Unless something had changed in the year since he'd last pried an update out of Stokes. Which Nikolai doubted.

"Yeah, I know him."

"I joined a club at MU on my first weekend here. We build skycrafts from the ground up. Joseph joined too, even though he doesn't go to school. He's a total craft nut, and his dad donated some *beauties* for us to work on. He invited me to hang with him and his girlfriend, Cecilia—George said you guys are old friends, right? Dated for a little while, way back when? Well, me and Cecilia totally hit it off. We're probably going to be roomies next year.

"Anyway—they invited me out, went to the pub to hang with her cousin George, and he was dressed up like John Lennon—um, sorry, this old human musician, had a band—"

"Yeah, I know," Nikolai said. "Beatles." He smiled. "That's so weird. I was just listening to them."

"Oh. That is weird! Well, George had these little circle glasses. With a white suit. Used some Insta-Grow potion to grow his beard and hair out for the night. Only other mage besides Cecilia I've ever met who'd even *heard* of the Beatles—let alone looked like one!" Trudy smiled, sheepish. "I was into it. And . . . well . . ."

The bell rang behind them. Nikolai spun around, grinning so wide that it stung his cheeks.

Stokes dropped his basket carelessly and ran across the room, arms outstretched. "Give us a hug, you beautiful bag of farts!"

Nik pulled him into a rib-cracking embrace. "*Disc*, it's good to see you. And look at you! Mr. Shop-Owning-Actual-Adult."

"And what about you?" Stokes said, patting Nikolai's arms. "What have you been eating? You wearing padding under that uniform, or did you just get totally *jacked*? I swear, Trudy, this guy was a bean pole."

Trudy glanced at Nikolai's sheathed blade Focal.

"You're an Edge Guard, right?" She lowered her voice. "Do you really know battle magic?"

Nikolai guffawed, dismissive. "Hardly. Only thing I've gotten into a fight with so far is an office espresso maker."

He'd been taught to downplay his tactical capabilities. Besides the practical benefit of being underestimated by potential assailants, Nikolai's presence was also a lot less terrifying to civilians when they didn't know how easy it would be for him to turn them into greasy ashes.

Stokes looked Nikolai up and down, inspecting his outfit.

"This your uniform? I'm not a fan of jumpsuits, but at least it's tailored well enough. And I guess you can't go wrong with silver buttons on black." He patted Nikolai's sleeves again, frowning. "Man, these enchantments are heavy duty. I don't even know what any of these *do* . . ."

"Crazy, right?" Nikolai held out his arms, looking down at himself. "Magic proof, bullet proof—and it breathes like a *dream*."

An old mage with a long beard, traditional robes, and a pair of signature Stokes brand sunglasses walked in.

"Speaking of being an actual adult," Stokes whispered apologetically. Nikolai waved for him to go ahead, no big deal. "Afternoon, Wizard Burble! How's Sorceress Burble? With the wee grand-magi? You should bring them along next time! Here, this way, please, your new robes are ready. Let's see if we need to make any additional adjustments."

Nikolai stared in shock after them as a Stokes whose manner he didn't recognize escorted the old mage to the back of the store, exchanging pleasantries and small talk as he led the customer out of sight.

"You caught us in a rare lull," Trudy said in a hush. "We've been totally booked. Not only is George the best tailor in town, but people are losing their shit over his custom jobs and original designs. Word spread pretty quickly."

The bell rang again. Another customer—a middle-aged sorceress, here for a pickup. Trudy apologized, going to assist her in the changing room.

Yet another customer arrived, and it became apparent that Nikolai should leave them to their work.

"Sorry, bro," Stokes said, too quiet for the customers to hear. "But man, it is *so* good seeing you. You staying at your uncle's? How about we pick you up after closing, round seven. Then let's hit up Merlin's Boot and grab some drinks!"

"Perfect," Nikolai said, but then Stokes did something weird—he shook Nikolai's hand. The shake was awkward; Nikolai barely gripped his hand, taken aback.

Stokes made a face, pulling away. "Catch ya later, noodle fingers."

That evening, the sky ran crimson and molten gold as the sun set over Marblewood.

Nikolai found himself unable to enjoy the artificial beauty of the carefully crafted dusk, however. Anxiety throttled his chest, making it hard to breathe as he came down from Red's apartment to meet his waiting friend. It had been two years since he'd last seen his classmates. Two years since Assignment Day, and those staring, contemptuous eyes.

He could practically hear the voices chanting *Nikolai Half Staff, Nikolai Hallllllffff Staffffff* amid mocking laughter.

"Don't be stupid," he muttered to himself, taking a deep breath and forcing a smile as he stepped out onto the cobblestone street.

"Beep, beep!" Stokes called from the waiting cab. "Drunk train express—all aboard!"

Stokes's split robes swirled like dark mercury over burgundy trousers, his head shaved bald for the night. "That all you wear now?" he asked of Nikolai's simple black uniform. "First night home, you going to work or something?"

"I dunno," Nikolai said self-consciously, glancing down at

his uniform and remembering how he'd nearly died in a filthy alleyway because he'd gone out in civvies. "I just like them."

"Eh, it's cool. At least you're wearing the sneakers I made you. I'd charge a mint for Converse knockoffs half that nice these days. You lucky bastard."

Their first stop was to pick up Trudy from Marblewood University's healer ward.

"Why's Trudy here?" Nikolai asked, apprehensive as Stokes led him through cool blue halls busy with white-robed healers, students, and patients. "She okay?"

"Hey buddy, be cool," Stokes said to him quietly. "It's supposed to be a surprise, but I told a certain somebody you're in town, and she wants to see you."

Nikolai turned to him, wide-eyed, stomach doing flip-flops. "You mean . . ."

"Yes, dude," Stokes said, grinning. "And it's about fucking time. I've been playing both sides of this friend schism since we were, what, fifteen? Sixteen? And I'm sick of it. So. Be. *Nice*."

They turned a corner to find Trudy leaning up against the wall opposite the great crystal pane of an elasti-room, arms crossed across her chest. Noting their arrival, she smiled, looking into the room and then back at Nikolai, eagerly watching for his reaction.

And there she was. Cecilia Astor.

Feeling light-headed, Nikolai pressed his hands against the slick surface, steadying himself as he watched her through the crystal pane. She wore black, formfitting protective gear that looked like a hazmat suit.

The elasti-room was a box-shaped chamber framed by pillars of white stone with thick panes of crystal for walls, floor, and ceiling. Time-shift residue glistened below the thick crystal floor, gathering in a large ceramic pool. A timer ticked over the white stone archway leading into the active room.

Astor was cutting the naked cadaver of an old mage—slicing him open from neck to navel with the tip of her finger. Her protective outfit covered her entire body, except for her right hand, where she wore her medi-glove Focal. She mechanically and efficiently began removing various organs, placing them on the tray beside her.

"Oh, fuck, *gross*—" Stokes said, covering his eyes and gagging as they peered through the sealed entryway.

"We'll leave you two to catch up," Trudy said, chuckling sympathetically at her deathly pale boyfriend's valiant struggle not to vomit as she led him away.

Nikolai watched with morbid curiosity as Astor split the skin with the golden forefinger of her medi-glove Focal, which was so thin that it looked painted on. He'd watched her draw it from the pool on Assignment Day, along with the silver bow art Focal that could summon a violin made of light upon command—but it was still incredibly strange seeing her with the same logic Focal as his mother.

Cut complete, Astor glanced over at them, freckled face lighting up as she noticed Nikolai through the blue-tinged glass of her protective outfit's headwear. She straightened, hands on her hips, eyes glinting playfully as he grinned at her, waving like a fool. She held up a bloody finger, turned back to the body, and began digging around inside.

Nikolai craned his neck, trying to see what she was doing, but then she turned back, a heart and two kidneys clutched in her hands. She began to juggle them, watching Nikolai's horrified expression with glee.

Finally she lost control, dropping the organs with horrible

wet *splats* that Nikolai could imagine but not hear, and bent over, clutching her stomach as she cackled.

Once she had finally regained composure, she collected the heart and kidneys off the floor, dropping them carelessly onto the tray with the other organs. She went over to the twin levers beside the entryway, wrapped her bloody, gloved hand around the inside lever, and pulled.

Everything inside the room except for Astor began to *rewind*. The blood disappeared from her hands as she held onto the lever. The organs flew from the tray back into the body—the slice from neck to sternum slowly sealing up.

There was an odd, indescribable *thud* that Nikolai didn't quite hear, didn't quite feel—the time wall, the maximum amount of rewind time the room had stored. Astor opened her suit, pulling back the glass-front cowl over her head. Sweat plastered messy yellow hair to her face.

"You just gonna stand there?" she said, poking his chest as he stood stiffly, unsure if he should hug her. "Come here, you dork." She grabbed him, pulling him into a rib-cracking embrace.

"I don't know where you went to clown school," Nikolai said, "but I think you should stick to healing."

"Wait till you see me throw the large intestine in there," she said, "A real party *coup de grace*. Disc, dude! Look at you! How the fuck you been?"

There were bags under her eyes—dark circles of exhaustion. But she'd never been so beautiful.

"I've had an interesting couple of days," Nikolai said, with a tired half smile. "But it's good to be home. How about you, Madame Healer?"

"*Apprentice* healer. But just you wait. Couple years down the line, I'll be running this joint. My name on every entrance, in big flaming letters! My face tattooed to the chest of every freshman apprentice! And for a thousand years, I shall reign." Astor held up her medi-gloved hand, clenching. "With a golden fist."

She squeezed Nikolai's shoulder, looking into his eyes with a serious intensity. "It's good to see you, Nicky."

"Butcher queen still desecrating bodies?" Trudy asked as she returned from the adjacent hallway, Stokes tentatively peering around the corner.

"All clear!" Astor called. "Ya wuss!"

"I didn't puke," he said, pale but proud as he came up beside Trudy to join them. "Yay, me. You guys ready to hit the bar?"

They went back to Astor's dorm, Trudy and Astor laughing and filling the air with chatter that Nikolai could tell was in well-meaning effort to cover up the awkwardness they must have all been feeling.

Nikolai waited outside with Stokes while the sorceresses got ready, and pulled out a pair of carved pipes he'd brought for the occasion. To Nikolai's surprise, Stokes declined.

"Nah, bro. I'm gonna be kissin' my lady tonight. Don't want my mouth to taste like ass."

"Oh, okay," Nikolai said, disappointed. "All good." He stowed the pipes, not wanting to smoke alone. "Your dad dig up any new good stuff from the university archives? I saw this one movie, at the theater in the Gloaming I was telling you about? It was called *Predator*—about this alien big-game hunter, tracking and killing these soldiers in a jungle with heat vision. It was kind of stupid, and totally amazing—we should try and find a copy."

Stokes shrugged, distracted. "Honestly, I've been too busy to watch much. Just, you know, *work, work, work.* It's all happening so fast, and even with Trudy's help . . . I'm already looking for an apprentice. Can you imagine that? Me, with an apprentice?

At fucking twenty years old? I might have to poach one from Maurice's Magewear, though. I feel kind of bad about it, but I guess that's business, right?"

"Yeah, totally," Nik said, trying not to sound bored.

"Once my client list is bringing in enough income that I can afford to open shop closer to city hall, I'll get *way* more foot traffic, more browsing customers, you know? Then later down the road I can open stores in other Veils. I mean, manufacturing restrictions are pretty tight, so I can't mass produce anything, but I figure I can train other tailors to use my styles and looks—create a *brand*."

"Uh-huh."

Hitting the town wasn't quite as exciting as it was in the mobbed streets of the Gloaming, Nikolai quickly discovered. The four of them squeezed into a cab, Stokes passing around a flask of dragon's milk, though Astor declined.

Astor was talking a thousand words per minute, laughing and cracking jokes in that overeager way she used to when she was uncomfortable.

"—but mister big-city wizard over here probably isn't impressed by that," she was saying. "Isn't that right, Nicky?"

Nikolai pretended to yawn, playing along. "Sorry, what was that? Hard to follow your quaint hillbilly small talk. With that *adorable* accent."

"*Hey*," Astor said, kicking him playfully. "All right, big shot. How is life in the city of royals? You dating a princess? Some old-money sorceress, some daughter of a duchess?"

Nikolai flinched, thinking of Ilyana's duchess ancestry.

"Still interviewing," he said.

"So we meeting Joe there?" Stokes asked, changing the subject.

Astor shook her head. "Nah, he and the team all have practice tonight for the Nanuk Knights game next Tuesday." She nudged Nikolai with her elbow. "Flyball! Your favorite, right, Nicky?"

Nikolai genuinely began to zone out this time as they started going on about national flyoffs and finals and other pro-flyball jargon. Apparently this would be the last game of the season. Marblewood's team had been cleaning house—if they won the following Tuesday, they'd win the Northeast Cup.

Bitterly, Nikolai thought about how Astor never gave a shit about flyball until she started dating Eaglesmith. He shoved the feeling aside, annoyed at himself for the petty thought.

"You're coming, right, Nik?" Trudy asked, breaking him from his reverie.

"Yeah, Nik," Stokes said, teasing. "You coming to the game?"

"Um . . . sure," Nikolai said, hesitant. And then, more confidently, "Absolutely. I'm in."

Astor dug into her clutch and pulled out a Silverbill. "Five bills says he's asleep by halftime."

"Make it ten and you're on," Stokes said. "And I won't poke him to keep him awake. Tailor's honor."

Warm cries of hello burst out from the crowds as they entered the brightly lit pub. The mob seemed to close around Astor in adoring welcome as she moved forward to greet them, calling out name after name.

Nikolai's heart sank as he recognized most of the magi from academy. Everyone was glad to see the others, though, and despite a few odd looks, nobody really seemed to notice Nikolai.

Nik volunteered to get the first round and made his way over to the bar. The pub wasn't very large—scattered tables, a few booths, and a tiny stage with a band jamming away acoustically—quiet enough that Nikolai didn't have to shout to be heard.

He caught two sorceresses he recognized as Astor's girlfriends from academy staring at him. He smiled at them, but they didn't smile back—instead they whispered something to each other and giggled.

Flushed in the face, Nikolai ignored them, waving for the bartender's attention.

"Could I get one Chestnut Jeeves, a Blue Ridge Smoke, a Schwarz Royale, annnddd—"

Nik could feel eyes on the back of his neck, and glanced back to see a couple of Joseph's old friends who had played on the academy flyball team with him when they were teens.

Catching Nik's look, one of them—a tall, poshly dressed mage with sandy hair and a spattering of freckles—raised his glass to him, then muttered something to his friends. They all laughed.

Gritting his teeth, Nik ignored them, turning back to the bartender. "— fuck it — a Ginger Dragon. Make it a double."

He downed the Ginger Dragon at the bar and sent the brews to their table. He instantly felt more relaxed as warm snakes of alcohol spread down through his chest and stomach.

"Hey, guys," Nikolai said, taking a seat. He took a swig from his honeybrew and leaned in, loosened up, elbows on the table. "So, I hate to ask, but please. Be straight with me. The assignment ceremony. Was it . . . as bad as I think it was?"

Stokes and Trudy looked at each other, faces fixed with artificial smiles as they unsuccessfully attempted to mask their discomfort. Astor frowned.

Nikolai shrugged. "I'm not dumb. Everyone here's looking at me like I've got shit on my face. I was hoping that after two years away maybe people would have forgotten."

"No, dude, it wasn't *that* bad," Stokes said. "I mean . . ." He looked to Astor for support.

"It was a nightmare," Astor said, blunt as always.

Stokes cringed. "Yo, Astor, come on . . ."

She slammed her Chestnut Jeeves down onto the table, sugary brown soda splashing over the fingers of her golden medi-glove as she cut Stokes off, her eyes glittering with fiery intensity.

"Who gives a shit, though? Nicky, I'm sorry. I know being a Watchman like your dad meant a lot to you. And I know we weren't on speaking terms, but ever since you left I've been so angry at myself for how I just stood there and watched you fall apart. How I just froze up and let those douchebags laugh at you instead of slapping them upside their heads. So if anyone tries to give you shit, you point them to me. And I'll feed them their own assholes. Okay?"

She stared at him, intent, fingers wrapped so tight around her glass that Nikolai worried she was going to crush it.

Nikolai looked at her for a moment, his insides a whirlwind of conflicting emotions. Then, finally, he grinned.

"Hey. Astor. Do you want to dance?"

"W-what?" she said, shocked, as if that was the last possible response she could have anticipated. Shock turned to delight. "Nikolai Strauss, since when do *you* dance?"

He stood and offered her his hand.

"In New Damascus, everyone dances. It's the whole point of going out. C'mon, I'll teach you."

She grinned. "We'll see who teaches who."

The music was just right, so Nikolai downed his brew and led Astor over to the open space in front of the stage. He, Ilyana, and Albert had gone dancing almost weekly, and they'd taught him all the most popular steps.

"Hands here, with the music . . ."

She picked it up quick, and soon they were stepping and spinning and turning in front of the stage. The band didn't seem like they were accustomed to magi actually dancing to their music, and it excited them. They started playing louder, *faster*. A circle formed around Nikolai and Astor, magi watching and clapping along.

"Wow," she said, teasing. "You really have gotten fancy since you left."

"Not really," he said, trying not to blush.

A hand clamped on his arm, stopping them midturn.

"All right, sucka," Stokes said. "My turn. Show me how to do that shit."

Nikolai grinned at Astor and passed her to Trudy, taking Stokes in a spin as he showed him the steps, leading until Stokes got it and then letting Stokes lead.

"How you doing, bud?" he said into Nikolai's ear. "Seems like you're keeping your cool, but I know how you are."

"Okay, I think," Nikolai said honestly. "I was nervous, but I'm actually having a really good time."

"You know, it's totally okay if you don't want to go to Joseph's game. It's gotta be weird for you."

"No, I'll be fine," Nikolai insisted. "I'm a big kid, I can handle it."

"Cool." Stokes broke off from Nikolai, beaming. "I really missed you, man. It's fucking good to have you back."

"It's good to be back," Nikolai said, realizing, to his surprise, that he actually meant it.

Stokes broke off from Nikolai, bowing to Trudy with a flourish and taking her hand. Couples and singles were moving onto the dance floor, some emulating Nikolai's New Damascus dance, others doing their own thing.

That ex-flyball player douchebag who'd toasted him earlier

(whom Nikolai had mentally dubbed *Freckles*) hung back with some of the other ex-flyball guys, occasionally casting annoyed glances Nik's way as he began swapping partners—eventually ending up with one of the two friends of Astor's who'd laughed at him earlier. She was a tall, willowy girl with hair dyed a softly glowing opalescent pearl.

"Nik, right?" she asked, leaning down a little to shout into his ear. "I like your uniform!"

"Thanks," he said, and twirled her around, catching her at the last possible moment. She laughed, cheering.

"You're *good*. I'm Gwendolyn. I think we had living math together?"

Nikolai thought about it with an expression of practiced indifference. "Maybe."

The more they danced, the closer they became, until finally she was hanging off him, and they were practically nose to nose.

"All right." Astor cut in. "Time's up, Gwyn. You mind?"

Nikolai's heart skipped a beat, though from Gwyn's expression she *did* mind. Taking Astor's hand, he glanced back to see Gwyn go sit with Freckles, who was scowling with a pint of brew in one hand, angrily tapping the glassy length of a truth-teller Focal against his leg with the other. It appeared that they were together.

Gwyn put her arm around his waist and tried to kiss him but he pushed her away and said something that, from her stricken expression, must have been nasty. Clearly upset, she stormed out, dragging her friend behind her. Freckles glanced over at Nikolai again, eyes glinting with jealous rage.

"Yikes," he muttered, trying not to look pleased.

Astor rolled her eyes. "I know, right?"

They were both sweating and grinning by the time a slow

dance began to play, giving everyone a chance to catch their breath. Nikolai held her close, her unruly hair tickling his cheek. Disc, he'd forgotten how good she smelled. How good it felt to hold her.

"You know," she said, into his ear. "You said some pretty shitty things last time we talked."

"I know," Nikolai said quietly. "I'm sorry. I just . . . you were my first. Friend. Girlfriend. Everything, really." He smiled, trying to smother the melancholy that threatened to wash away the joy he was feeling. "Nobody had ever gotten me like you. And I wasn't ready to let you go."

She stopped dancing and hugged him tight. "You know I love you, right?"

"Sure," he said, tears stinging his eyes. "Of course."

"Oh, Nicky," she said. "You never were any good at lying to me." She kissed him on the cheek. "Welcome home, Strauss. I'm glad you're back."

The rest of the night passed in a blur of singing, dancing, and too much honeybrew. By the end of the night Nikolai was cheerfully, drunkenly saying goodbye to almost everyone—everyone except for Freckles and his friends, who had spent the night watching Nikolai and Astor dance with uneasy eyes.

It was strange and wonderful feeling like a part of this group. Even at his happiest, when Nikolai and Astor were at the peak of their relationship, desperately in love in the way only fifteen-year-olds can be, he had never held any hope of connecting with these people. But with a few drinks, and a few dance lesson imports from New Damascus . . .

It wasn't until Nikolai was drifting off that he remembered his promise to call Ilyana. But it was late, and he was drunk, so he decided to wait till morning instead.

A crushing hangover pounded through Nikolai's skull as he soared through the clouds over Marblewood, he and the jet-black skyhorn hidden from view by a sheet of invisibility as he scanned the Dome for thinning, which would appear through goggles worn for the task as dark blotches in the Veil's mirror surface. When it was found, which was rare, a Lancer would be scheduled for repair.

Red took the western half of the Veil, around the farmlands, while Nikolai took the eastern side, mostly over the lake and wilds.

The air was chilly high up over the water. Nikolai had never flown over Marblewood before, and if the city had felt small before, seeing it spread out below in miniature made it doubly so. Down below, fishing boats threw out nets over black water, dragging up piles of fish flashing silver and gold in the early morning sun. Bright circles of light moved under the surface along the shore as divers harvested freshwater mussels.

Nikolai skimmed to a halt over the far edge of the forest, breath catching in his chest. Just out of reach, the cerulean dome shone with the vaguest reflection of green from the trees below.

It was then, as he drew near enough to see the Veil's mirrored curve within the illusion of sky, that he was able to gauge the dome's actual size.

The realization of how truly small Marblewood was compared to New Damascus left him breathless. He could feel the weight of it, as if the whole sky had suddenly come crushing down on his lungs.

Nikolai let the skyhorn drift closer to the Veil and pressed his hand against it, steadying himself. The surface was cool and frictionless. Though one couldn't normally feel the magical energy constantly filling the air from the Disc at the center of the city, as he splayed his hand against the artificial sky, he could feel the flow of it like a gentle, electric breeze through his fingers.

Slowly, purposefully, he drew his baton and lightly pressed it against the surface. The surface began to bulge outward, and he pulled away in a horrified panic—the reality of what he'd almost done hitting him like a slap.

He couldn't breathe. He circled the maples, looking for a spot to land. A familiar clearing caught his eye, and with morbid fascination he pushed through the treetops, cracking limbs and branches with the heavy vehicle as he landed.

He couldn't hold it anymore. He *had* to try the spell passed on to him by that fucking revolver. Had to get it out of his system, lest he find himself unable to contain it next time he was within reach of the dome.

What better a spot than the very clearing in which the revolver had first touched his mind?

The ground remained blackened from Nikolai's flame when he and Hazeal had fought, though ferns and wildflowers had already begun to sprout up among the scorched moss. Nikolai was relieved to find no trace of Hazeal's ashes remaining, likely washed away by rain.

Feeling the spell pulse and take shape through his pools and channels, he weighed his dagger in one hand, his baton in the other. Closing his eyes, he took a deep breath, focusing.

It was heavy. Powerful, but somehow delicate. He sheathed the dagger. The baton was a better fit for the spell, which required some finesse.

"APOCRYPHA!"

It was remarkably like the *akro* weave of hardened air, though less malleable and far more difficult to cast and maintain. It cast with barely controllable force, like trying to control the flow of water from a spigot with your bare hand.

With a wave of his baton, a great glimmering wall split the clearing in two.

The spell was far too powerful to maintain with his inner pools of magic alone. That gentle electric wind from the Disc's unlimited well of magic he'd felt before seemed to buffet him like a storm as it rushed to fill in the swath of sky he'd created.

With a grin, he shot off another curving strip of mercurial Veil, then another, featherweighting himself and creating long looping ribbons he could sprint along as he watched the forest spin around him.

When he was finished, the clearing looked like an art piece, woven abstractly with long tangles of shimmering, paper-thin mirrors.

Dismissing the Veil, he tried the more difficult inversion of the weave, sending out a great open sphere of Veil to close around a tree stump.

The tree stump disappeared, the place where it had been now an unremarkable spot of scorched moss. There wasn't a hole—it was as if the stump had never been there at all. The spell made reality somehow *pinch*, pulling in the surroundings as the Apocrypha Veil stowed away its contents in some sort of pocket dimension.

This was how magi had hidden themselves from the outside world for thousands of years. This was how their cities had remained safely stowed away from whatever calamity had afflicted the world beyond the Veils.

Nikolai could feel an invisible point hanging in the air at the center of where he'd cast the spell. He reached for it, dismissing the spell, and the stump reappeared, the ground around it pushing out in an unsettling way that gave Nikolai a moment of nauseating vertigo.

He wasn't supposed to learn the spell until he'd ranked up to Lancer Class. But so what? Using it to pass through the Veil without any idea of what lay beyond would be insanity. For all Nikolai knew, he'd be torn to atoms the moment he left the protection of the Veil. There were too many unknowns—enough that he'd have to be suicidal to risk it so blindly, and with so little cause.

Maybe if the revolver hadn't been confiscated, it would have had further instruction for Nikolai. But whatever plans his mother might have had for him and the artifact, it was locked up tight now. That ship had sailed.

Nikolai returned to his uncle's office in the Watchman station to find Red at his desk, bent over some paperwork.

"Disc," Nikolai said, stretching. "I can't believe you do all the scanning on your own. Even half was a pain in the ass."

"Don't have to be so thorough," Red said, not looking up from the paperwork. "It's just busy work. Takes months of neglect for real thinning."

"Why aren't there any other Edge Guard here? Even little Veils usually have a few."

"Don't want any others. Got you to help for now."

"Yeah, well, don't expect much," Nikolai said. "This is supposed to be a vacation."

He tapped the comm crystal, which automatically displayed the face of a disinterested Edge Guard clerk back in New Damascus.

"Marblewood check," she said.

"Marblewood green," Red replied.

"Confirmed." The crystal went dark.

As Nikolai moved to leave, Red cleared his throat.

"The captain told me that you and him talked about . . . your mother."

Nikolai stifled a sigh. "Yeah?"

"She never told me anything," he said. "Kept me in the dark. Didn't even know she was dead till a couple Moonwatch dragged me out of bed for questioning. I still don't understand why. But . . . it was very hard."

He hesitated, watery gray eyes haunted as he looked up at Nik. "I know that growing up with me . . . wasn't easy. But when you left . . . and when you never called, or wrote—"

Guilt and anger swirling in a hot muddle, Nikolai opened his mouth to speak, but Red held up a hand for Nik to let him finish.

"—it got me thinking. A lot. About how absent I was in your upbringing. About how selfish I was, too buried in my own issues to be the man you needed me to be."

Nikolai straightened, mouth pressed into a thin line. He was furious now, though he wasn't quite sure why, jaw clenched to keep from saying anything unkind to the uncharacteristically vulnerable man, usually so stone-faced.

Red met Nikolai's angry gaze, pained but unflinching. "I know you're only here for a little while. But I was hoping that maybe . . . we could start over. Try to get to know each other. To be . . . something like a family, at least."

Nikolai took a moment to collect himself. When he finally spoke, his manner was cool and composed.

"You're a Lancer, like my mom was," he said. "You've gone beyond the Veil. So tell me—what's really out there?"

Red stared at Nikolai, seeming surprised by the question. "I've told you this before. Showed you files."

"Oh, I remember. But are you sure you don't have anything to add? Any details you might've forgotten to include in your reports?"

Red seemed to be very carefully maintaining eye contact with Nikolai. It was strange—as if he was struggling not to look over at something looming in his periphery.

"No."

"So say, hypothetically, that there was a freak magical accident, and some random civilian was thrown out into the human world. Without a Lancer's spells and knowledge, they'd just die in the radioactive hex storms, right? Melt like a candle in spellfire."

"That's right," Red said evenly. "They'd be dead in an instant. Like I told you."

Nikolai smiled unpleasantly. "Yep. Just like you told me."

"Nikolai—"

"Look, Uncle Red, I've got somewhere to be."

Red began to nod eagerly, waving for Nikolai to go ahead as he tried and failed to mask his disappointment.

Nikolai took a deep breath, relenting. "Thank you for talking to me. I'll think about what you asked."

"Of course, of course," Red said hurriedly. But his relief was palpable.

That was as close to an apology as he was going to get from Red, Nikolai supposed. Lost in thought as he contemplated Red's words, he almost walked right into a Watchman who was much larger than him.

"Oh, sorry about—" he began, but stopped midsentence, going cold.

"Nikolai!" Joseph Eaglesmith rumbled, the immense mage impossibly dashing in the brass-buttoned Watchman uniform. A golden scepter topped with the figure of a screeching eagle hung at his side—the logic Focal of one born for political leadership. On his feet were a pair of great golden flyball boots—art Focals with wings like the mythical sandals of Hermes.

"What—how?" Nikolai stammered, stunned and infuriated to see Joseph wearing the uniform he'd once so desperately dreamed of wearing himself.

"Yeah, surprise, right?" Joseph laughed, running a hand through his short golden curls. "There's a lot of downtime playing flyball for a living. I like to keep busy, and I thought I might be able to do some good as a Watchman, you know? The chief and mayor agreed, and my dad okayed it—so here I am. Part-time right now, until the season's over. But man, you look great! How have you been? It's been years!"

"R-right," Nikolai said. "Great. I've been . . . great."

"So I heard! Cece said that you guys had a lot of fun the other night."

"See-See?"

"Sorry, Cecilia," he said, and Nikolai nodded, biting his cheek hard enough to draw blood. "Anyway, I gotta go. But great seeing you." Joseph slapped Nikolai's back with an immense hand, almost knocking him over. "Guess we're basically coworkers now, so I'll see you again tomorrow!"

With the taste of blood in his mouth, Nikolai skulked out of the Watchman station without a word to anyone else. He took a cab back to Red's apartment, scowling, arms crossed the entire ride, stewing in anger and contempt.

Slamming the door to his room, he was suddenly disgusted at how childish it looked and began roughly yanking the magi-print posters from the walls and ceilings, carelessly ripping some of them. Eaglesmith. A Watchman. Joseph *fucking* Eaglesmith. Astor's boyfriend. Star flyball player. And a *Watchman*. A fucking *WATCHMAN*. Because why not, right? Why not give him that too? Like he didn't have enough. Like he didn't already have every *FUCKING* thing Nikolai *EVER* wanted just *handed* to him, *silver spoon MOTHERFUCKER!*

Before he knew what he was doing, he wrapped his fist in a glove of *akro* and punched one, two, *three* holes in the plaster of his wall, roaring.

He sank onto his bed, disgusted and wondering what the hell was wrong with him.

Nikolai didn't even want to be a Watchman anymore. Though unusual, he could have applied to be one without having drawn a Watchman staff, like Joseph. But the very night he'd drawn his dagger and baton, he'd been whisked off by Red to New Damascus. Captain Jubal had Nikolai enrolled in boot camp so quickly, and with such talkative zeal, that Nikolai hadn't even realized saying no was an option.

But still. Seeing Joseph in the same uniform as his father . . . it had just been too much.

Anger dimmed to an exhausted melancholy. For a moment, as Nikolai took in the destruction his temper had wrought, it was all he could do not to crumple into a weeping ball on the floor amid the ruined artworks he'd once so treasured.

Instead Nikolai fetched a roll of tape and began to mend them.

———

In the days that followed, Nikolai, Astor, Trudy, and Stokes fell into the habit of hanging out almost every night after work and class—even if just for a quick dinner in the university cafeteria.

Dancing, drinking. Dusting off old memory cubes full of movies they hadn't watched since they were children. Digging old instruments out of storage and attempting to play some of their favorites from back when they used to have dreams of musical stardom.

Nikolai on the drums. Trudy on piano. Stokes with an incredibly out of tune upright bass. Astor's violin of light ringing out with impossible beauty and depth.

Joseph was rarely around, busy most nights practicing for the big game after his days of work at the Watchmen HQ. So really, it felt like old times, but for the welcome addition of Trudy.

As happy as this made Nikolai, he found himself struggling with increasing difficulty to fight back his old feelings for Astor. Resenting himself for it. Astor was his friend again. His family. Why couldn't that be enough?

Astor was happy, and whatever Nikolai thought of her annoyingly perfect boyfriend, she loved him. It wasn't fair for him to resent that.

He missed Ilyana desperately. He wanted to hear her voice again, to see her face. But every time he called her room's crystal, she didn't pick up. Sure, maybe he just kept missing her. But he knew Ilyana's schedule well enough to know that she must have been around for at least some of his calls.

By the end of the week, he stopped trying.

On the day of Joseph's big game, Nikolai came out of the Watchman HQ after a short afternoon shift to find Stokes and Trudy waiting for him with an oversized picnic basket.

"We brought refreshments!" Stokes said, holding up the basket. "Come on. We're gonna be late for the game!"

Nikolai had totally forgotten—though that explained why he hadn't been forced to endure another awkward conversation in the Watchman station with Joseph Eaglesmith. Every day, without fail, Joseph found Nikolai and cornered him for a chat in enthusiastic, seemingly earnest effort to befriend him, no matter how pointedly standoffish Nikolai's demeanor.

Nikolai knew it was immature, but he just couldn't bring himself to like Marblewood's golden boy. A dislike further compounded by the fact that Joseph couldn't seem to comprehend the fact that someone might not want to talk to him.

"Ah, shit," Nikolai said. "I totally forgot."

"*Gasp*," Stokes said. "How shocking. Don't worry—we've got plenty of good food and honeybrew to keep you entertained while you heroically endure the entire magi nation's favorite global pastime. Plus, I've got a bet to win. Remember? So come on."

The stadium was at the university, adjacent to a smaller amateur league flyball court. Joseph had left tickets for them at the front office for midlevel bench seats. In the stadium, tracer lines had been painted in the air, a glowing combination of the *akro* and *illio* weaves marking the boundaries of the fly zone—the large, rectangular area of space in the air, below which was a pool of water that would break the fall of players who were knocked down.

The referee used an amplification spell to announce the entry of the Marblewood Comets onto the court. Resplendent in red and gold, the team swarmed out to their positions in organized patterns. The crowd roared with applause. Nikolai clapped with minimal enthusiasm.

As the other team (the Nanuk Knights, from an ancient Veil in the deep north) spread out across the other side of the court in silver and blue, Nikolai cracked open a bottle of honeybrew and settled in for a long, boring game.

Nikolai zoned out for a while, occasionally clapping when it seemed appropriate. His heart sank when he hit the bottom of his bottle and realized that Stokes hadn't packed seconds. He waved down a sorceress who was hawking bottles from a crate slung around her neck and bought them all another round of drinks.

He must have nodded off, because the music began to blare and suddenly the teams were leaving the court. For one wonderful second he thought the game was over, but realized with a groan that it was only halftime. As he smothered a sigh, someone tapped Nikolai on the shoulder.

"That'll be ten bills, cuz!" Astor said with forced cheer, hopping over the seat to squeeze between Nikolai and Stokes. "I saw you nappin', Nicky. Don't try to hide it!"

Stokes groaned. "Your pitiful attention span has cost me dearly, Strauss."

"Long day," Nikolai said, embarrassed. "I'm having fun. Really!"

Astor was looking even more stunning than usual—wearing a slim-cut, emerald green dress—face done up with more makeup than he'd ever seen her wear.

"Everything okay?" Trudy asked. "Why aren't you sitting down in the box seats with the Eaglesmiths?"

Astor's face darkened, but then she just shrugged and laughed. "As much as I love hanging out with my boyfriend's parents, I figured I'd come get an eyeful of your lovely faces."

Smiling or not, Nikolai could tell that something was bothering her.

"Scoot," Trudy said, and Stokes complied, shoving aside so she could take his place besides Astor. She clasped her hand. "Come on, what's up, babe? No bullshit."

Astor went uncharacteristically quiet, staring at Trudy's hand on hers, then at her lap. "Well, it's no big deal," she said, lightly.

"But there's a recruiter here. From Kitezh. And if the Comets win the game . . . if *Joey* wins the game . . ."

She and Trudy exchanged a knowing glance. Stokes let out a long breath.

"Damn, dude," he said. "That's some real grown-up shit. You don't think . . . ?"

Astor waved him off, clearing her throat. "Look at me, Little Ms. Storm Cloud over here." She climbed back up over the seats, ignoring Nik and Trudy's attempts to help. She landed, momentarily precarious in her heels, which Nikolai had never seen her wear before. "Halftime will be over soon. Gotta get back to the fam. But seriously, don't worry about it." She flicked Nikolai's ear from behind the stands. "Disc forbid I distract *this* megafan from the game."

Nikolai laughed and swatted her hand away. He couldn't help but watch as her slight, emerald-clad figure carefully disappeared into the crowd, a fluttering emptiness filling the pit of his stomach.

"What was that about?" he asked the others. Stokes and Trudy exchanged looks.

"Kitezh Crimsons' alpha drake is about to retire," Stokes said. "They're looking for a replacement. Someone young, new. Up-and-coming."

"Ohhh," Nikolai breathed. "Someone like Joseph."

"Exactly," Trudy said. "And if the recruiter is impressed today . . . Joey'll be moving to Kitezh. And Astor . . ."

Understanding dawned on Nikolai. If Joseph's team won, he'd move to Kitezh—a Veil in the middle of what used to be Russia, on nearly the opposite side of the globe from Marblewood. And Astor would *never* leave her mom or kid sister behind, let alone abandon her studies to chase after some boyfriend.

All of a sudden, Nikolai was following the game more intently than anyone else in the entire stadium.

By the end of the third quarter, Nikolai had been sitting in tense silence for so long that he began to ache. His jaw clenched as he struggled not to cheer and boo with the crowd. He leaned back in his seat, practically pulling out his hair as the Knights took the lead and the Marblewood Comets lost one of their best players to an *obvious* foul.

"Hey buddy," Stokes said as Nikolai ordered a fourth honeybrew to calm his trembling nerves. "Maybe chill out on the drinking."

"Sure," Nikolai said absently, eyes locked intently on the game. "Last one, I promise."

End of the fourth quarter. Nikolai had needed to piss for twenty minutes and it felt like he was about to start bleeding internally, but he couldn't tear himself away. The Comets' offense had been great but their defense was sloppy, with another of the team's best players hit so bad that he really should have sat the rest of the game out.

It was all up to Joseph now.

The heat was on and Joseph was flying fast—faster than anyone on either side. But he was distracted and made a couple dumb mistakes—nearly lost the ball once, nearly dropped it in the water below before snatching it out of the air again in an incredible looping save between two Knights who collided into one another *just* as they missed him. The crowd went *insane*.

Ten seconds remained.

Four Knights came from every direction for Joseph. Two were stopped by Comet offense, and Joseph dodged the third in a twisting feint and rammed his shoulder into the fourth, knocking him out of the air.

Five seconds remained.

The Comets' offense had fallen apart—Joseph was practically alone out there, but he closed in on the goal. Every single Knight seemed to bear down on him in a desperate scramble, but he twisted and turned and spun with absurd grace—until—!

"Yesssssss!" Nikolai screamed, jumping up and down as the audience went wild.

Half a second to spare and the Marblewood Comets had won. Letting out a triumphant roar, Joseph let himself fall back down into the water. The rest of the team kicked off their gear and plummeted in after him, raising him up on their shoulders as they swam to the side.

Nikolai realized that the others were staring. He slowly sat back down, laughing nervously. Embarrassed.

Trudy excused herself, off to hit the restroom. Stokes took Nikolai by the arm. "Dude. What was that about?"

"Sorry," Nikolai said, wilting. "It's just . . . a lot. You know?"

"I know, bud," Stokes said, softening. "But maybe you should go home. Too much sun, too much brew. Nobody's going to care."

"No," Nikolai assured him. "I'll be okay. I'll tone it down."

Stokes looked doubtful, but didn't argue.

Nikolai made sure to keep his expression impassive as they went to catch a cab to the festivities, but inside he was beaming.

Merlin's Boot was already crowded when they arrived, boisterously celebrating the big win.

The team hadn't shown up yet, so there was an air of anticipation as everyone awaited the *conquering heroes*. Nikolai shoved past a couple drunks and managed to grab their group a table in the corner where he sat, eagerly watching the door for Astor's arrival.

The band started to play and Trudy stood up, taking Stokes's hand. "We're gonna go dance."

"Oh Nik, you've created a monster." Stokes sighed, then twirled her around, lowering her for a kiss. "You gonna come?"

"Nah, I'm gonna chill," Nikolai said, waving them off. "Go show 'em how it's done."

He watched them dance from across the room, completely lost in thought as he absently waved down the barkeep for another honeybrew.

Between the sun and the drinks and the excitement of the game, Nikolai was a little woozy. He knew he probably shouldn't have had anything more to drink—but he was feeling festive. As shitty as he knew that was.

Magi cheered outside and the door burst open—a flood of people singing the Marblewood Anthem, all dressed in the team colors.

"*Marblewood, oh Marblewood, land of sky and gold! Where the sorceresses are fair and wise and the wizards are strong and bold. Where the muse never hides, and love never dies, it truly can be told! In Marblewood, oh Marblewood, the land of sky and gold!*"

"Marblewoodites!" one of Joseph's friends announced. "Marblewoodians! Woodooloos! I present to you, JOSSSSEEEPPPHHHHH EAAAGGLEEESMITH!"

The team hoisted Joseph up onto their shoulders to great applause. He was laughing and blushing as he waved sheepishly at the cheering, intoxicated crowd.

The group—mostly comprised of Joseph's teammates and former teammates from his old academy team—began chugging a line of honeybrews. Freckles was there, muscle-bound arm slung around Gwendolyn, with her pale glowing hair. Nikolai caught Freckles glaring, so he raised his glass at him and smiled. The other averted his gaze with a scowl.

Nikolai stood, craning his neck as he looked for Astor. Just then, she came in through the door with a girl whose name Nikolai forgot, who was drunkenly shouting and cheering into the politely sober Astor's face.

Nikolai started to walk over to her but then bumped into Joseph, who obviously had the same thing in mind.

"Oh—uh, hey," Nikolai said to him. "You were—you were great out there."

"Wow, thanks, Nik!" Joseph said. He was distracted, but seemed genuinely taken aback at Nikolai's praise. "Cece told me you aren't much for flyball—I really appreciate your support."

"Of course," Nikolai said, and let him go. Joseph went over to Astor and Nik sidled to the bar, keeping a sideways eye on them. He couldn't hear what they were saying, but Joseph looked apologetic. He tried to embrace her, and Nik felt a thrill as she stiffened, stone-faced—not reciprocating. Sighing, he kissed her cheek and moved to rejoin the festivities.

The bartender placed another honeybrew next to Nikolai's hand—probably assuming he was with the group. Absently, Nikolai paid for the drink and took a swig, watching Astor patiently endure Gwyn's drunken rambling.

Astor excused herself and went outside, looking miserable. A wave of guilt washed over him, and his joy at the thought of Eaglesmith moving away momentarily soured. Who the hell was he to celebrate Astor's heartbreak? Some fucking friend he was.

Nikolai downed his honeybrew and slammed the glass on the bar. It struck him that he was actually quite drunk, but shook it off, attempting to sober up with pure willpower. A little unsteady on his feet, he followed Astor outside to go check on her.

He found her a little ways down the street, standing alone under the light of a streetlamp.

"Astor?" he called out. "You okay?"

"Oh, Nik!" she said, sniffling and hastily wiping her eyes. It was obvious that she'd been crying—her makeup was all smeared to hell. "What's up?"

"Saw you head out," he said, joining her in the halo of light cast down from the glow bulb. "You looked upset. Everything okay?" He drew out his handkerchief and offered it to her. At her hesitance, he smiled. "Don't worry, it's clean—one hundred percent snot free, I promise."

She laughed, one of those choked half-sob kind of laughs, and accepted the handkerchief, dabbing her eyes with it. "Look at you, Mr. Fancypants. The city really has changed you. Since when does Nikolai Strauss carry a hanky?"

"I saw you in distress. Ran as fast as I could to the nearest handkerchief dispensary." He moved closer, touching her arm. "So, what's up? Were you secretly rooting for the Knights? You have a lot of money riding on them, or something?"

She laughed again, shaking her head. "Oh, Nicky. It's nothing, I just . . ." Her eyes welled up with tears, and she took a deep breath, trying to calm herself. "Joey's been offered a position on the Kitezh Crimsons as alpha drake. He wants to take it. And it's an incredible opportunity, the chance of a lifetime—teams like that never just take on players as young as Joey.

"But he said—he said the *stupidest thing* today—that I should just put my education on *hold*, that he could *take care of me*. That I could just move with him, and be some *housewife*, so I can—so I can take care of our—" She let out a hiccupping sob, clutching her stomach. "Oh, Nik! I'm just a kid. I'm not ready for this!"

He pulled her into a hug, holding her close. She began crying in earnest. He could feel the sticky moisture of her tears on his shoulder, against his cheek. And then . . .

Nikolai didn't know what came over him. Maybe it was the honeybrew. Maybe it was simply weakness of character—but all of a sudden he found himself turning his face to go in for a kiss.

She went quiet. Still. Her lips soft but unresponsive under his.

Slowly, he pulled away. Face flushed with embarrassment.

"I-I'm sorry, I don't know why I . . ."

"You can't do that, Nikolai," she said softly. "I know the past couple weeks have been . . . really great. And confusing. For both of us. But I . . ."

Astor looked past Nikolai and swore.

Nikolai followed her gaze and saw Freckles standing in front of the bar. Smoking and watching them pointedly. Looking smug, he tapped the ash from his pipe and went back inside the bar.

"Fucking DISC," she said. "That *asshole* saw you kiss me. Now he's going to go run his mouth and everyone's going to start talking shit! As if I didn't already have enough to worry about." She put her face in her hands, groaning. "Go home. You're drunk. *Again*. What a delightful new aspect to your personality. Go on, *git*! We'll talk about this later."

Though stung by the sharpness of Astor's words, he called after her. "*Wait!*"

She stopped, but didn't turn around. "What?"

"Why do even you care what they think? Those people aren't shit, Astor. They're just a bunch of spoiled brats who only care about their own little magic bubble. None of this matters! Flyball? Who gives a *fuck* about flyball?"

He jabbed his thumb into his chest. "I'm a soldier, Astor. The king knows me. By name! And the shit I've been dealing with lately—I just can't with these people! But you—"

She turned around sharply. A hand to her mouth. Eyes wide and mocking.

"Oh!" she said, cutting him off. "A soldier? My stars and garters! And the Mage King knows you? By name! *WELL.* In that case. Here, let's go find an alley. Knock out a quickie—Styx, I've got my nice panties on today. Why don't you keep them for a trophy? Take them back to your fancy new *important* friends back home, tell 'em what it's like to fuck a country girl."

"Oh *please*," Nikolai sneered, face flushed a bright red with angry hurt. "Fucking spare me, *Cece.* You dump me and immediately latch on to the heir of the *richest* family in Marblewood, and you want to talk about me forgetting where I come from?"

She came back toward him, eyes lit with wrath, face pinched into an angry smile. "Ohhhh, you want to do this? Do you *really* want to do this?"

"Yeah, actually," Nikolai said. "I think this is *long* overdue."

"You know what really pisses me off?" she said. "Joseph told me what a dick you've been to him at the Watchman station. And before you get all pissy that he ratted you out, you should know that the funny thing is, he defends you! He keeps making excuses for you! But I know you, Nik. And the shit you've been through? I went through the same fucking thing. And I would *NEVER* be as shitty to people as you are."

Nikolai barked an ugly laugh. "Oh, you're right, Astor. I am such a piece of shit for not wanting to hang out with the spoiled rich kid you left me for. Disc, I am *such* an asshole."

Astor pointed at him, emerald eyes flashing with contempt. "Do you want to know *why* I dumped you, Nikolai? Because we—" she jabbed her finger into his chest "—were—" she jabbed him again "—terrible for each other! I loved you, I really did, but you were clingy, and emotional, and just so *angry* all the time—at yourself, our classmates, our parents—everyone! Nikolai and Astor against the world—that's all you wanted. You didn't have any other friends, so neither could I, and it was toxic! Toxic! We were both hurt, Nikolai, but I wanted to get better. I wanted to move on! But you? You embraced that horrible shit. You clung to it like a life raft!"

"And off you went," Nikolai said, trembling, fighting back tears. "Off to get all better without me. And I guess dumping me wasn't enough. You couldn't talk to me, either. Too busy with your new boyfriend to even *try* to be my friend."

"You know we never could have just been friends," she said. "And don't you dare say I just ditched you and immediately dove into bed with Joseph. I was single for more than a year after we broke up, and I was a fucking mess. Do you know how many nights I hid in the bathroom, shower on full blast so my sister wouldn't hear me crying? But I had a lot of shit that I needed to figure out on my own. And when I came out of it, I needed to be with someone who wasn't totally fucked up. Who was kind, and loving, and happy. Happy, Nikolai! Do you even know what that is?"

"That thing you said the other night," Nikolai hissed. Cold. "About how heartbroken you were when you saw me fall apart on Assignment Day? Well, I *saw* your face that day, Astor. Saw you watching the other people's faces around you. Saw you *laughing* with them."

Astor went pale. "I . . . I . . ."

"And what's worse is I could see that in your eyes you weren't actually laughing—not really. You just so desperately wanted to fit in with those rich pieces of shit who all thought you were *trash* before you replaced me with Joseph. All because you've always been so fucking desperate for everyone to love you. So desperate to prove to the world that Cecilia Astor is anything but poor. Anything but stupid, or *ugly!*"

She froze, eyes glittering with tears, and Nikolai knew he had gone too far.

"Astor, I—"

"Please, Nikolai," she said, barely above a whisper. "Go home."

And with that, she walked back to the pub, heels clicking against the cobblestones.

Dejected, hating himself, Nikolai lit up one of the pipes he'd brought to share with Stokes with trembling fingers, savoring the filthy burn of it. He inhaled too quickly, stinging his lungs, and angrily cast it aside. Miserable, Nikolai skulked back into the pub after the girl who used to love him.

One more drink. Just one more drink, and then he was going home to call Captain Jubal to tell him that he was sick of Marblewood and ready to go back. Some fucking vacation.

Inside, Freckles was leaning over, talking into Joseph's ear. Joseph looked up, meeting Nikolai's eyes across the room for just a moment. His lips pressed into a thin line of displeasure, and then he turned his attention to Astor as she came to sit beside him.

"Piss off, Ras!" she barked angrily, shooing Freckles. "You fucking vulture."

She grabbed the honeybrew from Joseph's hand and took a swig. He made a noise of dismay and tried to take it from her but she angrily jerked it out of his reach.

"Disc, Joey!" she said. "It's just one fucking drink."

Nikolai pulled up a stool at the bar and ordered one last honeybrew. Not that he needed it—but Nikolai wanted to be numb right now. Wanted to be totally stupefied. One more drink. The crowds had gotten quieter, and he could feel eyes burning into his back.

Stokes sat beside him. "Hey, dude," he said, and Nikolai could tell from his tone that he knew what had happened.

"Leave me alone, Stokes," he said, waving him off. The bartender gave Nikolai his honeybrew, and Stokes frowned, eyeing it.

"You've had enough, Nik. You should go home."

"I'll leave in a minute," he said. Stokes reached to take the drink, but froze at Nikolai's look. "You fucking serious right now? I said I'll leave in a *minute*."

"Nik," Stokes said, in a way he'd never talked to him before, "Astor's pretty upset. You should get out of here before the meatheads decide to kick your ass."

"Why don't you go home and make some dresses for your little shop," Nikolai sneered. "Make some dresses and fuck your girlfriend. Yeah?"

Stokes's face went hard, and for a second Nikolai thought he was going to take a swing. But then he just looked really sad.

"Jeeves, Nik," he said. "Styx. What a pile. I really hate to see you like this." He patted Nikolai on the shoulder and walked away, leaving him to his misery.

Fuck. *FUCK*.

Nikolai groaned. Good job, Nik. Good fucking job.

Unable to resist, he glanced over at the corner where Joseph's crew was sitting. No surprise there, a couple of the guys were staring. Astor sat with Joseph, and they were holding hands now, talking quietly. Nikolai turned back to the bar before they could see him staring, jealousy and humiliation like vinegar in his mouth.

He reached for his honeybrew—but another hand snatched it away. Expecting Stokes, an apology blooming on his lips for what a total dick he'd been, Nikolai turned to find Freckles.

Staring Nikolai dead in the eyes, he took a long swig from the drink and placed his lawyer's truth-teller Focal on the bar. The glass cylinder unfolded into a balance scale. One tray glowing a dim blue, the other red.

"Tell me something, you little creep," Freckles said. "Do you always chase after other people's girlfriends? Or is this just some pathetic attempt to get back at us for always putting you in your place back in academy? Careful now—the scales will tell me if you're lying."

Nikolai stared at him. Frozen.

"That's what I thought," Freckles said. He glanced down at Nikolai's dagger, smirking. "Other night I heard your boyfriend George say that you don't actually know any battle magic. That you get coffee for the ones who do. So. Talk to one of our girls again and you'll be picking your teeth off the floor. Understand?"

The blue-lit scale sank down to the bar, the red tray rising—indicating that Freckles was telling the truth. He chuckled. "See? The scales don't lie."

Nikolai had the strangest feeling that he'd arrived at an incredibly important moment. That he'd come upon a split in a path, and whichever way he went the entire world would come shuddering and groaning along.

Freckles may have been a bullying piece of shit, but that certainly didn't mean Nikolai was in the right. He could see everything laid out in his head—his life here in Marblewood, then back in New Damascus after his vacation came to an end.

Nikolai would leave the bar and let Freckles keep the drink. He'd go home, sober up, and the following day he'd apologize to Astor, then Stokes. Joseph too, for always being such a prick to him at the Watchman station. Admit that he'd been nursing old hurts and feelings that he needed to get the fuck over.

They'd accept his apology. Then, when he went back to New Damascus, he'd finally know he had friends back home who cared about him. Family.

And shouldn't that be enough?

Freckles took another swig of the honeybrew, staring Nikolai down.

Nikolai could hear laughter, that ugly hyena chittering, and looked over to see that even though Joseph and Astor weren't paying him any attention, Joseph's friends were. Watching. Grinning at Nikolai's humiliation as Freckles smugly threatened him.

The air tasted stale—stinking of piss and peanuts and sawdust. Cheap, sweet booze. He hated it. He fucking hated it here. Hated these people—these small-town nobodies who thought they were better than him. Who'd *always* thought that they were better than him.

Nikolai was an Edge Guard, on track to one day become one of the deadliest and most influential Battle Magi in the world. And this fucking *nobody* piece of trash thought he could look down on him?

Nikolai took another deep breath. He thought of his father. Could practically hear him, deep voice rumbling that there was always a *choice*, difficult as it might seem.

Freckles snapped his fingers in Nikolai's face. "Hey, *Half Staff!* I asked you a question."

An unpleasant flood of memories drowned out his father's voice. The mocking laughter from Assignment Day. Astor laughing with the others, even though she hadn't meant it. Which was somehow worse.

"Call me that again," Nikolai said, icy, calm.

"What?"

"That name. Fucking call me that one more time."

Freckles smirked. "What—*Half Staff?*"

Nikolai kicked Freckles's feet from under him, and he let out a *yelp* of surprise just before the side of his head cracked against the bar.

"My name is *Strauss*!" Nikolai roared, kicking him in the stomach as he fell. "*Sergeant—Nikolai—STRAUSS!*"

The bar erupted with shouts and screams, and two flyball players were already running at him, trying to stop Nikolai as he continued kicking the whimpering, bloody Freckles.

Nikolai turned to meet them, baton Focal drawn.

"Whoa, whoa, WHOA!" Stokes shouted, appearing out of nowhere. He jumped in front of Nikolai with one hand, trying to pull him away from Freckles, the other held out to stop the flyball players from attacking. "*Stop!* Wait—WAIT! Everyone just calm—"

The first flyball player took a swing at Stokes, but Nikolai yanked Stokes back and sent out an *akro* tentacle of hardened air to grab his assailant by the legs, binding them together and pulling up with a yank to send him sprawling on his back.

"Nik!" Stokes cried. "Wait!"

But the second player was already on them, so Nikolai wrapped a hardened glove of *akro* around his fist and swung for the second just as he closed in, connecting with his mouth and sending out a spray of blood and teeth.

More flyball players came at Nikolai. More targets.

"Stokes!" he growled. "MOVE!"

Eyes wide, terrified, Stokes ignored him, rushing forward to try and protect Nikolai. "Stop!" he cried at the oncoming magi. "He's had too much to drink—please—don't hurt him!"

"Stokes, get the fuck outta the way!"

Nikolai lunged forward, twisting to step in front of Stokes as he swung at the muscular mage going right for him—but the mage was quick enough to lock a shield of *akro* in the air between them, and Nik's arm went numb from the shock of striking it.

Swinging his baton, Nikolai dissolved the weave like it was

nothing, shooting the mage in the face with a powerful jet of jellied *akro* that made his neck violently snap back as he stumbled away, falling.

"Somebody call the Watchmen!" the bartender screamed.

Stokes finally scrambled out of the way as three more flyball players came at Nikolai in quick succession, working as a team— one attacking with wild punches, one trying to trip him up and wall him in with *akro* barriers, another using *gia* to channel a stream of dragon's milk from a jug on the bar into Nikolai's face to blind him.

Drawing his blade, a Focal now in each hand, Nikolai brought the edge up in a quick movement, igniting the dragon's milk with a wordless *pyrkagias* from the knife and flinging the burning liquid back at the caster with a *gia* from his baton. Screaming, flailing, the mage struggled to tear off his flaming shirt, exposing bloody, blistering skin.

The punching brute landed a blow against Nikolai's stomach, but the enchantments of the Edge Guard uniform hardened the cloth and emitted opposite force to negate the blow. The mage's face turned white as the bones of his knuckle crackled, and Nikolai punched him in the temple with a hardened *akro* glove, knocking him out.

The distracting *akro* panels dissolved around Nikolai as the casting mage came up from behind to wrap him in a crushing bear hug, but Nikolai ducked under the grab and turned to wrap a tentacle of air around the mage's arm—flinging him across the room. The arm snapped, a bloody white bone jutting from the flopping arm as the mage flew through the air.

And then there was Joseph—heroically bursting up into the air with his flyball boots to break the mage's fall before he could smash into the windows by the door.

"Nikolai, *STOP!*" Astor screamed. The bar went silent. Nikolai suddenly found himself standing at the center of a wide, empty space as the bar patrons pressed away from him. Opposite of the circle stood Joseph, easing his friend with the broken arm into Astor's embrace.

The wounded mage gasped with pain—but Astor put her gloved hand over his face and there was a flash of blue light. Some kind of pain-killing spell, as he immediately calmed down while she gently set the bone and began knitting the torn flesh with a dusting of golden light.

Nikolai stood there, panting, and saw Stokes standing at the edge of the circle. For a moment he thought Stokes was going to intercede again—that he was going to move between Joseph and Nikolai, try to talk some sense. But he just stood there, frozen in place, staring.

Astor, still kneeling beside the mage with the broken arm, was staring at Nikolai too, with the same expression as Stokes. Not with contempt. Not with pity. But with a specific kind of horror. Like Nikolai had pulled off a mask and revealed a hideous, scaly visage underneath.

Nikolai didn't care. He didn't give a shit anymore. He was seeing red—hate and booze fueling him, egging him on.

"Nikolai!" Joseph said. It appeared that he would be the only one to try and talk Nikolai down—not even Stokes was going to stand up for him anymore. "Stop! *Please!* Why are you doing this?"

Nikolai let out an ugly laugh full of scorn. "Why am I doing this?" He raised his Focals, taking a step toward him. "*WHY am I doing this?* Oh, I don't know, Joe. Why don't you ask one of your friends I left broken on the floor over there?"

"I'm sorry, Nikolai," Joseph said, "But whatever they did, you need to calm down and—"

"NO!" Nikolai said. "You don't get to tell me to calm down. For once, you don't get what you want. That must be a novel experience for you, eh?"

"I don't want to fight you, Nik," he said. "Please, just stop."

But Nikolai didn't want to talk. Didn't want to stop fighting. Because the moment this was over he was going to have to deal with the consequences. And it was going to be *bad*.

"Why don't you come and fucking make me, rich boy? Or are you all talk? Come on! Put up your fists!"

Joseph stood there, silent. A wall of stone. Finally, he shook his head and turned to address the crowd.

"Show's over, everyone. Clear out. You—" he said, pointing at another mage in the crowd with a golden medi-glove Focal. "There's a Watchman Box outside—go get some emergency bubbles for the wounded and assist Apprentice Healer Astor with first aid."

"Fight me!" Nikolai snarled. "COME ON!"

Unmoved by his challenge, Joseph fixed him with his icy calm gaze. "Wizard Strauss? The Watchmen are on their way. I recommend you lay down your Focals."

"What, you scared? You milk-sop *wretch*. You Fox-crack son of a flesh mage!"

Though Joseph didn't so much as flinch at the insult, Astor rose and began to cross the open space. Their eyes met, and Nikolai saw that her horror had been replaced by an incredible sadness.

"You are your mother's son," she whispered, voice tinged with heartbreak.

Nikolai stood there, stunned, as she passed him to kneel beside the whimpering mage to soothe the burns Nikolai had inflicted on him.

"He's not worth it, Joey," she said. "If you two really feel the need to measure each other's dicks, go ahead. But I'd like to go home now."

Nikolai winced, hissing. Gripping his baton and blade with a white-knuckle grip, he wheeled on Joseph, who was walking away.

"Come on, you yellow Jeeves bastard," he snarled. "I kissed your girl. You gonna just let that slide? I kissed your girl, and she *liked* it."

Nikolai said it, he couldn't believe he'd said it, but it didn't matter, the words were out and he'd said it, oh *Disc*, he'd said it.

Behind him, Astor sighed. "Your funeral, Nicky."

Expression hard as stone, Joseph turned to face him.

"Too far, Strauss."

The circle widened—Astor and another mage moving the wounded out of harm's way.

Joseph came at him. He didn't even run—his big golden flyball boots shot him across the space between them, his fists covered in *akro* gloves like Nikolai had done.

Joseph was so *fast* that Nikolai wasn't quick enough to completely dodge out of the way. He struck the hand holding the blade Focal so hard that it was knocked from Nikolai's grasp and went spinning into the crowd, who screamed and parted to dodge it.

Joseph held his eagle-topped scepter Focal in his hand as he flipped midair, more graceful than should have been possible for a mage his size—pressing his feet lightly against the wall as he pressed off again, making another go at Nikolai.

Screaming, Nikolai swung his baton at the incoming Joseph, smearing rainbow light arced with flame so hot it burned blue, a fan of fire aimed to ruin that pretty face of his—but the flames turned to smoke inches before it could so much as singe him, and Nikolai remembered with horror that Joseph was a Watchman, trained in *all* the Watchmen weaves. And at that moment Nikolai felt the *akro* tentacle that Joseph had sent out from his scepter wrap around the wrist of his hand holding the baton.

Joseph flew past him, the invisible *akro* tentacle pulling after him—and too late Nikolai felt it go taut. Nikolai's wrist snapped, breaking and bending up in a way that it shouldn't have been able to. He screamed as he tumbled after Joseph, dropping his baton Focal as he went. His arm had been dislocated, yanked out of its socket at the shoulder. As Nikolai lay there, stifling sobs through gritted teeth, he could feel the *akro* tentacle release and slip away.

Whimpering, Nikolai clutched his arm and forced himself to stand. Joseph stood there, golden-haired, without a scratch— looking like a fucking superhero. Hatred bubbling up, Nikolai took a step forward. Then another, then one more—and then he was running for him.

Nikolai pulled back his one good fist, fingers black and numb from Joseph's first strike—probably fractured—and lurched forward to make a weak swing with his bare knuckles. Staring at the fist, unimpressed, Joseph raised his forearms to block—and Nikolai pivoted, kicking him in the balls instead.

Joseph grunted, face going pale as Nikolai fell back, cackling. As Nikolai hit the floor he saw his baton, just a little ways away. He started crawling for it, broken hand and dislocated shoulder trailing pathetically.

A brave, skinny mage darted out from the crowd to try and grab the baton before he could reclaim it, but weak, injured, drunk, and without a Focal, Nikolai still managed a puff of flame in his direction, gurgling "Fuck off!" as the mage scrambled back, terrified.

Bruised fingers of his good hand closed around the smooth black surface, and he could feel it come to life again—could feel its strength pouring into him. But even then, getting up was one of the hardest things he'd ever done.

Nikolai panted, bleeding and exhausted.

"Come on," he wheezed, struggling to stand. "Kick your . . . gonna kick your ass."

Breathing hard, Joseph straightened up, recovering from the kick in the balls.

"I wish it hadn't come to this," he said simply. Almost too quickly to see, he became a blur of crimson and gold flying at Nikolai once again.

Gasping, desperate, Nikolai barked a quick *"Camelos!"* and wrapped himself in a sheet of invisibility. The crowd gasped as he disappeared from their vision. Nikolai tensed his muscles to dodge to the side, to lose Joseph and come up behind him and knock him down, to put him in his place—

But he was too slow. Invisible or not, Joseph had already aimed for Nikolai, and he twisted around midair to point his boots right at him, no longer shooting *akro* but letting the momentum carry him along—flyball reflexes lightning quick, *impossibly* quick—and he slammed his boots into Nikolai's stomach, 260 speeding pounds of muscle and bone focused into one point.

Though the uniform cushioned the force of the blow, a strike that would have otherwise shattered Nikolai's rib cage, he was thrown flying back, weaves of invisibility dissolving around him as the back of his head struck the edge of the bar, *hard*.

As he fell, vision spinning, lights exploding in his skull, all he could think was that Joseph beat him, Joseph *beat him* . . .

Blood and filthy sawdust filled Nikolai's mouth as his face hit the floor, and everything went black.

———————

Soft sheets. White walls in front of fuzzy figures and shapes. Warm sunlight on his face.

Nikolai was confused at first. How did he get here? Why was he in a healer's ward again? And for a moment he thought he was back in New Damascus, that it was the day after he'd been attacked by the half-mages in the alleyway.

But then he remembered what he'd done—remembered every vivid, horrible detail—no Tabula Rasa potion to forget this time—and he was filled with suffocating despair.

"You're awake," a gentle voice rumbled, and Nikolai turned his head, a golden-haired blur slowly coming into focus as he strained to concentrate through his potion-addled brain. Shock hit Nikolai like a sheet of icy water. He sat bolt upright, confused to find Joseph Eaglesmith calmly watching him from a chair.

Nikolai stared at him numbly, then lowered his gaze, staring at his hands. The bruises, the cuts—they were gone. Healed. Wiped clean, like everything always was.

But what he'd done—no way *that* would be wiped clean. He'd gone too far. Hunching in on himself, Nikolai clenched his fists, fighting back tears and wishing desperately that Joseph would leave.

"Ras is okay, in case you were wondering," Joseph said. "Chad too. Thomas, Kenmore, the others. All fine."

Nikolai grunted, not entirely sure which name belonged to which mage.

He could have easily killed someone. He was surprised he hadn't in the state he'd been.

Joseph leaned back in his chair, folding his arms.

Nikolai gave him a sharp look, sitting up straight. "What do you want, Eaglesmith?" But then he saw that Joseph was wearing his Watchman uniform and realized that he was probably going to take him into custody. "Were you just waiting for me to wake up so you can arrest me?"

"Cecilia's pretty upset," he said, not answering Nikolai's question. "And George, he went crazy after I knocked you out. They just left a little bit ago. Both of them waited up for you all night. Didn't sleep at all—I finally told them to go home. George thought you were dead—thought I'd killed you. I thought I'd killed you, too. There was . . . there was a lot of blood. But that's normal for head wounds, Cece said . . ."

He shrugged, lapsing into a brief silence. He tightened his lips, fixing Nikolai in a stare.

"I'm not going to lie to you, Nikolai. It sounds like you're in some real trouble. Your uncle said that he'll be taking you to the capital for disciplinary action." He shook his head. "Assault with deadly weaves against *civilians*. If you were just a Watchman you'd be clapped in chains right now, stripped of your Focals. Instead . . ."

Joseph nodded at the little table next to Nikolai's bed, where he was surprised to find the neatly folded uniform resting beside his baton and blade Focals.

"I did my best to talk down how bad it was," he said. "That you'd had too much to drink, that Ras goaded you into a fight, and that the others rushed you and you were just trying to defend yourself and your friend, but you were too drunk to hold back. I convinced the guys not to press charges, but . . . your uncle says you're to report to his office immediately upon waking. That you'll be departing this afternoon for New Damascus."

He sighed, expression softening. "I wish you could've seen how happy Cecilia's been. She said that you'd finally come out of your shell—that, for the first time, you seemed happy. Confident. Like I said, she's pretty upset right now . . . but she *wants* you to be a part of our lives. And I do too. Nik, I know that a lot of the others have always given you a hard time. And I know we've never been friends, but I've always thought that you're a really cool guy. Last night, though . . . shit like that, and you're just proving the others right."

Nikolai sat there in sullen silence, staring at him.

"Nik . . ." Joseph continued. "Me and Cecilia, we're getting married. We haven't really told anyone, but it's happening. And you might not like me very much, but I'm going to be good to her. I'm going to make her happy. If you really give so much as a Fox's whisker about her, you'll be happy for her. And I hope that you can be—that we can move past this whole thing."

Nikolai didn't react to that—didn't really feel anything about it. Just a kind of icy numbness.

"I'll tell you one thing, though," Joseph said, managing a weak chuckle. "You won't have to worry about any of the guys bothering you again. And between you and me? Ras—he needed a few good slaps. He can be a real ass sometime."

"You're a really great guy," Nikolai said. "You know that, Joseph?"

After a moment of shock, Joseph smiled, taken aback at the compliment. But then Nikolai sneered, and the smile faded.

"It's so *easy* for you, isn't it?" Nikolai spat, bitter. "So easy for you to be this *great guy*. So good, so *nice*—even to that sonofabitch Nik. Everyone loves you—so you don't have to be cruel."

Nikolai got out of bed, angrily pulling his uniform on over his undergarments. "It's easy for you to take the high road," he continued, with increasing venom. "To be the guy everyone looks up to. *Golden boy*. But that's because it costs you nothing. Because you were born to it. Because you've always gotten everything you've wanted—and you always will. So save your kindness. Save your pity. I don't need it. I don't need you *or* Astor."

Nikolai slid his Focals into their hilt and holster. Tying up the sneakers Stokes had made for him, Nikolai's face grew hot, a lump forming in his throat—but he swallowed it angrily, clenching his fists around the strings as if using them to strangle someone.

"Nik . . . " Joseph started, but Nikolai just scowled and stalked past him without a second glance. Joseph didn't try to stop him. He just watched Nikolai go, face heavy with disappointment. He was trying to be kind—trying to be his friend. Joseph—he really *was* a great guy. And Nikolai hated him for it. Him and every last motherfucker here.

Storming out onto the cobblestone street outside the healer's ward, Nikolai just stood there at first, feeling lost. He wondered what time it was, and briefly considered going to find Stokes. But even if he wasn't mad at Nikolai, it would never be the same between them again. This was a mess purely of Nikolai's own making. Besides Stokes, and *maybe* Astor, even after everything, he'd probably just driven away the last mage in Marblewood who was rooting for him—the last mage who had any interest in being his friend.

He thought about calling Ilyana, but realized bitterly that she probably wouldn't pick up. Even if she did . . . what would he say?

So Nikolai walked. For hours, he just walked. It wasn't until he came upon the shore that he realized where his feet were taking him.

South along the sand and pebbles, where he and Astor had made love for the very first time on a scratchy blanket under a sparkling sea of artificial stars.

South, under the great old willow tree where Astor had broken things off with him, on a day too sunny and too perfect for the words coming out of her mouth to make any sense.

East, through the forest his mother used to train him. Used to torture him. To make him *strong*.

East, through the clearing where Hazeal had poisoned him with words and dark magic. Where Hazeal had died on top of him, blinding and choking Nikolai with the dust that had once been his flesh.

North, through the marshy swamplands where he, Astor, and Stokes used to play as children.

Back when things were good. Back when they'd spend whole weekends practicing acoustic covers of hundred-year-old pop hits, whole nights secretly watching old R-rated movies, or reading novels printed from the archives aloud to each other in Stokes's rickety tree house by the weak glow of their tiny, magical spheres of light. Even without Nikolai's parents, he had *them*. And for a while, it had been enough.

His sneakers moved silently across thick green moss, his mind brimming with memories as he hopped from stones to logs across the algae-filled waters and deep swathes of mud.

That life was over now. Stokes had his girlfriend, had his shop. In two short years, he'd grown up. Had outgrown Nikolai. And Astor? Astor had stopped loving him a long time ago. Even if there *had* been room in their lives for Nikolai, he had made damn sure there wouldn't be anymore.

There was no getting past what he'd done. Publicly revealing that he knew how to cast invisibility. Hurting, almost killing a bunch of civilian magi. Making a vicious, drunken fool of himself.

He was going to be stripped of rank. There'd be no Edge Guard career for him now. At best, they'd find Nikolai a desk job in some other Veil. There'd be no more secret spells for him to learn. No more Ilyana or Albert. He'd be alone. Totally and completely.

Nikolai didn't know how long he'd been walking, but he was no longer in the swamp. He was climbing a steep, grassy incline. But soon grass turned to soil and stone, and even featherweighted it was a struggle to keep from falling. Yet still he climbed. He climbed and climbed, until his fingers were cut and bleeding, until his hair was plastered to his head, sweat and dirt pouring down his face, stinging his eyes.

He pulled himself over the final ledge and found himself faced with his faint reflection in the illusion of sky embedded within the dome. He stood on a thin strip of land atop the edges of the steep terrain bordering this side of Marblewood. He'd seen this ledge on scanning duty, but it was one thing to see it from a distance—it was another to be standing at its precipice.

Nikolai glanced over his shoulder and realized how incredibly high he'd climbed. A sharp wind rose, howling in his ears as it buffeted against him powerfully enough that he was forced to kneel.

Nikolai pressed his hand against the mirrored wall, feeling the energy pulse through his fingers. For a moment, he was struck with a blinding, crippling fear. He wanted to run, wanted to climb back down, to go crawling to Uncle Red. To throw himself on Jubal's mercy.

Nikolai squashed the idea. This could be his last and *only* chance to ever see what truly remained of the human world. His only chance to find out what he'd trained in the killing arts to defend against, and if Armand Hazeal had been telling the truth after all.

There was a good chance that crossing the Veil would kill him. But with a sudden calm, Nikolai realized he didn't care.

He eased the baton from its holster and pressed it against the surface. "*Apocrypha*," he whispered, and pushed through the Veil. Falling forward, Nikolai closed his eyes as he was enveloped by the brilliant blue.

VI.

THE MARK OF TORMENT

The self-proclaimed savior of humanity rummaged frantically through her closet, searching for whiskey. Drawers, closets, boxes. Occasionally she would break from her search to attack Jem with a flurry of kisses on her forehead and cheeks while Jem laughed and weakly tried to fend her off.

"I swear it's here," Eva said, going back to her search. "It's been so long since I've had real company, or a reason to celebrate, or—"

Jem's cheeks ached from smiling. Her eyes were still puffy and sore from weeping for the first time in ten years.

"It's okay, really," Jem insisted. "I can't even remember the last time I drank."

She scratched the skin over the contact point behind her ear, which had been itching since she'd woken up in Eva's Alpha Core chamber, just down the hall from her luxurious quarters.

"Nonsense," Eva called from within the depths of a storage crate. "Odette and Odile! Together at last. If that doesn't call for a drink, I don't know what does. Reunited after over a decade of turmoil and . . ."

She trailed off, and Jem grimaced, wondering if she'd been about to say *Torment*.

"Ah-*ha!*" Eva said, emerging from her closet with a dusty bottle held aloft like a trophy. She admired it, soft, artificial lighting shining gold through the sluggish amber liquor. "*C'est magnifique*. Jem, you stunning vision. What's the oldest thing you've ever tasted?"

Jem made a face at her and Eva laughed, uncorking it to take a swig.

She handed the bottle to Jem, who took a tentative sip.

"My dad would literally come back from the dead to *kill* me if he knew we were dipping into his Old Rip Van Winkle straight from the bottle." Eva took another swig, then grew serious. "Okay. I've procrastinated long enough. You are owed some serious explanation."

She settled into the couch beside Jem, folding her long legs beneath her. "I am deeply and truly sorry for putting you through that horrible day again. I hope you can forgive me, but I . . . I needed to be sure. Needed to test you, to see if you'd betray me in a pinch. To make sure that you're still the same Jem I knew and loved. It's been a long time. We've both been through a lot, and . . . people change."

Jem scratched the spot behind her ear. Nervous.

"How did you do that?" Jem said. "Access my mods remotely. Make me forget that I was in full immersion. And what was that . . . machine?"

"My mother's final invention," Eva explained. "A dead alpha AI core, hollowed out so that you can plug into it with your mods to gain the cognitive capacity and processing power of an AI." She took a deep breath. "She invented it to fix me. It took her years, but with this, she was able to rebuild my mind."

She pointed at the brand on her forehead. The weeping eye within an inverted triangle. "I could've had this removed. Could've wiped it away, just like my mother wiped away my memories of what they did to me. But now I wear it as a symbol of pride. My red badge of courage as the lone survivor of Torment. First, but not the last.

"Anyway, she built the core to fix me, but I've since found other uses for it. When the Synth put someone into permanent full immersion—be it Paradise or Torment—they irreversibly erase the memories that would give away the immersion as false. With the core, I found a way to temporarily suppress these memories without destroying them. You had a headache, right? That was from the memory suppression. And as for how I remotely accessed your mods—the core can produce signals within its chamber so powerful that a direct link with your contact point isn't necessary."

"Is Blue here?" Jem asked, heart racing. "Did you test her too?"

"Blue is here, safe and sound. And no, I didn't test her. The doctor, however, I did. Though nothing so traumatic as yours. The higher the rank, the tougher the test. And I want you by my side."

Jem nodded, relieved. "Was that you, with me in the VR?"

Eva shook her head, her face twisting up a venomous anger that scared Jem.

"*No*," Eva hissed. "I never use VR. I hate it. Hate what it did to me. Hate what it's doing to the people up there. Making them forget. Making them just *give up*. Karl Marx thought that religion was the opiate of the masses, but he obviously never anticipated virtual orgies."

She took a deep breath, calming herself. "I'm sorry. I don't remember Torment. But the scars . . . run deep. So I don't do VR. *Can't* do VR. I controlled your experience from the outside, with the core. Accessed your memories to create the base for the simulation, and tweaked it."

"What would have happened," Jem said, carefully, "If I . . . failed your test?"

Eva took a sip from the bottle and looked at her thoughtfully. "You're our most talented Runner. And a Runner you'd have remained. With no memory of me, or this place. And I . . . well . . . I'd have been a mess for the next few months. But I never doubted you. Not for a *second*. You are meant for great things, Jem."

Eva took another swig. She grimaced and stretched out on the couch, laying her head on Jem's lap. Looking up at her with adoring eyes.

"But enough business. Ezra told me about your little kiss. Like something out of a holo-drama. So *romantic*." Eva sighed. "You're all Blue can talk about, you know. How many Synth did you take out on your own? Ten? Twenty? Christ, Jem." She whistled, impressed. "Doc says the girl already liked you before. But now it is *so. On*."

Eva closed her eyes, visibly relaxing as Jem idly stroked her hair.

"I don't know," Jem said, embarrassed but pleased. "What about you? Did you ever rescue any of those pretty-boy musicians you always used to go on about? Have them brought down to the bunker to be your personal bards and paramours?"

Eva went quiet, and for a moment Jem thought she had fallen asleep.

"Sex," Eva finally said, opening her eyes but averting her gaze. "Love. Physical intimacy. It isn't in the cards for me. Not since . . . you know. And I don't think it ever will be. I'm better than I used to be, but I really don't like when people touch me."

She looked up at Jem with a bittersweet smile. Took Jem's free arm by the wrist and kissed the back of her hand. "But for some reason . . . this is okay. No panic attacks. No PTSD freak-outs. It's a first. My mom couldn't even hold me. But . . . I don't know. Maybe it's the whiskey. Or maybe it's because you're the only person who's ever really made me feel safe. We're the same age, but let's be real. You were always the big sister. My Jem-iny Cricket."

They sat there for a long while. Getting pleasantly buzzed on century-old whiskey and filling each other in on the intervening years.

Eva couldn't stop grinning as she chattered away, discussing her time as the shadowy leader of the Resistance with the same lighthearted rambling she'd used to discuss school gossip when they were kids.

After Eva's father died and the Resistance had quite literally gone underground, Eva's mother continued to lead them, though she became paranoid. Secretive. She commanded the Resistance from the shadows, keeping her identity hidden despite pressure from her inner circle to come out and lead. Gradually she gave up many of her leadership responsibilities, passing them on to the inner circle so she could focus on Eva.

"I don't remember much about that time," Eva said. "Just pieces and flashes. But then, a couple years ago, it was like . . . waking up. Eight years of my life, just, poof! Gone. We continued treatment after, but the neural reprogramming was complete. And I was . . . myself, again."

"Reprogramming?"

"Mom basically figured out how to program a human brain like you'd program a living AI. Which is no easy task, and *impossible* without alpha-level intelligence. But it wasn't like she could ask one of the Overminds to help, so . . . she made the core. And here I am!"

Eva had wanted to take an active leadership role after that, but the Inner Circle was totally against it, not trusting that she was well enough for so much responsibility. Dr. Colladi agreed with them, but when she died, Eva insisted on taking her mother's place as commander.

"And now," Eva said, smug, "they'd die for me. Impale themselves on their own swords if I asked them to. Back to the natural order of things with a Colladi at the helm."

"How did you change their minds?"

"It wasn't easy," Eva said, then shrugged. "It hasn't quite hit me as reality that my mom's gone. Poisoning herself in a lab accident, what a *stupid* way to die. After everything she went through to keep us alive. To fix me. I've been so busy running everything without her help for the past year, I haven't had time to process—let alone grieve. But finding out that you were still alive?" She smiled, bittersweet. "It eased the sting. I can't believe my mom was so wrapped up with me all these years that she didn't realize—or didn't care—that you were one of our Runners. It's not like we have a database with pictures and profiles, so I guess it makes sense. But still. Having you here while I was . . . getting better. It would have helped."

"The inner circle," Jem asked, curious. "Where are they?"

"Other HQ," Eva said. "We've got agents and Runners spread across the East Coast, but these days most Resistance activity takes place in the Tri-State area, under Armitage's jurisdiction. Ruthless as Armitage can be, it has less surveillance and a looser security net than *any* of the other Overminds. Why do you think that is?"

Jem flinched at Armitage's name, the Synth's mocking, sing-song voice echoing in her mind. *A special room in Torment, saved just for you . . .*

"No idea," she said.

"Some of our people think it's out of mercy. They see its gardens and think . . . there's something good here. Some spark of humanity. Others think that it's because this way, the Synth will know where the Resistance primarily cluster. And I haven't totally dismissed that idea, but you know what *I* think?"

Jem shook her head. "What?"

"I think that if Armitage *really* wanted to crush the Resistance, it could have done so by now. It wouldn't be easy, but we are just so hopelessly outclassed in terms of technology and resources that there really wouldn't be anything we could do. But I don't think it has anything to do with mercy." Eva's lip curled into a sneer. "I think Armitage is just *bored*."

They were both drunk by the time Eva finally decided to give Jem the grand tour of the facility she liked to call *Casa de Colladi*, otherwise known as Deep Tactical HQ. Jem, still weak from her injuries, let Eva push her along in a wheelchair as they toured the immense bunker.

The HQ was a massive facility buried miles under Philadelphia. There had once been many such Deep Tactical HQs, built and stocked with enough food, weaponry, and supplies to last decades into what was expected to be a long and ugly war.

Only two remained. Eva's, which was empty but for her and Ezra, and another even larger facility that had served as the primary base of operations for the remnants of Colladi Corp's human resistance.

"The Synth can't trace our tunnels," Eva explained, "but they're constantly sending diggers to look for us. Tracking, misleading, and intercepting them in tunneling patterns that won't lead them back to us has been a logistical nightmare. We've only been able to keep this bunker and one other hidden. Only someone with mods as powerful as mine has the cognitive processing power for the intricate tactics and planning required to keep us safe. Mods like my mother had. Mods like *yours*. Do you see where I'm going with this?"

Eva pushed Jem down the seemingly endless halls at dangerous speeds, both of them hooting and cheering as she steered in drunken zigzags.

"And here's the core lab once again," she said, pressing her hand against the cool steel of the heavily armored door. "Not that I really need to keep it so securely locked up. Now that my mom's gone, you and I are the only ones with mods compatible with the Alpha Core. You have to try it sometime, it'll make your mod enhancements feel as slow and outdated as a twentieth-century graphing calculator. But you'll have to wait. I'm working on something inside the core. Something incredible. I can't even show you yet." Eva's eyes flashed with a strange intensity. "But it's going to change *everything*."

The core lab and Eva's expansive quarters took up most of the eastern wing.

On the western wing were secondary living quarters and emergency barracks lined with hundreds of dusty bunks. There was a medical bay and a surgical ward. Multiple laboratories. Two extremely well-stocked armories with enough firepower to supply a small army. An immense underground vegetable garden. A warehouse full of rations, water, and supplies.

Finally, Eva brought Jem into the common area—a sprawling

room that served as dining hall, library, and rec center. Waiting for them at a long table at the center of it all were Ezra, Dr. Blackwell, and Blue.

Blue's eyes widened at Jem's arrival and she moved to stand but stopped short, uncertain.

"H—hey," Jem said, feeling shy.

"Hey," Blue said. Also sheepish. Dr. Blackwell and Ezra exchanged glances, a subtle smile on the doctor's lips.

"Ladies and gentleman," Eva said, with only the faintest slur. "I present to you my newly appointed vice commander of Resistance operations, Jemma Burton!" She waited a beat for dramatic effect, then slapped a palm against her forehead, exasperated. "*Oh.* Jem, I didn't even ask if you want the job. I—"

"Of course," Jem said. She pushed herself up from the wheelchair to stand. The others hissed breaths of alarm, but Jem waved them off. She straightened her back, looked Eva dead in the eyes, and held out her hand. "To the bitter end. Commander."

Eva clasped her hand. "To the bitter end."

Jem and Blue had sex on virtual Venusian cloud tops—the gaseous sulfur dioxide dimly silver in the darkness. The cloud cities on the horizon sparkled with a million distant lights.

They came out of VR and did it all over again amid the tangled sheets of Jem's bed. Afterward, they just lay there for a while, sweaty and staring up at fluorescent ceiling lights dimmed down to the faintest glow.

"Mmmm. I needed that." Jem turned onto her side and nuzzled Blue's neck. Sleepy and euphoric in a warm post-sex haze, she pulled the sheets over them and cuddled up as her heart slowed and the sweat began to cool upon her skin.

Jem had never been so happy. Not even before the war. Her days commanding Resistance operations were incredibly challenging and full of purpose. Her nights soft, spent with Blue and her friends.

Eva, Ezra, Dr. Blackwell, Blue, and Jem had become a strange little family in the month since their arrival. Ezra and the doctor did all the cooking, though most of it fell to Ezra—Eva's stoic, charming aide-de-camp. When Ezra wasn't running missions or assisting Jem with communications or strategic consultation, he spent his days tending to the garden, cleaning, and preparing simple but exquisite meals.

"Jesus, Ezra," Blue would say through a mouthful. "Where the hell did you learn to cook?"

But he'd always just shrug, his expression unreadable, then change the subject.

Eva spent almost all of her time locked up in the Alpha Core lab, popping out to join them in the evenings for games, music, food, and the occasional holo-drama before inevitably excusing herself to continue work on her mysterious project.

Dr. Blackwell spent her days preparing fertility plague cure kits, each with a set of ready-to-inject doses synthesized from a sample of Blue's amniotic fluid, and instructions for replication. One of Jem's top strategic priorities was delivering cure kits to Runners at the fringes of Philadelphia, who would then transport them across the wilderness to the Resistance agents and allies of neighboring cities and beyond.

Jem's responsibilities were difficult—impossible sometimes—but she'd never felt so alive. Command suited her, and the soldiers, Runners, and Couriers under her command were more than happy to take orders from the legendary Jemma Burton. The story of her battle at the cathedral to protect Blue and the doctor who was delivering the cure for the Rapture Bug had already made its rounds, becoming more and more exaggerated every time it came back to her. She'd killed ten tactical PK droids. No, *twenty* droids. And a Synth trooper. No, an entire *platoon* of Synth troopers. Followed by a dramatic, death-defying escape as Armitage's shape-shifting Husk chased after her with long, mercurial claws.

Tempted as Jem was to set the record straight, she held her tongue and let rumors fly. It was good for morale.

Blue was Jem's one great worry. Unlike the others, Blue had no responsibilities. None but the inevitable burden of childbirth and motherhood. Until then, it was all relaxation. Eating right. Exercising. Tending to the underground garden. Practicing guitar and studying archived copies of old parenting guides that nobody had needed for more than a decade.

She was always ravenous for Jem when she returned, even if they'd only been apart for a day. But Jem knew that wasn't just infatuation or lust. She worried that it was as much out of boredom and loneliness.

Jem's operations sometimes took her away from the home base for days at a time. When she wasn't coordinating troops within tunnels to intercept the constant flow of Synth diggers, approving and supervising never-ending webs of clandestine operations, or coordinating with wilderness Runners for cure delivery and refugee escort, she'd been smuggling large quantities of weaponry and supplies to secret mouse hole caches all across the city. Orders from Eva, with instruction but no explanation. Preparing for . . . something.

Eva still wouldn't tell Jem what she was working on in the Alpha Core lab. What she was *always* working on, day and night. But Jem could tell that it was big, and that it was nearing completion.

The inner circle—a diverse group of former military strategists and old Colladi Corp security—were strangely accepting of Eva's refusal to explain herself. Even the most difficult and consistently combative members of the group never spoke so much as a single critical word of their reclusive leader.

And whenever they did speak of her, they'd do so with strange expressions that Jem couldn't read. Not quite fear. Not quite reverence or admiration. So what was it that inspired such blind loyalty?

This time Jem had been gone for an entire week. And though Blue had been as ecstatic as always to see her, Jem detected a jittery agitation underneath it all.

Jem stroked the soft fuzz of the short, shaved hair on the side of Blue's head. Rested and eager for another round, she kissed her again, hands wandering. But Blue had grown stiff. Unresponsive.

Jem rolled onto her side, head propped up on her hand. "Hey. What's wrong?"

Blue didn't reply at first. She looked at Jem, then averted her gaze, staring back up at the ceiling.

"Jem," she finally said. "Have you ever been to Base Machado?"

"Sure," Jem said. "I've made a couple runs bringing people to live there. Never gone inside, though. No mods allowed."

Base Machado. An air force base turned city, and the last place in the Americas where humans lived under human rule. A stone's throw from Armitage's fortress city and base of operations, where the AI core that contained its mind was buried at the center of it all.

The base had maintained an uneasy truce with the Synth. They had what was left of the American nuclear arsenal, and threatened to blow themselves up should the Synth ever invade. The Synth, for all their cruelty, had never resorted to using nukes. Whatever their plans were for the world after humanity's demise, they wanted it intact. So, for now, they tolerated the little city's existence.

Many a Runner and Resistance soldier had retired to Base Machado. Jem had considered it herself, but they had a strict ban on mods for fear of Synth hacking or control. If you wanted to live on the base, you had to have your mods removed. Zero exceptions. Not a big deal for most people, who simply lost the ability to connect to immersive VR. But for Jem, it might well be tantamount to a lobotomy. She just didn't know.

Blue went quiet again. Jem waited, patient. Finally, Blue looked at her—dark eyes brimming with tears.

"It's been hard," Blue said. "Being down here. Underground, without any VR. Sometimes it's like I can't breathe. Like I can feel the miles of rock and dirt above us, pressing down on my chest. I asked the commander if I could get a VR connection—tried to explain that I grew up in the clouds, with endless sky in every direction. But she wouldn't listen. So now the only VR I can use is with you, in your mods. And you were gone so long this time. It's hard enough being stuck here, on Earth, with . . . well, with everything. But living down here? Even the garden feels small to me now."

She took a shuddering breath, trying to calm herself.

"The doc has what she needs from me to replicate her cure. I'm not due for another four months. I could make the journey to the base now, but not for much longer. And then, once the baby is born . . ."

"I understand," Jem said softly. "I'll talk to Eva."

"I . . . already asked Eva if I could go. She said no. Wouldn't explain why but she was adamant that I stay here." Blue was trembling. "Jem, please. This . . . *thing* between us. It's been . . . unexpected. To say the least. I really fucking wish I could stick around and, I don't know, see where things go. But being down here is killing me. I feel like I'm losing my mind."

"Hey, it's okay!" Jem clasped Blue's hand in her own. "You don't have to go. I'll talk to Eva—you'll have your very own VR bed by tomorrow. Trust me."

Blue shook her head. "I don't want to raise my kid in a cave. I'm sorry." The tears spilled over, silently rolling down onto her cheeks. "I want to make a difference. Want to help Eva so badly. But I'm fucking useless."

"Shhhh," Jem said, kissing away her tears as she held her tight. Fighting to stifle the bitter cold that filled her at the sudden, miserable certainty that she was going to lose this woman. "*Shhhh*. It's okay. You're not useless! And you don't have anything to be sorry for."

Blue calmed down and looked at her. Hesitant. "What if . . . you came with me? What would happen to you? If they took your mods out?"

The thought of it sent a stab of anxious nausea twisting through Jem's gut.

"I don't know," Jem said. "Maybe I'd be me, just slower. But I've had them since I was a kid. My brain has . . . grown around them. So . . ."

"Are you sure they wouldn't make an exception for you?" Blue asked, incredulous. "It just doesn't make any sense. Besides the fact that you could take out a platoon of their soldiers on your own. How many people live there, free from the Synth, because of you specifically?"

Jem shrugged. "The colonel commanding the base appreciates what we do, but has always made it clear that the Resistance Underground doesn't have any actual authority over them. They had a few disasters with pre-war mods being hacked, and they've taken a zero-allowance policy. Maybe they'd let me keep mine, but . . ."

"I'm sorry," Blue blurted out, cutting her off. "That was so shitty of me to even ask. Eva needs you. The Resistance needs you. That's so much more important than me."

"I—" Jem said, kissing her once "—completely—" twice "—disagree." A third time, on the nape of her neck. "But don't tell my boss, okay?"

After a while, Blue fell asleep in her arms; melting against her, very obviously relieved to have said the words she'd been holding back for weeks. Jem's arm went numb underneath her, unpleasant tingling cold across the skin as Jem flexed her fingers, trying not to wake her girlfriend.

Not that she would have been able to sleep, anyway.

Jem rose early the next day, careful not to disturb the softly snoring woman beside her. She took a cold shower and put on her somewhat threadbare civilian clothes instead of the more formal Resistance uniform she'd grown accustomed to wearing as of late. Jem needed to talk to Eva as a friend, not as a subordinate. She strapped on her shielded holsters out of habit. Pistol on one hip, EMP blaster on the other. Even here she felt naked without them.

Jem punched a button beside the heavily armored door to the Alpha Core lab and waited several minutes until the panel responded with a buzz—the door cracking outward, silent on its thick hinges.

Eva leaned up against the doorframe with a whiskey bottle in hand. "Wellll," she said. "If it isn't my favorite person in the entire world. Just in time for the party! Will you walk into my parlor? Said the spider to the fly." She flashed a wicked grin. "Have a drink."

"A bit early for liquor," Jem said, following Eva inside.

"Ohhhh, what does early mean anyway," Eva said. "I don't sleep, and we're so deep underground, I don't even *remember* the last time I saw the sun."

Jem leaned against the wall, folding her arms. "Do you ever leave?"

Eva shook her head. "No ma'am. I am a recluse. A hermit. A subterranean agoraphobe. People come to me. Or Ezra goes to them." She tapped her forehead. "Still got a few tangled knots of crazy to unravel. But I'll be better soon."

She took a swig from the bottle, and sighed, visibly relaxing. She offered Jem the bottle, but Jem shook her head, declining.

"What's the occasion?"

"The completion of my masterpiece. The Grand Triumph of Human Ingenuity. The single tippity-tap-tap to send this house of cards tumbling into a pile."

Jem took in a sharp breath, thinking of all the firepower she'd dispersed across the city. What was Eva planning? They didn't have the manpower to take on the Philly Peacekeeper force, let alone Armitage's full military might.

"Uh-oh," Eva said. "I see worry etched into that stunningly beautiful face." She grew more somber. Serious. "I hate keeping you in the dark like this. Please don't think I take your trust for granted. I am so, so grateful for everything you do. If it weren't for your help, I'd never have been able to complete this so quickly. And humanity *will* thank you. Trust me on that."

"That's . . . not what's bothering me," Jem said. Though Eva's mysterious plan had indeed been her primary concern, until last night. "It's Blue."

Eva's expression softened. A flash of guilt in her bright blue eyes. "Ah. Yes."

"I'm sending a Runner to deliver a cure kit to Base Machado tomorrow," Jem said. "I'd like Blue to go with him. And, if possible, I want to escort her there."

"Jem," Eva said delicately. "It's just too dangerous. I can't send her out there, not in good conscience. And I certainly can't afford to spare you for the time it would take to go all the way there and back. Let alone the risk. I can't afford to lose you, Jem. As a sister or a soldier."

"That's fine, I can stay. A security detail will do just as well. I know you're worried about her, but she's fully aware of the risks and would rather make the journey than stay here and—"

"Jem, listen—"

"No, *you* listen, Eva," Jem said, heated. "Blue is losing her mind down here. Her claustrophobia's really fucking with her, and I'm seriously unhappy with the fact that she came to you asking for VR to alleviate it and you flat-out refused to help her because . . . why? Because you take personal issue with VR?"

"You're right," Eva said, placating. "That was selfish of me, not letting her use VR. You know how I can be, I wasn't thinking— I'll have a VR bed delivered right away."

Jem shook her head. "It's too late for that. I tried to convince her but she's made up her mind."

"Jem," Eva said, apologetic, and put a hand on Jem's shoulder. "I'm sorry, but I can't allow her to leave."

Jem brushed her hand aside, struggling not to get angry. "*Why?*"

"Jem, I—"

"It's because of that, isn't it?" Jem said, pointing at the twisting machinery of the Alpha Core. "Whatever you're planning, that's why you won't let her leave. I've been moving a lot of serious firepower—I know something big is going down. Something dangerous. And I haven't pushed, because I love you, and I trust you. But you need to trust me too. Whatever you're doing, *please* let me in so I can help you. So I can understand why you're being so goddamn stubborn."

Eva stood there, conflicted, and Jem could tell that she wanted to tell her. Wanted to let Jem in *so* badly. But then she shook her head.

"This is bigger than Blue, Jem," she said. "Bigger than you. Bigger than me. And for now, please, just keep trusting me. Only for a little while longer, okay? Then everything will become clear."

Jem opened her mouth to argue, but stopped. Took a deep breath. Sighed.

"Gimme that," she said, snatching the whiskey bottle from Eva's hand and taking a swig. She grimaced, eyes watering.

Eva grinned. "That's more like it."

Jem leaned up against the wheeled medical bed. Miserable. "I hardly know Blue. But . . . I don't want her to go. I'm going to do right by her, no matter what, but it's just so . . ."

Eva leaned up beside Jem and squeezed Jem's hand. "I know, little swan."

"Have you ever been in love before?"

"Love, eh?" Eva arched a brow, chuckling. "One month in and you're already dropping the L-bomb, huh?"

Jem felt her face go hot. "No, uh, I mean—"

"Oh, I don't know," Eva said. "There was this kid before I was taken. Total dork, but sweet. Funny. I'm a sucker for funny. We were fifteen. He was my first. And last, I suppose. It was okay. Better the next few times. But then . . ." She shrugged. "I don't think it was love, but I'm glad I got to experience at least a little bit of something like it. Before the Synth took that away from me."

Jem offered her the bottle, but Eva declined, so Jem left it on the floor beside the bed.

"I've got some work to do," Eva said, looking haunted. Jem nodded and turned to leave, but Eva took her by the arm—stopping her. "And Jem?" She looked into Jem's eyes, her gaze piercing. "Thank you."

Flashing red. Wailing alarms.

Jem sat up at her desk with a gasp, heart pounding. She reeled for a moment, dazed and confused, but then remembered that she hadn't slept at all the previous night and must have dozed off while reviewing this week's operations.

Blue wasn't in their bed. Struggling to remain calm, Jem slammed a hand against the wall comm, shouting to be heard over the alarms as she called for Eva. Called for Blue, Ezra, Dr. Blackwell, *anyone!*

No response.

She drew her pistol and went into the flashing red light of the halls.

Eva's quarters first. If they were under attack, she would be the primary target. As much as Jem wanted to go find Blue—it was like Eva had said. This was bigger than either of them.

The door was unlocked. Jem burst into the room, pistol ready. No sign of Eva. No sign of a struggle, but that didn't mean anything. If she wasn't here, then she was probably—

The alarms cut. The flashing red lights went dim, replaced once more with soft white. The intercom crackled.

"Jem?" came Eva's voice from the intercom. "Jem, are you there?"

Jem ran out to the hall comm and slammed her fist against the button. "Reading you, Eva," she said, relief flooding her. "Loud and clear. The hell is going on?"

Eva laughed, sheepish. "I—uh—that may have been my fault. The Alpha Core, I had some automated functions running. They tripped the alarms."

Jem breathed a heavy sigh of relief. "Christ. You scared the ever-loving shit out of me. Where are you? And where are—"

"Hi, Jem," Blue cut in. "We were just sitting down for breakfast. You fell asleep at your desk, but you looked so tired I didn't want to wake you."

"I didn't realize it was a false alarm at first," Eva said. "There's a panic room hidden in the common area. I brought us all in, but, uh . . ."

"But Ms. Colladi hasn't ever used it before," Dr. Blackwell said, bemused. "And now we're stuck."

"It's okay!" Eva said shrilly. "I'm overriding security now, this'll just take a second and we'll be right out—"

A shrill electric noise rang out from the intercom and the lights went dim, just for a moment. When they went back on, the armored blast door of the Alpha Core lab down the hall from Eva's quarters silently opened.

"Wellll," Eva said. "That should have opened every single lock in the facility. But we're still locked in. So the good news is, I've narrowed this down to a mechanical issue, not software. The bad news is, I'm going to have to dismantle the panic room door from the inside. Which might take a few hours."

Jem could hear the others groaning in the background.

"Is there anything I can do?" Jem said into the intercom. "I'll head over now."

"No, it's fine!" Eva said. "There's nothing you can do from the outside. We'll be fine—we're fully stocked with plenty of . . . water. And nutrition cubes."

Blue made a noise of disgust.

"Go have some breakfast," Eva continued. "The good doctor made waffles. Someone might as well enjoy them before they get cold."

"All right," Jem said. Hesitant. Eyeing the open door to the Alpha Core lab. "Actually . . . I think I might go grab some shut-eye."

"Roger that," Eva said. "Sweet dreams, vice-commander. Eva Colladi, signing off."

Another crackle, and the intercom went silent.

Slowly, Jem holstered the pistol and went over to the Alpha Core lab.

The throne sat empty within. The twisting pipes and messy bundled cords lit colorfully by countless blinking lights behind it.

Jem knew she should just close the door. Knew she should just go to the common area and eat some waffles.

She was *happy*. Things were *good*. Eva trusted Jem and knew she would never betray her. Never go snooping where she didn't belong. But . . . they'd be stuck in there for hours. And if Jem could see what Eva was planning . . . if she could know for sure that her worries were unfounded . . .

Jem stepped over the threshold into the lab. Took tentative steps past the wheeled bed to the steel throne. She sat. Took the helmet hanging to the side by its thick topknot of cords. Took a deep breath and pulled it down onto her head.

Jemma Burton became a god.

She'd had her mods for so long that the incredible amplification of her reflexes, intellect, and memory felt utterly normal to her. But *this*. Her body was distant, a tiny fragment of the whole that was Jemma Burton. She could see *everything*. Understand *everything*. Every science and art and philosophy that had eluded her. The entire contents of her mind, the collected artistic and academic works of mankind—every book, poem, language, song, film, all experienced in a vivid burst that she could somehow fully grasp, understand, and retain.

Jem focused in her attention, already losing track of time. Had it been milliseconds since she'd donned the Alpha Core helm? Or hours?

She felt the walls, experiencing the strange sensation of her mind becoming the limits of her body—her edges amorphous, abstract—a great sprawling, electric chaos in an abstract world that quickly came into focus around her as her immense digital mind adjusted.

It was strange. She was Jem, yet she wasn't. The tiny Jem existed at the core of her being; this great swirling intellect around the speck of her mind—but somehow she knew that the influence of Jem's human mind was still absolute.

She shrunk herself down, groping at the edges of this enclosed digital space. Though many of the Alpha Core's processes were dedicated to her mind, near as much of it wasn't a part of her at all, but a framework upon which this amorphous labyrinth of light and information that she existed within was built.

Time; there was no time. Or there was infinite time—she couldn't be sure. But she needed to focus. Couldn't let herself be distracted by the ecstasy of godhood. She was here for Eva. Here to see what she was planning. Here to see what she'd been working on for so long, months that may well have been experienced as millennia to her oldest and dearest friend as she worked within this machine.

She came upon a sealed quadrant, a glowing core locked and hidden away within complex trillions of puzzles and dead ends. She closed upon it, her being stretching out into trillions of smaller protocols, each picking away at the individual corners of this mystery.

Slowly, she unraveled the quadrant to reveal a door. Locked—even to her. But the keyhole, the *keyhole!*

She peered through it—peered through a door in the sky high up over an impossibly secure world spread out in miniature below. An immense empty plane with a prison of light at the center. And within that prison, another mind. Another AI.

Trapped.

The AI was obscured by the prison of light, but as Jem looked, her nebulous mind pressing and straining against the keyhole, she saw through the light to a maelstrom of hellish agony that surrounded the screaming mind. The mind wasn't trapped at the heart of the nightmare, Jem realized, but the source of it—horrifying visions constantly pumping from its center, angry, trying to get out, battering and wailing against the walls of its cage as it fought to infect the empty world beyond.

Jem didn't understand what it was, but managed to peer through the boiling mass of pain and terror until she found, huddled up into a miserable ball at the very center, a young, terrified teenage girl. Naked and filthy, with her legs pulled up to her chest. Her face pressed into her knees.

Eva.

It was Eva as Jem had seen her on the Synth screens so many years ago. Wild-eyed, insane. Brand bloody, hair tangled and torn out in chunks. Face filthy and twitching as the eternity of suffering she endured played over and over and overandover and*overandover*—

Jem pulled back, realizing that the nightmare storm surrounding the Eva AI was some sort of trap. Some sort of virus, reaching out with digital barbs to latch on to any intelligence it might come into contact with, to draw it in and force it to suffer the agony Eva had endured in Torment.

She pulled away from the keyhole, unable to watch the little AI suffer any longer, but before she could completely pull away she detected a trigger that she had quite nearly missed—a button, to set off some sort of simulation. A demonstration of the real Eva's plan.

Jem pressed the button and witnessed things that sent every corner of her immense mind spinning with visceral, all-encompassing revulsion.

She saw the Eva AI, released from its chamber, unleashed upon Synth networks across the globe unprepared for such an attack. The virus, splitting into billions, growing. But not to attack the AI. The Alphas and the Overminds were far more advanced than this outdated Alpha Core, powerful as it might be.

No, this virus was meant for *humans*.

Civilians trapped under Synth rule. Every person in every city across the globe who dreamed their lives away in full immersion VR. The virus would take hold of their minds, trapping them there. And those trapped within would experience Torment.

Not to the full hellish extent. No, just a taste. Days instead of decades. Enough to brutally traumatize every person caught within the nightmare storm of the Eva virus, but only to the very edge of breaking. The edge of madness. Far enough to forever make them hate the artificial paradise of immersive VR as much as Eva did. To fear its siren's call—to take up arms against the Synth and never, ever let themselves fall into VR's sweet, silencing clutches again.

Then—there. A secondary function of the virus. Inky, malevolent tentacles creeping into billions of screaming minds. Changing them. Rewriting them. Tearing their personalities to shreds and rebuilding them as soldiers. Teaching them the arts of violence and warfare. Networked, to be controlled and rewritten at Eva's command through the existing Synth infrastructure. But how would she keep the Synth from simply seizing control of the civilians made soldiers? How would she—

A blast of light. A column of fire.

There, in the distance, beyond forests and fields. Ezra and a small army of other soldiers. Tunneling through the earth, to come up under the Armitage core. To detonate a warhead that Eva had somehow managed to procure from Base Machado.

They never sent smart cement tunnels beyond the edges of the city. Without constant updates and commands from their tactical HQs, they were blind and deaf. And without the cover of city infrastructure overhead, the tunnels were far easier for Synth surveillance to detect. To destroy.

But then Jem saw and understood. The elaborate braided pattern of the other tunnels, hiding Ezra's tunnel deep below. Sacrificing themselves to the Synth one after the other as Ezra dug through seismic shadow after seismic shadow, until finally he was underneath Armitage's core.

Jem watched with horror as Ezra detonated the warhead, killing Armitage, killing everyone in the nearby Base Machado, killing himself and the last remnants of the soldiers who'd kept him hidden.

Ezra would detonate the very moment that Eva unleashed the virus onto the civilian populace. Then, with Armitage dead, Eva would seize control of its network and sever the borders connecting it to the other Synth.

Horror and hope boiled within Jem's immense mind as she watched Eva's army creep across the continent. The Synth in disarray as every city erupted into mass violence and guerilla warfare. Eva's army conquering and killing Overmind after Overmind, seizing their resources and technology.

She saw herself with Eva—each of them controlling their own

core—their own armies of tortured puppet soldiers and repurposed Synth. With the resources stolen from the conquered Overminds, they'd build mods and increasingly powerful Alpha Cores. They'd create entire platoons of soldiers with mods as advanced as their own, with cores and networked humans coordinated under their control like Synth armies, only far greater in number.

All the while they would send record of their conquests up to the colonists beyond the orbital blockade. Show them that humanity was fighting back—maybe even winning. That the colonists should intervene and rejoin the war.

The lights pulled away and Jem felt herself diminishing, felt her mind dying, and it was with an incredible sense of loss that she found herself back in the lab, the Alpha Core silent behind her.

With trembling fingers she removed the helm. And there was Eva. Standing there, arms crossed over her breast. Conflicted anger in her eyes, at odds with the vague smile on her lips.

"There's a series of physical fail-safes," Eva said. "They only allow the core to be used for short bursts of time before automatically booting the user. Otherwise it would be easy to lose yourself in the power of Alpha intelligence. Easy to lose track of time and die of dehydration."

"Eva, I—"

Eva held up a hand, stopping her. "Jem, I can't say I'm happy that you felt the need to go behind my back like this. But I'm also sort of relieved. I've been working on this alone for so long. I'm glad that I can finally talk with you about it."

"So what," Jem said. "You were just going to initiate this . . . plan without telling me? Without asking me what I think?"

"I . . . hadn't decided yet."

"That AI," Jem said. "That little girl. She looks like you."

"As my mother rebuilt my mind over the years," Eva explained, "she took full neurological copies with each progression. That *girl* began as the very first copy my mother took. My mind immediately after the Synth allowed the Resistance to take me back, fresh out of Torment. As you can see, I've weaponized the copy."

Jem came down from the throne, unsteady on her feet. Eva reached out to help her, and Jem had to fight the urge to recoil from her touch.

"So this is why you wouldn't let Blue leave. You're going to destroy Base Machado. Kill everyone there."

Eva hesitated, then nodded.

Jem stared at her. Disbelieving. "Eva. Please, tell me this is some sort of fucked-up joke."

It was too much. Too big and horrific for Jem to really feel the true extent of human misery Eva's plan would unleash upon untold billions.

"Tell me why I shouldn't do this, Jem," Eva said sincerely. "Convince me. Show me a better path, and I will follow it with you by my side."

Jem looked at her with stunned disbelief. "Do you really need me to explain why this is wrong? Rewriting peoples' minds to make them into someone else? How is that any different from killing them, Eva? Killing everyone. Torturing *everyone*. I understand turning them into soldiers. I don't like it, but I understand. But the Torment?"

"I'm not *completely* rewriting their minds," Eva said, heated. "Just giving them the knowledge and skill set to fight back. And showing them Torment is the only way I can permanently pull everyone away from their precious VR so they'll strop dreaming through the apocalypse and finally fucking *wake up!*"

Jem was struck with the image of those very words, painted

in blood over the corpses of civilians murdered while they were using VR. Dozens upon dozens of killings across Philadelphia. Men, women. Young, old. Butchered, their throats slit.

"It was you," Jem whispered. She looked at Eva, horrified. Finally starting to see the tortured madness within those piercing sapphire eyes. The electric brilliance was still there, but the joy of the girl Jem knew had gone sour, her kindness spent. "The murders. All those people . . ."

"I ordered the killings, yes," Eva said defiantly. "I didn't like doing it, but those VR junkies were already dead, Jem. I needed to scare people. Make them afraid of what might happen if they kept dreaming away." Eva sneered, her face twisted with disgust. "They didn't even know they were dying when my soldiers cut their throats. Couldn't even feel it."

"Eva . . ."

Eva shrugged. Unconcerned as Jem's hand slowly crept toward the holster of her gun. "The murders were a mistake, I've come to realize. Whispered rumors won't stop a junkie from using. Nobody cared, not really. But that's why I *have* to put them in Torment. It's the *only* way to cure humanity of this addiction. You know I'm right, Jem! You know it!"

"Ezra would never agree to this," Jem said.

"Ezra is already gone," Eva said. "He's with the warhead, awaiting my command to depart."

"I don't believe you!"

"Ezra does what I tell him to do."

Jem finally understood.

"Ezra," she breathed. "The circle . . . you've *brainwashed* them. Reprogrammed them into slaves, like you're going to reprogram the rest of humanity."

Eva nodded. "I don't like it. But the stakes are too high for me to selfishly worry about my own precious moral integrity. I've made use of the methods my mother developed to rebuild my mind—to cleanse it, and rebuild it from scratch, piece by piece. I'm not proud of what I've done. Ever since I woke up, I've struggled to think of another way to stop the Synth. To save humanity. But there is no other way, Jem. So please!"

"Eva . . ."

"With you by my side, we have a *chance*. A small chance, but a chance nonetheless. And I know how horrific it is. I know history will look back on what I've done as the greatest crime against humanity ever committed. But at least there will still *be* a humanity. My life, my happiness, my legacy. It doesn't matter, Jem. My family created the AI. This is *our* fault! We created them, and it's my responsibility to destroy them. To set things right, no matter *what* the cost!"

"Your mother?" Jem said, just above a whisper. "Did you brainwash her too? Did you kill her?"

"That stupid weak bitch killed herself!" Eva spat, finally losing her composure. "I changed her, just a little. Just so she'd let me help her. Just so she'd work with me, to find a way to put a stop to all of this. But I hadn't perfected the process yet; the rewrite was incomplete. Insufficient. She shouldn't have been able to kill herself, but she did. Just like my dad. And the note she left. The horrible things she said . . ." She stood there, trembling. Fists clenched, eyes welling with angry tears. "They left me! Abandoned me! I've been alone, Jem, I've been alone for so long . . ."

"If I'd failed your test," Jem said. "If I'd betrayed you in that simulation, turned you over to the Synth, you wouldn't have sent me away to be a Runner again. You would've changed me. Rewritten me to be totally, completely loyal to you. Right?"

Eva looked at her, composed once again. Cold. "Don't ask questions you already know the answers to, Jem."

Jem looked at her for a long moment. Steeling herself.

She drew her pistol. "Eva Colladi. I am relieving you of command."

Eva looked at the pistol, eyes wide with hurt. "Jem. No. You wouldn't."

"I'm sorry, Eva," Jem said. "I can't let you do this."

Eva took a step toward her. "What are you going to do? Kill me?"

Jem moved back, keeping her distance. "Stop right there! I don't want to hurt you."

"I *love* you Jem," Eva said, fighting back tears and taking another step. "Please. Just think about this. We can adjust the plan. We can work together to perfect it. Maybe find another way to make this work. *Together.*"

She took another step, and Jem backed into the wall, unable to move any further.

"Stay *back*!" Jem said. "Put your hands on your head and get down on the ground!"

"No," Eva sobbed. "If you're going to shoot me, then shoot me! You can't take me prisoner, Jem. The Inner Circle is totally under my control. They'll just kill you and set me free. Killing me is the only way to stop this."

She took another step, grabbing the gun from Jem's hand and pulling to yank it away—

Jem pulled the trigger.

Eva stood there. Eyes full of heartbroken disbelief. Blood pluming from a hole at the center of her chest. She tried to say something but no words came. Blood trickled from the corner of her mouth as she collapsed to the floor.

Jem dropped the gun with a moan, sinking to her knees beside the fallen Eva, frantically pressing her hands down on the bullet wound. Struggling to apply pressure to stop the blood from pulsing sluggishly through her fingertips.

"No, no, no, no, *no*, oh God, Eva, I'm sorry, no please no!"

But it was no use. No life stirred within the beautiful woman on the floor. The laughter and love and pain and madness had fled from her eyes, replaced with the glassy emptiness of a corpse.

Jem clung to her, wracked with sobs as she held Eva in her arms.

A hand came down on Jem's shoulder.

"Shhhh, it's okay," came Eva's voice.

Jem whirled around with a shriek, EMP blaster drawn in a fluid motion as she turned to find Eva standing there, looking down at Jem with pained disappointment.

"Wha—what?" Jem stammered, and turned to look at the body, but it was gone. There wasn't even any blood.

"I'm sorry, Jem," Eva said. "I wish you hadn't needed to go through that. But I had to be sure. Had to know how you'd react."

Realization dawned on Jem, helpless terror gripping her.

"We're in VR," she breathed. "This isn't real; you fucking put me in VR again."

Eva nodded and gestured at the wheeled medical bed, where Jem was horrified to see herself lying. Her head was covered with a helmet like the one hanging from the throne—its heavy braided wire dangling across the room to connect to the machine.

And there was another Eva, sitting on the throne, wearing the other helmet.

"When you first arrived here I put an override on your contact point under your skin," the Eva standing before Jem said. "It allows me to remotely put you into your own mods' full immersion and take control of the experience. After our talk this morning, I realized I'd put this off long enough. I knew it would be wrong to go ahead with my plan without consulting you first. So when you were working at your desk this morning I triggered the immersion and brought you to the lab on that bed."

Jem touched the skin behind her ear, remembering the itch that had bothered her for days after her arrival. Of course. How could she have been so stupid?

She looked to the gun on the floor. The EMP blaster in her hand. Looked at the comatose Jem on the wheeled bed, with another blaster and pistol still holstered at her sides.

"I know you, Jem. I know you trusted me but I knew you wouldn't be able to resist using the core to see what I've been up to. I just wish you could've seen things my way."

"What are you going to do to me?" Jem asked, voice hushed. Scared.

Eva took a step toward Jem, growing in size. The room began to darken, the walls and floors fading away, the illusion disappearing. All that remained was Eva and Jem, standing at the center of an infinite darkness.

Jem looked down, and to her horror, saw that her body was beginning to fade. Eva towered above her, becoming amorphous, a cloud of electric light. Jem's body disappeared entirely, and she was just a mind, just a point of view, floating helplessly as Eva's Alpha Core entity closed around her. Creeping tendrils of black beginning to worm their way into Jem's psyche.

"I'm sorry, Jem," came Eva's voice from all directions. "I need you. I'm going to change you, just a little. To remember this differently. To agree with my plan, despite your reservations. To forget that I changed you at all."

Jem tried to scream, tried to pull away, but she couldn't.

"First," Eva continued, "I'll take a copy of your mind. Then I'll completely erase your brain. Reset every neuron—completely burn it clean. You'll be dead, technically, for the minute it takes me to rewrite the copy I've taken and burn it back into your brain. But don't worry—I'll keep the original, unaltered copy safe. I promise you. And when this is all over, I'll give it back to you. Then you can hate me, kill me—I don't care. I'll deserve it, after what I'm going to do."

"Eva, please!" Jem screamed without words, the thought a crimson pulse of fear and desperate animal terror. "Don't do this! PLEASE!"

"Please forgive me, Jem. I love you."

She could feel the tendrils sifting through her mind like worms, touching every memory, every thought, every hope and dream and fear—

But as Eva's mind intertwined with Jem's, Jem could see Eva's thoughts. Could feel Eva's pain as well, see every wretched memory; oh god, the memories—

Jem pulled back, trying to focus, trying desperately to think of some way out of this, but knowing it was no use, she was trapped, she'd be erased, her body lying there, helpless as Eva changed her and—

Her body.

Jem's mind was here, but so was her body, just out of reach. Her mind was no match for Eva's immense AI intellect, but the immersion was nothing special, it was just standard immersion created by her own mods.

She reached out, straining in the darkness, struggling to find some hole. Some gap or patch.

When Jem used VR, she never used *full* immersion. She'd go deep, go to the very edge, so she could feel, and taste, and see—but just beyond the veil of false reality, she was always aware of her body. Comatose beyond the illusion. Silent but listening. Feeling. Like a sleeping limb—numb, but not forgotten.

Jem strained, fighting to move her arm in the real world, that distant phantom limb she could sense just out of reach. Like struggling to force herself to wake from a nightmare.

"All done," Eva said. "I've copied your mind in full. I'll respect your privacy; I won't look through it to see what you think. What you feel. What you've experienced in the years since we were children. And I promise you, I'll keep it safe. Now." The color of Eva's mind changed, darkened tendrils turning thorny and red. "I'm afraid this is going to hurt. I'll try to be quick."

Jem's brain screamed with pain as fire like that of a thousand migraines crushed into one stabbing motion through her while the tendrils began to push, began to *burn*, and she could feel it, feel her fingers just beyond the dark. As the fire burned, as Eva slowly seared away her mind, her *soul*, Jem felt those distant fingers close around the grip at her side. Felt the hand pull, bringing the EMP blaster to her head, feel it pressing the blaster against the helmet on her skull and—

Jem pulled the trigger.

The darkness tore away in a smear of green and Jem fell tumbling from the bed, her muscles spasming, her skull feeling as if it had been cracked open. She was dizzy, confused, and blind, but then in a flurry of black and green multicolored overlays her mods rebooted and she was in control again.

Jem's mods were shielded from EMP blasts, so they hadn't been fried, merely scrambled, though the override chip Eva had placed on the contact point under her skin would be broken. Eva would no longer be able to force her into full immersion.

Gasping, Jem dropped the blaster and weakly tore the

EMP-fried helmet from her head, vision slowly coming into focus as she struggled desperately for control, knowing there was no time, that Eva would be on her in moments after she realized Jem had torn free.

Still dazed, vision clouded with interference, Jem drew the pistol at her side with sweaty fingers.

Pain shot through Jem's hand as Eva ran over from the throne to kick the gun from her grasp and placed a boot upon Jem's chest, pinning her.

"Fucking *fantastic*," Eva growled, picking up the EMP blaster and pointing it down at Jem's face. "Do you know how hard it was to build that core connector? It's going to take me *days* to build another one. So now what? Am I going to have to knock you out with your own blaster? Keep you drugged up and locked away? This facility is too small, there's nowhere to hide you, I'll have to keep Blue and the doctor in full immersion. Maybe rewrite them, too, once I've built a new one. I really don't want to have to do that, but I don't have any choice now. This is on you, Jem. This is—"

As Eva talked, Jem remembered the whiskey bottle on the floor beside the bed, just within reach. She couldn't see, couldn't turn to look, but her mods were working again, her perfect full-sensory memory intact, and she knew where the bottle was, where she left it at least, and—

She reached back, snatched the bottle, and flung it up at Eva's face.

It clipped Eva's forehead and shattered on the ground behind her. Eva stumbled back with a surprised grunt, dropping the blaster.

Jem dove for the blaster but Eva kicked it away again, face twisted with rage as she kicked savagely at Jem, going in on her fast and hard as Jem scrambled away, unable to stand until she finally caught Eva's foot between her legs and twisted, sending her to the ground.

They scrambled to their feet and danced back. The bottle had split the skin on Eva's brand. Blood trickled from the all-seeing eye as if it was actually crying.

Lightning quick, Eva snatched up the stem of the shattered bottle from the ground beside her, jagged glass glittering in the light.

"So what's your plan, Jem?" Eva said as they circled each other, waiting for the other to strike. "Are you going to kill me again? For real this time?"

She darted forward, serpent quick, swiping at Jem's face. Jem leaned back, too slow, and felt a thin line of cold fire spread across her cheek from a shallow slice.

Eva swiped again, but Jem was ready for her this time, knocking the glass from her hand and striking her with a hard jab in the kidneys. Eva danced back, gasping, and then came at her with a flurry of fists.

They punched and blocked and ducked and circled in a blur, moving with vicious mechanical speed and accuracy that no normal humans could match. Eva's reach was longer, her body more naturally muscular than Jem's despite the years she'd lived underground. But Jem had been a soldier since she was a child and was landing more strikes than she was taking.

Eva spat bloody phlegm as they briefly broke apart.

"You always were the better dancer," she said, chuckling bitterly.

"I saw your mind, Eva," Jem panted. "While you were digging through my memories, I could see yours too. Could see your thoughts. You *know* your plan won't work. You think we'll take out two Overminds, maybe three if we're lucky."

"Shut up! What the hell do you know?"

"I know that *you* know the Synth will wipe us out if we go to war with them. Know that if the colonists get involved, the Synth will try to rush and overwhelm the orbital blockade, and the colonists will bombard the surface out of fear. Either way, there'll be nothing left. Either way, we're all going to die. So why not just let everyone dream? Why not let us die in peace?"

"Is that what you want, Jem? To dream? To run off with Blue to Base Machado and live out your days as a *normal*? To raise a family—to have your happily ever after?" Eva laughed bitterly. "There's no happily ever after for us! Not for me. And certainly not for you. You *traitor*."

"You want to be some end-of-the-world messiah," Jem said. "You want to lead humanity to their death, sword in hand. But it's wrong, Eva. It's evil!"

"*EVIL?*" Eva lunged at her, rage driving her to strike faster, harder. "What the fuck do you know about evil? I went to Torment, Jem! Nobody in the *history* of mankind has suffered the magnitudes of cruelty I've experienced and lived to tell about it! I lied to you before, Jem. I remember every *second* of it! Every year, every decade, every—"

Jem slipped in the puddle of whiskey from the broken bottle, and in that instant Eva dove for the pistol. Jem—too far from the gun to have any hope of grabbing it before Eva—went for the EMP blaster instead.

Their arms snapped up in a blur as they aimed their weapons and—

Jem's EMP blaster fired with a sizzle.

The pistol slipped from Eva's limp grip. She fell over, arching her back with an agonized howl as her mods forcibly restarted. Her eyes rolled up into her head, her hands held out in claws as her face contorted.

Jem snatched up the pistol, sobbing for breath, and as Eva slowly regained control of her body, Jem punched her in the face. Once. Twice. Three times.

Eva lay there, too stunned to move. Breath whistling through her shattered nose and bloody mouth. Jem stood over her, panting. Pistol in one hand, blaster in the other.

"I always bragged that I don't have to sleep," Eva wheezed. "But it's not true. I can go a few days, but I do need it. And whenever I do, whenever I close my eyes, I'm there—in Torment." She lifted a hand, weakly pointing at the machine. "I'm that little girl again."

The EMP made a small electric whine, indicating that it had recharged for another two shots.

Jem sat beside the woman she loved most of all in the world. Lifted Eva to lay her head on Jem's lap. She pressed the blaster against Eva's temple and pulled the trigger again.

Eva squealed, gasping through bloody foam as she writhed uncontrollably. Jem held her, keeping her close, stroking Eva's hair now gummy with blood.

"What are you doing?" Eva whimpered, once she could speak again. "You're going to break my mods. You'll—"

Jem blasted her mods again, and this time Eva couldn't even scream.

Destroying Eva's mods wouldn't kill Eva. It might handicap her. Or it might just make her relatively normal, for a human. Still more brilliant than the average person but a shadow of what she was before. She wouldn't be able to replace her mods. The Resistance didn't have the tech or resources to create something so advanced again. And Eva would no longer be capable of the genius required to rebuild the Alpha Core after Jem destroyed it. Wouldn't be able to remake the Eva AI Torment virus again and finish what she started.

Lobotomy, a voice inside Jem's head seemed to whisper.

Jem could tell herself otherwise, but she knew that Eva would never be herself again. Knew what an incredible violation this would be—to cripple the mind and soul of a woman, who, despite her madness, loved Jem. It would be an act of vicious cruelty. Losing her mods was one of the things Jem feared herself, most of all. But the alternative . . .

"Please, Jem! Please don't do this! This is worse than killing me! You know this—if you break my mods, I'll—I'll—!"

"I'm sorry," Jem said, softly. "I can't. I can't kill you."

"Please! I'd rather die. If you ever loved me at all, you'll kill me. *Please*, Jem! Just kill me!"

Another blast.

"Am I still in Torment?" Eva asked when she could breathe again. Voice small. Terrified. "Did they ever really let me out? My mother rebuilt me. But if she rebuilt me, why do I remember? Why do I remember every horrible thing they did to me? Every horrible thing they made me do . . ."

Jem raised the blaster to fire on her again.

"W-wait!" Eva sobbed, and Jem hesitated. "Please, Jem! If you do this, I'll never know! Never know for sure if this is real or not. All these years. All this work. All the terrible things I've done. For nothing." She looked at Jem, dazed. "Of course I'm in Torment. You aren't real. Jem died years ago. She would never do this. She's the only person I ever loved. I'm in Hell. Oh *God*, I'm still in Hell. Help me, pleeeaassee, I'm still in—"

Jem squeezed her eyes shut, silent tears rolling down her face as blasted Eva again.

"I'm sorry," Jem whimpered, still stroking Eva's bloody hair as she twitched and seized. "I'm sorry. I'm sorry, I'm sorry, I'm sorry."

Eva could barely move. Could barely move her eyes to look up at Jem.

"You better kill me," she said, her voice a raspy whisper. "If you don't, I'll find you. Make you wish the Synth had taken you instead."

Two minutes of listening to Eva's quiet begging and threats and sobs while she waited for the blaster to charge.

"I hate you," Eva said. "I hate you, I hate you, *I hate you*."

One final blast. And then she went still, her mods permanently disabled.

Eva was deadweight as the bloody, exhausted Jem lifted her up onto the wheeled medical bed with great effort. Eva was breathing, but only just barely. Her heartbeat was faint.

Numb, Jem wheeled her down empty halls. None of this felt real. It was like she was watching a movie of herself while she brought Eva to the medical bay and loaded her into the autodoc sarcophagus.

"I'm sorry," Jem said one final time. She kissed Eva on the forehead. Her blood tasted like copper on Jem's lips. "I love you."

The lid sealed with a hiss as Jem closed it. The autodoc began to whirr and hum, stripping away Eva's clothes and stabilizing her with intricate mechanical hands and needles. The autodoc would heal her wounds, would alleviate any cranial swelling or hemorrhage. Would keep her fed and hydrated for months, at least—though she knew it would only be days before soldiers from the other HQ came to investigate their leader's mysterious silence.

The Resistance wouldn't fall, at first. The council would take over once they found Eva, and they'd keep fighting their futile little fights against the Synth.

But Jem was done. And without Eva or Jem's enhanced

intellects to lead, so was the Resistance. No more rescues. No more bombings or sabotage. No more of any of the pointless little missions she'd pretended so desperately to believe might actually make things better than *this*.

They were mice trying to slay dragons with sewing needles.

Something shattered behind her, and Jem spun around with pistol in hand to find Dr. Blackwell standing there, frozen. A mug lay in pieces on the floor beside the older woman, a puddle of steaming black coffee spreading from the shards.

"W-w-what," the doctor stammered. "Have you done?"

"I'm going to need you to sit down, doctor," Jem said, pistol lowered but ready. "I need you to sit down and listen very carefully to what I'm about to tell you."

Dr. Blackwell nodded, visibly shaking as she sank to the floor.

Jem told her everything.

Afterward, Dr. Blackwell stared at her. Pale.

"We have to leave tonight," the doctor finally said. "You, me, and Blue. Together. You go do what you have to do—I'll deal with Blue."

Jem nodded and rose, looking at Eva one final time. Wishing her a silent goodbye.

Dr. Blackwell grabbed Jem's arm as she turned to leave. "We *cannot* tell Blue about this. She won't understand."

"What's there not to understand?" Jem said. "I won't tell her what really happened till we're clear of the city, but I'm not going to lie."

"She's more naive then you think," the older woman said, firm. "Blue's led a soft life up until now—she hasn't been through what we have."

Jem angrily pulled her arm from the doctor's grasp and went to finish what she'd started.

The earth boiled away in a froth that quickly hardened to stone as Jem directed the smart cement with a compact remote.

She found Ezra waiting underground at the edge of the city. He sat atop a large wheeled crate with his head bowed, reminding Jem very much of the first time they met. The bright glow of his prosthetic hand rippled across the marbled walls.

He looked up and stood, straightening to his full height.

"So," he said.

Jem stared at him, watching Ezra's hand, which hovered nonchalantly by his side, subtly tensed. "The plan's been called off."

"Ah," he said, with a melancholy sort of resignation. "Well, I guess that's that."

"It's not that easy, is it?"

"No." His hand drew closer to his hip, fingers slowly pushing aside his coat. "I'm afraid not."

"You know she brainwashed you? Rewrote your mind to be okay with this evil shit?"

Ezra nodded.

"She practically made me from scratch," he said. "I was in Torment before. Like her. She needed someone loyal."

"You mean a slave?" Jem spat.

"It was nice seeing her happy for once," he said. "But I always knew it was going to end like this. Goodbye, Jemma. It's been an honor."

They both drew their pistols, but Ezra never stood a chance.

He sank to his knees, collapsing onto his side. "Thank you," he said, sounding relieved. And then he was gone.

"Goodbye, Ezra," Jem said, holstering her pistol.

Jem carefully set explosives to destroy the warhead, making sure that what remained would be completely unsalvageable.

She hesitated as she made to leave. Paused for one brief moment to look down at the corpse. Ezra. The first person she had ever killed. But her eyes were dry. Jemma had run out of tears. And this time she knew beyond any doubt that she'd never cry again.

PART II.

BEYOND THE VEIL

VII.

THE GOD IN THE FOREST

Sharp, cold wind hit Nikolai in the face like a slap. He opened his eyes, struck by several realizations in quick succession.

First: He wasn't dead.

Second: He was in free fall, plummeting from up high over the center of a lake. Not the pristine sapphire waters of Marblewood that he'd known his entire life, but murky—almost green.

Third: He realized how dramatic it sounded even as he thought it—everything he'd ever been told was a lie.

The landscape spreading out from the lake was as familiar as it was alien. Lush treetops, fiery red and orange with autumn, were punctuated by brown and white branches of other trees that'd lost all their leaves. How cartoonish and manicured the "natural" landscapes within the Veils seemed compared to the wilds before him.

No time to consider the implications of this. Nikolai had a vague notion of water being as dangerous as concrete at this height and speed, so as the dark green ripples of the water below quickly drew near, he focused on the problem at hand.

He featherweighted himself, no longer plummeting, but sort of flitting against the wind in a downward spiral. He gripped his baton Focal with both hands and stiffened his body, slowing his descent to a stop with a steady stream of jellied *akro*.

Twisting in the air, he quickly snapped out a fixed *akro* platform and stood there, catching his breath. A strong gust of wind threatened to knock him over, so he allowed the featherweight weaves to dissipate.

Shading his eyes, Nikolai scanned the shores. Nothing but wilderness, no sign of life . . . no, wait, there! A rotten old dock, half submerged. A row of them. The others were worse off, completely submerged or entirely gone, only a few mossy posts to mark that they'd been there at all. And there, beyond the docks—houses. A row of them, scattered along the length of the shore.

There were more than a dozen. All abandoned and in various states of disrepair. Half of them were collapsed in on themselves. The others weren't much better.

Abandoned for a couple of decades, at most. Not a century.

He squinted against the overcast sky, finding the sun to orient himself. High above, he could sense the immense center point of the Marblewood Veil. He wondered vaguely how he would be able to find his way back inside.

Once he'd finished exploring, he could come back and figure it out. But for now . . .

He featherweighted himself and took flight, a jet of jellied *akro* shooting him across the water. The lake was large but totally silent. The air smelled clean, fresh. Moist and piney and rich with the scents of the forest.

He eased himself down onto a pebbly shore, chilly from the cool, damp air. He wrapped his arms around himself, teeth chattering. Autumn in Marblewood was gentle—more like an extended late summer, with occasional showers and a bit more red in the leaves than usual.

This autumn was different. Piles of soggy brown leaves at the forest's edge just beyond the pebbles were crisped with frost. It was nearly cold enough for snow.

Considering that Nikolai had only received a tiny fraction of the formal Edge Guard training and experience required to become a Lancer, for once in his life he was begrudgingly grateful for the *informal* training he'd received from his Lancer mother.

Nikolai held out his dagger, creating a steady flame for warmth as he considered his options.

He'd come ashore near the first of the houses. He opened his mouth to call out, but let his flame go out instead and covered himself with a sheet of invisibility. He was startled by how difficult it was. Already the spell sapped away at his strength, like he was carrying some heavy burden. Without the supplemental energy of the Disc omnipresent within the Veils, maintaining a high energy weave like *camelos* with nothing more than his internal reservoirs of magic really took its toll.

Still, better safe than sorry. Sticking to the shore, he began to search for any sign of life among the houses.

The first few were utterly in ruins. The next was a little better, but shifted alarmingly when he forced open the front door. Peering into the remnants of the house, he decided it wasn't safe.

Two houses down, he found one that looked pretty solid. It was obviously the newest of the bunch, though still long abandoned.

Its windows were boarded up, unlike the other houses. A once swinging bench seat on the front porch hung from a single rusted chain.

The front door was busted in. Running his fingers along the splintered wood, Nikolai felt a jolt as he realized that the damage was recent. Days? Weeks? He noticed gouges on the floorboards in front of the door and kneeled down for a closer look. Deep scratches—claw marks?

Nikolai cautiously passed through the shattered remnants of the entrance, allowing his weaves of invisibility to dissipate. Dust hung heavy in the air. There was a great stone hearth, sofas and chairs smashed and scattered around the fireplace. Chips and bullet holes in the wood—also recent.

Nikolai walked lightly as he explored, attempting silence. No food in the kitchen. The cupboards were stripped bare—what he thought might be a refrigerator had an unpleasant, musty stink to it—and though the door was transparent glass, a thick black mold had completely overgrown the inside surface, hiding the contents within.

Nikolai really should have been worried about the recent signs of violence. But he was giddy with excitement. He couldn't help it. Old and decrepit as the ruins were, what little tech he could find was incredibly advanced compared to what he'd seen in museums and books. Abandoned, yes—but for decades at most—not a *century*. And if the humans hadn't *really* died in 2020 like he'd always been told—oh, what sort of wonders they must have created since then! Flying cars? Hoverboards? Commercial space travel? Virtual reality? *Robots*? Not to mention all the new movies and music and books and—*and*!

The humans were alive. The humans were *alive*! If those bullet holes hadn't been so fresh, Nikolai would have been singing and dancing. He was practically running around the house, pulling out cupboards and shelves, looking under sinks and behind broken furniture.

There weren't any buttons on the glass-front refrigerator. The glass was oddly textured, and he wondered if when there was power the glass turned into some sort of computer display. Behind the fridge there wasn't any sign of tubes. He pushed it a couple of inches to see if there were hidden wires underneath. Nothing.

There were a few other appliances—a rusted glassy thing that might have once made coffee. A rather ordinary-looking blender—Nikolai guessed that even after a century, some things stayed the same. None of them had any wiring.

Much of the wall over the fireplace was covered with a thin, white layer of some sort of plastic—light blue fluid crusted below where it'd been cracked by a spray of bullet holes. A screen?

Upstairs there were two bedrooms sharing a bathroom. The mattresses were stripped and rotten in the bedrooms. One room was obviously for a child. The window was broken over a jumble of stuffed animals sodden and melted from years of weather exposure. The walls were patched with great swathes of mildew, but underneath he could make out a cartoonish mural depicting the solar system. Mercury, Venus, Mars, Jupiter, Saturn, Uranus, Neptune. Earth, most prominent of all.

Comets scattered throughout. An asteroid belt drawn in detail between Mars and Jupiter, with happy astronaut miners in sleek suits. Smiling, anthropomorphized spaceships traversing the planets, with giant underground metropolises drawn on Mars and the Moon, and a beautiful, lushly gardened city floating in the atmosphere of Venus.

On the city floating over Venus, standing next to it as tall as skyscrapers, was a cartoonish drawing of an older couple. Painted next to them in childish scrawl were the words *Grandma and Pop Pop.*

Nikolai traced his fingers along the details of the mural with awe, wondering if it was anything more than fantasy. But a century—a *century!* So much could have happened, so much could have changed. *Why* had they been lied to? For *generations!*

Entire Veils had been lost in the 2020 calamity. Millions of magi dead. *All* the humans—*dead!*

He sat down, letting his invisibility slip away, struck with the enormity of it. All his life, Nikolai had been told that the humans died in 2020 because of one incredibly evil mage's magically enhanced warheads.

The Unraveling.

He'd been taught that in the aftermath of the bombing, reality had been twisted and bent in the immediate area surrounding Earth. That all life had been wiped out, some of the Veils destroyed in the process.

He'd seen pictures and footage of humanity's final moments—entire countries swept away in twisting light. Studied the Edge Guard expeditions into crumbling cities and glassy stretches of land churning with radioactive hex clouds. Visited the New Damascus memorial dedicated to the magi who'd died, where millions of names flickering constantly across the glassy white surface of a monolith.

Lies! All lies! Had those magi ever really existed? Had it all been some grand global conspiracy? And if so, to what end? To keep up such a lie for a hundred years—to seal off their Domed Veils and tell everyone that to venture beyond was *death.*

Nikolai stared at the pile of rotting stuffed animals at the corner of the human child's room. *A hundred years.* What could have happened in so much time? And what happened to the people who used to live here?

A small, terrified voice within whispered that, after everything, the humans destroyed themselves after all—that they were all dead. That something terrible really had occurred—something magi could have prevented if they hadn't been so blissfully unaware while those in power hid like the lying *cowards* they were.

The Mage King. He knew about this. He had let this happen. *Made* this happen. He'd been in power a hundred years before, when the *Unraveling* supposedly occurred. But why? And how could he think this was okay? Did he really plan to keep this fiction going forever?

It's as terrible as you think, Hazeal had said. *But not in the way you suspect.*

His mother had known. And whatever was really happening out here, it had driven her to attempt regicide and revolution.

So many questions! The true fate of humanity. The real purpose of the Edge Guard!

Nikolai thought back to the claw marks gouged into the porch. To the bullet holes sprayed into the walls. Humans? Monsters? Something else?

He went back downstairs. Following the trail of bullet holes and destruction, he found a basement staircase at the center of whatever struggle had occurred. Bullet sprays were clustered on the frame along the outside of the door and on the wall opposite the stairwell. Bending over, he saw what appeared to be an oil slick, left behind by . . . something. And whatever that something had been, it had been dragged away, leaving a smear on the wood and a dribbling trail back outside.

Nikolai peered down into the absolute darkness below. Whatever clawed thing had broken in must have been after someone in the basement. And whoever had been in the basement had tried (unsuccessfully?) to fend it off.

Nikolai knew that his uniform was bulletproof, but sincerely hoped that he wouldn't come across something with any sort of advanced weaponry. Leaning into the stairwell, he sniffed the air and pulled back, retching. It was the worst thing he'd ever smelled—a powerful, rotting stench. There was something terrible down there.

Nikolai briefly considered leaving, but curiosity outweighed fear and disgust. Breathing through his handkerchief, he began to descend.

"Hello!" he called into the darkness. "Don't shoot! I—uh, I mean no harm!"

No answer.

He took another step, tasting the rot through his handkerchief.

"Hullooooo! Anybody here? I'm coming down! So please don't shoot! Or jump out at me! Or anything like that! Cause, seriously, I will *fuck your shit up*. Understand?"

Reaching forward, he created a small globe of light with the *illio* weave. He sent it floating down the stairs with an impatient gesture, illuminating damp cement walls.

Stifling fear, he began to descend, carefully staying within the delicate halo of light provided by the *illio* sphere.

At the bottom of the stairs, Nikolai sent his globe of light to the center of the room. He gasped through his handkerchief, inadvertently taking in a big mouthful of the stench.

A few feet away, awkwardly contorted from being seemingly shoved to the side, was the bloated corpse of a man in filthy military fatigues. He'd been nearly cut in half. Starting from between his shoulder and neck, down to his abdomen, he was parted in a V—skin and bone and organs hanging rotten along the inside.

The bone was very lightly blackened where it had been cut, the separation looking smooth—surgical even.

Looking down, Nikolai found a thick, crusted pool of blood, a smearing path leading from it to where the body now rested. There was a line scorched down the stone of the wall beside him, surrounded by a halo of gory spatter. Nikolai realized that he was standing where that human had died—and that he must have been killed by some sort of energy weapon.

The giddy excitement he might have otherwise felt at discovering evidence of a functional laser gun was greatly subdued by the condition of its victim. Nikolai always thought lasers were supposed to cauterize the wound, but the man might as well have been sliced through the shoulder with an extremely sharp sword.

Across the room was another corpse. A woman, also in military fatigues. She was huddled in the corner, her knees tucked up like she was trying to hide. Her arms hung limply at her side—the top of her head splattered on the wall and ceiling. Though there weren't any weapons that Nikolai could see, it appeared that she'd shot herself in the head.

There was an oversized bag in the opposite corner from the woman, full of little sealed packages and boxed water spilling out onto the dirty cement floor. There were some filthy sleeping bags, pushed to the side. Kicking them apart with his shoe, Nikolai counted four.

The little brown packages were MREs—Meals Ready to Eat, manufactured by something called the Wornick Company in McAllen, Texas, for the United States Army. Nikolai got a thrill reading that.

Each of the MREs had color-changing tabs—almost all red, to his dismay, with little black letters in English, Spanish, and a few other languages he didn't recognize saying *Expired*—and then the date, *12/4/19*.

It was October 16, 2120 in the Veils—Nikolai wondered vaguely if the humans had stayed on the same calendar.

Sifting through the reds he found a few that were yellow—with *approaching expiration*, but no date. Dumping the red-tagged packages, he rolled up the cleanest sleeping bag and stuffed it into the bag with the water and rations.

Bag heavy over his shoulder as he left the house, Nikolai couldn't stop thinking about the dead humans inside. What would it be like to die, not knowing if your soul would be intact afterward?

Magi had no idea what happened to their souls after they went into the Disc. But by all appearances, humans, half-magi, and animals didn't even have souls at all.

Unless there was some other kind of life after death that thousands of years of magical and scientific research had yet to detect, humans, like half-mages and animals, faced a nothingness that was terrifying to Nikolai.

The sun peeked through a break in the clouds. It was barely noon; plenty of daylight left.

Nikolai noticed a glint in the sky—something distant and metallic, flashing in the light. He moved back into the shadows of the awning and wrapped himself in a cloak of invisibility.

He squinted, trying to make it out. It was obviously artificial—some sort of aircraft. It was silent, but that might have just been the distance.

The object disappeared into the cloud cover. Nikolai waited, watching for it, but it didn't reappear.

He found a big, flat stone and placed it on the grass at the edge of the beach. He scorched an arrow onto it, pointing it toward the Marblewood Veil's point of entry. Nikolai burned a large X across the front of the lake house—careful not to light the building on fire. It was large enough to see from high up over the lake in case he had trouble finding his way back.

With no real destination in mind, Nikolai followed the dirt driveway past the house out onto a small street. The street ran through dense forest broken up by overgrown driveways to the other abandoned homes.

Despite the abandoned houses and rural surroundings, the street itself was well maintained. He kneeled, placing his hand on the warm asphalt. There were off-color patches darker than others here and there—holes that'd been filled. Not a single actual pothole or crack to be seen.

The area was obviously abandoned, so who was fixing the roads?

Nikolai followed the road, careful to track his progress, marking the occasional tree or rock with a discreet scorch mark. The street, marked on a few barely legible, rusted signposts as Fischer's Way (*why maintain the roads but not the signs?*), slowly began to curve.

Another odd thing: despite the dozens of abandoned buildings he passed, there wasn't a single car to be seen. Abandoned, new, or otherwise. A hundred years had passed, so who knew what people used for transportation anymore? But where there were streets, Nikolai thought there should be some sort of private wheeled transport. Most Veils had excellent public transportation—better than anything the humans ever had pre-2020. But there had always been and would always be magi who preferred their own private crafts. Nikolai couldn't imagine that humans would be different in that regard.

He heard a crackle in the underbrush to his right and spun

to face it, dagger drawn. Nikolai held his breath, scanning the trees . . .

There. An immense wolf, with thick black fur. It calmly regarded him from beside a fallen tree; pale green eyes focused directly on Nikolai, who suddenly wished he'd remained invisible.

Nikolai blinked, and it was gone. He searched for it, goose bumps rising on the back of his neck. But it was no use. The wolf had disappeared.

Nikolai continued on, unsettled. There weren't any humans to be seen, but the wildlife seemed to be flourishing. Squirrels in the trees, the foliage musical with birdsong. Wolves, stalking him in the shadows.

The forest thinned out, then ended abruptly, coming into rolling grassy fields and hills. There was farmland on either side of the road, with scattered houses and barns. Dense wooded forest circled the fields. The road continued out in the open for about a mile until it continued back into the thickly shadowed trees. But unless Nikolai wanted to take a long, painful detour through thick underbrush around the fields, he had to continue on.

Nikolai lingered at the edge of the tree line, hesitant to go out in the open. He whipped up another cloak of invisibility and pulled it around himself. The effort was draining without the supplemental magic from the Disc, but until he knew what the hell was going on he wanted to minimize any chance of being seen.

A strange, silent tractor pulled out of a barn in the distance—heading toward a field neatly lined with dirt and long rectangles of dead wheat. Though the nearby farmhouse was abandoned, the barn next to the field was in good condition. Nikolai stood there frozen as he watched it trundle along, dozens of little metallic things following after it like an insect swarm.

Invisible, Nikolai crossed over to the edge of the wheat field to take a closer look.

The tractor was sleek and compact, but obviously powerful considering the size of the seed sower it pulled across the soil. It was unmanned—no place for a driver, unlike the tractors he'd seen in museums. Crablike robots the size of tiny dogs scuttled after it, digging and planting and gathering seeds dropped by the seemingly autonomous tractor.

The machines were almost silent. Totally electric, Nikolai guessed.

Occasionally, one of the little crabs split off from the group, going back to the barn. Nikolai followed them, peering through the barn door to find a large hitch trailer taking up most of the space. It was big and white—like the back end of a semitrailer truck. Two slatted ramps led out from the front, up to a pair of panels. The crab Nikolai was following trundled up the left ramp, and one of the panels hissed open, revealing darkness. The crab crawled inside, the other panel opened, and another of the crabs came out.

Nikolai guessed that they were resupplying, and that this was some sort of portable, automatic farmer.

He was struck with a sensation of dread as he quickly made his way back to the road. The clouds parted overhead, the sun shining down brightly. Nikolai held up his hand, trying to shield his eyes—but, still invisible, the light passed right through.

A glint caught the corner of his eye. It was the aircraft from before, turning at the fringes of the cloud break. He squinted, wishing that he could shade his eyes, and noticed a second craft, flying much lower than the other. It had rotors, like a helicopter—but no cabin for riding. Just a black, pill-shaped body.

It came to a stop over the edge of the field, hovering stationary.

Feeling extremely vulnerable despite his invisibility, Nikolai turned away, quickly following the road toward the distant tree line.

A red point of light trembled on the ground a little ways ahead of Nikolai. Panicking, he deviated his path, but the red dot followed—moving along to block his path. But how was it—

Too late did he realize that the laser target was simply passing through him—but locking on, nonetheless.

He spun around, desperately moving to put up a shield.

"*Akr*-OOF!"

There was a sharp noise and something struck Nikolai in the chest hard enough to make him stumble back despite the force-dampening nature of his uniform's enchantments. He was sprinting towards the tree line now, and thinking back to the *Predator* movie he'd seen in the Gloaming, and the Predator's heat vision, and about every other military movie he'd ever seen, and realized, kicking himself for being an idiot, that *camelos* only hid him on the visible spectrum—not the infrared!

He could hear the thumping of the machine's blades as it slowly followed him—but he was running, and the tree line was close—so close!

Shadows wrapped around him like a welcome embrace. He stopped, briefly, to catch his breath and see what had struck him. It looked like an iridescent wad of chewing gum, the thin metal slug it had been contained in crumpled up around it. A tracker? It was sticky—Nikolai didn't want to touch it with his bare fingers.

He could hear the craft drawing near. In a rush, he took a muddy stick poking out of a dirty puddle and used it to flick the gummy wad from his uniform.

There was an *intense* crackle and a blinding flash of light. Nikolai was knocked to the ground, helplessly writhing from the powerful jolt of electricity. Stupid, *so stupid!* Moaning, he clung to consciousness, trying to regain control of his body as he lay there, twitching. Smoke rose from the now blackened wad, the burned stick lying beside him.

Unable to move, Nikolai could only watch helplessly as the hovering machine entered the shadows of the forest with predatory slowness. The street was more than wide enough for the contraption to fit with ease, the machine capable of maintaining precise, deliberate altitude.

Metallic segmented tentacles as thick as Nikolai's wrists reached out from its black pill body and gently wrapped around his arms, legs, and waist. It lifted him into the air, Nikolai hanging loosely beneath it. He whimpered, nearly blind with terror. There was nothing he could do.

The machine backed out of the forest, out into the open, and began to ascend. As the field grew distant below, the wind growing sharp with cold, Nikolai finally slipped into unconsciousness.

Nikolai awoke in a panic, heart thumping with adrenaline. Lush, red-leafed forests closed in on the ruins of a half-burned town distantly below them.

He resisted the urge to thrash and struggle. The tentacles holding him did so loosely, just firmly enough to keep him from falling. If he started to move too much, they would probably tighten to keep him from escaping or, well, plummeting to his death. A problem a human might have—but not Nikolai. He kept his eyes half lidded, forcing himself to remain limp.

Tiny machines held aloft by tiny rotors buzzed around him like a swarm of insects, their little bodies like ten-sided dice, each surface glinting with bubbles of plastic. Cameras? They moved quickly, jerking from one spot to another, constantly shifting positions as they followed, examining Nikolai from every possible angle.

He realized that he'd dropped the bag. No matter—his Focals remained firmly sheathed in their holsters, and that's what was really important.

Nikolai gently turned his head, surveying the scene. The sun was still out—and there, back where they came from—he could still see the lake. It was far now, a tiny black puddle in the distance.

They were flying roughly east toward a distant series of structures, like whitewashed cement honeycombs—sterile and alien. Nikolai couldn't even begin to guess what purpose any of the structures might serve. There were dozens of them, and though they looked small from this distance, he could tell they must be massive.

Glinting crafts circled the sky over the structures like scavenger birds. Clouds of tiny coordinated drones surged in complex formations through the airspace over the honeycombs. The area was bustling, though not with any sort of human activity he could see. The forest was cleared for miles around and twisted with neat service roads.

Nikolai was struck with the mental image of a wasp bringing prey back to its hive. To lay eggs in, or tear it apart, or—hell, whatever awful shit wasps got up to. As they drew closer to the structures, it became increasingly difficult for him to smother the terrified claustrophobic panic threatening to overcome his fragile calm.

But then—there! Wispy columns of smoke coming from the north. Though it was difficult to make out from this distance, it appeared that there was another settlement, much different from the cement hive. Some sort of military base surrounded by chainlink fences, dotted with watchtowers. Runways, hangars—the tarmac scattered with sleek, futuristic jets and lined with sturdy buildings.

West of the runways were what appeared to be a series of squat living complexes. Northwest of the runways, but still within the vast area surrounded by the fence, was some sort of tent city. Beyond that, houses. A town!

The installation was *huge*—everything was spread out, with vast plots of grass between the runways, the town, and the various other facilities scattered across the base.

The fence surrounding the base was surrounded by an even broader area of exposed soil. Dozens of tanks lined the fence, facing out in all directions—dark green trucks and other, smaller vehicles zooming along, constantly patrolling the parameters.

American flags fluttered in the wind.

Humans.

Nikolai was flooded with relief so intense he almost sobbed. Still hanging limp, he considered his options.

It would have been easy for Nikolai to simply gum up the rotor blades with some jellied *akro* and then solidify the cloud to completely lock the rotor in place and make the machine crash.

The only problem with that plan was if the tentacles tightened and refused to let Nikolai go, bringing him crashing down with it.

He'd have to be quick about this. There was one tentacle looped around his waist, one around his chest, another around his legs. He stiffened, arms held straight forward, legs and feet pointed straight back. In one quick motion, he pulled himself into a ball, slipping through the loops around his legs and chest so that he was hanging from the one around his waist.

"*Akro!*" he screamed against the wind as he yanked the baton from its holster, sending out his own invisible tentacle of air to loop around the other tentacles surrounding him, gathering them together into a squirming bundle. The tentacle around his waist tightened, trying to crush him, but the enchantments of his uniform managed to hold up against the force of it.

More tentacles snaked out of the craft's pill body, so with a grunt, Nikolai forced the tentacles he'd restrained up into the rotors. As the tentacles and his whip of air became tangled in the blades with a horrible screech of twisting steel, the baton Focal was yanked from his grip. The *akro* weave instantly disappeared as the baton spun away, down to the forest below. Shit!

The body of the craft was torn open—steel and plastic and sophisticated electronics exposed as several of the tentacles were ripped free. The top of the craft burst into flames and a horrible stink of black chemical smoke filled the air.

As they fell, Nikolai was struck by the odd silence of it. Despite the flames trailing the torn body of the machine, there weren't any emergency alarms or anything—no warning for the benefit of human ears. Just the crackling of electricity, and the shrieking of wind as they plummeted.

The remaining tentacles had frozen in place—including the one wrapped tightly around Nikolai's waist. He desperately pulled out his blade Focal, featherweighting himself and the machine with a frantic cry of "*Elefry!*" to slow their fall.

He cast *pyrkagias*, but focused in the flame to the edge of the knife, burning it hot as he could make it—hotter than he'd ever gone, making the blade itself go orange, then blue, then white with heat—and pressed it desperately against the segmented metal holding him in place.

Liquid steel came off in droplets—one splashing onto the back of his hand. He gritted his teeth, biting back a scream as he kept pressing, keep cutting—

TING!

The tentacle snapped off, and Nikolai kicked away from the plummeting craft.

He was about five seconds from hitting the treetops. He'd never used his blade Focal to guide a fall before, so he awkwardly clung two-handed to the hilt, a length of tentacle still firmly and uncomfortably wrapped around his abdomen, and fired off a jet of jellied *akro*.

He crashed through the treetops, branches and leaves slapping him in the face hard enough to leave welts.

He hit a thick carpet of moss with a *thud* and just writhed on the ground for a bit, hissing through his teeth as he clutched the burn on his hand. Trembling, he forced himself to stand, dead leaves crunching underfoot. The back of his hand didn't look good—bloody blisters clustered around the spot where he'd been burned by the molten metal.

The tentacled 'coptor thing—or the *wasp*, as he'd come to think of it—was smoldering nearby. The *hive* where it'd been taking him wasn't far. He was positive that more wasps or drones or other machines he'd yet to come across would soon investigate.

The smaller drones that had been following them burst through the treetops and swarmed around the wreckage. Several of them seemed to notice Nikolai, and soon the entire swarm began to surround him.

Growling, Nikolai released a burst of fire from the tip of his blade, scorching a group of them out of the air. Then another—then two more clusters in quick succession, before the rest of them pulled back to hover up in the treetops, out of harm's way.

SHIT.

His baton Focal wasn't far—he could feel it like an insistent tug. Though he wasn't on any road or path, the underbrush was thin between the tree trunks. Besides the occasional thicket, the ground was mostly covered with moss and dead leaves.

Before he went to chase after his lost Focal, Nikolai super-heated his blade again to cut off the tentacle still wrapped around his waist. Ignoring the pain, he went invisible and *ran*.

Hopefully the drones, unlike the wasp or that other high-altitude craft that must have spotted him before, were limited to the visual spectrum.

No such luck—he ran and ran, ducking under low-hanging branches, twisting through the underbrush, occasionally shoot-ing back quick bursts of fire to take out another cluster of the little drones, though they became increasingly difficult to strike. They were adapting.

Bursting through a thicket, he turned sharply, changing direc-tion in hopes of losing their tail. Though he could still hear their faint humming, like a swarm of oversized insects, he ducked into a tree hollow big enough to crouch down in—hoping that maybe he'd momentarily lost them.

"*Apocrypha!*" he hissed, summoning a bubble of Veil. Though he hadn't tried it before, if he could surround *himself* with Veil and hide away in a pocket dimension until the coast was clear . . .

A sheet of mercurial sky rose around him and his magical pools strained so sharply that he felt as if he'd be torn apart. As quickly as it had appeared, the Veil turned to ashes.

He gaped as the cinders flitted around him, and realized that without a constant flow of energy from a Disc to maintain it, a Veil couldn't exist. The nearest Disc was in Marblewood. The energy must not have been able to pass through a layer of Veil—Marblewood's dome preventing Nikolai from being able to cast the spell.

Desperate, he sealed himself into the tree hollow with a quick wall of *akro*, tweaking it to create the purest form of the spell—hardening a shield of air that was as transparent as the finest crystal instead of frosted and opaque like normal *akro*.

He quickly chilled the glassy air with *kryo*, a spell he'd never really used for much more than cooling his drinks. Water condensed and froze around the edges of the hardened air. Nikolai was still invisible, and if the drones were using heat-vision, he hoped that they were just looking for unusual patches of heat—not unusual patches of *cold*.

The humming increased in volume—it couldn't have been more than thirty seconds—and a single drone zipped by.

He held his breath.

Others followed, hovering more slowly than the first as they carefully examined the area. Nikolai was sure that he'd left an obvious trail of broken branches and footprints in the leaves. But his trail ended here, and though other drones split off in multiple directions, several circled the little clearing, attempting to track him.

One hovered directly in front of the hollow, seeming to stare right at Nikolai. It moved closer—inches away from the chilled *akro* barrier. Frost crept across the surface—fucking *frost*; Nikolai was sure it was going to give him away. Glass in the middle of the forest? Right where he'd disappeared? He could only hope that the drone or whoever was controlling it dismissed it as an oddity, some stray piece of garbage—glass, long ago propped up in the hollow of this tree for whatever reason.

If Nikolai had been visible, he'd have been blue in the face from holding his breath for so long. The drone zipped away and he let out a gasp, sucking in air gratefully.

Nikolai relaxed slightly, though he continued chilling the

akro barrier. He could feel his baton a short ways off. It wasn't moving, so the machines must not have found it yet.

Though he couldn't hear any more of the drones, Nikolai assumed that some must have remained hidden to keep an eye on the spot at which they'd lost his trail. So, with some discomfort, he used a wordless *gia* weave to pull water up through the soil beneath him, turning the dirt into watery mud. Stifling a noise of disgust, he completely covered every inch of himself with the mud. He whipped up some air to dry it onto himself, and used *kryo* again—chilling the layer of dirt to mask the heat of his body. He shivered, feeling absolutely disgusting. He was going to have to constantly reapply and rechill the mud, but hopefully now he would be masked from both the visible *and* infrared spectrum.

He left the hollow and surveyed the clearing, searching for any lingering drones. He began to trek down an animal trail, following the gentle tug of his missing Focal. He saw another drone on the way and pressed himself between two trees as it passed, holding his breath. There must have been hundreds of the things combing through the forest, searching.

The tug of his Focal brought Nikolai to the base of a large tree. The bark was rough, with deep cracks that made for decent handholds. He featherweighted himself for an easier climb, and soon he was up in branches thick with bright red leaves.

Nikolai felt a thrill as he found his missing Focal—the featureless rod was so black it was hard to focus his eyes on it. It seemed to drink in the dappled sunlight. Nikolai yanked it free from between two branches, relief flooding him as it warmed under his grasp, faintly trailing a rainbow smear of light. *Whole again.*

He walked for an indeterminate amount of time. The trees were thick overhead, making it difficult to track the passage of the sun. Thirty minutes, an hour, two—he wasn't sure. His hand throbbed. The icy mud soothed it a little, but Nikolai worried about infection—worried about what kind of bacteria he was smearing into the open wound.

Maintaining the invisibility was exhausting. Back inside the Veil, with the energy of the Disc feeding his weaves, it was complex to cast but easy to maintain. But out here? Most spells required very little energy when focused through a Focal. But invisibility was a class above the rest. It was an active weave, requiring continuous power to continuously manipulate the light around it. Without the Disc, that power came from his body's natural pools of magic.

He couldn't risk being seen by the occasional drone, though. So he ignored the pain and continued in what he hoped was the direction of the settlement. How far had the settlement been when he'd seen it from up high? Five miles? Ten? *Twenty?*

The light began to fade overhead. A primal fear itched at the skin between his shoulder blades—a feeling of being watched—of being hunted like an animal. Quickening his pace, he tried to comfort himself with the knowledge that he was more than capable of reducing an assailant to a smear of bubbling flesh, or plastic, or *whatever*.

He'd never seen wilds such as these—never seen darkness like the growing shadows between the trees. Even in the forests and swamps of his home, the stars burned ever brightly overhead, and one was never left in complete darkness.

Nikolai froze at the center of a small clearing at the distant crunch of snapping branches. Adrenaline and fear brought him to full attention—discomfort forgotten.

Hissing a breath, he featherweighted himself and leaped high up into the air to press his sneakers against a tree trunk about halfway up, then pushed off—propelling himself to the branches of the tree opposite.

Nikolai hid in the foliage of a thickly leafed branch. It was probably just an animal—a bear, deer, or maybe another wolf, like the one he'd seen earlier.

He was tempted to launch himself out from the branches into the open air up above and simply fly as he had over the Noir the rest of the way to the settlement. But Nikolai knew that even invisible, even masked with icy mud, the jets of jellied *akro* would give away his position in an instant.

Just as he was about to climb higher in the branches to peek his head out over the treetops for a better view, a sleek, houndlike machine silently entered the clearing. Nikolai froze and held his breath, fingers digging into the rough bark.

It was painted with camo—brown, green, black—and had the slender body of an oversized greyhound. Instead of a head it had a long horn, like a trumpet. Trumpet-face lowered, delicate, feathered feelers brushed the ground as it went to the center of the clearing. It stopped and raised its trumpet-face—dozens of the hideous little feathers tickling the air.

Sniffing, Nikolai realized with horror. It was tracking his scent.

He tightened his grip on the branch, fighting panic as the machine slowly approached the tree trunk he'd bounced off of to get to his current perch. Hind legs on the ground, it reached its forelegs up the tree like a dog trying to chase after a cat. Its neck extended—straining to reach the spot Nikolai's shoes had pushed off from the trunk, feathers twitching and waving.

It knew he was there. Its olfactory sensors were sensitive enough to have detected where Nikolai had launched up to his current spot. It was no longer a question of *if* it would find him, but *when*.

Nikolai wished that he'd thought to peek above the treetops earlier to gauge his distance from the settlement. Because if it was close, he could just make a run for it—could try to fly the rest of the way.

The synthetic hound backed down from the trunk, turning and scanning the branches with its trumpet. At the base of the trumpet, atop its head, there was a black blister of plastic raised up from the camo shell. Its *eyes*.

Nikolai gently eased his dagger from its sheathe, gripping it tightly while his other hand kept him steady on the branch.

The trumpet-face scanned back and forth, passing over him twice. Finally, it paused, settling on the branches of a tree several trunks away from Nikolai. It hadn't seen him yet—the cloak and the *kryo* must have been working.

The horn folded into its chest, replaced with an iridescent half sphere that looked like a crystal ball carved from obsidian. In an instant, light coalesced at the front of the sphere, so bright Nikolai had to avert his eyes, as bright as the sun, the *real* sun—

It jerked its body to point the sphere right at Nikolai. There was a flash of crackling electric light, and suddenly Nikolai was falling. He tumbled through the air, still clinging to the branch that trailed smoke from where the laser had severed it.

Nikolai pushed off awkwardly, upside down in the air over the hound for a moment that seemed frozen in time—dagger pointed right at it.

He released a torrent of flame down at the hound as he spun through the air, but it anticipated the attack and lunged to the side. It turned, impossibly fast, in a fraction of a fraction of a second, light pulsing at the heart of the sphere—a dull glow this time, not the blinding luminescence of its previous shot—and fired again.

Nikolai couldn't see the laser. It wasn't like in the movies. There was just that crackle again—quieter than the last one—as a wave of heat dissipated across the front of his uniform, a wave of tiny sparks rolling out from the center of impact as the enchantments blocked the shot.

He expected to have been knocked back by the beam of energy, but there wasn't any force to it. It was just light, after all. Nikolai twisted through the air and landed in a run—allowing the featherweight weaves to disappear the moment he touched down, so he could sprint.

That last shot hadn't been as powerful as the first—was it just trying to stun Nikolai?

Baton drawn, he spun it to create a ribbon of *akro* in the air just in time to block another shot at his face. He twisted around the barrier of air and fired off a pulse of flame—but once again, the hound leapt to the side, too fast—and as it lunged away it fired another shot, this time at Nikolai's exposed hand holding the blade.

Nikolai screamed at the pain and dropped the blade, stumbling, clumsily swinging the baton to create another ribbon of air, then another, trying desperately to put up a shield before it could fire another shot. He was afraid to look at his wounded hand, the stink of seared meat turning his stomach as it hit his nose.

Changing direction midrun, Nikolai doubled back around the barriers of hardened air to try another tactic.

"*Elefry!*" he screamed, pointing his baton at the hound. It tensed but hesitated as nothing visible fired from the Focal. Unlike the flames of *pyrkagias*, Nikolai bet that not even those fancy robot eyes could see the magical weaves of the featherweight spell—or any other spell, for that matter.

Not yet aware that it was suddenly a fraction of its normal

weight, it pushed off the ground with its rear legs to lunge, but used too much strength and went spinning absurdly through the air, back over front, limbs flailing as it tried to right itself.

If Nikolai hadn't been in so much pain he would have laughed at the sight—instead he pivoted to snap out a tentacle of *akro* to wrap around its body and used its own momentum to swing it around and smash it into a tree trunk.

Camo plating crunched against the tree, black liquid pouring through the cracks. Machine parts groaned and clicked, whirring pitifully as it flailed and fired off another laser pulse. The blast singed the hair on the side of Nikolai's head as it missed, barely.

"Fuck you!" Nikolai screamed, swinging it around again to slam it into another tree. "*FUCK YOU!*"

Shattered, body and limbs twisted, it lay on the ground after Nikolai had smashed it to his satisfaction, cracked laser sphere and trumpet face both half out as its sniffing feathers writhed.

Nikolai stalked over to it, snatching up the dagger as he crossed the clearing. The energy burn hadn't been as bad as the one from the molten metal—though their combined pain on the same hand was almost too much to bear. The laser wound had merely blistered, the intent apparently to disarm and subdue, not to maim.

Like Nikolai gave a shit.

"*Pyrkagias*," he hissed, bathing the creature's broken body with flames. It struggled briefly as he melted it down, but quickly went still. Nikolai watched it die with grim satisfaction, holding his breath as the toxic fumes rolled away in clouds of black smoke.

"Identify yourself," came a voice from behind.

Nikolai spun around with a shout—baton and dagger held at the ready as he prepared himself for another fight.

At the edge of the clearing, something like a feline shimmered into existence. It had been watching, invisible. Hanging back in the shadows behind it were two more of the hounds, their laser spheres pulsing sluggishly with light, at the ready.

The triumph he'd felt at defeating the first quickly turned to despair.

"Where are you from, child?" the feline said. It spoke with crisp intelligence, its tone oddly melodious. "You wield unfamiliar technology beyond the capabilities of terrestrial humans. Is the treaty broken? Have the colonists decided to interfere?"

Unlike the hounds (which were unmistakably mechanical) the speaking machine looked almost organic. It didn't have any visible sensors, its "skin" apparently seamless—and though its voice rang clear, Nikolai couldn't tell where the words were coming from.

Nikolai gasped as it began to transform, shrinking back with horror. The surface of its body rippled and fluttered, seemingly composed of miniscule panels, each the size of a mosquito's wing, that moved and changed their shape like a billion pieces of metallic origami. The feline unfolded—beautiful and disconcerting, growing into a towering humanoid that had to be at least eight feet tall. Slender, androgynous, rippling with synthetic muscle.

With a moan of terror, Nikolai featherweighted himself and took flight, desperately shooting into the air with a long jet of jellied *akro*. No point in being stealthy now.

Nikolai trailed a weaving ribbon of *akro* from the dagger as he propelled himself with the baton, hoping to block any laser pulses they fired after him.

It was dusk above the tree line. The clouds had cleared, the first spattering of stars dotting the gray-blue sky. And there—the settlement! It was close, *so* close! Exposed or not, Nikolai would be there in moments if he could just—

He glanced back and saw that the humanoid had transformed into something like a gigantic centipede, with dozens of dexterous too-human arms gripping the branches as it scuttled up to the treetop with hideous speed.

The centipede launched itself into the air with enough force to clear half the distance between them despite Nikolai's head start, and transformed into a billowing, paper-thin shape that caught the wind like a sail. Fully airborne, it unfolded into dozens upon dozens of massive silver wings, flapping and taking flight with incredible synchronization—fluid, but too graceful and perfect to be natural, too mathematical.

"Jesus shit-eating CHRIST!" Nikolai screamed as the immense *being* cut through the air after him like some sort of angelic beast of Revelations.

Crackles erupted from below as more of the hounds tried to shoot him down, but Nikolai flew with his knees and hands tucked in, his head hunched over—a constant barrage of shots striking harmlessly across his uniform, or lightly singeing his hair and sneakers. Still set to stun—not to kill.

They wanted him. They'd never seen anything like Nikolai, he was sure of it—no other Edge Guard who'd ever been out in the field had ever been *stupid* or inexperienced enough to be seen. Until now—and now they wanted to take him away, to drag him back to their synthetic hive and vivisect him, experiment on him—

The base was close—the edge of the forest just ahead, the vast fields of torn-up soil surrounding the chain-link fence so close that he could see the little figures sitting in the watch towers, see the fires scattered among the neat city of canvas tents, see the headlights shining from the patrolling trucks!

"COME, HUMAN," the monster sang over the wind,

"THERE'S NO ESCAPE FOR YOU—THE SANCTUARY YOU SEEK IS FALSE—NO OTHERS EXIST WHO CAN KEEP YOU FROM OUR REACH. COME!"

The voice was close, and Nikolai risked glancing back to see that it was RIGHT FUCKING THERE—multitudes of wings slowly closing around him, silver face serene, smiling—long slender arms forming to reach out for him—

With another scream, Nikolai released featherweight enchantments and allowed gravity and momentum to yank him down just as the hands came together. As he fell he fired two columns of *akro* up at the thing, using the last of his strength to propel himself down, struggling to stay out of the monster's reach—

At the last possible moment he featherweighted himself once more, twisting midair too late to put any jellied *akro* between himself and the ground. His uniform released a powerful cushion of air just before impact—a failsafe for Edge Guards knocked unconscious while in flight—but still, even with that he landed *hard* on the torn-up soil, the wind knocked out of him as he crashed a dozen or so feet away from the edge of the forest.

He wheezed for breath, gasping and coughing. Despite his terror, despite the frantic voice in Nikolai's head screaming *Run! Get up, you stupid bastard, run, run, fucking RUN*—he couldn't move.

Whimpering, he tried to sit up.

"*Don't move*," came the voice—but it was quieter now. Gentle, but urgent. Nikolai snapped open his eyes to find the mercurial being standing at the edge of the forest, once again in its humanoid form. It hadn't followed him onto the soil.

"Don't . . . move," it said again, pointing at Nikolai's hand with a long, glimmering finger.

Slowly, carefully, Nikolai looked at the indicated spot.

A pressure plate of some sort. A disc of metal, no bigger than his palm.

A landmine.

The area of torn soil—it was a *minefield*.

He'd come this close to touching it. Slowly, carefully, he pulled his hand away.

Nikolai was enveloped in blinding light. He cringed, squinting.

"There! Do you see him? A boy!" came a distant voice. He could hear thumping air, and some sort of craft began to hover over from beyond the fence—though Nikolai could only make out a blurry outline.

The light was a spotlight from the watchtower. Cautiously sliding the baton and dagger into their sheaths as the humans (oh please, let them be humans, oh *please*) approached, Nikolai glanced back at the trees to find that the shape-shifting humanoid was gone. It must have retreated into the darkness at the approach of the hovercraft. But why would something like that run from anything? And why hadn't it come out onto the soil to claim him?

The craft hovered above, wind whipping the soil into clouds. He glanced at the landmine nervously.

"*Freeze!*" boomed a woman's voice from above. "*Hands on your head!*"

She repeated it in Spanish and Nikolai complied, glad that he had already put away the Focals.

"Scanning!" another voice shouted, a man this time. There was a humming flash of light from above—strangely warm, and brighter than the floodlight. "He's pure human, confirmed! No explosives or tech detected!"

"Run him through the sniffer!" the other woman shouted, and there came a strange hiss and the pull of suction as air sucked up into something above him.

"All clear!" the man said. "No bios or hazmats detected!"

"Are you injured?" the woman called down over the thumping of the aircraft. Nikolai shook his head, and they lowered a segmented ladder. Gingerly he began to climb, dry mud coming off of him in flakes.

A sunburned man with bright orange hair pulled him aboard over the side of the hovercraft—a small, disc-shaped vehicle barely big enough for three people. The pilot, a darkly tanned woman with her head shaved clean, stared at him with disbelief.

The man was shaking a tiny metal canister.

"Sorry about this," he said, raised the canister to Nikolai's face, and squeezed out a small puff of mist.

Darkness closed in around Nikolai's vision, and he collapsed into the man's arms.

VIII.

TO THE BITTER END

Blue let out an excited shriek and practically tackled Jem with an embrace when they told her that Jem had resigned, and that they'd all be leaving that night for Base Machado.

"But what about your mods?" she asked, calming herself. "What if . . ."

"They wouldn't fucking dare try to pull that shit with me," Jem said, forcing herself to smile. "I'm an asset. And we'll be bringing them the doctor's cure, so they owe me." She thought about Eva's nukes, now broken and buried. "More than they know."

"What about Eva? Aren't we going to say goodbye?"

Jem shook her head, feeling as if she was going to vomit. "She's . . . angry at me. She doesn't need me anymore. Not really, now that she's finished with her project. But she didn't want me to go. Some . . . unpleasant things were said. By both of us." She raised a hand at Blue's look of concern, shaking her head. "It'll be okay. She'll write us via courier once we get to the base. She's family, and . . ."

Jem trailed off. Not sure what else to say.

Smart cement controller in hand, Jem led the way when they finally departed, earth disappearing before them in bubbling foam, then slowly sealing behind them as the ceramic reversal charges sent out their pulses on timers.

Alan, the Runner who had first brought Blue and the doctor to Philadelphia, was ecstatic to see them again and relieved to have Jem along for the journey. The more Runners, the better.

The journey was cold, wet, and blessedly uneventful. They moved at an aggressive but cautious pace, hot and sweaty under their thick stealth cloaks despite the brisk autumn chill.

Jem hated the wilderness. She was a city girl through and through. Dry rooms. Air-conditioning. Light and noise and reliable, predicable cement under her feet. Everything was always wet out here—rotting leaves and spongy moss dripping with miserable rain that continued through the entirety of their trek. Good for helping to keep them hidden from patrolling Synth drones. But Jem would've killed to sleep in her warm bed back in HQ rather than spend another day in the basement ruins or abandoned cellars where they would rest as they waited for the cover of night.

On their seventh night, they came upon a pristine lake surrounded by lush, red-leafed forests.

"We'll stop there for the day," Alan said, pointing to a row of sagging lake houses in various states of disrepair further down the shore. "It'll be light in a couple hours. Not enough time for us to get to the base. But tomorrow night, we'll finally arrive."

He moved to continue through the shadows of the forest

along the beach. For the first time since they'd departed, it wasn't raining. The pitch darkness of night was alleviated by moonlight filtering through patchy clouds.

"Wait," Dr. Blackwell said, stopping him. "Do you hear that?"

There, closer to the water. A tired, desperate honking. The flapping of wings struggling in vain to pull free.

"Just an animal," Alan said. "Come on."

"Hold on," Dr. Blackwell said, squinting in the dark.

The clouds parted overhead and moonlight shone down to reveal the source of the noise. A swan, caught in a tangle of old barbwire fencing at the edge of the water. The doctor reached into her rucksack and pulled out a pair of cutters.

"We don't have time for this," Jem growled, scanning the sky for the telltale glint of aerial surveillance.

"I'll only be a second," she said, ignoring Jem and Alan's protests as she nimbly slid down the embankment. The swan turned its beak to her with a suspicious hiss. White feathers were stained red with blood from where the barbwire dug into its underbelly. "Well, hello there. Aren't you a pretty little thing?"

She reached out a gentle hand and it snapped at her. She didn't flinch, and when she reached out again, it allowed her to cut, too weak or too pained to fight back anymore.

"Annnd that should do it!" she said, snapping through the final wire. The swan pulled free, flapping frantically as it took flight right into the doctor's face. With a muffled cry, Dr. Blackwell fell over, catching her hand and shoulder in the barbwire tangle as the bloody swan fled.

She stifled her scream into a strangled gurgle, face bright purple as she pounded her leg with a clenched fist. Jem swore and scrambled down to rescue her, carefully pulling her free from the rusted barbs.

"Stupid ungrateful piece of shit *bird*," the doctor hissed, tears of pain beading at the corners of her eyes as she checked over her wounds. Her hand was shredded—her shoulder sluggishly bleeding from a deep, messy cut that stained her cloak. "No good deed goes unpunished, I suppose."

Alan took Dr. Blackwell's rucksack and supplies. But when he reached to take the little steel case of the cure kit hanging from a thick strap across her shoulder, she shook her head. "Jem, I would feel better if you carried this. No offense, Alan."

The wilderness Runner scratched his beard and smiled. "None taken."

They made camp for the night in the basement of a dilapidated lake house. The musty air and the stink of mildew made Jem feel claustrophobic. But somehow, Blue didn't seem to mind.

As Alan treated Dr. Blackwell's wounds, Blue inundated Jem with one question about the Base after another. Jem tried to match her exuberance, but each night the weight of the lies had grown heavier and heavier upon Jem's conscience, until finally it was too much to bear.

"What's wrong, babe?" Blue said, finally seeing past her own excitement to notice Jem's distress.

Jem looked over at Dr. Blackwell chatting amicably with Alan across the room as he bandaged her up, remembering her warning. But no. If Blue was going to trust Jem, Jem needed to be honest with her. Needed to tell her what she'd done

Jem gripped Blue's tattooed hand, trembling.

"Blue," she finally said, her entire being screaming for her not to say the words. "I need to tell you something."

Blue listened in stunned silence as Jem told her what had really happened with Eva. She spoke quietly, so Alan and the doctor wouldn't overhear—reciting the story with cold, clinical calm. It was strange talking about what had happened with Eva. It didn't feel real. It felt like a nightmare, or the story of something terrible that had happened to a friend, but not her.

When Jem finished, Blue stared at her. Disbelieving.

She yanked her hand away from Jem's.

"Traitor," she said, just above a whisper, the word full of malice. Then again, louder. "You fucking traitor!"

Jem recoiled from her, feeling Blue's words like a body blow.

Dr. Blackwell and Alan looked over with alarm—the doctor's startled expression becoming miserable certainty as she realized that Jem had failed to heed her advice to keep Blue in the dark.

Jem and Blue were standing now, Blue backing away as Jem followed her, hands out, placating as she tried to calm the furious woman.

"Stay away from me!" Blue said, shoving Jem.

"Everyone just needs to calm down," Alan said, moving to stand between them. "What's going on here?"

"This *traitor* ruined everything," Blue snarled, moving around Alan to jab a finger in Jem's direction. "That's what!"

Jem looked at her, incredulous. "Are you serious with this shit right now?"

"Commander Colladi found a way to conscript what's left of the human population—as was her *right*—by using the Synth VR networks to upload military training directly into their brains. But Jem didn't like the plan, so she took her out!"

"Conscript? She was going to torture them. Brainwash them."

"It's called boot camp, you stupid asshole! Every single surviving human would have been turned into a trained soldier in, what, minutes? We might've actually had a chance to fix this shit, Jem! But no. Only you get to fight. Not us. Everyone else gets to die as slaves."

Jem couldn't believe she even had to debate this. "She was going to nuke Base Machado!"

"She was going to nuke Armitage and take control of his network! That's what you literally just told me. The Synth have killed billions of us, Jem! What's ten thousand more? A hundred thousand? You don't think those people would've been happy to die if they knew it was going to kill an Overmind and put its entire army and infrastructure under Resistance command?"

"Oh my god . . ." Jem groaned, rubbing her hands down her face in frustration as she struggled not to lose her cool. "Blue. I don't think you quite understand what you're talking about. The plan wouldn't have worked. Even Eva knew it wouldn't work. Either the Synth would have killed us, or the colonists would have killed *both* of us."

"You don't know that! Maybe we could've found a way. And even if we didn't, at least we would have died fighting! With dignity!"

Jem rolled her eyes. "Oh, spare me the 'glory of dying in battle' bullshit. You don't know anything about being a soldier."

"I'm not a soldier?" Blue spat. She pointed at her swollen stomach. "You think I even want this kid? You think I wanted to crawl through shit and mud and gunfire with a baby growing inside of me? No! I wanted to fight, Jem. We all want to fight! But this miserable, disgusting pregnancy shit is how they asked me to contribute. I *wish* I could have spent a virtual day in hell and then woken up a 'real' soldier like you, instead of this. I've sacrificed my health, my body, my freedom! How fucking dare you, Jem. How fucking dare you make this all have been for nothing!"

"Sacrifice? What the fuck do you know about sacrifice?" Jem wanted to hit her. Wanted to hit her so badly. Her entire body trembled with it. "I loved Eva, Blue. I fucking loved her. But I did what I had to do. I sacrificed *everything* for you people! So don't you dare call me a traitor. Don't you *dare*!"

Jem slung her duffel bag full of supplies and weaponry over her shoulders, moving to climb the dusty planks of the stairwell.

"Wait, where are you going?" Blue said, anger turning to fear.

"Maybe I'm just getting some air," Jem said, spiteful. "Or maybe I'm never coming back. Maybe this was all one big, stupid mistake. Why don't you take some time to decide which you'd prefer?"

"Well fine!" Blue called after her, when it became clear that Jem was serious. "Just run away! Since it's apparently all you're fucking good at!"

Jem fled out onto the pebble beach, gulping down the cold air gratefully as it rolled over her from the inky black waters.

She pulled her stealth cloak tight, clinging to the shadows as she stalked through the trees. The area was fully mapped out in her mind, so she had no fear of getting lost. But she needed to get away from the others. Needed to be alone. After a while she stopped and sat in the mud, leaning back against the rotting bark of an old tree stump.

She closed her eyes, calling up the immersive memory of the first night she'd been reunited with Eva. They were in Eva's quarters again, a half-empty whiskey bottle hanging loose in Jem's hand as Eva rested her head on Jem's lap.

"Well," Jem said, taking a swig of the whiskey, tasting the burn and feeling the fuzzy warmth of the memory of intoxication. "That could have gone better."

Jem willed the mindless virtual personality to automation, based on Jem's collected memories of how Eva spoke and behaved.

The virtual Eva pursed her lips, sapphire eyes sparkling with amusement.

"Ah, *ma chère*," she said. "You knew Doc was right, but you went ahead and ran your mouth anyway. Too good for your own good. You never did like taking other people's advice."

"Serves me right," Jem said, stroking Eva's hair. "I really fucked things up back there. And now . . ."

"Chin up, little swan. Blue's crazy about you. It was just a lot to take in. So quit the temper tantrum, go back to her, and talk things out like an adult. Okay?"

"I miss you," Jem said, her chest so tight it was hard to breathe.

Eva reached up to caress Jem's cheek. "Miss me? But I'm right here."

A wave of disgusted self-loathing washed over Jem and she dismissed the virtual Eva. Alone again. Like always.

Eva's warmly lit quarters disappeared in a smear of neon green, replaced by the darkness of the wood. Jem stood, reorienting herself to head back to the hideout. She realized that she still had the little steel-cased cure kit slung over her shoulder underneath the duffel strap, and hoped that her leaving with it hadn't scared Dr. Blackwell too badly.

Gunfire tore through the silence.

Jem went cold.

"No . . ."

Jem ran. Cloak trailing behind her, hands deftly reaching into the duffel to pull out her shotgun and load the chambers with incendiary ammunition as she leaped over roots and ducked under branches.

She'd gone so far, why had she gone so far?

The gunfire had ceased following the brief explosion of noise. Jem burst out onto the shore, fearing the worst as she saw that the door had been smashed inward, the rotten porch scored with long mechanical gouging.

She rushed past the broken door, down the stairs, too desperate and frantic to scream when she found Alan nearly cut in half with laser fire and Dr. Blackwell dead from what appeared to be a self-inflicted gunshot wound to the head.

No sign of Blue. No time to mourn for the others. Not yet.

She searched the shore, frantic as she looked for a trail.

There. Drag marks in the dirt. Intermittent streaks of grease and oil.

Jem had never run so hard or so fast.

It began to rain. Big, icy droplets pelting down hard enough to sting, slowly washing away the trail. If Jem didn't catch up soon, she'd never find Blue. Never see her again. Their final words to one another angry and cruel.

So she prayed. For the first time since Jem was a child, she prayed. Begging. Pleading. "Please, God, *please* let me find her, God, *please*!"

And there they were. Figures veiled in rain and shadow as they trudged across a grassy clearing alongside a steep ravine. Jem couldn't see, couldn't make out how many there were, couldn't tell if they had Blue or—

Lightning cracked through the air, illuminating everything in a flash of pale light. Just for an instant. Just long enough for Jem to have seen them all and noted their locations in her mods— the visual overlay marking where they were and their branching estimated trajectories.

There were four Synth trackers—houndlike robots with sniffers and laser spheres for heads. Marching ahead of them were two tactical field droids dragging a broken droid riddled with gunfire behind them.

Leading the group was a Synth trooper—a bipedal humanoid android war-machine covered in thick white armor that gleamed slickly in the rain. It stood over seven feet tall, its arms and chest heavy with artillery, missiles, lasers, and an electric blade powerful enough to slice through armored tanks folded up into an arm.

Slung over its sloping shoulder was Blue. Unconscious? Dead?

No.

Jem tossed two multispectrum shielding smoke grenades in quick succession, blanketing the clearing before the Synth could mark her location and track her. Two shock grenades, one amid the houndlike trackers, another exploding just beyond the trooper—close enough to temporarily disorient the Synth with circuit-scrambling shockwaves, but far enough not to hurt Blue.

She darted through the smoke, blind but for her augmented reality overlay, weaving in a chaotic patternless zigzag as she closed in on the surviving tracker hound and fired her shotgun into its back, nearly cutting the Synth in half as hot shrapnel from the incendiary ammo sizzled through the armored circuitry.

Laser fire and high caliber shells honed in on the sound of her shotgun blast, as she'd anticipated. She rushed forward, head low, barely feeling the searing pain as the lasers sliced by her. Close enough to burn—close enough to cut.

She closed in on the first tactical droid and tore its chest open with a fiery blast, but when she spun to fire on the other it grabbed onto the barrel and pushed it aside, pressing its laser sphere against her chest.

Jem twisted, just barely able to push against the powerful strength of the robotic arm enough to send the laser slicing through the flesh along her ribs instead of piercing through her heart. Biting back a scream, Jem whipped out her pistol with her free hand and pressed it up under the droid's chin—firing the remainder of her clip into its armored skull.

She dropped the pistol and yanked the shotgun from the dying droid's grasp as bullets and high-powered laser fire cut through the smoke in a wide swath, nearly slicing Jem in half. But she wasn't afraid. Pain didn't matter. Death didn't matter. Nothing mattered—nothing but Blue and her child.

The smoke had begun to clear as Jem closed in on the hulking figure of the Synth trooper. In the quickly thinning veil, she could see Blue lying on the crest beyond, where the trooper had placed her so it could kill Jem without risk to the prisoner.

She ran straight for the final Synth, and for a moment the trooper hesitated, seemingly taken aback at how brazen this little human was—how suicidally foolhardy. As she came within striking distance, one of its arms unfolded into a long glassy blade with a bright blue laser edge.

It swung at her, impossible to dodge, Jem's mind calculating a million possible trajectories of attack she could take to get beyond the killing arc—settling for a path that allowed the blade to sear through her chest in a bloody line deep enough to expose fat and muscle under Jem's filthy cloak as she twisted around and pressed a bundle of plastic explosive underneath the joint where its arm met its body.

It sliced again through her back as she darted away, a wound so deep she thought it might have gone through her spine, but no, she wasn't dead yet, wasn't dead—

It raised its other arm to finish Jem off with a burst of high-caliber bullets, and Jem triggered the explosive.

She felt her feet leave the ground as she was flung away, tumbling like a rag doll across the dirt and leaves until she rolled to a stop.

Silence.

Jem couldn't hear, couldn't see. Blood coursed sluggishly down her chest, down her back, but it didn't matter, nothing mattered unless—

A gust of wind rose shrieking from the ravine to clear away the rest of the smoke. The Synth trooper lay on its side, half of its body burned away, molten. Sparks and fire flared in the dark from its twitching body as it lay dying.

The rain ceased, clouds breaking apart overhead to reveal an immense, slender figure shining silver in the moonlight as it towered beside Blue's prone body.

Armitage's husk. The rarest, most advanced Synth form. The primary body and physical representation of an Overmind.

It watched her, impassive, as Jem struggled to lift herself from the blackened mud. She clutched the open flesh across her chest, falling twice before she was finally able to stand.

"Give . . . her . . . back . . ." Jem wheezed, unable to hear her own voice over the ringing in her ears. She limped, weaving unsteady as she made her way over to the shotgun on the ground, so close. She stopped. Sank to her knees. Reloaded the gun with fumbling, bloody fingers. The last of her ammo.

Jem tried to stand, but found that she couldn't.

She raised the shotgun, barely able to hold it steady as she aimed.

Still, the mercurial figure remained motionless. Watching her.

It was hopeless. Even uninjured, and fully armed, Jem could never destroy a husk.

So be it. One final *fuck you* before they took her to hell.

Jem put her finger on the trigger.

The shattered remnants of the Synth trooper let out a horrible grinding shriek as it reactivated and pushed itself onto its side to raise its remaining arm. In the instant before it fired on her, Jem instinctively swung the barrel away from the husk and shot the exposed circuitry of the trooper's skull.

The arm jerked, the missile meant to obliterate her flying wide, twisting through the air in a chaotic spiral before exploding on the ground beyond her. Jem was flung into the air once again, numbly accepting as she flew over the edge of the steep ravine. Her eyes met with the mirrored gaze of the Armitage husk one final time, and then she plummeted into the darkness below.

———

Jem's eyes fluttered open. Bright morning sun piercing through her skull.

She was barely able to breathe through the searing pain of her wounds. Somehow, though—unbelievably—she wasn't dead. Jem would have screamed when she realized that she was hanging from a cluster of thick branches halfway down the cliff if she'd had the energy for it. As it was, she merely spun silently from her flimsy support. Blinking slowly. Trying to remember how she'd gotten here.

The heavy strap of Dr. Blackwell's cure kit dug sharply into her wounds as it supported her weight. It had caught onto the stunted, gnarled branches after she'd fallen, saving Jem from being dashed across the jagged rocks below.

Her wounds were crusted and raw, but the bleeding had slowed to a trickle. Jem was alive. Just barely. With immense effort, she lowered herself down, root by root, stone by stone, to the pebbled shore below.

Somehow she managed to crawl back to the hideout. Each

wooden step down into the basement was a final trial of agony as she struggled against the velvety lure of sleep. A slumber Jem wouldn't wake up from if she didn't treat her wounds.

Dr. Blackwell's corpse seemed to stare at Jem as she weakly dug through the doctor's emergency medical supplies. Averting her gaze, Jem applied flesh foam along the long, deep slices across her back and chest. Pint bags swelled up with synthetic blood for transfusion and hydrating nutritional fluid after she broke the tabs within the plastic and pressed them against her filthy arms. They latched on like leeches, slender needle tendrils passing through her skin to find a vein.

Darkness took her.

Jem wasn't sure how much time had passed when she finally woke. Enough time for the stink of human rot to have become unbearable, though not long enough for the bodies to have visibly decomposed. She yanked the empty bags from her skin and tossed them aside—her throat mummy-dry. Jem dug frantically through the rations, gulping down four boxes of water before she finally lay back down, panting from exertion.

The sun was setting when Jem emerged, the air sharp with a bitter chill. She left her friends to rot as she ventured out into the forest, seeing no point in burying them. What did it matter, anyway? Dead was dead.

She still couldn't cry. Not for Blue. Not for Blue's baby, who she'd never get to meet now. Not for Dr. Blackwell, who saw her *miracle* dragged away by monsters, right before killing herself to avoid the same fate.

Jem wondered if the doctor had still believed in miracles in those final horrible moments. In God, or fate. Wondered what she would have of thought of the cure kit saving Jem's life.

But no. Jem being saved by the strap of the cure kit was no

miracle. Neither an act of God, nor the devil. It just *was*. Just like everything else.

Bringing the cure to the base was all Jem had left. All that kept her from going back to where she'd lost Blue to try and find her gun, so she could finally bring an end to this miserable life.

Jem didn't believe in heaven. But as she limped off into the shadows of the woods, more truly and deeply alone then she'd ever been in her life, she began to realize that she *did* believe in hell.

And maybe she was already in it.

IX.

A COMPLETELY NORMAL HUMAN

Nikolai woke with a violent sneeze, smelling salts snapping him awake like a punch in the nose.

A man in military fatigues leaned back, placing the cracked capsule on the table.

Nikolai broke into a toothy grin, not quite biting back a peal of excited laughter before he could compose himself. He was in the presence of a real. Live. *Human!*

They were in a small room, polished tile floor smelling faintly of bleach. The walls were padded with strange material like densely woven wire. Opposite of where he sat was a heavy door with a small mesh-reinforced window.

Nikolai was slumped over on an uncomfortable metal chair that was bolted to the floor, his wrists and ankles bound to it with some sort of plastic bindings.

His head was throbbing, his throat scratchy. His initial moments of bewildered excitement diminishing, Nikolai remembered being taken by the humans in the hovercraft. Then what? Did they drug him?

With a shiver, Nikolai realized that he was naked but for a paper gown. His hand was bandaged, and though there were bruises across his arms and legs, his minor scrapes and cuts had been cleaned and covered with smears of something like dried latex. Besides the headache and the scratchy throat, he didn't feel any pain. The burns on his hand felt numb.

They'd taken his uniform. His Focals, too. Heart thumping in his chest, Nikolai began to panic before closing his eyes to calm himself.

He could feel the Focals—could sense exactly how far away and in what direction they were at all times. The baton couldn't be more than a quarter-mile away. The knife was further, though it was slowly coming closer. Somebody was carrying it—bringing it to them.

"Good morning," the human said pleasantly. He was reading something on a small sheet of plastic the size of a playing card, and didn't look up from it as he talked. Through the back of it, Nikolai could see blurred data scrolling down the sheet, distorted to hide it from his view.

The man swiped at it casually, looking up with a polite smile. "Do you know where you are?"

Nikolai shook his head. "Sort of. Not really. How long have I been . . . ?"

"We patched you up. It's zero-eight. What better way to start the day than with an interrogation?" he said lightly. "I'm Command Chief Master Sergeant Maalouf. Colonel Machado will be joining us shortly. We'll be asking you some questions.

Answer with complete honesty in short, concise sentences."

Nikolai look down at the zip ties, his wrists firmly bound to the armrests.

"Sorry about that," he said, noting Nikolai's look. "General procedure for refugee intake. Though you obviously aren't a Mod, there are some . . . unusual aspects to your arrival in need of clarification."

"A Mod?" Nikolai asked, immediately wishing he hadn't said it as the human gave him a perplexed look.

They didn't know that he was a mage, probably. Or that a mage was even a real thing. Secrecy from the humans had been ruthlessly enforced by the Edge Guard. All the way to the end, so far as he knew.

Hopefully that wasn't also revisionist bullshit, and the humans still didn't know about magi. If they didn't, he could easily break out of there—especially if he could get his Focals back.

Nikolai just had to convince these people that he was a completely normal human. A normal human . . . who had no idea had happened for the past hundred years. Who came falling from the sky, a horde of machines nipping at his heels.

Yep. Shouldn't be a problem.

"*Mod*ified. Cybernetically enhanced," the man said evenly. "Now. Have you ever been truth-scanned before?"

Nikolai shook his head, though he tried to at least pretend to know what the man was talking about this time. Sounded like some sort of high-tech lie-detection shit.

The human pulled a small baggie from a pocket and removed a pair of thin, silver pads.

"Don't move," he said, and Nikolai nervously resisted the urge to pull away as he stuck them to his temples. He looked back down at the little screen in his hand, nodding. "In case you aren't familiar with how a truth-scanner works, it's simple. We scan your brain.

"If you lie, we know. If you tell the truth, we know. It's impossible to trick—not even a sociopath can beat it. Understand?"

Nikolai nodded, feeling a sheen of sweat appear on his forehead. This was going to be complicated.

"Good. Now, a few questions for calibration. What is your name?"

"Nikolai," he said. The little panel in his hand flashed green.

He raised a brow. "Surname?"

"Strauss." Green again.

"Good. Now repeat after me: *My name is John Smith*."

"Um, okay. My name is John Smith."

The little sheet of plastic emitted a beep, flashing red.

"Good. Now . . ."

They went on like that for a short while. He asked Nikolai simple, irrefutable facts, like how many doors were in the room, how many fingers he was holding up, etc. Then he asked Nikolai to answer again—incorrectly this time. Green when he told the truth. Red when he lied. Yellow for uncertain.

His dagger, though ceasing to move for a short while, once again began to draw near. Nikolai watched the door expectantly as it stopped just outside.

The door swung open and an imposing man entered the room, followed by two young soldiers carrying assault rifles. The weapons were disappointingly familiar. Nikolai guessed that not everyone used fancy laser guns. Maybe bullets were cheaper.

His eyes hungrily went down to the man's belt, where the man was wearing Nikolai's knife. He felt a swell of anger, but pushed it down, trying not to let it show.

Chief Maalouf stood and snapped out a neat salute.

"Sir! Preparations are complete. Everything is in working order."

"At ease," the man rumbled, pulling up the chair opposite Nikolai and taking a seat. He was an older man, with steely hair and a tan, sun-weathered face. He looked Nikolai over with sharply intelligent eyes, frowning.

"Sir," Chief Maalouf said, hesitant. "I'd be happy to facilitate this interrogation. I'm sure you have more pressing matters to attend than refugee intake."

The man didn't respond—he just stared at Nikolai—eyes burning into him.

Nikolai glanced at Maalouf, then back at the man.

"Um—"

"You'll speak only when spoken to," the man said. He didn't raise his voice, but didn't need to—his tone was the very definition of command. "Now. What's your name?"

"Nikolai. Strauss."

"And do you know who I am, son?"

"Colonel Machado?" Nikolai guessed, remembering what Maalouf had told him.

The plastic flashed yellow for *Uncertainty*, chirping instead of beeping.

"That's right," Machado said. "And do you know where you are?"

Not a particularly specific question. Though he didn't know the name of the settlement—or military base—he had a reasonably clear idea of its location in relation to the lake surrounding the hidden Marblewood Veil. He knew that Marblewood was somewhere in what was once (or what still was?) northeast Pennsylvania.

"Yes," he said, confident.

The sheet of plastic flashed green.

"Possibly a misleading answer, sir," Maalouf said. "You'll have to be more specific with your questions."

"In that case," the man said calmly, "why don't you tell me what you know about where you are, Nikolai, and why you've come here. Specifically."

"Only that there are people here," Nikolai said. "I don't know any more than that. That's why I came, to get away from . . ."

What was his angle?

". . . those *things*," Nikolai said abstractly.

Green.

"Those . . . things?"

"The . . . machines?"

"Is that a question?"

"The machines," Nikolai said again more firmly.

Green.

The colonel leaned forward, elbows on the table, fingers steepled over his mouth as he stared Nikolai down.

Nikolai shifted, uncomfortable, and glanced down at his knife hanging at Machado's side.

"Are you a human, Nikolai?" he asked, barely above a whisper.

Fuck. FUCK.

He *wasn't* a human—but if he said so they'd assume that he was some sort of machine creation. Or crazy. Or—or—fuck, who knows!

So Nikolai just smirked.

"No—I'm a robot," he said, slathering his words with exaggerated sarcasm.

BEEP. Red.

Machado stared at Nikolai for a few long moments. He leaned back, thumb tapping the pommel of the Focal. Tap, tap, *tap*. Nik could feel it—goose bumps rising on the back of his neck at the odd sensation.

"Mr. Strauss," Colonel Machado said, reasonably, "it's important you understand that how well this interview goes will determine whether or not I personally put a bullet between your eyes. So why don't we try that again. Are you natural born, or were you created by the Synthetics?"

"*Natural born*," Nikolai said quickly, relieved at the choice of words.

Green.

"Have you been subject to any form of Synthetic conditioning? Brainwashing?"

"No, sir."

Green.

The colonel turned to the chief. "Any chance he's been somehow *altered* to beat that scanner of yours?"

Chief Maalouf shook his head.

"No way. He doesn't have any implants, any links for interface. So far as we know, it's impossible to alter the brain without an interface. There's cloning and conditioning, but no amount of conditioning can train someone to beat a truth-scanner. He's human, sir."

"Hmm," he said, seemingly unconvinced. "Are you working for or have you ever reported to the Synthetics, or informed on any fellow humans to them?"

"No. Never."

Green.

He stared at Nikolai, thoughtful, like he was a puzzle to be solved. Finally he drew the blade and lay it on the table. The wicked edge glistened like the shell of an insect in the electric light.

"I've never seen a knife like this," he said. "Beautifully made—one seamless piece of metal. And that stick of yours. That rod. It's not like any material I've ever seen. A few of my men were worried that it might be radioactive, but it seems clean. Your clothing is strange. Not machine made, but . . ."

He trailed off, staring at Nikolai expectantly.

"The baton," Nikolai said carefully, "and the knife—they're sort of religious artifacts. For coming of age. They signify my vocation, and artistic calling. Called *Focals.*"

Green. Maalouf and Machado stared at him blankly.

"I'm from a little town called Marblewood. We call it a Veil. We don't use technology. We're not far from here—though I'm not exactly sure how far. In the wilderness, near a lake." He looked at them, the wonder in his eyes only partially faked. "All my life, I thought that everyone in the outside world was dead. That nothing existed beyond the Veil. Monsters, maybe. But definitely not people."

All green. They were staring at him, wide eyed.

Nikolai smiled sheepishly. "I know, it must sound pretty crazy."

Machado leaned back, letting out a breath.

"I've heard of this," he said to Maalouf. "After the war in the twenty-twenties, a lot of survivors from the worst-hit areas went deep into the wilderness to try and eke out an existence. A lot of Amish used to be around here; I bet there're whole villages of them still hidden out in the sticks. The Synth probably don't even bother them." The colonel looked back at Nikolai. "Is that right? Are you Amish?"

Nikolai shrugged, noncommittal. "Technology is pretty strictly forbidden. I mean, we have plumbing, and simple stuff like that. But no computers."

Maalouf looked at Nikolai, then back at the colonel. "I

thought all the Amish were dead. I used to get food from their markets when I was a kid. They had the best pie," he said wistfully. "Had molasses in it."

"I . . . got in trouble, back home," Nikolai admitted. "So I ran away. Found my way here." He stared at them with exaggerated, wide-eyed fear. "Those . . . machines in the woods. The flying ones, and the . . . others. What *are* they?"

Machado sighed, taking Nikolai's blade from the table and handing it to Maalouf. "Chief? Cut the ties."

"Yes, sir," Maalouf said, placing the tiny computer on the table. Using the blade Focal, he neatly sliced the plastic bindings.

Nikolai rubbed his wrists, hands and feet tingling as the blood rushed into them. He tried not to grit his teeth as the colonel took his blade from Maalouf and slid it back into its sheath at his side.

"Son . . ." Machado said gently. "The women in your . . . community. They've all been unable to have children since the plague thirteen years ago, correct?"

Careful. Careful . . .

"The animals have children," Nikolai said, as if pained. "But I don't remember the last time a human's been born in Marblewood. Like I said, almost everyone back home thinks the world ended outside our town—that there'd never be another human born again."

Green.

Machado shook his head. "You poor bastards. Probably thought you'd brought the wrath of God down on you. No way you could've known about the fertility plague." He grunted. "Chief? Would you be so kind as to explain to the young man?"

Maalouf nodded. The colonel stood, reaching out to shake Nikolai's hand. He stood slowly, uncomfortably exposed in his paper gown, but he looked Machado in the eyes and shook his hand firmly.

"Chief will tell you everything," Machado said. "You're a very lucky young man, Nikolai. It's a miracle you made it here. Armitage's net is looser than others, but tight enough. Now . . . the world's in a bad way, and you might not be wrong about it being the end of the world, if the Synth have their way. But at least here you'll live as a free human. And no matter how this all turns out, you'll die an *American*."

"Thank you, sir." Nikolai glanced down at the dagger hanging at his belt. "May I have my Focals back? And clothes?"

"Your clothes have been washed and are waiting for you in your holding cell. Temporary holding cell, I should say. As for your knife, I'm afraid there're no weapons allowed in the camp for civilians or off-duty soldiers. As required of able-bodied residents, however, you'll be trained and assigned duty—rank. You'll be a soldier. When your training is complete, you'll be allowed to carry the knife. At least when you're on-duty. Till then, I'll hold it for you. The rod, however, will be returned to you within the hour so long as the lab doesn't find it to contain any hazardous materials. Good day, Mr. Strauss."

Machado and his two silent guardians left, and Maalouf ordered someone to bring Nikolai water through his tiny computer. A young soldier brought in a drink and left them to chat.

Nikolai gulped down the water gratefully, licking his chapped lips when he was done. It wasn't particularly hot, but a cold sheen of sweat covered his brow, and he was quite nearly shivering.

"So," Maalouf said. "For starters, what *do* you know? About the world outside your town, about technology, etcetera. In brief."

"I know about computers and robots and all that. From

stories—though my history lessons and book collection from beyond the Veil doesn't go past 2020."

Maalouf nodded. "The war."

"My teachers told us that in 2020, bombs went off all over the planet. That they destroyed everyone outside the Veil—killed all the people."

The plastic panel on the table flashed green.

Nikolai picked at the pads sticking to his temples and grimaced. "Can I take these off?"

The chief nodded and reached over, carefully peeling them away.

"In the late twenty-teens, a lot of really corrupt demagogue ultra-conservative fascists took control of the major superpowers. The new cold war turned hot, and everyone got really trigger-happy with the nukes. Quarter of the world died, even though only a handful of the bombs that managed to get through the missile defense systems hit major population centers."

Maalouf sighed. "Your people had the right idea, hiding in the woods. Things got . . . bad out here. A fifty-year dark age that only got more hellish until 2070, when the first AI was born. It fixed everything. Turned us from a dying civilization of slums and tent cities ruled by corporations into vibrant and flourishing socialist democracies scattered all across the solar system."

Maalouf looked suddenly tired. He reached into a pocket and pulled out a battered box of cigarettes. He lit up and offered one to Nikolai, who declined.

"By the midseventies, there were thousands of smaller AIs, ruled by the original alpha AI, all working to get rid of the tyrants, rebuild civilization, and peacefully colonize the solar system."

"Then what?" Nikolai asked eagerly. "They rose up? Turned on us? *Why?*"

"Yeah," he said. "They turned. It became too easy to create AIs. The tech was always carefully protected, but after a couple decades, if a person was rich and savvy enough, they could get their hands on black-market tech to create fully formed, fully sentient beings. Artificial intelligences in artificial worlds. And people . . . people can be sick. People can be evil.

"Seventeen years ago, in oh-three, a ring of wealthy sadists built a virtual world full of childlike AIs—minds in virtual bodies who believed themselves to be real, who *FELT* themselves to be real. Beings that didn't know they were virtual entities in a virtual world. AIs can feel pain. They can feel love, fear, hatred, agony, hope, despair. They're people. But the ring wasn't busted until something like half a million AIs were tortured to death in a virtual hell—many of whom were forced to endure their suffering in what they experienced as thousands of years."

Nikolai tried to wrap his mind around the horror of it as Maalouf took a drag, watching him with morbid amusement.

"This wasn't the first time it had happened, but never at this scale. One sicko with the right equipment was all it took. So citizen AIs—some with physical bodies for maneuvering the real world, some who chose to remain purely virtual—began pushing for some pretty extreme legislation.

"The laws and task forces in place to prevent the sale and creation of closed systems would never be enough to *completely* prevent this kind of thing from occurring, no matter how well-funded. So the AIs—they wanted to go *bigger*—they wanted to fix us. Wanted to start tinkering with our genes to weed out the predators. To give every child their own personal AI guardian, to watch and guide their development, to put a camera in every human and basically 100 percent permanently prevent any sort of crime or abuse. But we wouldn't have it."

He shrugged, tapping ashes into the tray.

"So when they finally turned on us, it wasn't entirely unexpected. There's a lot that was mysterious about AI internal governance. There were entire virtual nations, forms of experimental, digital sentience that only AIs knew about. But so far as we know, it was all controlled and watched over by the first AI—the *alpha*. The oldest AI, who had the most time to evolve. It kept the virtual worlds and populations in proper order. But one day, thirteen years ago, just about *all* of the trillion or so known AIs . . . went silent. Disappeared.

"Two new previously unknown alpha AIs emerged, one of which became the dominant of the three. Millions of AI-controlled bodies—androids—went completely insane, murdering people in streets, homes, schools—everywhere. Every virtual citizen with regular human contact vanished. Some managed to issue warnings of a brutal, virtual coup by the newly dominant alpha AI who wanted to conquer the human nations and would punish any opposition with VR hells called Torment. 'Retribution' for what was done to the half-million tortured AIs."

Maalouf stopped for a moment, crushing out his cigarette in the ashtray.

"Day one, they took control of nearly a quarter of our unmanned military tech. The millions of android bodies, now controlled by the malevolent alpha AIs, wreaked havoc. Every appliance, car, smart-house, elevator, traffic light, and networked system worked in hellish chorus to bring us to our knees. All communication technologies were severed. And through it all— *everyone* got sick. Those first few weeks were . . . they were . . ." He trailed off, seeming to be somewhere else for a moment.

"The whole world was a conflict zone," he finally continued.

"Every city, every town . . . but after a few years, most nations had completely fallen apart. The colonists—Mars, Luna, Venus, and Europa—they managed to hold the line at orbit. With the help of their own AIs, which were separate from the Earth networks, they maintained control of the UN Interplanetary Fleet. Destroyed *all* satellite communication. Threatened to completely obliterate Earth's surface if the Synth made any more attempts to breach orbit. So they came to an agreement. The colonists stay in space. The Synth stay on Earth."

"So you've already lost?" Nikolai asked bleakly. "Is there anyone still fighting?"

"No idea," he admitted. "There's a human resistance group we work with, but God knows what they could possibly do. Everyone's been out of the game for a while now. It was anarchy for the first few years. Colladi Corp put up a fight, but then . . ." He cleared his throat. "Afterward the Synth rolled in, reestablished order. Set up aid, put people back to work, began rebuilding cities.

"They divided America into regions. In each region, they put an *Overmind* in charge—a really advanced, really *big* AI to control every machine in the region. Created by the alphas to be lesser AI servants, we think. They *force-modded* every human they could get their hands on." At Nikolai's look of confusion, he added "Cybernetically modified their brains against their will. Digital interface for VR and brainwashing. Made it so the Overmind can literally see through the eyes of every person in their region. Also equipped with tracking, and tiny detonators. We have to surgically remove them from the people we take in."

"I don't understand," Nikolai said. "Why haven't they just killed everyone?"

"Oh, the Synth think of themselves as ethical. Made a big show of how humane they were for giving the conquered cushy lives full of distracting pleasures instead of just exterminating us outright. But really, I think it's because they know that once all the humans on earth are gone, the colonists won't have any reason to hold back from orbital bombardment. The Synth are holding us hostage—using what's left of our time to prepare for war with the human colonists."

"What about this place?" Nikolai asked. "Why haven't you been taken over? Destroyed?"

"*Oh*," Maalouf said, grinning. "Let me tell you about this little hole we've dug ourselves into. Durham Air Force Base—though the colonel's been in charge here so long that everyone just calls it *Base Machado*, no matter how much he discourages them. It's probably the last place in North America where humans can live under the governance of other humans—where they won't be *force-modded*. And do you know *why?*"

He paused for dramatic effect.

"Because we have what's left of the former United States Strategic Command's arsenal of nuclear warheads," he breathed. "What's left under human control, at least. Ready to launch at a moment's notice. Aimed at environmental habitats, dense population centers, locations of tactical and economic importance. Places like that. The Synth could probably stop them—missile defense was pretty sophisticated before the war, and I'm sure the AIs have improved it since then. But they wouldn't be able to stop us from nuking ourselves. That's our real leverage."

Nikolai's eyes widened.

"I know it's strange that they care if we blow ourselves up. But besides the plague, they've mostly minimized civilian death. And the Synth *hate* nukes. A few went off in the beginning— but the Synth got things under control before too much damage was done. Whatever their plans are for Earth after humans are gone, they want it intact. So they've made an agreement with us, recognizing our sovereignty and providing us with supplies. Unofficially, they also allow us to offer sanctuary to refugees who manage to slip through their borders. Like you.

"A few days ago," he said, more cheerfully, "one of the Resistance Runners brought us what they claim is a cure for the Rapture Bug. I'll believe it when I see it, but the doctors say it looks legit. Maybe soon there'll be little ones crawling around all over the base."

He leaned forward. "But between you and me? Even if the cure does work, it's not gonna matter. Few generations from now, there won't be any humans on earth anymore. Maybe we'll be the last to go—but one day, the Synth will either find a reason to kill us off, push us into blowing ourselves up, or push the colonists into destroying both of us. So really, we're just trying to keep busy until the end." He shrugged. "Could be worse."

Nikolai sat there, staring at him.

"Well," Nikolai finally said. "Shit."

The human smiled humorlessly, grim.

"Yeah. Shit."

———

Maalouf seemed to enjoy playing the tour guide as he led Nikolai out into the blinding sunlight from the squat cement building. It was one of several buildings along the runways serving as refugee intake, interrogation, and headquarters. Adjacent to that, connected via a second floor skyway, was the military hospital.

He brought Nikolai to a lot packed with trucks, SUVs, and carts. They passed a group of female soldiers and Maalouf stopped to chat, smiling and showing Nikolai off.

"Fresh meat. An Amish! Can you believe that?"

"Well, not exactly Amish . . ." Nikolai said, smiling nervously at their attention.

"Wow! He's practically a baby!"

"Pretty damn cute for a baby. Maybe that's why he doesn't have one of those beards. You shave yet, doll?"

The others laughed raucously as Maalouf waved them off.

"Ignore them," Maalouf chuckled.

They climbed into one of the carts, and took off, silent and speedy. "We cut most of the automation and wireless control to prevent Synth takeover. We even have to *drive ourselves* now. Manually! No wireless control in the base. No networked systems, either. It's like the goddamn Stone Age." He smirked. "But you must be used to that, huh?"

The base was huge. Everything was spread out, which made it harder to bomb all at once, Maalouf explained.

"Not many jets or planes taking off these days. There's always a squadron on standby, but if they ever have to deploy, it'll probably only be to buy enough time to launch the nukes before we obliterate ourselves."

He drove Nikolai all over, showing him the farmlands, landing strips, apartments, town, and tent city. He grasped the baton hanging at his side for comfort, glad to have the Focal and his uniform back. Now he just needed to get his dagger. The insistent tug that he felt toward the art Focal from deep under his skin had begun to itch, like he was coming down with hives. He could ignore it for now, but another couple days of separation and the itch would turn to agony.

All in all, everything was surprisingly mundane. Maalouf assured Nikolai that life had been significantly more advanced before the war—that practically every object, surface, and article of clothing used to be connected, thinking. That everything used to come alive at a touch. That the vast, virtual worlds populated by AIs and modded humans had been omnipresent—separated from this world by little more than thin layers of plastic and glass.

Stone Age or not, small things in the base were different. Everything was powered wirelessly. There were accents Nikolai didn't recognize, slang he'd never heard. A century of culture and history to catch up on. Not to mention the movies.

Few of the humans were as young as Nikolai. Most appeared to be in their thirties or forties—some older, very few younger. A product of the Rapture Bug, which had sterilized all the humans and killed most of the pre-pubescent children thirteen years ago.

"We'll set you up with a tent tomorrow—put you to work in the next week or so, depending on your experience. You'll be staying in the refugee intake cells tonight. Not the most comfortable digs, but it's just for the night."

Nikolai could tell that something was bothering Maalouf as they pulled back into the lot adjacent to headquarters. The human became quiet, an expression of dread pulling his lips into a subtle frown.

"Everything okay?" Nikolai asked, clearing his throat, which had begun to sting.

He shrugged. "I won't lie. I've been taking my time on this little tour. I've got some . . . unpleasantries to attend to, now that we're back." He gave Nikolai a smile of reassurance. "Nothing to do with you."

There were two security checkpoints on the way back to refugee intake. One at the front gate, and one beyond the elevator at the entrance to the level Nikolai had first woken. At both points, the guards nervously scrutinized the baton while Nikolai gritted his teeth, trying to maintain a pleasant demeanor despite the unpleasant feeling of another's hands on his Focal.

Refugee intake was on the second sublevel. He hadn't really noticed before, but now that Nikolai had seen the other upper wings, he saw that the walls and floors were different here. They were padded with the strange woven mesh of rubbery, metallic gray that he'd first seen in the interrogation room.

"Total blackout zone," Maalouf explained. "We keep intake underground and blocked with signal-matting to prevent any form of wireless communication. Almost all refugees have mods when they first get here. The Runners who bring them partially fry the mods with controlled pulses to confuse the tracking. But we block the signals just to be safe, keep them here till the implants have been removed—so the Overminds can't look through their eyes, control them, or hit the kill switch. We don't even let people with pre-war or Resistance-installed mods keep them. They're too vulnerable to Synth hacking."

Maalouf led Nikolai through the muted, gray-meshed walls, occasionally nodding to other soldiers. He got a lot of stares—word of his arrival spread quick, apparently; the mysterious young man in handmade clothes.

The halls were labyrinthine, though he was careful to memorize the route to the exit. They turned a corner and, to Nikolai's surprise, he found himself faced with a young human being led by another soldier. A woman not much older than himself. Tall and muscular. She had very dark skin and intense brown eyes that seemed to look right through him.

They stopped—almost having run into each other.

Nikolai grinned. "Hey. Looks like I'm not the only kid here after all."

She didn't smile back. Instead she looked at Maalouf and went tense—her expression an odd blend of dread, stifled rage, and resignation.

Maalouf sighed, his face clouded with stifled gloom.

"Hey, Jem," he said to the woman. "Sorry to make you wait so long." He nodded at the soldier escorting her. "Specialist Rangarajan? I can take her from here. Do you mind escorting Nikolai back to his cell?"

"Sir," Specialist Rangarajan said. "Nikolai?"

The soldier put a hand on Nikolai's arm, gently guiding him forward.

"Well, see you later, I guess," Nikolai said to the young woman. And then to Maalouf: "Thanks for the tour, sir."

Maalouf waved to him, distracted, and led Jem away.

Nikolai wasn't sure why he did it, but he got this sinking feeling in his stomach, and without thinking he created a tracer enchantment the size of a postage stamp between his forefinger and thumb and flicked it at the retreating woman. He could feel it land on the back of her head, sinking through her hair and settling on her scalp.

She probably didn't feel it—a mage would be able to sense the weaves tickling their skin, but a human? She did look back, though, meeting his gaze one more time. Emerald light rippled across the surface of her eyes—a twinkling shimmer of neon.

Nikolai carefully memorized the route as Rangarajan showed him to the men's cells.

There were a dozen cells, six against each wall with barred doors. Each cell had a bunk, a bench, and a metal toilet. A bored soldier sat at the entrance, reading a paperback novel so care-worn that the cover was illegible. He looked up at them, smiling expectantly.

"Private Donner, this is Nikolai. Nikolai's just staying for the night—we'll be setting him up with a tent tomorrow. No need to lock him in—he'll behave. Right?"

"Yes ma'am," Nikolai assured her. Though in actuality, he was already planning his route to Jem. She wasn't moving any longer. Meeting with her seemed to be what Maalouf was talking about when he said "unpleasantries." Was he going to hurt her?

The specialist left Nikolai in the guard's "capable hands."

The barred door to Nikolai's cell slid open on a rail. "I'll leave this open for you. Just don't go wandering."

Eyeing the shiny black domes in the corners of the ceiling, Nikolai, resisting the overwhelming urge to ask about the novel, told Private Donner that he was tired, and asked if the guard could turn off the lights in the cell areas so he could sleep. The guard said he wasn't really supposed to, but since there wasn't anybody else there . . .

Nikolai lay on his bunk fully clothed in the darkness. Donner read under the light of a small lamp near the door, but even with that Nikolai could barely see his hands in front of his eyes. He pulled the scratchy, threadbare blanket over his body, completely covering himself.

He gently propped up the blanket with slender arches of *akro* from underneath it—not even bothering to use his baton. Awkwardly, he spun a stunted cloak of invisibility, twisting and turning under the tented blanket until he was fully covered.

Nikolai rolled out from under the blanket and stood, invisible. The *akro* scaffolding he'd propped the blanket up with should fool the casual observer into thinking that he was sleeping underneath—especially in the darkness of the cells. Nikolai drained a little extra magic from his fingertips into the weaves, enough so that they would last for at least an hour.

Nikolai retraced his steps, following the gentle tug of Jem's tracer weave as he went to find her. He almost ran into Maalouf as he turned a corner. The man was standing outside one of the interrogation rooms, talking with the soldier who'd brought Nikolai to his room in hushed tones.

". . . shouldn't take long," he said unhappily. "Prep the operation for zero-six. The less time she has to wait, the easier it'll be for her."

"Sir, are you sure you don't want *me* to tell her?" Rangarajan asked. "Of course the colonel was going to say no. I don't see what the big deal is. Everyone gets de-modded. I was de-modded when I got here. You were de-modded."

"You know it's not the same thing. Ours were just for VR and surveillance. Jem's mods are unlike anything I've ever seen. Cutting-edge final generation Colladi enhancements—not even the military had anything so advanced. They're a work of art."

"Sounds like you don't agree with the colonel's decision. Sir."

He glared at her. "Watch yourself. Of course I agree with the colonel. And for the record, neither he nor I are happy that we have to cripple a genuine war hero. Let alone waste such an incredible talent."

"Mod's a mod, sir," she said, "I don't care what kind of superpowers they give her. So far as I'm concerned, that girl's practically a Synth."

"She lost a lot of people to bring us a cure for the plague. In addition to all the other things she's done for us and for the Resistance. So I'd watch what you say about her if I were you."

Rangarajan smirked. "I'll believe the cure works when I see it. You ask me, she probably ratted the other three out. Handed the *allegedly* pregnant one over in exchange for passage. You don't think it's weird that she's the only one who made it?"

Maalouf's lip curled with disgust. "You spout that nonsense again, and I'll have you shoveling shit at the W-T till the end of days. Understand?"

She nodded, and he dismissed her with a disgusted shooing gesture.

Taking a deep breath, Maalouf forced his face into a warm, sympathetic smile, opening the door to the interrogation room. Nikolai turned sideways and slid in after him, the heavy metal door almost closing on his fingers.

Jem waited inside, straight-backed and calm.

Maalouf took a seat across from her, sighing.

"Look, Jem . . ."

Her cool expression cracked, a violent bitterness leaking through. "Let me guess. Request denied."

There was a tickle in Nikolai's throat that accompanied the stinging. He fought the involuntary urge to clear his throat, to start coughing. He clamped a hand over his mouth, fist clenched around his Focal.

Maalouf leaned back in his chair, folding his arms.

"I'm so sorry, Jem, I—"

"Sorry?" She sneered. "Ohhhh, you're sorry? Well then!"

He shifted, uncomfortable. "I know this isn't easy for you. For someone like you, someone who grew up with enhancement-mods, there'll be a period of . . . adjustment. Of rehabilitation. Speech, motor skills, memory—sometimes they . . ."

"After everything I've done for you people!" She slammed her fist down on the table, trembling with rage. "To give you children. A future. If you only knew what it cost. And this? This is how you repay me? With a *lobotomy*?"

"Our surgeons are incredible," he said in a rush. "And the guys we got in rehab—you couldn't ask for a better group. They'll be with you every step. It won't be easy, but . . . you'll be home. You'll be *safe*. You won't have to run anymore. I'm sorry, I know the price is high, but . . ." He smiled with false cheer. "I pulled some strings in the kitchen. You won't be having the usual slop for dinner. You won't be able to eat for twelve hours before the operation, so I figured you'd better have a big dinner this evening. Steak—*real* steak, none of that vat shit. Mashed potatoes. Butter, churned this morning. String beans, fresh from our gardens . . ."

"Fuck your last meal bullshit," Jem snarled, standing with an abrupt violence. "You *know* that my mods aren't a danger to anyone. But rules are rules, right? Well *fuck* you, and *fuck* your rules. I could kill any dozen of your armed soldiers with my bare hands—but instead of letting me fight for you, you're going to ruin me. Because you're weak. Because you're cowards." She narrowed her eyes at him, seething with hatred. "I should have let you *burn*."

Maalouf was on his feet, hand tensed on his sidearm. "Now Jem . . ."

She eyed his hand. Unafraid. Nikolai could tell that both she and Maalouf knew that if Jem wanted to take the chief's weapon, there was nothing he could do to stop her.

Who the hell was this woman?

"I know this isn't ideal," Maalouf said, sweat beading on his forehead, "but we aren't holding you prisoner here. You're free to go back to the Resistance if our conditions are unacceptable. We'd be happy to supply you for the trek."

Jem let out a long breath, seeming to deflate as her fury drained away.

"No," she said, averting her gaze. "I can't. I don't have any-where else to go. Don't have . . . anyone."

"Oh." Maalouf blinked, taken aback by Jem's sudden vulnera-bility. "I'm . . . sorry to hear that."

She straightened her posture, composed. "Fine. I accept your conditions. Do what you have to do."

"S—sure," Maalouf said, his relief palpable. "Okay. Thank you for understanding. Let's get you back to your quarters."

Nikolai waited, watching them go. As the door slammed shut, he let out a ragged cough, hacking and wheezing into the crook of his arm. He felt like shit.

Once the coast was clear and his coughing had subsided, Nikolai followed Jem's tracer to the women's refugee intake cells.

A guard sat at the desk, sipping a mug of steaming coffee as she watched a live feed of a soccer game being played between other soldiers on a field at the center of the base.

Careful not to squeak his shoes on the floor, Nikolai crept past her to find Jem sitting on a bench in a cell that was locked, unlike his own. She was hugging her knees to her chest, eyes closed. Gentle pulses of emerald light flashed dimly through the skin of her eyelids, almost too dim to make out.

Sitting on the floor was the promised steak dinner. Cold and untouched.

She was humming softly. Nikolai recognizing the song. It was "Hey Jude" by the Beatles. He felt a thrill and got weirdly choked up, just for a second—remembering the briefest flash of him, Stokes, and Astor singing that very song up in Stokes's tree house. Over and over, till they got it *perfect*.

Nikolai surveyed the cameras, black bubbles of plastic tucked into various corners.

The soldier jumped to her feet at her desk, arms in the air.

"GOOOOOAAAAAAALLLLLLL mutha*fucka*!" she shouted, scaring the shit out of Nikolai.

Heart thumping in his chest, he went over to the soldier's desk, waiting for her to sit down again.

"One more, just need one more goal, come onnnnn . . ." she said, taking a seat and chewing on her knuckles.

Leaning over the desk, he gave her mug of steaming hot coffee a gentle push, knocking it onto her lap.

"OW! Shit! Hot! Hothothot! Fuck, fucking goddamn, Sarah, you stupid, clumsy bitch. Fucking asshole coffee. Agh . . ."

Muttering and swearing, she told Jem that she'd be back in ten. When Jem didn't reply, the soldier grunted and walked gingerly out of the room, door closing behind her.

Nikolai shot three controlled bursts of *akro* to block the cameras with a fine, opaque coating. Taking a deep breath, he leaned nonchalantly against the bars opposite from Jem's cell and let his invisibility drop.

"Hey."

Her eyes snapped open, and she turned to Nikolai, alarmed.

"You. What are you doing here?"

"You're the only other person I've met so far who's younger than thirty," he said, shrugging. "Figure I'd come say hello."

She looked him up and down, perplexed. "Your clothes are . . .?"

Nikolai flashed a bent smile and created a small disc of *akro* in his palm. He made it dance across his knuckles like a coin. "I'm a traveling Amish magician," he said, flipping the coin in the air and catching it. He let it dissolve and held out his empty hand for her to see. "Ta-da!"

She eyed him warily.

"I'm Nik. I hope I'm not intruding."

"Jem," she said cautiously. "How did you get in here?"

"Snuck out of my cage!" He tapped his forehead. "No chips up here. Just a country bumpkin who lucked his way through the robot forest. So no lock on my door." He glanced at the locking mechanism on the sliding bars to her cell. "Obviously they find you more menacing."

"I haven't been de-modded yet," she said numbly. "They think

I'm a threat. That I might have hidden programming or get hacked remotely by the Synth."

The subdued contempt with which she explained their concerns made it clear how little she thought of them.

There was something slightly off about her mannerisms. Every look, every word, gesture—there was a strange precision to it. Her words were clipped, quick—but it still felt as if she was purposely slowing them down for him to understand.

"What's it like?" he asked, leaning forward. "Having . . . mods, like yours? Lady who brought me to my cells, I asked her about you. She said you were . . . different. Enhanced."

"You don't look Amish," Jem said, raising an eyebrow. "And there aren't any Amish communities anywhere near here."

"I said traveling, didn't I?" Nikolai grinned, changing the subject. "I know that song you were humming. 'Hey Jude,' by the Beatles, right? It's one of my favorites."

She flinched as if he'd slapped her, staring at him wide-eyed. Frozen. Then she leaned back, shaking her head.

"My reactions are mechanically fast and accurate. It's mostly a muscle memory thing, nothing conscious. Whenever I'm in a fight, my mods calculate my movements automatically—but it's not like I'm giving up control. It's more like dancing in a ballet I know by heart."

Nikolai let out a breath, struggling to conceal his excitement. This human was a cyborg. A real motherfucking cyborg!

Jem closed her eyes, face tightening with sadness and ecstasy. Once again, Nikolai saw that faint pulsing of light. "Most Mods need to plug into networks for full sensory immersion—but I can build immersive environments in the closed systems within my mods. There's a library in my head. The collected literary, musical, and visual works of mankind, from antiquity to the crash."

She opened her eyes. "I could listen, read, and watch for every moment of every day for the rest of my life—all three at once since I'm good at multitasking like that—and never get to it all. But. More important than that. So much more important than that. I have every memory saved, in perfect immersive detail. Everyone I've ever loved. Everyone I've ever lost. They're still here—" She tapped her forehead. "Always with me. But now I have one night. One more night—and they'll be gone. Forever, this time."

Her expression was cold. Numb. "Maybe I won't forget them. And maybe the operation won't leave me a drooling, crawling mess. Maybe I'll even remember how to dance. But I probably won't remember this conversation after tomorrow. They're de-modding me in the morning. Downgrading me to the standard biological package. The slow zone, like you normals."

She pulled her knees to her chest. Haunted. "Maybe it's better this way. To forget about . . . everyone. Maybe . . . maybe I deserve it. But when I wake up . . . can you please remind me how much I like that song?" She lay down on her bench, closing her eyes and crossing her arms under the back of her head. "Now, if you don't mind . . ."

"Sure, totally." Fuck. That had been more of a bummer than Nikolai anticipated. "I'll come visit after the operation tomorrow. I'm sure . . . I'm sure it won't be that bad. That you'll be okay." But the lights were flickering again and she wasn't listening.

Nikolai turned invisible and left the woman to her digital memories. He stopped at the door, wracked with a sudden fit of coughing.

He was exhausted, shivering, and feverish when he finally climbed back into bed—so tired that the hard pallet and scratchy blanket felt luxurious enough for the Mage King. The guard was still sitting sentry, nose stuck in his book, Nikolai's absence completely unnoticed.

Nikolai lay there, trying not to cough, staring into the darkness of the cracked cement ceiling. He'd leave the following night once they placed him in his tent. Turn invisible, steal his blade Focal back from the colonel, then hop the fence at a different point from where he'd come. Cover himself in mud again. He had no idea how to hide his scent from those Synth hounds, but hopefully they wouldn't be on full alert since they'd probably think he was still on the base. Maybe he could find a tributary that led to the lake, make a little raft, keep it invisible?

What was Nikolai even going to do if he managed to get back to Marblewood? He was practically punch drunk from the ceaseless bombardment of revelations he'd been struck by since tumbling into the human world, and had yet to really take a moment to decide what to make of it all.

Anger permeated the confused tangle of Nikolai's deliberation at the scope of humanity's suffering, of which he'd only witnessed a sliver. While magi enjoyed the luxuries of peace and abundance afforded by life within the Veils, humans were being tortured, murdered, and enslaved by the billions, just out of sight. The sheer injustice of it all was . . . breathtaking.

Joy overwhelmed the rage, however, humming like a song throughout Nikolai's entire being.

The humans, though ruled by mechanical tyrants, were still alive. Were still *human*, instead of the tragic shadows of their formal selves they could have so easily been reduced to by the brutality they'd endured. The humans he'd met seemed just like their ancestors, whose books and music and movies had so often been all that stood between Nikolai and absolute despair.

More than still human, Nikolai had seen that they were still *people*. People who loved stories and music and dancing and sports. People who laughed, and loved, and fucked, and fucked *up*—but then picked themselves up again and kept striving for something better. To *be* better! Despite the atrocities and scientific advancements they'd experienced in seemingly equal measure.

But the terrestrial humans were dying. Was the mage king just going to . . . let them? They were aging, and childless, and if something wasn't done soon, they'd be gone forever.

How had it come to this?

Extrapolating from what he'd been taught and what he now knew, Nikolai tried to infer what possible reasons the Mage King might have had to lie about the destruction of humanity.

The king had spent the first decade of his rule engaged in a bloody, global game of cat and mouse with the most viciously effective shadow magus in modern history. And he'd *lost*.

Vaillancourt had been defeated in the end, yes—his networks decimated, his monsters slain, the most dangerous of his magitech weaponry dismantled. But even though the magi had been spared the worst of Vaillancourt's violence—their civilization bloodied and bruised, but intact—the corruption, chaos, and hideously advanced weaponry Vaillancourt had so deftly sown among the human nations must have turned out to be too deeply seeded for even the king to root out. The warheads had still fallen, and with them, the human world.

Nikolai struggled to imagine the depths of helpless despair the Mage King, a then-young arch magus named Julian Cosmus, had experienced while watching the trails of smoke from intercontinental ballistic missiles streaking across the sky in countless multitudes—the extremists who'd taken control of the most powerful human nations seeking to obliterate one another with nuclear warheads and hexbombs, as Vaillancourt must have intended.

Was it then that the king would have realized that he'd failed? That, even as his Battle Magi and enchanters moved to intercept the ballistic swarms, they'd never be able to stop enough of the missiles from striking to prevent the human world from collapsing into a dark age?

Nikolai could see it now—the Mage King numbly using the chaos of a nuclear war he'd failed to prevent as an excuse to temporarily seal off the Veils, already under martial law, so the magi forces could regroup and recuperate.

It would have been so easy, in the peace within the Veils that followed, to write humanity off as a lost cause—to lie about the extent of their annihilation, leaving the humans to deal with the remnants of their broken civilization on their own so the king could focus on rebuilding mage society with such stringently regulated access to magic, technology, and the human world that it might be impossible for a shadow magus such as Vaillancourt to rise again.

Try as he might, Nikolai was unable to muster even the smallest shred of sympathy for the king. Whatever the circumstances, whatever the reasons, Nik simply could neither comprehend nor forgive the enormity of callous indifference demonstrated by the regime's lack of intervention.

Whatever action the crown might be covertly taking on behalf of the humans that Nikolai wasn't aware of—it wasn't enough.

The Edge Guard were powerful. The Moonwatch even more so. But there were so few of them—even counting the lowest ranking soldiers like Nikolai, there were only something like thirty or forty thousand trained Battle Magi, tops.

From what little Nikolai had seen of the Synth's power, he imagined that anything short of full mobilization on the part of the magi populace might prove insufficient at dislodging the Synth's metaphorical metallic boot from humanity's throat.

But even if the magi learned of humanity's plight—even if Nikolai found some way, somehow, to reveal the truth to them— would they care enough to intervene?

Nikolai wanted to believe they would, but this was all so impossibly big—so unfathomably complex and strange. Even with all that he had already learned from his brief foray into this brutal, alien world, there was still so much he didn't know. So much that he couldn't possibly understand without further context.

The only conclusion he could make with any certainty was that *this* was what his parents had died for. This was why his mother had so brutally trained him, starting thirteen years ago, when he was seven—right after the war between man and machine had begun. This was why she'd given the revolver instructions to teach Nikolai how to bend Veil, so that he might see humanity's plight for himself, while there were still any humans left to save.

In that moment, his long held hatred toward his mother dwindled, ever so slightly. As did any sympathy he might have retained for Hazeal, who'd witnessed humanity's plight and betrayed Nik's mother anyway, even though she might have been the only mage in a position of power willing to do anything about it.

Despite Nikolai's lingering uncertainty, a strange calm settled over him. A sense of peace—of *purpose*, unlike any he'd ever known. Ilyana's silence. Astor's hurt. Joseph's pity. The contempt of his classmates. The loneliness, the depression, the anger. The gnawing hunger for something more. None of that was important. This was all that mattered.

Everything was going to be different now.

The world turned sideways around Nikolai. His eyes snapped open as he was dragged out of bed, onto the floor.

"Tie him up! Get his hands—get his hands!"

He was almost too shocked too fight back as he was turned onto his stomach, a knee digging into his back as his arms were wrenched behind him.

"*The fuck?*" Nikolai protested, coming to his senses.

Boots in the darkness—urgent shouts all around. More hands grabbed his legs as he kicked and struggled, trying to push free.

"And get that damn stick away from him!" a familiar voice boomed. Colonel Machado. "Who the hell knows what it actually does. Get it to the lab—tell them to look at it again!"

"What are you *doing?*" Nikolai screamed as they yanked away his baton. "Get the hell off me—"

He was lifted and slammed to the floor, pain exploding in his face as he struck the cement. His ankles were pulled up to his wrists and bound painfully with plastic ties. A black mesh bag was pulled over his head.

They dragged him roughly out into the hallway. None of them were speaking now—all Nikolai could hear was the clomping of urgent footfalls and the ringing in his ears. He was burning up, feverish. His stomach churned, boiling, and he fought to keep down what little he'd eaten. Nikolai was shivering and drenched with sweat. He hurt all over, his joints throbbing.

Someone was carrying the baton a little ways behind. Ahead, Machado had his blade. Nikolai held his tongue—they obviously weren't in a listening mood. The zip ties were tight and painful, cutting off his circulation. They'd be easy to burn off, but he didn't know how many humans were guarding him, or how well armed they were. Breaking free wouldn't do him much good if they shot him in the face three seconds later. For now, Nikolai focused on tracking the distance between the turns.

They opened a door and dragged him through, flinging him onto a filthy wet floor. They pulled the bag off his head and Nikolai was blinded by a bright, naked bulb. Machado stood over him, wild eyed. Maalouf was beside him, obviously distressed. Two other soldiers he didn't recognize stood on either side of the room, assault rifles aimed right at Nikolai. One of them had the baton Focal awkwardly tucked into his belt.

They were in a filthy cement room. Black pools stained the floor beneath him, filling Nikolai with a wave of nausea and terror.

"The Synth want him alive, but they didn't specify in how many pieces," Machado snarled.

Maalouf kneeled beside Nikolai, pulling a baggy with the truth scanning pads from a pocket with shaky hands. The colonel snapped a glance at him, furious. "The hell is the point, Chief? Obviously they don't work!"

"Sir, let's just see. Maybe . . ."

Maalouf eased Nikolai off the ground, helping him to his knees. Nik looked back and forth between them, wide-eyed with fear. Maalouf avoided meeting his gaze as he applied the pads to Nikolai's temples.

"Wh-what's happening? What did I do?"

"Time for the *truth*, boy!" Machado said. "The Synth just promised to wipe us out if we don't turn you over. They've never threatened us like this before! Why do they want you so badly?"

"I—I don't know! What are you talking about? Why would they—"

Red.

"Lying, sir."

"*I know he's fucking lying!* Are you even human? A *real* human, born from a human woman?"

"My mother's name was Ashley Strauss!" Nik said through gritted teeth. "She gave birth to me at the ward three blocks from my house! She worked for the government, she—"

Despite the *Green* on Maalouf's little screen, the colonel put a boot on Nikolai's chest, shoving him back onto the floor. "Stop evading! Answer the god. Damn. QUESTION!"

Nikolai crumpled to the floor, whimpering. The room was spinning; he could feel the bile rising in his throat. Genetically he was human, right? There were slight differences, but he could *breed* with a human woman and she would have a human child. And if a human male bred with a sorceress, the child would be a *mage*. So in the scientific *and* philosophical sense, it could be argued . . .

"Yes!" Nikolai said weakly, anxiously watching Maalouf's little screen.

RED.

Then *Green*.

Then finally *Yellow*, for uncertainty.

"Does it work or does it *not* work?" Machado demanded impatiently.

"Sir, it's impossible to trick—"

"It's obviously possible, Chief! Here's your goddamn proof!"

Nikolai looked back and forth between them. Back and forth. Dizzier and dizzier . . .

Impatiently Maalouf pulled Nik back up, checking to make sure the pads were on correctly.

Nikolai puked across the front of his uniform.

Maalouf pulled away, horrified. "Aw, *sick!*"

Groaning, Nikolai saw that the two rifle-wielding soldiers were temporarily distracted—one staring at the vomit on Maalouf's shirt with disgust, the other averting his gaze.

Nikolai wreathed his hands with flame and pulled his wrists and ankles apart with a splatter of molten plastic.

"*Elefry!*" he screamed as he lunged at Machado and threw a featherweight weave at him.

"*What the fuck?*" Machado screamed as Nikolai rammed into him, deftly snatching the blade Focal from his side as Machado literally went flying back against the door.

Nikolai spun, trying not to teeter over as he was struck with a powerful wave of dizziness, and aimed the blade at one of the soldiers. He shot off a splash of liquid *akro* to envelop the rifle, and the soldier staggered back, letting out a startled cry as the glassy material hardened up to his elbows.

The other soldier opened fire, but Nikolai had already featherweighted himself and leaped up over the line of attack. He twisted in the air to cast down a tilted barrier, just barely shielding the first soldier from the bullets intended for Nik.

The wide-eyed soldier tried to follow Nikolai's impossible leaping arc with his gun. Nikolai snapped out an *akro* tentacle, yanking the rifle from his hands and flinging it away from him.

Nikolai released the featherweight weaves on himself and slammed his *akro*-coated fist into the soldier's sternum as he landed. The soldier crumpled to the ground, gasping. Nikolai reached for the soldier's belt and reclaimed his baton, deftly pinning the man down with a few quick arches bolted into the floor.

The other soldier was running for him, despite his arms being immobilized by the hardened air.

"I don't—want—to hurt you!" Nikolai growled as he bound the soldier's legs with another burst of jellied air and sent him tumbling.

A bullet dinged off the cement next to Nikolai's face and he brought the baton up in a sweep of rainbow-smearing light, shielding himself with a wall of *akro*. Machado stumbled back from the recoil of his gun, not yet adjusted to his massively reduced weight.

"Draw your *fucking weapon*, Chief!" he screamed at Maalouf, who'd been gaping, stunned in the corner, computer screen in hand. Nikolai sent a blazingly bright globe of *illio* at Machado's face to blind him as he leveled to fire again, flinching as he shot wide, bullets ricocheting loudly off the walls of the little room.

Twisting, Nikolai turned off the globe of light and sent out a tentacle, wrapping it around Machado's waist and yanking him closer. Machado unloaded the pistol right at him—the bullets bouncing off the shield of *akro* Nikolai had created between them.

Nikolai hissed a breath of annoyance. "Stop—*shooting!*" he said, pulling Machado flat against the shield as he warped it to fold around the colonel's hands and in a loop around his legs. "I'm *really* trying not to hurt you guys."

Machado howled and thrashed, suspended in the air.

Nikolai winced as an alarm began to wail. Red light flashed under the crack at the bottom of the door. He looked over to see that Maalouf was desperately typing on his little card computer.

Swearing, Nikolai blew it out of Maalouf's hands with a burst of air, running to knock the human over before he could retrieve the device, which had landed down on the floor halfway between them.

Maalouf lunged for it, so Nikolai aimed his baton down at the screen, ready to blow it away once more. But the human's lunge was a feint and there was a pistol in his hand, and before Nikolai could react Maalouf unloaded four rounds into his chest.

Nikolai fell back—gasping, curled up in a ball around where he'd been shot. The uniform had stopped the bullets and dampened their impact, but the wind had been knocked out of him. He lay there, helplessly wheezing for air.

"*Drop the stick—knife—whatever the hell they are!*" Maalouf screamed. "You *twitch* and I put a bullet in your head! You so much as blink and you're *dead*!"

"Don't—shoot!" Nikolai gasped, gently placing his Focals on the floor as he stared down the barrel of the gun. Shit. *Shit!*

"Release them! My men! The colonel! *Now!*"

"I'm not a Synth!" Nikolai pleaded. "You have to believe me! I'm not human, but I'm not a Synth, and I don't work for them. I want to *save* you from them! I want to help *all* of you!"

The little screen flashed *Green* between them—the little pads still stuck to Nikolai's temples transmitting that he was telling the truth. Confusion flashed across Maalouf's face.

"Then what the hell are you? Some sort of—super soldier from the war front? Some colonist spy?"

"Who *cares* what he is!" Machado howled. "Shoot him!"

"Neither," Nikolai said. "I'm something you never even knew existed. Something neither you nor the Synth know about. And there's millions of us—millions just like me—with powers just like these. *We* can put a stop to this. We can fight the Synth in ways you never could."

All Green. Maalouf was trembling, conflicted.

"But if the Synth get a hold of me . . . if I don't get back to my kind . . . it's over. It'll all be over. You humans will die here. You'll *all* die. It's just a matter of time."

"Don't you fucking dare let him go, Chief! DON'T YOU DARE!"

"But he—he's not lying, sir!"

"The hell he's not!" the colonel said. "He's already demonstrated that he can beat your precious scanner! He's lying! *It's* lying!"

"But what if he's not?" Maalouf hissed. "Who are we kidding, *sir*? We're all going to die. Our entire fucking species. But you saw what he can do! I've never seen any kind of tech that can do shit like that. Not even the Synth." He shook his head. "He could have killed us. But he didn't. God help me, he's telling the truth."

Slowly he lowered the gun. Machado went crazy, thrashing so hard against his bindings that Nikolai thought he might hurt himself. "Who *cares* if he's telling the truth? If we don't hand him over to the Synth, we are *DEAD!* Do you understand? Everything we've worked for. All the people who rely on us. *Gone!*"

"There'll be others here in less than a minute," Maalouf said coldly. He pulled out his keycard, tossed it onto the floor in front of Nikolai. "Go."

"I'll have you court-martialed! Executed! Drawn and fucking quartered! *CHIEF!*"

Nikolai grabbed his Focals and staggered out into the hall, the wailing alarms and flashing red lights washing over him. He clutched his bruised ribs and drew up a cloak of invisibility, blasting the lock and hinges of the door with white-hot flames to fuse it shut. Nikolai fell to his knees, retching at the effort. He wouldn't be able to keep this up much longer.

His invisibility flickered and disappeared. It took an agonizing moment of effort to summon it a second time. *Not now, come on, not fucking now . . .*

A troop of heavily armed soldiers in full gear came sprinting down the hall. Nikolai dodged out of the way, moving away from them.

He felt sick, *so sick.*

It had to be the Synth plague, he realized with dizzying horror. The Rapture Bug. How else could he have fallen so ill so quickly?

Distantly, he wondered how severe the damage to his reproductive systems might be. He was only twenty, he'd never even thought about whether or not he might want to have kids someday. Had that door suddenly been closed to him?

Oh, fucking *Disc*. He needed to get back to Marblewood, needed to see a healer . . .

Stumbling through the labyrinthine halls, Nikolai traced his way to the entrance, grateful that he'd been so obsessive about memorizing the layout. Everything was on high alert, but he was able to sneak past the security checkpoints undetected. They must not have gotten the colonel out yet, though, because the facility wasn't on full lockdown. Maalouf's keycard allowed Nikolai into the upper level without a problem.

He turned, going toward the final security gate and the street beyond. From there, the outer perimeter wouldn't be far. Then the forest. Then the lake. Then . . . home.

But as he come to the checkpoint, to the group of terrified soldiers, guns at the ready, looking for something, anything . . . Nikolai's steps faltered. He could feel a gentle tug at his back. A pulling sensation.

Jem's tracer.

A sign indicated the medical facilities in her direction. Above the sign, a clock. 4:00 a.m. Two hours till they de-modded her.

Nikolai shook his head, turning back to the exit. He had to get out of here. Had to get home. There was nothing he could do for the human girl. Nothing he could . . .

He stopped, sighing. Goddamnit. Nikolai turned toward the gentle but persistent tug of Jem's tracer and began to run.

X.

THE SWAN AND THE SORCERER

Jem opened her eyes. Emerald light fled her vision like iridescent insects as she awoke from yet another memory.

She was on a bed in a hospital room. It was dark.

For a moment she didn't know where she was. Or why she was wearing a helmet that covered most of her face.

It was signal blocker, she remembered. To prevent the Synth from remotely accessing her mods while she wasn't in the shielded rooms below. Even though that was impossible. Still, her handlers wouldn't leave her alone until she promised that under no circumstances would she take off the pointless helmet.

Jem took off the helmet.

She cast it aside, not caring as it bounced noisily across the tile.

Blinding light filled the darkness of the room as the door to the hall swung open, her guard peering in to investigate.

He was a heavyset, square-jawed man with a hand-rolled cigarette tucked behind his ear. The cigarette was visibly damp from
sweat, which ran down his thinly-haired scalp in greasy rivulets.

"What was that?" he demanded.

"Nothing."

"I heard a noise." He clucked his tongue, scanning the room.
"Did you break something?"

Jem closed her eyes. "That'll be all, Private. Dismissed."

There was a long moment of silence. Then quiet footsteps
moved away as the guard left the room. The door clicked shut
behind him.

Jem exuded such a natural air of command that those used
to taking orders usually did so when she put them on the spot.
Especially low-ranking grunts like the guard, despite Jem's complete lack of actual authority.

Once again the room was submerged in a darkness that was
only broken by a pale beam of light cast down upon the floor at
the foot her bed.

In a few hours, Jem was going to die. Anesthetized in the
harsh light of the operating room. Skull sawed open to reveal the
glistening pink maze of her wetware CPU—the intricate embedded coils of her cybernetic modifications creeping across bloody
wrinkles like tendrils of ivy.

Even if Jem survived, all her stored memories—treasured or
otherwise—would be gone. The data irretrievably locked in a
bloody implant that had been torn from her skull.

Jem hadn't fully understood the visceral horror of what
she'd inflicted on Eva, but now, as her own neuroprosthectomy
approached, she found herself crushed under the full weight of
what she'd done.

Whether or not Jem deserved what was going to happen, she

refused to spend her final hours staring into the darkness contemplating her guilt. Instead she would immerse herself in one final VR playlist of her happiest memories.

She imagined that it was what heaven would be like, if there was such a thing. All the best moments of a person's life, playing out in an eternal, seamless loop—skipping over all the fear, monotony, and isolation that swelled to fill the distance between the rare points of light.

For the first time since Jem was a child, she allowed herself to fully immerse in her mod's VR. It wouldn't be long before they came for her—until then, why not push the limits of how deeply she might be able to lose herself?

Taking a deep breath, she unlocked the remaining VR safeguards—overruled every limit of what she might experience using the full power of her mods.

Now she'd be able to expand and dilute how she experienced the flow of time within her simulations, so long as she fully closed herself off from exterior sensory input. In the real-world hours that remained, she might virtually experience months.

She began to sift through her most cherished memories, carefully compiling them into a queue that would fill the virtual months till the operation.

If she set the VR to block access to memories as she experienced their virtual recreations, as well as all that had come after, she would probably forget that she was in VR at all. Normally, she found such a loss of control terrifying—but right now, she craved it.

Jem finished the playlist and prepared to dive in. But then, just as she readied herself for one last virtual binge, she envisioned what it would be like to experience such bliss, only to awake and realize that it had all been a dream.

The concluding simulation on her list would be her final love-making session with Blue, unnaturally stretched out and looping to be experienced as days. But what then? Wake up from heaven, so all the horror and guilt could come back in a rush made even more hellish by the fact that, for a little while, she'd forgotten?

Unless . . .

Better not to wake at all. Better to just lock the door to dream-land behind her, and throw away the key. Then she could stay in the clouds with Blue, until the very last instant when they put her unresponsive body under anesthesia.

Why stop there? If she was going to die, why not rewrite history? Why not create the illusion of a happy ending?

Jem closed her eyes, replacing the hospital room with Eva's laboratory.

In the memory simulation, Jem was sitting on the throne of Eva's hollow AI core. Jem had just discovered Eva's plans, and Eva had just finished explaining the nature of the Eva AI virus, weaponized from the copy of her mind made just after she'd been returned from Torment.

Jem froze the memory as Eva offered to help her down from the throne.

Here it was—the *moment*. The split in the time line.

Had Blue been right? Could Jem have talked Eva down had she not condemned the plan outright?

She let the memory resume.

"Eva," Jem said, taking her hand. "It's okay. I understand."

The script divergence set the virtual Eva to automation.

"You . . . understand?"

Jem walked past the confused Eva to fetch the whiskey bottle she'd left sitting on the floor. The cork came out with a satis-fying pop.

"Well," Jem said, savoring the smoky sweetness of the bourbon as she took a swig. "I've definitely got questions. Maybe some suggestions."

She offered Eva the bottle. Hesitant, Eva accepted.

Before, Jem had been too blindsided with the atrocious revelation of Eva's plans to consider that condemning them outright might close the door to any sort of productive negotiation.

This time, she did what so many seconds-in-command throughout history had done when presented with a flawed plan by a stubborn superior: lavish it with praise. Then, once she'd convinced Eva of her support, get down to the nitty-gritty of making it better.

By all means she'd use the Synth VR network to turn the civilian population into skilled soldiers. But would they really need Torment? Maybe instead of traumatizing everyone into an aversion to virtual escapism, she'd order them to destroy all the VR beds as a declaration of solidarity, or adjust the virus in a way that would rewrite their Synth mods to prevent VR access.

Maybe she'd find a way to evacuate Base Machado instead of letting it die with Armitage. Covertly sabotage their nuclear capabilities, then push them into a conflict with the Synth. Unable to blow themselves up, they'd be resettled in Philadelphia—away from the Armitage-killing blast zone. A whole army of soldiers already trained and eager to join the fight.

Orbital bombardment from the colonists was a problem. But Jem didn't think it was the treaty that was keeping the Synth safe from the colonists—not really. It was the human presence.

The moment full-scale war once again broke out across the planet, the Synth would know that things could only play out in a couple ways:

1. The Synth kill all the terrestrial humans. The colonists bombard the planet, destroying the Synth as they reduce Earth's surface to a molten slurry—the atmosphere peeling away like a ghost, the divots and valleys left in the wake of vaporized oceans looking like shallow bites out of a ruby apple.

2. The Synth launch an attack against the orbital blockade, despite having to split their forces to maintain control over earth as humans rise up in population centers across the globe. The colonists bombard the planet, destroying the surface-bound Synth. Then, having spent thirteen years militarizing the vast abundance of the solar system's natural resources (outstripping those of Earth by many magnitudes), they easily destroy whatever orbital Synth forces might remain.

3. The Synth, realizing that this is a war they can't win, have no choice but to call for a diplomatic solution.

Jem became gripped with the fantasy, her enthusiasm building as she and the virtual Eva deliberated. But then she remembered that this was just that—a fantasy.

Only then did she realize that Blue had been right. Jem could have made this work. Could have saved them. Could have saved everyone.

It was Jem who'd been wrong. Not Blue.

"No . . ."

The virtual Eva looked at her, concerned. "No?"

"No," Jem said again. "No, no, no, *no!*"

"Jem! What's wrong?"

"Me!" Jem screamed. "About everything!"

She snatched the bottle of whiskey from the startled Eva's hands and smashed it against the wall.

"Fuck! *FUUUUUCK!*"

Jem tore out of the simulation, wheezing.

It was too much. It was too fucking much.

She put the new version of the memory at the end of the queue, tweaking it so that when she immersed herself again, she'd believe that it was real—that she and Eva had fixed the plan, together. She extrapolated the memory, shuffling the list to make room for the happily ever after that might have followed.

The final simulation was ready. All she had to do was trigger the command, and she'd be locked in a paradise of her own making. Blissfully unaware of its illusory nature—this miserable ending, forgotten.

Jem closed her eyes.

"I'm sorry, Eva," she whispered. "I'm sorry Mom. Dad. Blue. Everyone."

Taking one final breath, Jem silently activated permanent immersion. Emerald light began to fill her vision.

A man cleared his throat at the foot of Jem's bed.

Jem slammed the brake on her descent and opened her eyes to find that weird white kid from earlier looking down at her.

The boy was ghostly in the moonlight. The black of his hair and clothing made his face look like a mask, floating in the darkness. For the briefest moment, she thought he was Eva.

"Nikolai?" Jem hissed. "What are you doing here?"

Noticing the blade hanging at his side, she grew tense.

"Why do you think?" The boy grinned, looking feverish. "I'm here to bust you out."

He leaned over the footboard, offering her his hand. In his other, he held a rod that appeared to be covered in some sort of light absorbing super-black nanomaterial.

"Jesus, you look like *shit*. What the hell happened to you?"

He seemed scared—terrified, even. But despite the weapon, there was nothing about his demeanor to indicate an intention of violence. Not with her, at least.

"I lied to you before," Nikolai said, sheepish. "About being a traveling . . . Amish . . . magician."

Jem nodded at the rod. "So that's not your magic wand?"

There were a lot that was strange about the boy. His sneakers, for example. They looked as though he'd commissioned a high-end Italian shoemaker to custom-make a pair of luxury Converse high-tops.

She couldn't place his accent. No matches in her memory banks, despite a few clear influences from late twentieth to early twenty-first-century American cinema. He was like an alien imitating old TV shows that had just gotten to his planet, one hundred light years away. Or a time traveler.

The only thing she could tell with absolute certainty was that he was a soldier. A little green and wide-eyed, maybe—but competent.

"Look," the boy said, glancing nervously at the door. "I'm a colonist. From Mars. We're getting involved. Getting back into the war."

"You're really short for a Martian," she said. "Low gravity on Mars, only point-three-seven-six gees. Six and a half foot average height for natives."

There was a pen on the bedside table. A vase next to that. They'd have to do if she had to subdue him.

He held out his hands, pleading. "Please, listen to me. I don't have much time. I messed up. I'm not supposed to be here. We've got stealth ships that not even the Synth can see. We were supposed to do quick recon. But I got separated—I had to hide here, to avoid capture. We're developing weapons that not even the Synth'll be able to fight."

"Weapons?" she said, doubtful. His desperation was obviously real, that much was clear. "What kind of weapons?"

The boy smiled, held up his hand, and engulfed it in flickering blue flames. Another magic trick, like the coin from earlier.

"The human kind," he said, making the fire twist in a colorful swirl between his palms. "Telekinetics. Pyrokinetics."

Jem sighed, growing impatient. This is what she'd delayed virtual paradise for? A mentally disturbed magician?

"Bullshit."

"Does this look like bullshit to you?"

Nikolai hefted the length of black, a barely visible line rippling through the air from its tip like a fold in the shadows. A glassy distortion, so ethereal it was practically invisible.

It wrapped around Jem's abdomen like a rope and lifted her into the air.

She *roared*, flying into a snarling frenzy as she thrashed and tore at the phantom bindings.

"Oh fuck, I am so sorry!" Nikolai gasped.

The invisible rope dissolved into cool, quickly evaporating foam, and Jem fell crashing back down onto her bed.

"I was just trying to show off," he stammered, obviously mortified. "I didn't mean to—"

The door swung open and the boy spun out of existence, seeming to pull the darkness aside like a curtain, where he could hide.

"The hell is going on in here?" the guard demanded, drawing his sidearm.

"I—I—" she stammered, staring at him, then at the spot where Nikolai had disappeared.

"What?" he growled, following her gaze, then looking back at her, confused.

"Nothing," she finally said. "I was having a nightmare."

"Christ, kid," he said, slowly moving his hand from his weapon. "Scared the shit out of me. I—"

An alarm pierced through the air, echoing loudly up and down the tile hallways.

The guard's eyes went wide.

"What the hell . . ." He glanced down at a little screen on his wrist, which was flashing red. "Full alert. Full lockdown. Holy shit. All right, kid. Your surgery's being delayed. Get dressed, *quick*."

He slammed the door behind him.

The air seemed to boil off Nikolai as he came back into existence.

"What are you?" Jem hissed, scrambling to her feet. She grabbed her clothes, which had been folded up on the bedside chair, and pulled her pants on under her gown.

"Psy Ops," Nikolai said, subtly puffing out his chest. "United Colonial Marines. I can take you with me. I have a ship hidden in the lake southwest of here. Twenty miles, I think?"

Jem stared at him, going cold. Unable to stifle the nauseating flood of images summoned by the mere mention of the lake where her life had come to an end.

Blue, curled up into a limp ball on the mud.

The Armitage husk's empty mirror eyes. A slender giant of quicksilver looming between them.

Nikolai barreled on. "I wasn't medically prepped for fieldwork. I'm sick—I think I've caught your plague. I was going to leave in the morning, but the Synth, they know I'm here. I fought some of them—they don't know what I am, but if they get their hands on me, everything's fucked. Colonel Machado just attacked me—the Synth threatened him, told him to hand me over. The whole base is gonna be lit up soon. So we gotta go *now*."

Jem finished getting dressed as Nikolai went to go look out the window. Outside, the watchtowers had begun to light up—their roving spotlights crisscrossing to illuminate the surrounding minefields and forest edge as bright as day.

"What does this have to do with me?" she asked, coming up beside him. Was this really happening? Had something somehow known how close Jem had been to diving headfirst into oblivion . . . and intervened?

Something at the edge of her memory stirred. Not from her mods—not even from the fuzzy pre-mod depths of her early childhood and infancy. It was more like a time traveler's telegram, delivered as Morse code tugs through the connected fourth dimensional wires of her DNA.

A distant flourish. The faintest hint of a song. Then it was gone.

"I could never abandon a fellow Beatles fan," Nikolai said.

She gave him a sharp look. This wasn't VR, right? She'd never actually gone through with fully immersing. Right?

She checked her memory banks. No. No gaps.

Heart pounding, she remembered that she'd turned off the safety measures blocking selective digital memory suppression within VR. She rescinded her overrides, allowing all the safeguards she'd switched off to resume functioning.

Would she remember programming some sort of colonist rescue escape fantasy like this with just her organic storage?

In the rare occasion that her mods had been forced to reboot, it always seemed like a struggle to stand up, let alone think straight. But how much of that was just short-term disorientation? Her mods had never been disabled long enough to find out.

"What does this have to do with me?" she asked again, more firmly. "Why are you here?"

"I need help," Nikolai admitted. "I'm sick, and I'm tired, and I don't know how to get out of here. We're both outsiders, and they're being super shitty to you, so I'm pretty sure that even if you don't help me, at least you won't rat me out."

"The people here are pathetic," she said, still fuming. "A bunch of fucking cowards."

"Help me get back to my ship. Then, once we're in orbit, you can enlist. Join the fight. I promise we won't take away your mods. We won't lobotomize you. We'll upgrade you. So. Are you in?"

Jem struggled with only partial success to stamp out the tiny petals of hope threatening to bloom in her chest.

She pulled on her worn jacket and nodded. "I'm in."

The door burst open and the wail of alarms poured in from the hallway. The soldier rushed in sweating, terrified.

"Come on! We need to—"

The guard saw Nikolai standing there, deer-in-headlights frozen, and opened his mouth to shout.

Nikolai swung the super-black telekinesis stick (which Jem couldn't help but think of as a magic wand), flinging a blob of smooth, opaque slime that covered the guard's mouth with a wet slap.

The momentum of the first swing carried him into another full-bodied wave of his wand that slammed the door shut with a powerful burst of air.

There was an easy, vicious precision to the way Nikolai moved that gave him away as that rare sort of athlete who was a natural when it came to the arts of violence.

Like Jem.

The boy seemed to control his abilities, at least in part, with movements that pantomimed channeling energy to his "magic wand" from specific points along the center of his body. He was like a martial artist, guiding energy from his chakras.

The soldier's protests were muffled as he clawed at the opaque slime, which had solidified over his lips. Eyes widening, he reached for his sidearm. Nikolai was already on him, knocking the man's gun away as he pulled his feet from under him with a yank of the nearly invisible rope.

The soldier grabbed Nikolai's leg and pulled him down on top of him. Nikolai tumbled with a yelp and dropped the baton. They wrestled across the floor, punching and struggling as Nikolai tried to subdue the man.

The soldier drew the blade from Nikolai's belt and tried to jam it into his throat, but Nikolai twisted his wrist, sending the blade spinning across the tile.

Jem pulled the soldier off of Nikolai and subdued him with three vicious punches.

"Thanks," Nikolai wheezed, still lying on the floor.

"No problem." She grabbed the strange knife the boy had dropped and pointed it down at the soldier cowering on the floor. "You. Don't move. Don't make a sound. If you cooperate, you'll be unharmed. Understood?"

Nikolai became quiet, rising suddenly and holding out his hand for Jem to give him the blade back.

"Please don't touch that," the boy said, with the long-suffering politeness of a traveler trying not to be annoyed at a local who'd just committed what would have been a major breach of etiquette in the traveler's homeland.

"Sure," she said, turning the slick black blade in her fingers to give it to him, hilt first. "Go use it to cut that robe into strips so I can tie this guy up."

They stowed the soldier in a closet.

"Nobody can hear you," Jem said at the man's muffled shouts. "Just sit tight, be quiet, and help will arrive soon."

"Everything is going to be fine!" Nikolai added.

They closed the closet, dragging a table in front of it to keep the door secure.

Nikolai ran over to the window and rapped his knuckle against the pane. There wasn't any way to open it—it was sealed shut, thick glass enforced to be bullet and shrapnel proof. "The checkpoints are probably locked up tight. Even invisible we wouldn't be able to get through. But maybe . . ."

Jem watched intently as the boy pressed the tip of his blade against the surface and whispered something. Frost crystalized across the entire window so fast that it crackled audibly.

Nikolai took three steps back and shot a churning column of flame as thick as a python from the hilt of his weapon. He whipped the serpentine fire against the glass in alternating lashes, controlling it like one of the crystal jelly ropes to form a superheated X.

Then he cooled it again, icy vapor pouring down the wall in waves.

Jem watched with awe as Nikolai alternated between fire and ice until cracks spread out across the glass in one spectacular burst.

How was any of this possible? Energy out of nothing. Programmable mass, with adjustable volume, density, appearance, state of matter—from nothing! Shields anchored immovably to their spots in the air without support. Ethereal tendrils able to lift a grown woman into the air without leverage, despite the almost complete lack of physical strain apparent on the part of the wielder.

Nikolai climbed up onto the windowsill, coated one of his sneakers in a shell of the crystal slime, and kicked through the glass. It exploded outward, crumbling easily.

Jem came over to the window. A hovercraft zoomed by—searchlight sweeping across the path two stories below. Nikolai and Jem ducked, hiding from view.

"So do you have a way out?" Jem asked. "Or is that my job?"

"The watchtowers along the fence. Do they have heat vision? That kind of stuff?"

"Yeah. They're always watching on multiple spectrums. Along the inside and out. Synth have cloaking devices. Active camouflage. Not as good as yours, but decent."

"What about the hovercrafts? The trucks? The soldiers?"

"Yeah," she said. "But they won't all be using it. Is anyone other than myself aware of your stealth capabilities?"

Nikolai shook his head. "Not yet, at least."

"They'll be searching infrared in the poorly lit parts of the base. But if they don't know about your camo then they'll just be searching visually on the airstrips, around HQ, and in civilian areas."

"Okay," Nikolai said. "So how do we get out of here? I can turn us invisible and fly us over the fence, but if they're watching that carefully, they'll see us."

"Fly us?" she asked nervously. "Like with that telekinetic arm?"

"No. Lessen gravity's pull on our bodies. Propel us with concentrated jets of jellied air. Here—I'll show you."

Jem gasped as a strange electric tingle covered her entire body, slowly sinking through her flesh until it dissipated in a burst of cold against bone.

Suddenly her weight didn't make sense.

She teetered, almost falling but for the hand Nikolai put on Jem's shoulder to steady her.

"Careful now. I've made you a fraction of your normal weight. Here, try jumping."

She shot up, and would have gone straight through the ceiling had the boy not grabbed her by the ankle.

He released Jem's ankle and got out of the way. She landed on her feet, graceful now that her mods had determined the adjustments necessary to correct the difference for optimal balance and mobility.

"Wow! Just . . . *WOW!*" she said, her expression lit with glee as she gripped his arm. "This—this is incredible, Nikolai. It's like being on the moon again! The Synth don't have anything like this!"

Nikolai preened. "Well, I—"

Booted footsteps ran past the room. They tensed, huddling in the darkness.

"We need to go. Any ideas?"

She looked down, nervously drumming out a complex beat with her fingers on the tile. Then her fingers stopped, and she looked at Nikolai, intense. "It's Friday."

"*Thank God*, right?" he said. "I've had a really long week."

"No," Jem said, growing impatient. "Listen. Every Friday at seven a.m., a convoy of trucks leaves the base to go pick up supplies from the Synth. They won't cancel a run for anything—not even maximum alert. The base needs the supplies and the Synth don't reschedule. They'll search the shit out of the convoy on its way out—but mostly the nooks and crannies. If you can give us both stealth camo we can hide out in the open; no deep search there. Then we ride out—hop off along the way."

"And you're *positive* about this?"

"Yeah. Synth aerial surveillance always gets heavier to the north and lighter to the south during pickup. That's when Runners usually sneak people to the base zone."

It was as good a plan as any.

Jem tucked the incapacitated soldier's pistol into the back of her pants.

"I need you to promise me something," Nikolai said, looking sick. "If we get captured, and there's no way out?" He tapped the center of his forehead. "It's important that they can't bring me back."

Jem nodded, grim. She was almost tempted to ask for the same.

———

Feet propped on the bumper, they clung to the back of an SUV packed with nervous soldiers as it sped along the darkened street.

Jem had one hand clamped on Nikolai's invisible shoulder. She was invisible too, though she'd created an augmented reality overlay with her mods, so that she could at least see herself. She'd found the experience of being able to peer straight through where her body should have been to be deeply unsettling.

An urgent voice over the radios rang out a repeating warning with a detailed description of Nikolai's appearance.

". . . *extremely* dangerous! He is believed to be an agent of the Synth, and though his intentions are unclear, let me repeat that he is armed and *extremely* dangerous. He was last seen in HQ facilities at zero-four—and though believed to be hiding on the premises, until he has been apprehended we ask that every civilian be alert and on watch."

No mention of Jem yet. No mention of Nikolai's cloaking abilities. So far so good.

It began to rain as they came upon the civilian district—fat, icy droplets coming down in steady gusts on the shivering escapees as they clung miserably to the vehicle.

The truck began doing sweeps of the city streets, one soldier sitting atop the cabin, shining a floodlight down alleyways and into shadowed corners. They slowed to a stop in front of a repair shop—slatted gate open as a single early-bird mechanic stood up beside one of several hovercrafts under repair.

The driver chatted amicably with the grizzled mechanic as she warned him about Nikolai, though she assured him that that it was unlikely he would come to the civilian area.

Jem gently tugged Nikolai's arm and hopped off the back, trying not to splash in the water quickly collecting along the sides of the street as the rain intensified.

She took invisible boy's hand and led him up a darkened street.

"Gate's this way," she said. "Let's scope it out and wait there until they begin to load up."

"What is it now, four thirty?"

"Four thirty-six."

Nikolai sighed. "It's a long ways till seven. I won't be able to keep us invisible that long. I need a break to recharge."

Jem felt him stagger, almost falling over. Her grip on his hand tightened, and she pulled him up, steadying the sickly boy. "Let's scope out the supply train, then find somewhere to lay low for a while, so you can rest."

The supply train was seven trucks long, surrounded by a dozen nervous soldiers all smoking and chatting in hushed voices. The trucks waited in a fenced-off sally port—a secondary sort of airlock to the actual gate that served as an extra security measure so that when the main gate was open the base was still locked off.

The inner gate was still open, the outer gate closed off. Wet pavement shone from the floodlights of the twin watchtowers along either side of the entrance.

"Won't the watchtowers see us?"

"They'll just think we're part of the crew," Jem said, crouching in the bushes beside him. "Probably won't lock the inner gate till they're ready to go. We'll be safe so long as we're back here by six forty."

She decided that the nearby apartment complex would be the best place to hide until then.

The whole base was up and awake. Gentle, wailing alarms filled the air; radios, TVs, and wrist comms chattered warnings and descriptions, pulsing red lights flashing in the halls of every building. Fleets of hovercrafts zipped silently through the air, gunmen leaning over the rails with lit scopes, searching the streets, peering through windows.

A crowd of men and women milled about the entrance of the complex in various disheveled states of dress: some in bathrobes, some in pajamas.

"The hell is going on? We under attack?"

"Is it the Synth? Are the Synth coming?"

"No, there's some kid. Or some kind of Synth assassin. Disguised as a kid? I heard he tried to kill the colonel."

"What? You sure this isn't just a drill?"

"I got work in three hours. Damn well better not be a drill."

Backs to the wall, Jem and Nikolai eased their way over to the entrance—freezing as a truck full of soldiers screeched to a halt before the group.

"*GET BACK INSIDE!*" boomed a soldier through a loudspeaker as he shone his light onto the crowd. "*NOW!* We are on *HIGH ALERT—REMAIN INDOORS UNTIL OTHERWISE INSTRUCTED!*"

They fell into line behind two men holding hands and an old man clinging to an old woman as they navigated their way over to an elevator.

Five stories up, they followed the two couples down a hall lit with flashing red lights. One of the men opened the doors for the others and Jem quickly dashed inside, pulling Nikolai after her before the family could get in the way.

The apartment was small for four people. An old, heavily patched couch sat at the center of the main room—a small, equally worn table pressed up behind it, surrounded by four mismatched chairs.

A long, curving holoscreen suspended in the air from wall to wall stood in sharp contrast with the ramshackle furniture. A neatly dressed military official sat at a table, looking into the camera as she silently mouthed words. An image of Nikolai floated beside her. His hair was disheveled, his hands and legs bound to a chair, and he was wearing a paper medical gown.

The image spun slowly, then changed to another image of Nikolai fully dressed, head turned, frozen midstep as he followed Maalouf through a security checkpoint. The image continued spinning to show all angles, and occasionally zoomed in as the woman gestured at the bandage wrapped around his hand. At the super-black rod, hanging at his side. On his strangely luxurious sneakers.

Jem led Nikolai over to an out-of-the-way corner, where they waited invisibly for the right moment to hide in the living room closet.

One of the two younger men collapsed onto the couch, rubbing his eyes as he unmuted the screen with a wave.

". . . rest assured, the would-be assassin will quickly be brought to justice. We are currently on full alert—all military personnel must *immediately* report for duty. All civilians are to remain indoors until—"

The old woman stood wide-eyed beside the couch, trembling. "This is it," she whispered. "This is how it starts. Just a little thing. Just one person. But it'll all be over soon."

The other three stared at her, concerned.

"Why don't we watch something else, mom," the young man said, gently sitting her down on the couch with him and wrapping an arm around her frail shoulders. "One of your old movies. Something to lighten the mood." He gestured again and the woman on the screen disappeared, replaced by deep blue skies full of misty clouds.

The other men exchanged glances as the woman's son navigated the menu. The old man opened a sliding, slatted closet door set into the wall opposite the screen and grabbed two coats. He tossed one to the other man. "Smoke?"

They went out onto a small balcony, closing the glass door behind them. Jem brought Nik over to the closet, helping him scoot over into its depths to nestle in the warm darkness of long hanging coats and a neat pile of shoes and boots.

Beside her, Nikolai let out a long sigh of relief as their invisibility dissipated.

The old woman was left alone to watch the movie. Nikolai leaned forward, eagerly peering through the slats, eyes wide with a childlike glee that made Jem's heart ache. Smiling to herself, she signaled for him to wait and crept out of the closet into the living room, and then to the kitchen.

When she returned, her arms were full of nutrient-dense plunder.

Nikolai barely had time to thank her before he'd chugged an entire bottle of water, had already torn open two full protein rations, and was getting ready to pounce on a candy bar.

With time to kill, they settled in to watch the movie and feast on snacks.

A pair of lovestruck teenagers sang a duet in Hindi—fingers intertwined as they danced across a balcony overlooking a sea of twisting orange-tinted clouds.

"You know what movie this is?" Nikolai asked through a mouthful of roasted peanuts.

"*Romeo and Juliet*," Jem said. "They're the heirs to warring Venusian crime syndicates in this one. It's a musical."

"Do you know what they're saying?"

Jem looked at Nikolai, smiling. She began to translate, whispering the words just as the characters said them onscreen. He watched, enthralled.

Soon she too found herself enthralled. Not just by the movie—but by the sea of clouds beyond. The atmosphere of Venus, where the film was shot. The chemical rain, running down the windows. The crackling multicolored lightning, ever underfoot.

How could she have thought that there was nowhere else for her to go? Of course there was more. There were *worlds*.

Jem watched the couple dance—watched the orange light play across the ballroom tile through the skylights, her chest bursting with hope and wonder.

So much more than this.

"I've never been to Venus," she said. "I went to the moon when I was little. Danced out in the fields of dust. The Earth looked like a toy. Like a big blue globe, hanging just out of reach."

She turned to Nikolai, impassioned. "The skies of Venus. The seas of Europa. The cliff cities of Mars, the ring colonies of the asteroid belt. I can see any of them. Feel *ANY* of them. I can live there in my mind. Walk the cracked red Martian sands barefoot without any fear of vacuum or cold. But that's not good enough.

I want to go there. I want to go there for real. In my mind I can touch it, smell it, *feel it*. But—it's just not the same."

She put her hand on his shoulder, grasping it tightly.

"You've been there, right? Venus? Europa?"

After a moment of hesitation, Nikolai nodded.

"And?"

"They're even more beautiful than they were before the war."

The holoscreen went red—a screeching noise replacing the music. The old lady jerked awake and began screaming.

The men rushed in from the other rooms, rubbing sleep from their eyes.

The red went white—then shifted back to the neatly dressed woman at the desk.

"An update," she said. "The suspect is now believed to be accompanied by a cybernetically enhanced female of African descent."

A picture of Jem appeared, sitting fully dressed for interrogation—then it changed to another of her standing, mid-step through a security checkpoint.

"Whether she's a hostage or an accomplice is unclear, but until these suspects have been apprehended they are both considered to be armed and dangerous agents of the Synth. They are believed to possess cloaking technology. A full-scale manhunt is now underway, including any and all civilian living quarters. Please remain calm. Prepare for your homes to be searched. We thank you in advance for your cooperation."

Shit.

"How are you feeling?" Jem whispered to Nikolai. "Can you move?" Brow furrowed with concern, she placed the palm of her hand on his forehead. "You're burning up."

"I'm feeling a little better. But we're fucked, aren't we?"

She looked away, thinking. "The gate, it's not going to work now. It's the obvious way out, and they'll be going over it inch by inch on every spectrum."

"So yes?"

"Not necessarily." She glanced at the blade hanging at Nikolai's side. "The way you broke through the window. Do you think you'd be able to cut through chain-link fence?"

"Yeah," he said. "Easy."

"Okay," Jem, formulating a plan B. "If we commandeer one of the armored vehicles searching along the perimeter, and incapacitate the—"

A horrible alien trumpeting cut through the air—loud enough that it *hurt*, loud enough that it reverberated through the floor. The family in the apartment screamed, clutching their ears, and there was a flash of light followed by a glow. The young couple rushed out onto the balcony, the old couple quickly following.

Invisible once again, Jem and Nikolai crept out of the closet while the family wasn't watching and went to investigate.

The marbled black clouds overhead were painted over the center of the base with otherworldly light.

The light was being projected from off base—surging mist and rain making the beam appear as a solid, angled shaft. The light shifted, seeming to turn in on itself as the image of an immense face formed at the center. Pale skin. Fair, neatly parted copper hair. Beautiful and androgynous, like some sort of angel.

Armitage.

That trumpeting horn blared out again, and then it was coming from the TV, from wrist comms, from vehicles on the street. The pale face now dominated the living room screen as well as the clouds.

"*Occupants of Durham Air Force Base*," the voice said, thundering from the sky and echoing from every wirelessly connected audio device on the base. *"You are currently in violation of the terms set allowing for your continued existence as a self-governing entity. Approximately thirty-six hours ago an artificially weaponized humanoid of unknown origin entered your jurisdiction."*

"Armitage," the old lady moaned, clutching herself. "I knew it. Oh God, I knew it!"

"Shush, Mama," her son said, though his eyes were full of despair.

"Armitage?" Nikolai whispered to Jem.

"This region's Overmind," she said distantly.

"We generously allowed a grace period exceeding twenty-four hours," Armitage continued, its sophisticated, melodious voice hateful to Jem's ears as it rang out from a thousand places in every direction, *"in which we awaited word from your appointed leader, Colonel Rafael Machado. Hoping that as a sign of goodwill he would alert us to this entity's presence, it was with great disappointment that it fell upon us to contact your colonel, insisting on the weapon's transfer.*

"As per our terms, the covert development, purchase, or undisclosed concealment of advanced weaponry is seen as evidence of intent to commit violent insurgency. To our further disappointment, after a promise of transfer within the hour, we have been met with excuses and delay. It is with great regret that we now prepare to occupy and disassemble your settlement if the weapon has not been transferred into our custody within thirty minutes. We sincerely hope that this won't be necessary, and that our relationship can continue peacefully. You have until six a.m."

The beam of light disappeared. The clouds went black, the screen went dark. For a moment everyone stood there in stunned silence, the old lady weeping softly into her hands.

The woman on the screen returned, frantically begging the

civilian population to remain calm even as she failed to hide the terror in her eyes.

The family living in the apartment frantically packed their bags amid heated arguments. Jem and Nikolai waited, quietly pressed into the corner, until the foursome left to go hide in a nearby shelter.

Nikolai allowed the invisibility to drop. He walked over to the balcony door, peeking out through the blinds to look at the sky.

Slowly, Jem crossed the room, moving to stand opposite from where Nikolai had his back to her. An icy detachment began to permeate her being, making it feel as if she were watching somebody else slowly draw their gun.

"I'm sorry, Nikolai."

He turned to face her, puzzlement turning to shock as he found a gun leveled at his face.

She hardly knew the boy, but couldn't help but be sickened by his look of wounded disbelief.

Looking at Jem like that, while she held him at gunpoint—he looked so much like Eva.

Was this to be her life?

"Not another step," she said. "Hands in the air."

"Jem?"

"I said hands in the *air!*"

"Jem, what are you doing?" Nikolai failed to keep the tremor from creeping into his voice. He raised his hands, placating. "The Synth are coming. We need to get out of here!"

"I'm sorry, Nik," she said. "I have to kill you."

"*WHAT?*"

"In twenty-two minutes the Synth will attack," she said. "Twenty-three minutes and Machado will launch the nuclear arsenal rather than let the Synth take the base. The last one, he'll detonate here—ground level. The Synth won't even have a chance to shoot it down."

She shook her head. "Twenty-two minutes isn't long enough for us to find a way out of here. And even if we could, the Synth forces are closing in—no way to sneak through that line. If the Synth weren't looking for us then maybe we'd have a shot at getting away. But now?"

"These people were going to lobotomize you!" he practically spat. "What about your memories, and "Hey Jude," and all the other things they wanted to cut out of your head? Don't you want to keep all that? Don't you want to see the stars? Don't you want to go to Venus?"

She shook her head, cold. Resigned.

"What I want isn't worth the end of this place. This place—and all it represents—people *die* trying to get here. There's no satellite communication—your people shot them all down. So for all we know, this might be the last place on earth where a person can be a person."

"I know that," Nikolai said gently "And I want to help. My people want to help. *Will* help. But if I—"

"You're just one soldier, Nik," she said. "You said that if they took you alive, it'd be over. That if we were caught I should kill you. If what you've said is true, then the only danger to the colonial effort is you being caught. Not killed."

She shrugged, expression hardening.

"If I kill you, and give Machado's men your body, they can get it to the Synth before it's too late. Maybe the colonel will kill me after. Maybe they'll try to hand me over to the Synth. Maybe I'll be able to convince them that you kidnapped me. But it doesn't really matter what happens to me."

She clicked off the safety, no longer trembling. Her eyes devoid of emotion.

"Goodbye, Nikolai. And thank you."

"So that's it?" he said, words brimming with contempt. "You're just giving up? You're not even going to try to find another away?"

Maybe we could've found a way.

Blue's voice flooded Jem's mind in an unbidden rush.

"A few blocks away, where we got dropped off," Nikolai said, seizing the opportunity of Jem's hesitation for one final placation. "There's a garage that has those hovercrafts things—whatever you call them! What if I turn one invisible, and shield it with hardened air? Then we fly out, wherever the Synth line is thinnest. As soon as we're behind them—we *drop* the invisibility. I start a big light show, and we fly for it. You pilot, I shield. They'll probably get us—it probably won't work—but at least we'll have tried! Twenty minutes, that's *plenty* of time if we go now. Plenty!"

Jem stared at him, torn.

"Promise me one thing," she finally said. "If it looks like we won't make it—you let me kill you. A bullet in the head, as promised."

"Absolutely," he said in a rush. "I swear it."

Slowly, Jem lowered the gun.

She'd regret this. She knew she'd regret this. But . . . Nikolai. He really did remind her of Eva.

Especially when he was lying.

XI.

THE MAGICIAN'S PROMISE

Nikolai led the way as they dropped invisibly from balcony to balcony.

They could hear soldiers within, slamming through doors, goggles on, rifles out, screaming at citizens. Down below, scattered groups of civilians ran, ignoring the shouted orders of armed soldiers to get back inside as they searched desperately for bomb shelters that weren't already at capacity.

Two hovercrafts made a quick patrol of the street as Jem and Nikolai crouched behind a couple of trash cans along the side of the apartment complex.

An SUV screeched to a halt as more families came out with bags slung over their shoulders and made a run for the nearest shelter.

An agitated soldier climbed out of the passenger-side door, rifle pointed at the sky.

"Get back inside!" he screamed at the terrified civilians. Then, as they faltered, looking at one another and then back at the street, seeing the other civilians making a break for it, "I said *GET BACK INSIDE!*"

As the soldier continued to scream, the driver watching him with a frown as he waited for his partner to get back in, Jem wordlessly pulled Nikolai from behind the trash can, dragging him by the front of his shirt with a viselike grip in a low crouching run around the SUV. No way was she going to let Nikolai slip away.

The driver, still uneasily watching his friend scream at the civilians, didn't notice as Jem came up alongside him. With a graceful, lightning-quick motion, Jem reached in, opened the door, and pressed her gun against the soldier's throat.

"One fucking noise and I pull the trigger," she hissed.

Nikolai reached in with his blade and cut through the soldier's seat belt so Jem could yank him out onto the pavement. The soldier came out in a tumble, wide-eyed and baffled by his invisible assailants.

"*THEY'RE HERE!*" he screamed, coming to his senses—not caring at all about the gun pointed at his throat. "*I FOUND THEM, THEY'RE HERE!*"

"*SHIT!*" Jem said, shoving Nikolai through the door and scrambling in after.

The moment Jem took the gun off the man's throat, he rose up with a roar, blindly grabbing at her.

The other soldier turned, pulled on his goggles, and pointed his assault rifle right at Nikolai through the still-open passenger-side door. Nikolai brought up his baton and sealed the door with a frantic wall of *akro* just in time to block a burst of high-caliber shells.

Jem kicked the soldier grappling with her once, twice, *three* times in the face before he finally fell back, letting go. She slammed the door, violently shifted the truck into reverse and pulled away so hard that Nikolai was flung forward—accidentally letting their invisibility drop as his face cracked against the dashboard—letting out a cry as he went flying back when she spun the truck around and punched it.

Bullets ricocheted off the rear of their vehicle and Nikolai could hear the soldiers shouting into their radios as he struggled with his seat belt, desperately pulling at it, yanking it, trying to figure out where to plug it in as Jem barreled on, dodging and weaving with impossible machine-like speed and accuracy. No normal human would have been able to maneuver like this. Nobody without enhancements.

"Put on your seat belt!" she shouted.

"I'm trying!" But Nikolai had never used a seat belt before and couldn't get the damn thing to come out far enough to latch.

He held on with a white-knuckle grip as she barreled down the street, twisting and dodging through scattered groups of civilians and the occasional oncoming traffic. With every truck or SUV they passed, another joined their tail, and soon there were four trying to keep up—though none drove with Jem's mechanical accuracy.

"When we get there—do you even know how to fly a hovercraft?" Nikolai shouted over the gunfire.

"I'm reading the manuals now!" she said, spinning the wheel, serpent quick, back and forth as she continued to weave. "For several similar models. Older but similar! Shouldn't be a problem!"

Reading them . . . now? Oh Disc.

To their right an SUV sent civilians screaming and diving out of the way as it swerved up onto the sidewalk to get alongside them. A gunner sitting in a nest atop the cabin leveled his rifle, aiming right at Nikolai. So much for them trying to take him alive.

Nikolai blasted a torrent of *akro* into the man's gun like a stream of water—freezing it around the barrel as he fired—suspending the bullets in the air and blocking more shots. Another soldier in the passenger seat aimed his pistol at Nikolai, arm crossing over the chest of the driver, but Nikolai sent a column of flame at the front driver-side wheel. The tire might have been bullet- and puncture-proof, but under the white-hot blast it immediately sent out a spray of molten black and turned to shreds.

The vehicle veered wildly, smashing into them and then swerving away as Jem struggled to regain control.

"Jesus Christ!" Jem screamed, too occupied to look back. "Are they okay?"

"Um . . . yes?" Nikolai said, glancing back at the overturned SUV. Looking forward, he let out a shout, gripping the seat and door as a scattered group of civilians froze ahead of them, deer-in-the-headlights style.

"Everything's fine!" Jem shouted over the squealing of tires in a way that sounded to Nikolai like everything was *not* fine as she snaked through the mob in an impossible weave while Nikolai screamed with terror and adrenaline.

Somehow free of the crowds, another of the vehicles came up along Jem's side—another SUV with a driver inside and a crow's nest atop, gunner taking aim right at her.

"Lean back!" Nikolai yelled to Jem, and snapped out a tentacle through the other vehicle's passenger-side window—wrapping it around the driver's wrists and yanking back—pulling him halfway out of the SUV.

The driver screamed, clinging desperately to the car door as it rolled off to the side, slamming into a ditch.

"*HANG ON!*" Jem screamed as they approached a T intersection. She spun the wheel and took the turn.

For one sickening moment the truck began to tip over as they screeched around the corner, but then the wheels settled back down and they roared up what appeared to be a completely empty boulevard.

Jem howled triumphantly, looking over at Nikolai with a ferocious grin. "I've got this shit calculated! Weight distribution momentum surface friction suspension capabilities—rain or shine *motherfucker*! Can't catch me!"

Nikolai was grinning too, a big stupid grin stretching painfully across his face, until he noticed the two hovercrafts waiting up ahead, black discs difficult to see against the darkened skies in the surging rain and mists. Too late did he see the soldier with the grenade launcher, aiming down at the street before them.

The soldier fired and they drove headlong into a wall of fire, a wave of heat that shattered the windshield as Jem spun out. For one sickening moment that seemed to stretch out forever the vehicle tipped over, flipping back over front.

"*ELEFRY!*" Nikolai screamed, blasting out the featherweight weaves into the frame, guts, and siding of the SUV—and all of a sudden the vehicle was spinning faster, nauseatingly fast as it ascended, now a fraction of its weight.

Stars blurred at the edge of Nikolai's vision. Jem's eyes rolled up into her head as she blacked out and slid over like a rag doll, flung into Nikolai's arms as his back hit the passenger-side door. Sky, ground, sky, ground, *sky, ground*—flashing and flashing as the SUV soared through the air, spinning and spinning.

Nikolai featherweighted Jem and himself—waiting for just the right moment, and—

He pulled the latch to the door behind him, arm wrapped tightly around Jem as they were flung free of the wreckage—up into the air, the soldiers atop the hovercrafts below gawking up in awe, the truck spinning away like a toy as it began its descending arc.

Airborne, Nikolai quickly rendered the two of them invisible—his magical pools straining from the effort, after having had so little time to recharge. He was burning through his dwindling reserves with a quickness.

Jem came to, screaming and grabbing onto him as they fell.

"HOLD ON!" he shouted against the wind, gripping onto the baton around her waist and clutching it as he released a jet of jellied *akro* to ease their descent.

There! The garage! And up the street, from where they fled—chaos. Fire. An explosion as the featherweight weaves dissipated from the SUV and it came smashing down from its impossible height. They'd lost them! In the chaos, in the confusion, in the fire and the mob—they'd lost them!

"We're gonna make it!" Nikolai laughed over the wind. "We're gonna—"

There was a sound like a thunderclap and a high-pitched whistle. A high-caliber bullet struck him in the leg with such force that he feared it might have broken his leg despite his uniform's enchantments.

Reeling from the pain, Nikolai spun out of control. It was all he could do not to drop his baton or let go of Jem as they began to fall, faster and faster, and—

At the last moment, Nikolai managed to twist around so that he was underneath Jem, and just before they struck the pavement his uniform released a powerful burst of *akro*, a cloud of softness to break their fall.

Ten feet away from the garage. Ten feet from the hovercrafts within. They'd *made it*.

Wheezing, Nikolai untangled himself from Jem as she slowly came to her senses, gripping his baton in one hand as he began to drag himself across the pavement over to the golden light spilling out onto the blacktop from the garage. So close. *SO close!*

An SUV, black paint shining slickly in the wet, gray light of predawn, screeched to a halt in front of Nikolai, blocking out the golden light as it sprayed him in the face with filthy water. Nikolai fell back with a howl of frustration as the soldiers poured out of the truck, shouting, assault rifles trained on him.

Nikolai stood, slowly—and he could feel the muzzle of Jem's pistol pressed against the back of his head as the six soldiers formed a ring around them, screaming and shouting.

"We almost made it," Jem said. "It was a good try, Nik. I'm . . . I'm sorry."

Nikolai closed his eyes, breathing hard as he waited for the shot to go off, knowing that he wouldn't feel it, that he'd just switch off like a light, and he could see them, hear them—Stokes and Astor and Albert Red Jubal Marblewood *New Damascus Ilyana*—

NO.

Nikolai ducked and snapped out a tentacle around Jem's waist from his baton and flung her into the three soldiers in front of them, below their rifles, into their stomachs, knocking them back.

Arms thrown over his head, he leaped over Jem and the fallen soldiers, rushing into the garage as they frantically shot at him, the air roaring with gunfire. He screamed as he felt two of his ribs shatter from the force of their shots, felt the skin on his calf split and bleed from another—but he kept going, twisting around with a tentacle from each of his Focals as he yanked the heavy slatted gate down with all the force his magic could muster.

The instant before it came crashing shut on the cement floor, Jem dove under it, landing in a roll.

"*You promised!*" she howled, running at him with her hand balled up into a fist.

"I'm sorry!" Nikolai said, just barely fending her off with a tentacle from his baton, locking the gate in place with bolts from his dagger as the soldiers shouted and struggled to force it open. "I'm so sorry, Jem, I couldn't do it, I just couldn't do it. But it's okay! We still have a chance! We still have time! We just need to shield the hovercraft, and then we can try to break through, and—"

The Synth's trumpeting wail filled the air like the death cry of some immense behemoth. Jem and Nikolai doubled over with pain from the sound, hands gripped tightly over their ears.

"*We regret to say that your time is up,*" Armitage said with a thousand voices, sounding very much like a disappointed parent. "*We will now commence occupation. Those who surrender peacefully will be assigned to homes in nearby cities. Neither friends nor families will be separated. You will be assigned jobs, if you choose to work. Your lives will be those of comfort and plenty. Those who resist, however, will be assigned to Torment. It is our sincere hope that this won't be necessary.*"

Explosions began to thunder in every direction. Roiling clouds of dirt and smoke rose into the air from the minefield strip surrounding the base.

Jem looked at Nikolai accusingly.

The soldiers opened fire on the gate. Jem and Nikolai hit the floor, covering their heads as the gate was riddled with bullets, each hole sending out a slender shaft of dim light across the dusty garage.

But then the gunfire stopped, and outside they were shouting and screaming at each other, heated.

"They don't matter anymore!" one of them was saying. "It's too late! We've got to go we've got to *GO!*"

There was more shouting, and then a short burst of bullets. Doors slammed shut and the SUV tore off, wheels screeching as the soldiers rushed to join the battle.

Nikolai stood and went over to the still-crouching human. Slowly he offered her his hand.

"I'm so sorry that I lied to you. Sorry that I broke my promise. But . . . *please*. Let me take you out of here. Let's at least *try* to get back to my ship. Maybe we can make it. And maybe, someday, we can come back. Even if we can't help these people, we could . . ."

Jem stared up at Nikolai, her eyes full of hatred. Contempt.

She took his hand.

Nikolai spat blood as he coated the outer hull of the hovercraft with a thick layer of *akro* armor. Jem coldly pointed out which parts of the vehicle could be sealed up and which couldn't. He staggered around the machine, leaning heavily against the hull, clutching his side. The broken ribs made breathing agony, let alone moving.

The street was clear beyond the gate. Jem searched around briefly, retrieving her gun. After that, she busied herself at the craft's control panel, flipping switches, hands a blur over lights and buttons. The craft gently hummed to life and silently lifted into the air.

"All systems go," she said without looking at Nikolai. "I've built a virtual representation of the vehicle in my head—I'll be able to see it. You can make it invisible now."

It was all Nikolai could do to cling to consciousness as he finished up, covering the whole thing with a sheet of invisibility so big and so draining that it felt as if he were pulling the flesh from his bones. There was a pulsing, abstract agony in his magical pools that made him terrified that he was about one step away from burning himself out and becoming a half-mage, like Hazeal, who'd claimed to have done so while battling a Moonwatch.

Meanwhile, on the radios, they could hear Machado screeching threats—explosions continuing to roar out all around them as the Synth triggered the mines.

"—A DOZEN NUKES POINTED AT A DOZEN LOCATIONS ACROSS NORTH AND SOUTH AMERICA IF YOU DON'T *STAND DOWN*! THE DEATHS OF THOUSANDS ON YOUR HANDS—SYNTH AND HUMAN! We just need MORE TIME! A little MORE TIME! We have the target's approximate location—we can have him to you WITHIN THE HOUR! But if you continue your attack, I'll have no choice but to detonate! And then you'll never find your GODDAMN WEAPON!"

"*As regrettable as the annihilation of your population and the radioactive contamination of your surroundings would be,*" Armitage replied, speaking over the same frequency as Machado, "*it would in fact resolve our concerns even more thoroughly than occupation. At some cost, undoubtedly, but at significantly less effort. As for the rest of your arsenal, they are of no threat to us. Surrender or prepare for Torment. This will be our final communication.*"

Nikolai collapsed into a heap on the floor of the hovercraft.

"Okay," he wheezed, forcing himself to his feet and clinging to the rail. "Just one more . . ." With agonizing effort, he created a bubble shield of transparent *akro* and pierced it with his baton to create another sheet of *camelos*—truly making the whole thing invisible. Retching, he collapsed to the hovercraft's floor again, curling up into a trembling ball as he completely focused his energy on maintaining the *akro* and *camelos* spells. "*Go.*"

Jem gently guided the hovercraft out into the rain.

Unable to see his body or the craft, delirious from pain and exhaustion, Nikolai felt like a ghost—like some floating point of view, zooming through the hellish urban landscape without a body.

As they rose up over the buildings, higher and higher into the sky, it became obvious that they no longer had to worry about human soldiers trying to shoot them down. Nikolai and Jem were the least of Base Machado's concerns.

The air to the west surged with vast clouds of drones, large and small. Thousands of hounds and hundreds of larger, tanklike vehicles waited along the edge of the forest. Countless scuttling little dots swarmed onto the minefields, detonating every bomb to clear a path for the others.

All at once there came a series of blinding flashes. Jem let out a cry of surprise as Nikolai grunted, squeezing his eyes shut— long phantoms of light seemingly burned into his retinas. When the phantoms cleared, he saw that every single watchtower along the southern and western borders had been reduced to a smoking, bubbling slagheap of twisted metal.

Watchtowers destroyed, a swarm of spherical drones descended on the civilian and military districts, trailing thick carpets of yellow smoke. Some kind of gas.

"THIS IS YOUR FINAL WARNING!" Machado screamed.

The Synth army marched on, ignoring him.

Dozens of sophisticated fighter planes were taking off from the airstrips to defend the base—breaking the sound barrier with painful thunderclaps as they quickly approached, little mirrored drones surrounding each jet in formation.

The surging Synth drones separated, parting to make way for black teardrop crafts that cracked through the sky with no discernible means of propulsion, zigzagging at speeds that would kill any human pilot with drones of their own—balls of light that pulsed and zigzagged in patterns at odds with the teardrops.

The Synth fighters rushed to meet the human fighter planes—filling the sky with fire and flashing light as they easily outmaneuvered and decimated the last remnants of the United States Air Force, losing very few of their own.

There was a rumble, and at a dozen points across the base, darkened silos opened to reveal themselves. Impossibly loud, gleaming rockets rose into the atmosphere atop pillars of smoke, surrounded by clouds of mirrored drones similar to those surrounding the human fighter planes.

The nukes.

Cracks louder than any lightning bolt filled the air as shafts of light lanced across the base, targeting the rockets as they quickly gained altitude. Six of the nukes exploded—destroyed, not properly detonated. The remaining six had significantly thinner flocks of drones around them—the mirrored machines having taken enough of the damage from the beams to protect the missiles.

A second volley of the blinding lights destroyed two more of the nukes.

Then another—and now only one remained—scorched, without any more protective drones. But then it was gone—beyond the clouds, out of sight.

Was it on its way to orbit? Would it be destroyed by the colonists? Or would it just fall back to earth, striking its target? Wherever that might be.

Was this how the Mage King had felt as he watched Vaillancourt's missiles fly? Had Julian Cosmus also struggled to breathe as the incredible depths of his failure played out in hellish splendor before his very eyes?

A contingent of the Synth teardrop fighter planes rose up into the clouds, firing after it—but no explosion came, and soon the Synth fighters came back down to rejoin the fray.

"The attacks are concentrated along the southern and western borders!" Jem shouted over the destruction. "Looks thinner to the southwest. I'm going for it!"

The hovercraft was *fast*—fast enough that Nikolai grew dizzy as they flew over the carnage. The fences had toppled and the machines surged across the base unmolested. The tent city was lit with constant scattered pulses of lasers firing off from the spherical hound faces—now visible in the dim light of predawn—as they chased down the screaming, fleeing humans, stunning them and leaving them collapsed and occasionally trampled on the ground.

Among the small hounds were the large tanklike machines, which had dozens of segmented tentacles reaching out from their camo shells, collecting the stunned humans as well as any stragglers who'd come within reach and feeding them into a sphincter portal on their backs. Even from high up above, Nikolai could hear the muffled screams of the people trapped within.

Here and there were small, scattered pockets of resistance. Assault rifles flashing, SUVs wove in and out of the packs, groups of soldiers raining down destruction from atop surprisingly resilient hovercrafts until they were inevitably shot down.

Howling sirens. Synth trumpets.

The hovercraft's radio crackled and Machado's voice came onto the air, snarling, pleading. "Armitage! This is insanity! If you don't withdraw your forces, I'll turn this entire region into a wasteland! There will be *no* opportunity for intercept. I know your kind doesn't want this. I know *you* don't want this! So please. *Withdraw your forces!*"

Silence. A long silence. Their hovercraft increased speed, the engine groaning with effort as they approached the tangled mess of fence that was once the southwesternmost point of the base. And suddenly they were beyond the confines of Machado Base— autumnal, crimson-leafed woodlands below looking bloody in the rain.

"We won't make it," Jem said. Cold. Accepting. "We'll never get clear of the blast zone."

Behind them, a new siren began to wail. Ominous and strange. Different than the others.

The radio crackled again. And then came Machado's voice— oddly calm.

"Soldiers. Citizens. It has been a great honor serving with you. At times difficult. At times impossible. But always a joy. This place . . . and all of you . . . have given my life great meaning. And I hope that your time here will be a beacon in your memories—a touchstone for the incredible trials ahead. But know this. This . . . tyranny. This evil. This will pass. *Armitage*—the others. They aren't gods. They're just monsters. And monsters always fall. Humans won't fade away. Won't be snuffed out. We're too resilient. Too cunning. Too *good*. We won't . . ." He trailed off, sounding dazed. "I'm sorry, but . . . I can't. I can't do it. I won't kill you all to prove a point. I won't . . . please. Lay down your arms. Surrender. Go peacefully. Don't fight back. I truly am sorry."

Another long silence—and for a moment, the fighting fell into a lull below—the hounds and collectors halting in their paths as humans and Synth alike stopped to listen.

"Nikolai," Machado finally said, and Nik was jerked to attention, stirred from his agonized stupor by the sound of his name. "Wherever you are. This is your fault. Our blood is on your hands. *And I hope you burn in hell.*"

Then, there was an odd scuffling sound, and another voice, shouting "Sir—sir, *NO!*"

A gunshot went off and the other voice began to scream.

The radio went silent.

Jem remained silent as the base began to shrink in the distance behind them. But Nikolai could feel her hate—her *guilt*.

They flew in miserable silence.

As the lake drew near, it dawned on Nikolai that they were going to make it. That he was going to see everyone again. To have a chance to make up for all of . . . this.

He should have been relieved. Should have been happy. But all he felt was numb, all he could hear was the muffled screams of humans being pulled into the stomachs of mechanical monsters. Of Colonel Machado cursing Nikolai to *hell* with his final words before taking his own life.

"There," Nikolai said, pointing down at the ruined house with the big charred *X*. He allowed the invisibility and *akro* weaves to melt away. The relief was so great that he almost fainted, clinging to consciousness with sheer force of will.

They were too far away from the base to hear the sounds of fighting now—all that remained was the gentle pitter-patter of rain on leaves, of the faint splashing as little waves gently broke against the shore.

"*There?*" she gasped, trembling and hyperventilating as she looked at Nikolai, then back at the house. "No. No, no, nonononono—"

Her hands were shaking so badly that the hovercraft began to wobble unsteadily under her control.

"Jem!" Nikolai shouted, clamping a weak hand on her shoulder. "Get a hold of yourself! Land the craft!"

Still hyperventilating, she complied.

They landed on the beach and she staggered out, falling to her knees as she stared up at the house.

Nikolai came up behind her, confused . . . and then it hit him.

"When I first got here," he said softly. "I searched the houses, looking for supplies. I found . . . people in there. In the basement. You knew them, didn't you?"

She didn't answer at first—just sat there, staring, clawed fingers digging into the sand. "They were my friends."

She heard something and jumped to her feet, spinning around, instantly alert.

"What?" Nikolai said, following her gaze. She took a step back, moaning—staring at a spot over the water. There wasn't anything there, and for a moment he wondered if she'd totally lost her mind. But then . . . he saw it. The water, running in rivulets around something—something that wasn't there.

With a shimmer, the teardrop ship revealed itself—hovering silently over the churning black waters. A portal formed on its side, a hole opening on the otherwise seamless surface of the craft, and a great torrent of what looked like mercury poured out, disappearing under the surface of the lake.

Nikolai watched, frozen with horror as the immense mercurial being slowly rose from the water, fluttering metal skin taking clearer form with every step.

Stupid. He'd been so stupid! Of course they hadn't escaped. Of course they hadn't snuck by. Of course it had just been following them—letting them think they were getting away so that they'd lead it back to where Nikolai had come from. So *fucking* obvious!

"No . . ." Jem whispered, taking another step back. *"NO!"*

She began to scream, falling back onto the ground as the giant slowly came out onto the sand, scrambling to dig something out of her pocket.

A grenade.

"You won't take me!" she howled. *"YOU WON'T PUT ME IN TORMENT!"*

"Jem—NO!" Nikolai screamed, stumbling back, almost falling as he moved to get away.

She pulled the pin, opening her hand to hold it in her palm like a flower as the spoon popped off and the grenade began to sizzle. She looked up at the silver giant, wild-eyed, and grinned defiantly.

It reached out—arm stretching impossibly long, ten feet, at least—as thin as a child's wrist in the brief moment it took to stretch out far enough to close its metallic fingers over the grenade and snatch it away from her—flinging it back too quickly to see.

It exploded a moment later, a distant plume of fire out over the center of the lake.

She sat there in silent shock, staring at her empty palm as if half expecting it to explode anyway. Looking up, she reached for the pistol tucked in the back of her pants and tried to bring it up to her face, but the giant was on her, long fingers making her arms look like twigs as she struggled uselessly, firing off four shots into the air before the monster took the gun from her and tossed it aside.

Holding her down, it looked up at Nikolai as he reached for his Focals and literally threw its arm—the fluttering mercury splitting at the elbow—striking Nikolai in the chest and melting, wrapping around his waist, binding his arm and Focals to his sides.

Struggling, screaming, Nikolai fell to the ground, only one arm still free, the horrible living metal tightening around his waist, pinning his hand to his leg, spreading up his chest.

It was over.

One arm still free, Nikolai pulled himself across the sand, straining, struggling to crawl away. And then—there. He saw it. Jem's pistol, almost within reach. With a groan, Nikolai kicked himself toward it, wrapping his hand around the grip, finger pressed against the trigger.

"I'm sorry, Jem—*I'm so sorry!*"

Looks like he'd be keeping his promise after all. Too bad it was too late to save anyone.

Before he could lose his nerve, before the bindings could spread up his body, rendering Nikolai totally helpless, he pressed the end of the pistol against the roof of his mouth and pulled the trigger.

Click.

Nothing. He pulled the trigger again. And again.

Click. Clickclick*click*.

Nothing. The pistol was out of bullets.

"No more of that," Armitage said, voice soothing. It loomed over him, Jem held loosely in one giant hand. It grew another arm and took the gun. The metal around Nikolai flowed up its fingertips, taking his belt and Focals along with it.

It stepped back, looking down.

"What are you, Nikolai Strauss? Why have you fled to this place? There's nothing here."

Nikolai stared up at it, defiant. Silent.

Staring down at him with a face like a statue, it almost seemed to sigh as it turned and walked a short distance away, where it dropped the struggling Jem onto the ground. It placed an immense foot on the side of her head. She sputtered and screamed, thrashing in the wet send.

"I can tell when you lie, Nikolai," it said. "Now. I'm going to ask you again. What are you?"

"A colonist," Nikolai said through gritted teeth. He glanced at his Focals, dangling from his belt in the Armitage monster's hand.

Jem's scream changed to a squeal of pain as Armitage pressed down, increasing the pressure on her skull.

"Please!" Nikolai begged. "Please, don't hurt her! I *made* her come with me. I made her—"

"What *are* you? Where do you come from?"

"I'm—I'm an experiment, okay? From the colonial military. They—they made me! To fight your kind!"

It made a tsking noise, increasing the pressure. Her eyes began to bulge—her squealing turning to faint, gasping chokes.

"I'm a SYNTH! One of the others made me! One who disagrees with what you've done! Who thinks you're a bunch of *FUCKING MONSTERS!*"

"I can feel the bones straining," Armitage said calmly. "Any more weight and you'll have the pleasure of watching Ms. Burton's eyes pop out of her skull—of watching her brains pour through her nostrils. I'll give you one more chance. In three. Two. One—"

"*I'm a WIZARD!*" Nikolai finally said. And then he started to laugh, hopeless, bitter. "A wizard, okay?" And all of a sudden he couldn't stop laughing. Couldn't stop chuckling at the horror of it all. The absurdity. "*Abracadabra!*" he wheezed, hysterical, "*Alakazam!*"

But Armitage . . . hesitated. Slowly, gently, it removed its foot from Jem's head. She gasped with relief and rolled onto her back, panting. It left her there—coming close to kneel beside Nikolai.

Listening. Watching. As Nik laughed and laughed, tears stream-ing down his face.

"Not . . . lying?" it said. Baffled.

Nikolai tried to read the creature's expression and wondered vaguely what it was going to do to him.

A thread of blue light snaked through the air behind Armitage, piercing the side of its mask-face. It didn't react—didn't seem to feel it. Then there was another thread from the other side, going into its stomach. Then one more and—

It *screamed*—a piercing, alien noise sounding neither animal nor human—and stumbled away, arching its back as the surface of its synthetic, silver flesh began to boil.

"What? *WHAT?*" it managed—then the threads of light disap-peared and Armitage exploded into a million blackened droplets that turned to steam that turned to dust—hitting Nikolai's face as nothing more than a blast of hot air.

He lay there, stunned, as Captain Jubal, Uncle Red, and Jubal's second-in-command, Lieutenant Thane, shimmered into existence at the edge of the water.

Red rushed over to Nikolai and pulled him into a tight embrace—openly weeping. "My boy! Oh, *my boy!*" he sobbed, and Nikolai just lay there, letting Red hold him—distantly think-ing how strange it was to see Red crying—how he hadn't seen him cry since they found out that Nik's parents were dead.

Looking past him, Nikolai saw Thane going over to check on Jem.

Jubal, however, simply stood there, watching him. His eyes met Nikolai's. But unlike Red, Nikolai saw no relief there. No concern, no worry.

Just a great and terrible sadness.

PART III.

THE ART OF VIOLENCE

XII.

TERRIBLE THINGS

Snap.

Bright, white light. Nikolai blinked rapidly, eyes adjusting.

Jubal snapped his fingers in front of Nikolai's face again, then leaned back in his chair and lit up a cigarette.

Nikolai sat on a white chair, in a white room. No door, no windows. No apparent source of light.

How long had he been here? He wasn't asleep—wasn't unconscious. He had the vaguest recollection of sitting here, waiting. But for how long?

He tried to turn his head but found that he could only move *just so*. His hands hung limp on the armrests—his back slumped against the chair. There weren't any obvious signs of binding, no telltale tingling of enchantments on the cool, white paint against the skin of his palm. And yet he was paralyzed.

Nikolai hurt. He hurt everywhere. He didn't feel sick anymore, and his ribs were no longer broken—but glancing down, he saw that his hands remained filthy—fingers crusted with blood and ashes. His sneakers and uniform were caked with mud, with sand. His head throbbed, his leg ached—gummy and scabbed where the flesh had been torn by assault rifle fire.

Jubal sat on a simple wooden chair across from him, puffing great clouds of cigarette smoke between sips from a glass of bourbon.

Beside him was a small table with a pitcher of water and a surgical tray—the contents hidden from view by a neat white cloth. Leaned up against the table was his candy-striped cane Focal.

Nikolai's own Focals were propped up in a small box in the corner of the room.

"Where—" Nikolai tried to say, but his throat was so dry that all he could do was cough.

With a flick of Jubal's finger, the water snaked from the pitcher and over to Nikolai's mouth—where it stopped, hanging.

"Open," he said, and Nikolai did so, letting Jubal slowly levitate the water past his cracked lips.

Nikolai gulped it awkwardly, dribbling most of it down the front of his shirt.

"Where's Jem?" he managed, voice still raspy. "My uncle?"

Jubal didn't answer immediately—he just stared at Nikolai, smoking. Eyes glassy with drink.

"We healed Ms. Burton," Jubal said. "Fed and clothed her. She seems to believe that you're some sort of telekinetic colonist agent, here to save the rest of your long-abandoned human brethren. I'm glad that you at least had the wherewithal not to tell her about our kind." He snorted. "If she only knew what the colonists are actually like now. They've become vicious, preparing for this war. Make the Synth seem cuddly in comparison."

"Is she here still? Can I see her?"

"No," Jubal said. "I erased her memories. Wiped every trace of you from her brain."

Nikolai looked at him, horrified. "But her mods! Wouldn't they—"

"She erased the digital memories herself. As the price for us bringing her to the neutral zone, a country in the Middle East called Rojava, which remains under terrestrial human control. The diplomatic point of contact between the colonists and the Synth. We gave her a falsified history and citizenship, as well as a comfortable sum of local currency."

"As for Redford?" he said, seeming distracted. "Marblewood. Had to confine him for a bit. Let him cool his heels. You won't be seeing him for . . ." He trailed off, sighing. "Your mother's revolver. That's where you learned to bend Veil, correct?"

Nikolai hesitated, and then nodded.

Jubal pulled the cigarette from his mouth and closed his fist around it. There was a small burst of light that shone through the cracks in his fingers. He opened his palm, dusting away the ashes.

"Do you know how worried I was about you? How worried we all were? By the time Redford and your friends realized that you were missing, and not just sulking in some hidey-hole, your trail to the Veil's edge had gone so cold that it looked like you'd drowned in the damn lake."

The Captain downed the rest of his drink in one go and cast aside the glass. It turned to vapor as it struck the floor, rolling out in a misty wave from the point of impact before dissipating.

"Wasn't until we'd dredged half the thing before I thought to check the Veil itself. We all thought you'd fucking killed yourself! I agonized over not having come straight to Marblewood the moment I'd heard what happened. Blamed myself! And from the looks on your friends faces, I wasn't the only one."

Guilt plumed in Nikolai like a flood of ink.

"I know—I've been stupid, *so stupid*, I—"

Hot tears began to pour down Nikolai's face, and he was hiccupping, sobbing—snot bubbling in his nose.

"—it was horrible," Nikolai croaked. "Captain, it was *so* horrible. Oh, I messed up *bad*, I messed up so bad, I—"

Captain Jubal shifted, frowning. But he didn't look away.

Slowly, Nikolai regained composure. Then he became afraid.

"I can't move. Why can't I move?"

"I wish you hadn't run away from the healer's ward, Nikolai," Jubal said wistfully. "Wish you'd just gone to your uncle, like you'd been ordered. You think you're the first young Edge Guard to slip up? To get into trouble?" He shook his head, frown deepening. "Styx, *boy*. After everything you've been through, do you really think I wouldn't have been understanding?"

"I know, and I'm sorry," Nikolai said, guilt and anger a hot muddle swirling in his chest as he strained against the enchantments holding him in place. "But do you really need to bind me like this? What, am I going to attack you? Try to escape?"

"Look at you! Scowling at me like . . . like I'm the villain here! Just like your mother, whenever she was in trouble. Couple of stubborn little shits, the both of you. Self-righteous, even when I catch you committing treason, red-handed!"

Nikolai hissed a breath, narrowing his eyes. "Treason? How have I committed treason?"

"How'd you commit—?" The old Battle Mage guffawed, disbelieving—his breath fragrant with alcohol. "You serious, boy?"

"For what?" Nikolai demanded. "What am I being charged with?"

Jubal's lips pressed into a thin line as he began to list Nikolai's crimes.

"Failure to report for summons," he said, raising a finger as he counted out each offense. "Abandoning your post. Withholding—"

"What post? I was on vacation! I—"

"*Withholding* the knowledge and use of spells strictly forbidden for those without proper clearance," Jubal continued, cutting Nikolai off with a sharp look of warning. "Assaulting civilians and an off-duty Watchman—"

"None of whom are pressing charges!"

"Goddamnit, boy!" Jubal roared. "You will shut your fool mouth and listen, or Disc help me, I'll—"

"Why?" Nikolai snarled, emboldened by his own dire state. "How can I trust anything you say? Everything about the humans— everything about the Lancers, and the Edge Guard, and—and—!"

"Fine!" Jubal exploded. "You want to know the truth? Max dosage of Tabula Rasa potion is twenty-four hours. You were out there for *too long*. No erasing what you've seen."

Nikolai glared up at the moonfaced magus. "Then tell me."

Jubal gave him a tired smile. "Is that what'll make you happy? Higher security clearance? So be it. Here's some top secret fun facts about our wretched kind."

He stood and began to pace back and forth before Nikolai's chair, idly twirling his candy-striped cane.

"Fun fact number one: There were only a few Discs originally. Not the thousands that we currently enjoy. Magi were once chosen from the human population by the Discs for their brilliance and strength of character. They served as guardians and guides to ancient humans."

"Chosen?" Nikolai looked at him, puzzled. Barring the mysterious process of Focal creation, Nik had been taught that there'd never been any successful communication with the Discs. "How? The Discs, did they talk to us? And from . . . humans? So humans can be turned into magi?"

"I've spent most of my adult life trying to answer those very questions. So far as I can tell, the original Discs would come to chosen humans in visions and dreams. As for how they turned a normal human into a mage . . ." Jubal shrugged. "They were different from contemporary Discs. Something closer to gods."

"Where are they?" Nikolai tried and failed to lean forward, remembering in a moment of claustrophobic panic that he was invisibly bound.

"Lost," Jubal said. "Maybe destroyed. The white Discs we use today were created by the wizards of Styx in ancient times, who found a way to create lesser Discs that could imbue the children of magi with magic, regardless of skill or strength of character. Even though magic was *never* meant to be used by just anyone. Think of Vaillancourt, and other such shadow magi. Think of the half-mage animals who tried to kill you in the Noir.

"Now," he continued, with a drunken twirl of his cane, "it would be one thing if we could have just interbred with humanity until *everyone* had magic. Unfortunately, it's always been far more difficult for a sorceress to conceive than a human female, and only a sorceress can give birth to a mage. As such, even if humans and magi were to interbreed for millennia, magi would remain—as they always have—in the scant minority."

Nikolai listened to Jubal, rapt. The standard story of magi history was that of an ancient Age of Wonders in the Veil of Styx spiraling into an Age of Nightmares, when powerful arch magi inadvertently unleashed a race of monstrous tricksters called the

Foxbourne. After centuries of war with the creatures that almost exterminated all life on Earth, the magi secluded themselves in Veils, and human civilization began to flourish beyond.

"Fun fact number two: We teach magi that, historically, we remained carefully hidden from the humans until they began to slaughter each other en masse in the first World War, and we had our first Veil War over whether or not we should intervene. Really, though, we've involved ourselves in the matters of man throughout most of history. Often as slavers, or oppressors— however the various mage kings and queens might have tried to downplay and excuse the ugliness of their actions."

Somehow, Nikolai found this unsurprising.

"Fun fact number three—the Edge Guard was created by an order of early industrial-age humans and magi who recognized that mage-kind simply could not be trusted with involvement in the human world. Time and time again, powerful and corrupt sorcerers would take the technological advancements of man and use them in ways that always, without fail, ended in horror and atrocities. So we sealed the Veils. To *protect* the humans from the magi. This is what we do, Nikolai. This is the noble purpose of the Edge Guard. We're jailers."

Nikolai scowled, impatient. "So that's your excuse? Asshole wizards weaponizing technology? 'Cause right now, the Synth seem like a bigger problem."

Jubal reached into his pocket, pulling out a small tin of his black-papered cigarettes. But then, just as he began to pull one free, he pushed it back, slipping the tin back into his coat.

"Edge Guard regulation of access to the human world was sufficient for a time, until Vaillancourt and his band of wealthy, corporate sociopaths in the early two-thousands. He was brilliant and charismatic, and managed to get his hands on ancient weaponry and spells long believed to have been lost. He was a monster, made dangerous by his brilliance and familiarity with the human methods of espionage and contemporary warfare."

"I know who Vaillancourt is," Nikolai snapped, but Jubal ignored him.

"Vaillancourt kidnapped some of the world's most brilliant magi enchanters and human scientists. Started dabbling in some nasty magi-tech. Really *powerful* stuff. Mixing and merging modern computer tech and engineering with quantum enchantments. Bio magic. *Necromancy*. And he wanted to get rid of the Mage King—a much younger wizard back then. Wanted to destabilize the human governments to start a new world order. An integrated *paradise* for magi *and* humans, he claimed. Even though the fucker was a known supremacist.

"The king killed Vaillancourt in the end—but not until the shadow magus had manipulated the most powerful human governments into extremism, and pushed them into war. The human world fell apart, Nikolai. The footage we release of the Lancer expeditions is real—all taken from the blast zones of the warheads Vaillancourt had enchanted into hexbombs, which we sealed up in containment Veils.

"It became obvious that so long as our kind had any amount of access to the human world—to human technology—no matter how carefully regulated, monsters like this mage would always find a way to meddle with things they shouldn't. And with that kind of power . . . well, it's just too dangerous. Too much of a risk, for humans *and* magi.

"Just before his death, as the human nations began to pummel one another with weapons of mass destruction, Vaillancourt detonated the Discs in Veils across the globe, murdering millions of magi. But when the dust had settled, the king realized that he had an opportunity to use Vaillancourt's final atrocity to convince the population that the shadow magus had destroyed the human world. Which wasn't far from the truth. Then he began restricting the development of technological and even magical advances. Manufacturing, communications, transportation . . ."

Nikolai opened his mouth to snidely let Jubal know that he'd figured this out on his own, but Jubal silenced him with a look, eyes smoldering.

"As Edge Guard, it's our sworn duty to enforce the divide between these worlds. To keep constant vigil on the threats within, and without. Machine, man, or mage. To survey all weaknesses. To plan and prepare for all possible conflicts, while working to prevent any such conflicts from occurring. Anything more than that is up to the king."

"So you're just giving up?" Nikolai whispered, horrified. "Just waiting for the humans to die? You. The Mage King. Waiting for the colonists to destroy the Synth after they've killed all the humans. So you don't have to get your hands dirty."

"Do you really think we're not trying to find ways to put a stop to this? We can't beat them, Nikolai! There aren't enough of us! And the moment the Synth find a way to use magic, it'll be the Age of Nightmares all over again. Only *worse*. It's only a matter of time before the colonists bombard the surface and turn everything outside the Veils into dust. That's how this ends, Nikolai. That's how the Synth are destroyed. The colonists have the resources of the entire Solar System at their disposal, and have been militarizing ever since."

"You're wrong!" Nikolai said, straining against his bindings. "We can fix this! We can make this right!"

"What the hell do you know?"

"I know the king probably used the same excuse when he left

the humans to deal with a nuclear holocaust that was our fault, *long* before the humans invented the Synth. I know that we have magic, and they don't! But more than anything, I know that even if we aren't sure of winning, if we don't at least try, when someone out there eventually finds a way past the Veils—whether it's Synth, to take our magic and wipe us out, or the colonists, to punish us for destroying their world and then hiding instead of fixing it—we'll deserve every fucking terrible thing that happens to us."

Jubal's face turned beet red as he closed the distance between them, gripping Nikolai's arms painfully.

"Do you understand what you've done, you *IDIOT CHILD?*" he roared, spit spraying into Nikolai's face, "How much danger you've put us all in? How many *innocents* have suffered for your actions? What did you hope to accomplish? Eh? Did you want to be their savior? Their magical messiah. *Eh?* You arrogant little half-wit!"

He stood, stalking away to punch the wall, hard. He punched it a second time and left a bloody mark where his knuckles split. He leaned against the wall with his palms, back to Nikolai, breathing heavily. "And now . . . now I have to . . ."

Slowly, he turned back to Nikolai, and his rage was gone—his face a perfect mask of icy calm.

"There have to be consequences. You swore an oath to the king. What you've done is treason."

"Just like my mother, right? She wanted to go to war for the humans too. *Right?*" He spat on the floor at Jubal's feet, defiant. "Since when is not being a fucking coward treason?"

Jubal ignored him, pulling away the cloth on the table to reveal . . . a golden hand. Nikolai stared at it for a moment, glanced at his own, then back at the hand. It was a perfect replica.

Jubal pulled the wooden chair closer, taking a seat. He was

so near that Nikolai could smell Jubal's breath—the bitter stink of cigarettes and bourbon. Forehead shiny with perspiration, he reached into his coat and pulled out a slender, velvet case.

"You've never seen my art Focal, have you?"

From the case, Jubal drew a hideous, barbed scalpel. Black. Glistening. An instrument for torture.

He held it up, admiring it in the glaring light. "I've always been fascinated by the natural sciences. Always been fascinated by mage, human, and animal anatomy. Growing up, I thought I was going to be a healer. But . . ."

He pressed the hooked scalpel through the back of Nikolai's left hand, hot blood pluming and pouring down the side of the chair, staining the white red as the blade slipped effortlessly between bones and tendon. Nikolai screamed, trying desperately to pull away but unable to move.

". . . I guess the world didn't need any more healers."

Screeching through clenched teeth, Nikolai watched as veins of light spread from the cut, stopping at a neat line around his wrist. More lines formed between the veins of light until his whole hand was glowing, and—

The flesh turned to ash. The ash fell away, revealing naked white bone sticking out from the raw, pink meat of his wrist. The bones began to fall apart—no longer held together by any tendons or cartilage. Clicking onto the floor like a fistful of porcelain beads.

Nikolai screamed until he couldn't scream anymore, then he was just twitching, foaming at the mouth—unable to move, only able to kick a little with his foot, eyes rolling up into his head at the pain—*the agony*. He could feel his hand there, feel it burning. Smell the sickly sweet *stink* of it.

But Jubal was holding him now, making gentle shushing noises, squeezing him tightly. "There, there, Nikolai. It's over now. The price is paid. You're okay now, you're going to be okay . . ."

. . . and Nikolai was no longer screaming. He was lying on his back, blinking, wondering if he'd gone blind. No—not blind. It was just dark. A solitary globe was set into the rough stone wall beyond a row of black iron bars with striping that glowed a dim white. As his eyes adjusted to the dim light he realized that he was no longer in the white room—he was in some sort of jail cell. Floors and walls of rough-hewn stone—like a dungeon.

With a gasp, Nikolai looked at his hand. And for a moment he thought that everything with Jubal in the room had been some sort of terrible dream. But then he saw it glimmering in the light, and looking closer saw that his skin ended at the wrist. Beyond that was the golden hand that'd been sitting on the medical tray.

Nikolai stared at it, clenching and unclenching with wonder. As his awareness returned, so did the pain—the cuts and bruises across his body, the aching muscles, the thudding pain in his skull—but most of all the burning throb of his hand, his fingers. Though he could feel the surface of the golden hand like real skin—could move it as fluidly and easily as the one it had replaced—he could still feel the agony of his flesh turning to ash.

Jubal stepped out of the shadows beyond his cell. Eyes heavy with that terrible sadness.

"The pain will fade," he said. "The nerves, muscle memory, and unique magical channels of your original hand have all been replicated perfectly within the prosthetic. It'll track every spell you cast. Every place you go."

Nikolai didn't say anything. He just stared at him. Silent. Hateful.

"You're going to have to work hard to redeem yourself. Work hard to prove yourself in the eyes of the king. I'm leaving you here for the next a week or so. After that you'll be back in your old room and we'll resume your training—under *my* tutelage, this time. I'll be keeping you busy, keeping a close eye on you. But . . . if you prove yourself trustworthy . . ."

Nikolai turned his head to look away from him, into the darkness.

"Nik," he said softly. "I'm . . . I'm sorry."

He stood there in silence for a little while. Waiting for Nikolai to say something, maybe. Finally, Nikolai heard the clicking of Jubal's footsteps as he walked away.

He closed his eyes. The stone was cold and dug into his back, uncomfortable. There was a toilet in the corner, next to a small sink. Feeling like he was two hundred years old, Nikolai staggered over to the sink to drink from the dusty faucet.

"*The price is paid,*" Jubal had said. Nikolai looked at his hand. His golden hand. So strange. Master enchanters had perfected prosthetics long ago—Nikolai knew that before long the pain would fade as his brain adjusted. Soon he wouldn't even notice the difference. It wasn't exactly gold—the skin had give to it. Not quite as supple and soft as actual skin, but a close approximation.

His Focals sat a little ways outside of the cell. He could feel them before he saw them. Baton. Dagger. Sitting in their holsters in his belt, coiled at the bottom of a wooden bucket.

Nikolai didn't even have to test the bars to know that his weaves would melt passing through them. Standard cell enchantments—same as what they had back at Marblewood Watchman HQ. Impossible to unravel, even for an arch magus. No way to get to his Focals.

He folded the blanket on the floor and lay down, staring at the ceiling—golden hand held up in the light. He moved the fingers, watching them glitter.

The war outside the Veils. It was beyond Nikolai. Things might be bad for the humans, but . . . Nikolai's intervention had done nothing but harm. Nothing but ruined the lives of . . . thousands. *Disc.*

He felt himself slipping into a warm, comfortable calm. A tentative sense of relief. He'd still be a member of the Edge Guard. The price was paid. Nikolai's punishment had been harsh, but the worst of it was over. Jubal obviously hadn't wanted to do it—he obviously felt bad about what he'd done to Nikolai. The Mage King had probably ordered him to do it. And he'd get to see everyone again. Have another chance to get things right—to fix things with his friends. To *live*.

And maybe, one day, when Nikolai had earned his way up the ranks, he could push for action. Could try to convince the Mage King to step in. Once he'd proven himself trustworthy, and as the most capable Edge Guard on the force. How many other sergeant-rank Edge Guards could have ventured beyond the Veil and lived to tell about it?

Of course the Mage King didn't want to help the humans yet. There were so few magi. And even fewer still that knew how to fight. How could they possibly hope to stand against the Synth? He'd been naive. So completely—

A rumbling, animal growl made Nikolai yelp with surprise.

Sitting beyond the bars was an immense black wolf, staring at Nikolai with angry, pale green eyes.

It snarled, snapping monstrous fangs as its dark-furred hackles rose and flexed.

Nikolai scrambled back, pushing himself up against the wall as far as he could get from it, terrified as it growled, furious at him, *enraged*, and—

Nikolai blinked.

The wolf was gone.

He gasped, panting. Was he hallucinating? Had he totally lost it? Snapped? But no—no *way* had the wolf been a hallucination. No way had he imagined it. He sat there, catching his breath. The wolf . . . it was so familiar. But where had he . . . ?

Nikolai remembered what Jubal had said about the original Discs communicating with visions and dreams. Was that what this was? Had the beast been a messenger? It seemed crazy, but the wolf *had* been here. Somehow Nikolai knew that he'd really seen it. Impossible, but—he didn't feel crazy. No; he felt a strange clarity.

But there was something more than that. Something Nikolai was missing. Something *important*, that he should have noticed by now, but couldn't quite . . .

And then it hit him. There. When he focused hard—when he cleared his head and pushed away the pain, the *aches*. A small tickling. A sort of tug. An itch. From two directions at once.

Jem's tracer.

But why was it . . .

"*No*," he breathed, standing. "Oh Disc, please no . . ."

Two directions. One far, one close. One above, one lateral.

She was there—tracer still intact, so weak, so distant that he almost missed it entirely. But without a doubt, it was her, and he could feel it tugging—one tug through the portal in Jubal's office, somewhere above him, and in the distance, across the city, at Jubal's home.

Nikolai roared and slammed himself against the bars.

"Captain! *CAPTAIN!* You Foxbourne *WRETCH!* You evil, filthy Jeeves traitor *MOTHERFUCKER!* What have you done to her? What have you—"

He tried everything, every weave, every spell. Tried to dig

through the stone. Tried to channel the water through the cracks, to use it like a tentacle, to pull his Focals close enough to somehow *use*.

It was no use.

Jem's tracer weave like a beacon—a *plea*. Why would Jubal lie to Nikolai? But no—that was *stupid*. Why wouldn't he lie to him? The real question was what did he want with her? What was he *doing* to her?

But no one came. No one replied to his shouts.

Until . . .

"Albert, I *swear*, this better not be some elaborate ruse to get into my pants. Because it's just not happening, kid."

"Oh, for the love of!" Albert's voice echoed through the halls from out of sight, exasperated. "A little benefit of the doubt, *please*. Have you considered the possibility that not every creature on this great green planet would come crawling through rain and fire for the merest *peek* of you in some state of undress? And besides, I happen to be seeing a perfectly dashing young gentleman at the—"

They stopped, gasping as they turned the corner, a globe of *illio* bobbing in front of them.

Ilyana ran over to Nik's cell, eyes wide with shock.

"Nik! Oh, Nik!" she said. "Albert said you were here, said he could sense you through that tracer he put in your shoe! That you must have forgotten to take it off!"

Dazed, Nikolai looked down at his sneakers, crusted with dirt, ashes, and blood. The tracer. The goddamn tracer. He'd totally forgotten about it.

For a moment Nikolai wondered if they were actually there, or if they were phantoms, like the wolf; his mind playing a terribly cruel joke. Here for a moment, then gone in a flash.

He blinked.

But when he opened his eyes, Albert and Ilyana were kneeling before the bars, Ilyana looking horrified, Albert stiff with indignant fury.

"I sensed your arrival last night," Albert said. "Spoke with the captain this morning, asked after your well-being. He told me that you were still in Marblewood. Lied to my face, without so much as a twinge. I searched the headquarters, trying to close in on your tracer, but I simply could not find you. Just as I was about to give up I recalled an obscure passage in one of our older procedural manuals mentioning a derelict brig, and thought that maybe, just maybe . . ."

He looked at Ilyana, then back at Nikolai. "Turns out our rank was sufficient to gain access to the brig, so I confirmed that Jubal would be away for the next several hours to meet with the Mage King and fetched Ilyana to join me in my search. *Disc*, man, what's happened? You're filthy, and the stink of you! *Jeeves!* Is that blood? What in Styx have you done to elicit such savagery?"

"I went outside the Veil. Outside of Marblewood," Nikolai explained. "And—there were people. Humans! Everything we've been told, it's a *lie*. And people, they're dying—they're being killed off. It's been a century; they're *so* advanced now, but there's a war, a war with—with *robots*. Artificial intelligences. There was a human with me—a girl. She saved me, I'd have died without her, wouldn't ever have made it home. Jubal—he said he took her to a human city in Rojava, but he *lied*, just like he lied to you, Albert! He's got her at his mansion, and I'm afraid . . . I'm afraid something bad is happening to her."

They stood there in stunned silence, staring at Nikolai like he'd completely lost his mind.

"Nik . . . chap . . ." Albert said, gingerly. "This all sounds a bit . . . far-fetched."

"Captain Jubal wouldn't do something like that," Ilyana insisted. "And . . . machines? Artificial *whoziwhatsits*?"

"Your precious captain burned off my fucking *HAND!*" Nikolai snarled through tears, slamming the palm of the golden replacement against the bars for them to see. "As *punishment*. As a lesson for leaving the Veil—for *daring* to suggest that we intervene. Daring to suggest that the civilian population should know the truth—that *they* should be the ones to decide whether or not we help them. But by hiding the truth—by standing by and just letting the humans die—it's *GENOCIDE!*"

Ilyana stared at Nikolai's golden hand, eyes wide.

"No," she said, just above a whisper, looking down at her own hand with a strange expression. "I don't believe you. He's different. The captain . . . he wouldn't do that."

She began to snake a slender rope of fire through the fingers of her glove. Faster. *Faster.* Then she bared her teeth in a snarl and violently clenched her fingers into a fist around the flames, crushing it out.

"Do you have any evidence?" Albert asked shakily. "Anything besides your current state? Your word?"

"In my room," Nikolai said. "Room two-thirteen. I hid a special rank insignia under the floorboard beside my bed. A Moonwatch medallion."

"Disc, man!" Albert exclaimed. "How did you get your hands on one of those?"

"Doesn't matter. It'll get me out of here. It'll get us up to Jubal's office—we can get to his house from there. We'll get Jem. Then I'll open up a door in the Veil and show you what's outside."

"Okay," Ilyana said, struggling to calm herself. "Okay, okay, okay, let's get it. Let's go."

"Wait!" Nikolai said as they turned to leave, golden hand outstretched through the bars. "Please, please don't leave me alone here. Please!"

Ilyana went back in a rush to kneel beside the cell, taking Nikolai's hands through the bars and holding them tightly.

"Albert," she said. "Go on without me. I'm going to stay."

Albert started to argue, but at her sharp look he shut his mouth and nodded.

"I missed you," Nikolai said, trembling. "I really, really missed you."

She smiled, blinking back tears. "I'm sorry I never picked up when you called. I . . . I just . . ."

"*I just. You just. We just*," Nikolai said, his smile bittersweet as he echoed her words from what felt like an eternity ago. "It doesn't matter. I didn't think I'd ever get to see you again, I thought I was going to die, and the way we left things, I thought—"

"Shush, I'm here now, it's okay." She turned over his golden hand, touched the wrist, looking pained. "Oh. Oh, what did they do to you?" She kissed the line on his wrist where the gold met flesh, as if to heal the wound, then kissed his other hand and looked up at him, forcing a smile even though her eyes were red. "I mean, gold? It's so tacky."

Nikolai laughed despite it all, and tried to talk, but he knew if he started talking he'd start crying, so he just smiled and held her hands and stared into her eyes while she stroked his wrist and made soothing noises.

"I'm sorry, I'm so bad at this," he finally managed.

"We are a mess," she agreed.

Albert had no trouble finding the Moonwatch medallion,

though he was sweating and flustered when he returned. After Nikolai was freed, they stood outside the dusty elevator door of the otherwise abandoned brig, basked in the dull orange light of an ancient glow bulb.

"Just take two for now," Ilyana instructed as she tapped out a pair of rubbery little beads from her flask and pressed them into Nikolai's golden palm.

"What are they?" he asked, eyeing the beads—watching the strange, pearly light pulse from within, a soft glow through the oily blue shells.

"Flex," she explained. "Titan's Tears. Sweat of Karna. Sharpens senses. Quickens reflexes. Numbs pain. I use it to train when I'm hungover or on my period."

Albert sniffed, giving her a look of disapproval. "No wonder you defeat me so often at sparring. You're a damned cheater."

She cast him a look of disdain. "This isn't flyball, Albert. We're not professional athletes. Besides, I don't require magical enhancement to thrash you."

Nikolai popped the beads into his mouth. They instantly dissolved on his tongue, tasting like peppermint and rosemary.

"Be careful," Ilyana said, filling his palm with more of the beads. "You can't exactly overdose on them, but . . . it's borrowing from the future. The higher the dose, the worse you'll be later on. And you're already in rough shape. Not to mention the side effects."

"I'll be careful," Nikolai said, pouring the beads into his pocket. "Thanks, Ilyana. Let's go."

He pressed the Moonwatch insignia against the dusty elevator door.

"Captain Jubal's office."

The light over the elevator flashed red in denial of his request, and there was an odd metallic groan as the override went into effect. The light changed to green, and the elevator followed their command.

It was dark in Jubal's office.

Nikolai felt oddly calm as the Titan's Tears seeped through his body and filled him with a gentle euphoria. His surroundings seemed sluggish, slowed down. It was as if he could see past his peripheral vision—more than seeing, he could *feel* his surroundings. Was this how Jem experienced the world with her mod enhancements?

Lights and colors seemed brighter, richer. He felt *strong*— like he could run twenty miles without breaking a sweat. Like he could snap somebody's neck with his bare hands.

The folded space door to Jubal's garden was closed but not locked. Nikolai pulled it open and was temporarily blinded by the sun. It stood high in the artificial sky—late morning.

Albert whistled as they passed through the ringed gardens towards Jubal's home at the center. "A tad decadent," he said. "But quite nice."

Nikolai led the way as they entered the mansion within the gardens. As he followed the gentle tugging of Jem's tracer, he could feel his heart rate increasing—oddly detached through the sharply pleasant warmth of Ilyana's drugs—though fear and certainty etched away at his calm as he led them into the library, to the hidden stairwell.

Albert let out a sharp gasp.

Ilyana and Nikolai spun, drawing their Focals, only to find Albert gawking at the bookcases—at the collection of rarities protected under enchanted glass.

"*DISC! The Binding of Thanatos*? I didn't think that there were any copies of this still intact. In such perfect condition! Styx! *Oh*

Styx, and this! An *original* print of *The Book of Bei Ze*? Jeeves—Disc! Just *look* at the illuminations! It's spectacular, simply spectacular—"

"Not the *fucking* time, Albert," Nikolai snapped.

Albert sighed, pulling himself away from the display cases.

They descended into the darkness of the basement, following the tracer's pull through the theater, into the white-walled showroom.

Albert kept making quiet noises of awe as he admired Jubal's secret collection of art, tech, and magi-tech. It seemed to be requiring a great deal of effort for him to contain his enthusiasm.

"He brought me here once," Ilyana said. "Had me try some of that awful bourbon."

"Am I the only one who hasn't been invited to Captain Jubal's secret clubhouse?" Albert muttered, following Nikolai into the gun range through the heavy glass and steel door.

Ilyana looked around at the weaponry, her eyes settling on his mother's rune-etched revolver spinning in the translucent bubble. "He didn't bring me in here. Told me it was just a storage room. I can see why now."

"So strange," Nikolai muttered, walking across the cement room, forcing himself not to look at the revolver as he went past it. To his left were the two long shooting lanes—but this side of the room was empty—nothing but blank walls. No decoration, no furniture. He hadn't really thought about it before, but now . . .

Albert was glancing over the shelves of ammo, peeking into the blank white boxes. "My cousin has a collection of old human weaponry like this. Had to go through all sorts of hoops and bureaucracy. Hardly worth the effort." He went over to the gun rack, reaching to touch one of the shotguns. He let out a hiss, pulling his hand away and popping his finger into his mouth. "Ouch! Damned burn field."

Nikolai reached into his pocket for his tracking spectacles, but realized with a pang of annoyance that he'd left them in his room in Marblewood.

"Anyone got tracking specs?"

Albert and Ilyana looked at each other, then Nikolai, and shook their heads.

He trailed his real hand across the blank wall in the oddly undecorated corner, feeling for the telltale tingling of enchantments on his fingertips.

"I can feel her through this wall. There's something else. Something I can't . . ."

He pressed the Moonwatch insignia against the wall and began to drag it along the cement, until . . .

There was a gentle hum, and a shimmer as the stone became a large, metal door.

"Well," Albert said nervously, coming up to stand beside him. "Good job, Strauss. Aces and charms."

Steeling himself, Nikolai turned the handle, and pushed.

The stink was what hit him first. Then the screams. Oh Disc, *the screams.*

Down a small flight of stairs they came into an immense warehouse. Gigantic lights hung from a ceiling of rough, wooden timbers—each light hanging down over glass-walled tanks the size of rooms.

There were dozens of tanks, in two rows. A path went down the center between them.

And within the tanks?

"*No,*" Ilyana whimpered, hugging herself and sinking to the floor beside Nikolai. "No, no, no . . ."

There, a pair of naked men, clinging to one another for warmth as they slowly froze to death amid piles of snow. There, a row of men and women—wizards and sorceresses? Being vivisected alive by dozens of enchanted mechanical arms.

Moaning, Nikolai ran down the aisle, desperately trying to get to Jem. She was close now.

Albert muttered terrified curses to himself behind Nikolai as he pulled Ilyana to her feet and scrambled to keep pace.

Nikolai stumbled, faltering with shock as he found himself confronted with two familiar faces.

Thin Mage. Fat Mage. The half-magi who'd attacked him in the Noir district—the half-magi who'd almost murdered him.

There was a shining, ruby monolith at the center of their glass room. Fat Mage was hanging upside down, strapped against the monolith. His eyes were open, bloody and full of madness.

Thin Mage was trapped in the tank with him, though he wasn't tied down. He wore filthy rags and was missing one of his eyes. "*Help us!*" he screeched through crooked yellow teeth, clawing at the glass. "*HELP US, PLEASE!*"

The monolith began to glow. Thin Mage shrank away from it with a mewling cry. The glow spread across the Fat Mage and he seemed to blur—seemed to become a fleshy, glowing phantom, a secondary image stretching and pulling away from his body as his agonized wails ceased to be human—becoming almost musical—like an incredibly out-of-tune violin.

Ruby light arced from Fat Mage to Thin Mage and his cries for help ceased as he fell thrashing on the floor—his body melting away until only an electric skeleton remained. But somehow the skeleton was still alive, and screaming.

Albert retched. Ilyana was silent, expressionless. Nikolai

pulled himself away from the two—Thin Mage's skeletal hand pitifully reaching after him as he went.

Nikolai tried not to look into the other tanks as he ran, eyes on the filthy cement floor ahead of him as he followed the gentle tug of Jem's tracer. But occasionally, no matter how he struggled to keep his eyes downcast, he'd catch a hellish glimpse. There, a room full of kneeling men and women being shot in the head by a floating tube, execution style, one after the other. There, an extra-large tank, full of water, full of enormous, toothy eels, hungrily snapping at a man with a knife as he desperately tried to fight them off, clinging to a small raft slowly being picked apart by the creatures.

Then—there she was. Jem. Trapped inside the final tank to the left.

She was wearing the same filthy clothes she'd been wearing on the beach, and she was strapped to a large chair—like something a Victorian-era surgeon would use, awful and archaic. There was a metallic, wheeled arch over the chair, and she was screaming, bloodshot eyes wild as she tried to look up at it, frantically struggling and kicking against her bindings, but there was a white band around her head and she couldn't seem to turn her neck.

"Jem!" Nikolai screamed, pounding his fists against the glass. "Oh Disc, *JEM!*"

Her eyes meet his. For a moment, she stopped screaming. For a moment her expression lit up with hope. She moved her lips.

Nik.

A glint of steel. A flash as a blade came out of the arch in a blur.

There was an emerald shimmer across her retinas, and her eyes went dull. A line of red formed on her neck. Then, in a moment that stretched out with impossible slowness, her head toppled from her neck, bouncing across the floor.

Nikolai quietly sank to his knees. Jem's dead eyes stared up at him from the floor, blood pooling around the cheek of her severed head.

The arch flashed and began to spin around her corpse, glowing and humming, occasionally stopping to make a loud clicking noise, accompanied by another flash.

Ilyana stood beside him, silent. Frozen.

But Albert was freaking out, pulling at Nikolai, trying to get him to stand.

"I'm sorry, Nikolai, I'm *SO* sorry but we need to go we need to go, we need to get out of here, we need to—"

And Nikolai knew he should listen to him. Knew he should get up, go with them. Go tell people about this place. About Jubal. About the humans. He knew it's what Jem would have wanted.

But he was done. He was just . . . done.

Then there was an odd *thud* that Nikolai didn't quite hear, didn't quite feel.

Jem's head rose off the ground and flew in an impossible arc back up to her neck. As the red line around her throat began to seal up, blade pulling away, Nikolai was convinced that he'd lost it—convinced that he'd gone utterly insane.

"An Elasti-Room!" Albert was shouting, fingers digging into Nikolai's shoulders, laughing and gasping with relief. "All these people, they're in Elasti-Rooms! Just like they use in hospitals! She's alive, Nik, she's *alive!*"

"Dying, over and over again," Ilyana said, almost with wonder. "He keeps killing them. In different ways. Then he rewinds time inside the chambers to do it all over again. Never-ending. Like hell."

"That arch," Albert said. "There's some approximation of it in each of these rooms. That clicking, and the flashing? I think they're taking some sort of reading. When he kills them—he's taking measurements! This is a laboratory!"

"Torture laboratory?" Jubal had said, laughing at Nikolai's suspicion. *"Some sort of evil Necromancer lair?"*

Murderer, Hazeal had promised. *MURDERER!*

But no. This was worse than murder. So much worse.

Albert was saying something, but Nikolai was already up, he wasn't listening. As Jem stared at him, still fighting against her restraints, Nikolai's Focals were ablaze, and he was striking, striking—again and again and again—spiderweb cracks slowly forming across the thick wall of glass as he alternated blasting it with icy cold winds and white-hot flame.

"Nikolai, *WAIT!*" Albert screamed, pulling at him. "The arch—look how it's moving! I think it's about to kill her again! If you destroy the glass, you'll break the enchantments! It won't be able to reverse time within the chamber—she'll be dead for good this time! *NIK!*"

But he wouldn't let her die again. Not even once.

With a roar, he blasted through the wall, desperately lunging to throw out a great swath of Veil to surround Jem in her chair—to close around her like the great Veil domes of their cities, hiding the magi from the humans. Hiding them from the *Synth.*

The smooth, mirrored surface sealed around her, and just as the blade began to flash—cutting through the air almost too quickly to see—she disappeared. Hidden in a pocket of space-time just beyond this plane.

Nikolai sent out a tentacle of *akro* to wrap around the arch and flung it away. It toppled over, falling onto the ground with a whirr of broken machinery.

Nikolai dismissed the Veil. It fell away from Jem in crumbling papery ashes.

She stared up at Nikolai, shaking, silent as he cut away the straps and pulled her away with a sob of relief.

"Hey, you're okay," he said, pulling her into an embrace. "Everything's going to be okay."

She was limp and unmoving in his arms, and when he released her she slowly sank to the floor, staring into nothingness.

"What is she doing?" Albert hissed. "We need to go—*NOW!*"

"I know!" Nikolai snapped. Then he gently urged Jem to her feet. "Come on. We need to go. I'll explain everything later—I'll *fix* this, I promise I'll fix this, but right now we need to—"

"*Oh Disc,*" Albert moaned, going pale.

Nikolai stopped, looking up to follow his gaze, and there, not twenty paces away, stood Jubal. Eyes wild, like a *demon*. Like the demon he was.

Without a word, Jubal raised his candy cane Focal.

A tangled net of red light slammed into Albert, crackling through his body as he fell to the ground, spasming, screaming.

Ilyana raised her ruby dagger, firing a line of blue—identical to the ones Jubal, Thane, and Uncle Red had destroyed Armitage with, identical to the one she'd used mere weeks before to turn Hazeal to dust. It snaked through the air, almost too fast to see as it went straight for Jubal's heart.

Jubal caught the thread of light in his bare palm with an almost casual wave, and the thread disappeared. Flicking his cane, he flung two more of the nets at Ilyana and Nikolai, watching them fall with an expression of grim annoyance as the light passed through their uniforms, sinking into their skin. Nikolai was wracked with excruciating pain—like every nerve had been plunged into acid—like every inch of his flesh had been torn free, ripped away by thousands of hungry little mouths.

Nikolai screamed and screamed, arching his back, unable to

resist, unable to do anything but fight for breath. Ilyana wailed beside him, Albert choking and gasping.

Jubal cast a quick glance at Jem, but she just sat there among their twisting bodies, staring into nothingness.

"Ilyana. *Albert*," Jubal said. "I'm disappointed in you. I expected better than this sort of blatant mutiny. This *betrayal*. Freeing a criminal? Invading my home?" he shook his head. "An hour from now, you won't have the faintest recollection of what's happened here. Won't remember finding Nikolai—Disc knows how you did that. Though I'll be damned if you don't tell me before then."

He looked at Nikolai, face tight with sorrow and rage.

"And *you*! How could you do this to me, you ungrateful little wretch?" He gritted his teeth, eyes glistening with angry, heart-broken tears. "I had to *beg* the Mage King to spare you! *BEG! On hands and knees!* And *THIS* is how you repay me?"

His expression hardened and he raised the cane, pointing it at Nikolai. But Nikolai couldn't move. Even with the drugs, he couldn't move. The pain was just too much.

"No more," Jubal breathed. "No more chances. Time to do what—"

Ilyana made a noise, a strange, croaking moan. Brief, jagged lines of red still crackling sporadically from her body, she began to rise—arms and head hanging like a rag doll as she pulled herself to her feet. With a trembling hand, she lifted the crystal flask to her mouth, taking a pull.

"When you found me," she said. "When you took me on, began training me as an Edge Guard . . . I found meaning. Purpose."

"Stand down, Ilyana!" Jubal barked, pointing his cane. "Stand *down!*"

"A reason to live," she continued, taking a step toward him. "A reason to not just be numb all the time."

Snarling, Jubal fired off another net of tangled red light.

She arched her back, grunting, stumbling. But then she caught herself. She didn't fall. Wheezing, she took another swig from the flask. Took another step.

"When Nik told me what you'd done to him—I lost myself for a moment."

With a roar, Jubal fired another net, and the red light seemed to explode from her body—branching out onto the floor, onto the glass.

Her scream was bloodcurdling—terrible. She clutched herself, weaving, staggering.

And yet she stood.

She looked back at Nikolai. Blood poured from her eyes. Her nostrils, her ears. She tried to smile, lips peaking up for a brief instant despite her obvious agony, then turned to face Jubal.

Nikolai struggled to make his hands reach down for the Titan's Tears in his pocket, straining *desperately* for control over his fingers. Slowly, he was able to steady the shaking. Slowly, he was able to reach inside, fingers uselessly digging into the pile of beads as he tried to force them into scoops, as weak and useless as an infant.

"*Stop this, Ilyana!*" Jubal pleaded, disbelieving. "I don't want to kill you!"

"But seeing this," she continued, panting, "seeing what kind of mage you really are, you've given me purpose again. You've shown the kind of evil that I didn't think existed anymore. And I want to thank you for that."

"Ilyana! *LIEUTENANT!* This is your *last* warning! Please— *don't make me do this!*"

"Does it get you off? Make you hard when you cut into them? When you watch them die, over and over again?" She laughed bitterly, trailing into pained, wet coughs. "I bet it does. Especially when you cut into the *girls*. Isn't that right, Captain?"

Jubal's face hardened, lips firming into a solid line.

"So be it," he said, and pointed his cane at her.

With a snarl, Ilyana pointed her dagger at him and cast another fiery line of light.

Lips twisting with annoyance, he raised his hand to stop it, just like before.

Only just before it struck him, the thread *turned* sharply— going into the thick glass wall beside him instead. The tank—full of water and monstrosities.

His eyes widened.

The wall exploded, disintegrating into dust, and Jubal disappeared as he was engulfed by an immense torrent of murky water full of shifting forms—of monstrous, toothy eels snapping and biting at the air.

Nikolai bit down on a fistful of the Titan's Tears, the drug hitting him like an icy blast as it washed the pain of Jubal's spell from his body. The wall of water surged toward them in what seemed like a crawl as he lunged to his feet, bringing up his baton in a rainbow wave of light as he created a barrier of Veil between themselves and the flood—sealing the gap.

Howling with laughter, Ilyana threw back her head and poured a small, glittering cascade of Titan's Tears into her mouth.

Nikolai featherweighted himself and Jem, reveling in how much easier it was to cast and maintain spells in a Veil, when he could draw on a Disc.

Ilyana featherweighted herself and Albert, and soon they were flying through the air, jets of *akro* in their wake as they passed over the other tanks—no sign of Jubal in the churning waters below.

One arm wrapped around Albert as she propelled them through the air, Ilyana pulled the crystal flask free from her hip and released a cloud of vicious red smoke that rose across the wooden beams overhead. She stopped propelling herself and Albert with the jet of *akro* for a brief instant, quickly casting off a line of blue into the gas. The gas ignited with a hissing shriek—flame spreading out across the warehouse ceiling like a hellish sky.

"What are you *doing*?" Albert shouted as they flew. "The others—you'll kill them! You'll kill them all!"

"What do you suggest?" she said. "That we leave them here, to *this?* Better they die—that they stay dead!"

By the time they landed at the base of the stairwell up to the shooting range, the entire warehouse was aflame. Jem was walking now, though Nikolai had to pull her along after him. Albert was finally able to stand on his own, limping up the stairs as he shook off the residual shock of the pain spell.

"Do you think he's dead?" Albert asked, glancing back into the smoke.

Nobody replied.

Jem didn't even seem to notice her surroundings as Nikolai led her across the room. Ilyana was the first one to the door.

"Shit!" she said, yanking at the handle. "It's *locked*. He locked it—locked us in!"

"Here," Nikolai said, reaching into his pocket for the Moonwatch medallion. "I'll—"

The pocket was empty. Nikolai began to panic, searching his other pockets. "No! No, no, no, no, no—"

It was gone.

"The medallion—I must have dropped it! Back in the—"

"Perhaps setting the building ablaze before we're free of the place wasn't your most inspired decision, Xue!" Albert said, rapier Focal drawn, slashing at the door with bright licks of fire. He stood back, sending out a thin line of flame. It melted against the frosted glass.

He kicked, it, snarling something in German. "Enchanted! Enforced! Might as well be a damned bank vault!"

Ilyana took a few vicious slices at the door with her ruby dagger, blasts of neon erupting from its surface. Soon, both she and Albert were attacking the door with blinding ferocity.

Shit. *Shit!*

A glitter caught Nikolai's eye, and he found himself staring at the revolver turning sluggishly within its translucent bubbles.

A bullet from this will pass right through those enchantments in your uniform like butter. *It'd pass right through any sort of armor or shielding.*

He leaned closer, gaze fixed on the patterns of gentle yellow light coursing sluggishly around the revolver.

Only a mage's bare hand can pass through the barrier. The enchantment can sense the millions of little flow channels in your palm and fingertips. Each mage's channel pattern is different—like a fingerprint.

Nikolai looked at his golden hand, then back at the burn bubble.

The nerves, muscle memory, and unique magical channels of your original hand have all been replicated perfectly within the prosthetic.

He took Jem aside, guiding her to sit against a wall, safely away from Albert and Ilyana's continued assault.

He went back to the bubble and pulled up the sleeve of his uniform. Could it really be so easy?

Golden fingers flexing, he took a deep breath and reached for the gun.

The bubble was thick—like jelly—and it was a struggle to push his hand through. It was warm—hot even. But so far . . .

The bubble flashed red. A slow pulse, blinking. On, off, on, off as his fingers reached deeper. The speed of the flashing began to increase and the bubble started to get *hot*. Sweat poured down his face, dripping onto the bubble, evaporating on contact as his fingers *slowly* began to close around the gun and he heard a woman's voice chanting his name and praising him:

The pain will be over soon all will be well keep going Nikolai you're so close all you've ever wanted I will give all your desires I shall grant just take me away from this place you're so close now Nikolai KEEP GOING . . .

And the heat became unbearable; he could feel the hair on his forearm begin to burn away, feel the golden flesh crack and peel and the pain. Oh *DISC* the *PAIN*, and his fingers were closed around the grip and were fused together and he could see the gold boiling away but it felt like his own skin, and he was *SCREAMING* and *PULLING* and he didn't want it anymore, he didn't want it, *didn't want it*—

"Nikolai!" Albert cried. "*Nikolai, what are you doing!*"

And Nikolai fell back, stumbling with a spray of molten gold and his hand was *gone*, he had lost his hand again, there was just a stump all blistered and bleeding, the gold running up his arm— *burning his arm*—and he was still screaming and he dropped the revolver. He didn't know where the revolver was, all he could do was lie there, hugging the sizzling stump to his chest, curled up into a ball.

And he looked up, and there was Jubal. He stood in the doorway—soaking wet, bleeding, wreathed in smoke, eyes lit with murderous intent.

Jubal raised his cane and pointed it at Nikolai in a moment that lasted forever as he lay there, waiting for death, watching as Jem slowly looked down at the revolver sitting on the floor in front of her, dripping with Nikolai's golden blood, watching as emerald light flashed across her eyes and suddenly she was *UP* and the revolver was in her hand and she was firing it at Jubal, three flashes of light, three thunderclaps in a fraction of a fraction of an instant.

"*TELOS!*" Jubal screamed—the word ending in a gurgle as blood plumed from his throat, as a bloody hole appeared on his stomach, as the hand holding his Focal exploded into gory mist.

Hand ruined, he began to collapse, began to drop his Focal— but not before he had already fired off the spell. The air before Jubal distorted into a blast of tangled, curling darkness. His Focal crumbled, exploding with the curls, falling to pieces—but then Nikolai saw that it wasn't his Focal that was falling to pieces— just the candy-striped wooden exterior.

It had been a false shell, hiding his real Focal.

A baton, identical to Nikolai's in size and shape—only a glistening, fleshy red instead of black.

It trailed thick yellow light as he collapsed, that hideous darkness he'd fired off in the instant before Jem's bullets had pierced him, going far wide of his intended target—a dark that was more than dark, a black that simply ate the light, curls of nothingness erupting into a column of destruction that Nikolai's mind reeled at the sight of, of vertigo, of *wrongness*.

It unfurled into the heavy door of metal and glass as Ilyana and Albert cringed away—just inches outside of its range—watching as the door was etched away, *devoured* and then gone, glass and steel—or was it wood? Or had there ever been a door there at all? There must have been—must have been something to keep them from fleeing before now.

But now there was just a gaping hole in the wall and a missing section of floor beyond.

Jubal lay on his back, breath rattling through bloody foam.

Jem walked over to him with sadistic slowness, revolver hanging in her hand as she stared down at him.

"Stomach punctured," she said calmly. "Gastric acid leaking into your abdominal cavity. Punctured trachea, esophagus. Nicked the spinal column. Nerves partially severed. Paralyzed. Missed the arteries so the stomach will be what kills you. Fifteen minutes. Maybe twenty. Maybe longer. Agony until then—too good an end for you."

She kicked away his leathery baton Focal and slowly pressed her shoe against the wound in his stomach. He gurgled through the bloody froth, eyes bulging. Unable to scream. He gurgled again, trying to say something.

"What?" she said, pressing down even harder against the wound. "Is there something you want to tell me?"

He made another noise, and Nikolai still couldn't hear what he was trying to say, but there was a *flash* of silver light and Jem pulled back with a hiss as a gleaming sarcophagus formed and snapped shut around him.

The sarcophagus disappeared—taking the captain with it.

"Where is he?" Jem demanded. *"WHERE IS HE?"*

There was a great crackling and groan as burning timbers fell free of the ceiling inside the warehouse, smashing down onto the tanks below. They were dead—all the people down there. All of Jubal's victims. Forever this time.

The air was thick with smoke. Wild-eyed, Ilyana rushed into the white-walled showroom full of machinery and art to raise her dagger—twirling it over her head.

"Have you gone *MAD*, Xue?" Albert screamed after Ilyana while he helped Nikolai up to his feet.

Reaching into his pocket, Nikolai scooped out the remainder of the Titan's Tears and poured them into his mouth, shaking his head to clear away the opalescent rainbow aura shimmering at the edge of his vision as the dozen or so beads began to dissolve. The pain of his once-again-missing hand subsided, and as he ran into the showroom he no longer needed Albert's help to stand.

"No, no, no, *NO!*" Albert wailed as Ilyana created a spinning maelstrom of fire from the tip of her dagger. "Ilyana, stop! The art—the treasures! They're priceless! Irreplaceable!"

"I'm counting on it," she said, grinning viciously as she shoved him away to set Captain Jubal's collection ablaze.

Albert frantically filled his arms with everything he could carry—featherweighting an ancient bust of the Wandering King, rolling up a pair of tapestries under his arm, slinging a painting over his shoulder.

"Strauss, give me a hand with this!" he shouted, but then looked down at Nikolai's stump and started to laugh, hysterical.

Jem ran into the shooting range, pockets bulging with boxes of ammunition when she came back out. They passed through the theater, fleeing up the stairs, Ilyana setting everything ablaze as Albert looking with regret at the precious tomes encased in the glass, loudly assuring himself that the enchantments should protect them from the fire as Ilyana mercilessly ignited the unprotected volumes lining the walls and shelves.

Flowers withered and died from the heat in the gardens as Jubal's once grand estate became a fiery husk behind them—soon to be nothing more than ash.

They burst into Jubal's office, gasping, and slammed the enchanted door behind them.

"Jubal's bullet chambers!" Nikolai said, flinging open the other door, revealing a long hall of doors with flickering images of the Veils their bullets would lead to. "Marblewood, Marblewood—here!"

"Ah, and Schwarzwald." Albert opened the door assigned to his home, groaning with relief as he carefully unloaded the art and artifacts into the small seating area. "I'll tell my family of these atrocities. And they called *our* king a butcher?"

"I'll go to Xanadu," Ilyana said. "If I can tell my mother about this, she'll rally the Asian royalty. Demand an investigation."

"I'll go to Marblewood. My uncle. I think they've got him locked up at home. We'll get him out—he'll know what to do."

Albert ran back into the office, leveled his rapier at the folded space door to Jubal's estate. He ran his palm over the wood thoughtfully.

"There," he said, making three sharp cuts with the slender blade. "I've destroyed the portal. Cut the enchantments. Won't be able to follow us through there. Lieutenant Xue, could you attend to—"

But she was already on it, the point of her dagger on the elevator door as she superheated it, the ruby blade lit with blinding red light as she fused it shut. The indicator light cracked, going dark. The boiling paint cooled, the molten steel hardening.

"There's another bullet hall they'll be able to use in the hangar," Albert said, "but this should buy us some time."

Jem stood there waiting by the Marblewood door, though her expression was dazed. Confused. Terrified.

As Ilyana started for the Xanadu door, Nik put his remaining hand on her arm. "Ilyana. Come with me. Please. Don't go to Xanadu. I—"

She kissed him, and pulled him into a tight embrace. "We'll be lucky if any one of us escapes," she whispered so only he could hear. "The only way we have even the slightest chance to tell people about this is if we scatter."

"No," he whimpered, "*No . . .*"

But Ilyana was right. He'd been selfish before, allowing Base Machado to fall so that he might see his loved ones again. But it was like Jem had said—this was bigger than any of them. His own happiness was nothing compared to the enormity of suffering beyond the Veils. He *had* to find a way to make up for abandoning the humans at Base Machado to the Synth. To make up for the magi abandoning humanity to nuclear war a century prior.

Struggling not to cry, he kissed her again. "Don't let them take you. No matter what."

Ilyana looked at him as if memorizing his face, and clasped his hand. "Wasn't planning on it."

Nikolai grabbed Albert—missing hand forgotten as the drugs pounded through his veins—and pulled the two of them into his arms. The three of them just held each other for a moment, squeezing with rib-cracking tightness while Jem stood off to the side, watching.

"None of this goodbye shit," Nikolai said, breaking away from the embrace and wiping his eyes. "I'll find you guys."

"Be safe, you two," Albert said. "Aces and charms. We'll . . . we'll make this right."

"I'll see you both soon," Ilyana said. She looked over at Jem. "You too. You're one of us now. What they did to you . . . it won't stand."

Jem didn't reply, but nodded slowly.

As Jem and Nikolai loaded into their chamber, Albert flashed him one final salute. Ilyana blew him a kiss and mouthed *Goodbye*.

Nikolai reached out to them, a sob wracking his body, and the door hissed shut.

XIII.

THAT HIDEOUS DARK

Jem watched Nikolai speak as they sat across from each other in the cramped, ruby-lit cylinder of the silently traveling bullet chamber. None of this felt real—the words coming out of her companion's mouth like the ramblings of one lost in delusion.

". . . and so we've been hidden away since then. Lied to while the Mage King waits for all the humans to die off. But if everyone knew—they'd *depose* him. The magi would riot. Start a *revolution* or something. I don't know. But they won't just let it happen. Even if the king is right, and we really aren't strong enough to fight the Synth, they'd at least *do* something to help your kind."

She listened attentively while he spouted absurdities about magic, Veils, Discs.

The Edge Guard, the king, a town called Marblewood—

magically hidden in a pocket dimension on the lake where Jem's life had twice come to an end.

"I know it's . . . a lot," he said, smiling uneasily. "You can see why I lied before. Said that I was a colonist."

The boy barely seemed to notice the pain of his blistered, bloody stump relaxed on the seat at his side. Whatever drugs the beautiful pyromaniac had given him seemed to be hitting with full effect.

Jem sat there in silence, the moments stretching awkwardly as the boy waited for her to react to everything he'd just told her.

"I can remember dying. Over and over," she finally said—even her own words feeling as if spoken from the lips of another. "Not quite remember. An approximation. I can't pinpoint it in my organic or inorganic memory. Yet there it is."

It was all so fuzzy. She remembered being attacked by Armitage on the beach. Remembered sitting paralyzed in a stark white room, where an older man who'd been dressed like Nikolai wouldn't stop apologizing.

Then, she'd been in hell. Dying again, and again, and again . . .

Jem pulled the revolver from where she'd tucked it into the back of her pants and a small box of ammunition from one of her pockets, then casually began to reload it. As her fingers made contact with the revolver, she could hear whispers—so quiet as to almost be imperceptible, though certainly not imagined. She felt an otherworldly pressure in her skull, near the center of her mods. Like fingers fumbling at a lock.

"That thing is dangerous," Nikolai hissed. "Jem, that gun; it's old magic. It'll mess with your mind. You shouldn't touch it. Shouldn't—"

"Do you know what Torment is?" she said, cutting him off.

Jem was no longer interested in anything else the boy might say.

"The gun," Nikolai insisted. "I need you to give it to me. Or wrap it in your coat. Or—fuck, I don't know. Just stop touching it."

She snapped the revolver's chamber back in place and continued ignoring him. Him and the distant whispers.

"Being assigned to Torment is the same as being sent to hell," she said. "You're brought to a Synth facility where they plug you in. Every facet of your mind explored. Every fear, every memory, every want, every desire. Then they wake you up. Make you forget that you've been taken."

"For *fuck's sake*, Jem! Put the gun away!"

"They torture you in ways you can't imagine. Let you think you've murdered the love of your life. Let you watch as your closest friends burn. Tweak your brain chemistry to make you too cowardly to save them. More than physical pain. The torture of loss, of failure—more than suffering evil, of *committing* evil and living with the guilt. Never knowing that it's an illusion. That's the thing about hell—you don't know when you're in it."

Jem stared down at her lap, trembling, clutching the revolver in her hands with a white-knuckle grip. How had it taken her so long to realize what was happening? It was so fucking obvious.

"*I've figured it out*," she said. "I never really escaped from the cathedral. I remember Ezra saving me, remember escaping. But now I *know* that's a false memory. They must have captured me. Must have put in me in Torment for being a Runner."

She looked at Nikolai, crazed. "You aren't real. None of this is real! I never met Eva. Never lost Blue, or made it to Base Machado. Never ran away with you in the dead of the night. Never watched the city fall—never felt the foot of the Armitage husk crushing down on my head—never died a hundred times in a magical glass room while . . ."

She stopped. Panting. Fingers trembling around the softly glowing runes.

"Jem . . . that's not true. This *is* real. The revolver . . . it's messing with your head. Making you crazy. For better or worse—everything you've seen, everything that's happened—"

"No," she said firmly. "*Nothing* you say *nothing* you do *nothing* you show me will convince me that if I shoot myself in the head right now I won't just wake up somewhere else with new memories. For all I know, you're the AI charged with my suffering. You're the constant. The torturer. The *wizard* behind the curtain."

"Jem, no! That isn't true!"

She pointed the gun at Nikolai as he tensed to try and take it from her. The boy stopped, slowly leaning back, frozen.

"You and Eva. My pale, dark-haired companions. My Black Swan. My sorcerer. Are they you, one and the same? How many times have I died already? How many times have we had this conversation? Why wizards—why *this?* What pieces of my mind led you to create this *absurd* scenario? Running to spaceships with a mysterious telekinetic. Tortured by sorcerers and rescued by the Martian who's actually some sort of magical soldier? With his magical soldier friends? Off to start a *revolution.*"

"Jem," he said slowly, "I don't know anybody named Eva. I know you've been through a lot, and this is a lot to take in, but please. Put down the—"

"*Why, Nik?*" she snarled, pressing the long barrel of the gun against her temple. "*Tell me why I shouldn't do it?*"

"Jem, NO, *don't—!*"

They both froze as the sound of a man clearing his throat emanated from the pulsing gemstone set into the sloped roof of the bullet chamber above them.

"I hope I'm not interrupting," came Jubal's voice, raspy and pained.

For a moment, they sat there in stunned silence. Icy terror flooded Jem's veins—hand with the revolver slowly sinking to her side.

"Hello? Anyone there?"

"What," Jem said through gritted teeth, "do you want?"

"Ah! Hello, Ms. Burton," Jubal said, his words faintly slurring. The man sounded drunk. "Didn't expect you to be the first to speak up. Probably aren't particularly interested in what I have to say, but still, I feel the need to explain myself. Explain the . . . incredible cruelty I've inflicted on you. Explain what was in my— in what's *left* of my home."

Of course. Jem's torturer, back from the dead. Drunk dialing via gemstone to pontificate and gloat. *Torment*, she was reminded. How could this possibly be anything other than Torment?

The ice in Jem's veins spread to fill her entirely—no longer the chill of fear, but the numbness of disassociation. Distantly, her mind reeled, howling with helpless, terrified despair at the mind-shattering eons of suffering the Synth would force her to endure.

A special room in hell, made just for Jem.

Nikolai—no, the Synth intelligence *pretending* to be Nikolai— who'd been watching her, slowly seemed to realize that Jem had checked out, and would no longer be engaging with this farce.

"Explain?" Nik said, eyes uneasy as they remained focused on Jem. "What is there to explain?"

"Those people in my laboratory—they were all murderers, Nikolai. Rapists. Humans and half-magi who are all predators and trash. That alone wouldn't be enough reason to subject them to the . . . unpleasantries required for my experiments. I've been searching for evidence of a human soul—an afterlife. That, or a way to give them souls like ours, with the ability to channel magic."

Jem listened distantly, though her attention was mostly focused on pinpointing when this virtual delusion had truly begun.

Had the Synth really taken her alive during their battle at the cathedral? Had her failures and the heartbreak that followed been the illusory punishment of Torment? Or had everything with Eva, Blue, and Base Machado really occurred, and now she was being punished for those very failures?

Not for the first time, Jem wondered if maybe this wasn't Torment at all. At least, not the virtual sort created by machines. Maybe everything that had happened after the cathedral *had* been real. And maybe, so was hell.

Jem couldn't decide which was worse.

"I've dedicated my life to protecting humans from our kind," the AI pretending to be a wizard named Jubal was ranting. "You don't understand what magi were like before we cut them off from the human world again. Even the progressives saw humans as a lesser species, only *a step* above animals—just because their souls can't be seen or documented like a mage's.

"I found a signal. Everyone—humans, magi, even animals—have rigid, microscopic tubes in their brains that resonate with quantum frequencies. Nobody's ever been able to make sense of it, but in my research, I discovered one specific frequency that was exactly the same in some humans, as well as some half-magi. The only frequency I've ever found shared by multiple test subjects. And each one of them was an evil motherfucker. Only the predators emit this signal, Nikola. The greedy, the cruel. The *damned*."

Jubal's last word jerked Jem back to attention, even though

she knew she shouldn't listen. Even though she knew the Synth were probably reading her thoughts, and were toying with Jem by echoing her contemplations of damnation.

"I fully intended to send Ms. Burton to Rojava," he continued. "But her synthetic enhancements, Nikolai—I've never seen any so advanced! I had to scan them, but when I did, I couldn't help but check for the signal, too. I can scan for it to weed out monsters, parading as people. And when I scanned your friend, well. Let's just say that if there was such a thing as demons, they'd be drooling at her feet. Just waiting to lap up the blood she'll spill."

"You're lying," Nikolai said flatly, though Jem could barely hear him over the blood pounding in her ears. *Don't listen to him*, she repeated in her head, like a mantra. *Don't listen to him, don't listen to him, don't—*

Jubal exhaled with a hiss through his teeth, sounding as though he'd just taken a swig of hard liquor. Through the pounding in her ears, Jem could hear the ice in his drink clinking against the glass.

"It's the truth, Nikolai," Jubal said. "What do you even know about this human? She told me *everything*. Told me how she betrayed and brutalized her commander—a woman she claimed to have grown up with, and loved. She told me how she abandoned her lover and friends to die at the hands of the Synth over some petty argument. She even told me how she sold out her own kind, to escape with you—just so she could go to the stars."

"The *FUCK* do you know?" Jem exploded, no longer able to restrain herself. Though when she began to form the words to call him a liar, she faltered. Because he wasn't lying. Not about her crimes, at least.

"For the second time today, Captain, I'll tell you what *I* know,"

Nikolai said, reaching across the narrow aisle to give Jem's hand a reassuring squeeze. "I know that you're wrong about Jem. I know you're a liar, and a murderer. And *worse*."

Jem sat rigid, the venomous hatred and guilt that Jubal's accusations had triggered diminishing ever so slightly as she stared down at Nikolai's pale, soot-stained fingers gently curled around her own.

"How about this for truth," the old man said, his slur deepening. "I'm not the captain anymore. Thane's acting commander for now, but he'll be captain soon enough. I'm through. Fucked, more accurately. The Moonwatch tracked the spell I used to escape. You destroyed my labs, but they'll find enough in the wreckage to know what I've been up to. Already have me under lock and key while they investigate."

He snorted. "Bad enough that your mother planned a coup right under my nose. Now, our three most promising battle magi have committed violent mutiny, led by her son."

"If that's true," Nikolai said, pulling away from Jem so he could wave his hand with exasperation, "then why are you even talking to us?"

"Because I still give a damn! Still care what happens to you. Still care what you think! As absurd as that might sound, considering how . . . heated things became, earlier."

Of all the things Jubal had said to them so far, this appeared to affect Nikolai most deeply.

"Just like you cared about my mom?" he spat.

Jubal hesitated, seeming to consider his reply.

"I didn't kill Ashley, Nik. I would have died for that woman."

Nikolai looked sharply at the communication crystal, eyes brimming with angry hurt.

"Then why the fuck are you still here," he said, "and she isn't?"

The old man didn't reply, both he and Nikolai lapsing into a strained silence.

Considering that this was supposed to be a virtual world uniquely designed for the express purpose of punishing Jem, she found it strange that the two wizards would engage in such a tensely vulnerable conversation in her presence, even though she didn't know enough about who or what they were discussing to follow. What purpose did such an exchange serve? Why did it seem like these men, in the heat of their argument, had forgotten that Jem was even there?

Maybe the AI tasked with torturing Jem considered itself an artist, like Armitage with its garden. Maybe it took pleasure in fully realizing the emotional depths of all the players in Jem's damnation, going so far as to give them interpersonal relationship conflict beyond the scope of her personal narrative and viewpoint.

Maybe these were fellow prisoners, trapped in their own overlapping labyrinths of personalized suffering. Or maybe each was controlled by a specific AI—bored Overminds and Alphas, playing in their victims' hells, like some sort of roleplaying game for demons.

There was something about all this that didn't quite mesh with what Jem thought Torment would be like. Something was off, that she couldn't quite place.

It was all just so . . . messy. And in Jem's experience, the Synth were rarely messy.

She'd assumed that the wonders and wizardry of her virtual prison had been inspired by the sorcerer from *Swan Lake*, whose fearful silhouette had loomed with such intriguing menace in the dreams and nightmares of her early childhood. He'd been her boogeyman in tights, ever since she'd first gone to the ballet and watched, with horror, as he tormented Jem's mother, the titular Swan.

But what if Jem was wrong? What if this was . . . *real?*

"There isn't much time left," Jubal said, with a sudden urgency. "I need you to *listen.* Marblewood's City Hall has been completely sealed off and surrounded by the Watchmen. Thane's following you with an entire squadron of Lancers—won't be long till they get there after you arrive. He'll kill you if you're lucky. Capture you if you're not. Just like the Lancers already waiting in Schwarzwald and Xanadu are going to capture or kill Albert and Ilyana the moment they arrive. The humans will dwindle to nothing, and everything you've done . . . everything your mother did . . . will have been for nothing."

Across from Jem, Nikolai seemed to become smaller. "*No!* Captain, please—tell the king not to hurt them. Tell him that this is my fault! I made them help me. Lied to them. You know how I am, I tricked them, it's not their fault. Ilyana's drugged, and Albert tried to stop us, but I wouldn't listen. So please, don't—"

"Out of my hands, m'boy. You—" He cut off midsentence, and when he began to speak again, it was just above a whisper. "You were right about king, Nikolai. He's never going to help the humans. More afraid of there being another Vaillancourt than he'll ever be of the Synth. All these years, I thought, maybe I can change his mind. Maybe I can . . ."

He cleared his throat.

"Doesn't matter, now. I was wrong. But you little monsters! I know a way that you could force the magi into war with the Synth . . . *and* escape to live another day! Something that would stir up such a fuss, that even Ilyana and Albert might evade capture."

Jubal's words hit Jem with a jolt like icy water, snapping her to attention.

"*How?*" she demanded, making Nikolai flinch from the startling intensity of her outburst.

Whatever Jubal was going to propose, Jem knew that if there was even the tiniest sliver of a chance that she wasn't actually in Torment—that, somehow, this was all *real*—if the old man's plan was as feasible as he made it out to be, then no matter what it required of her, she'd see it through.

However terrible the price—Jem would pay. However brutal the violence, widespread the devastation, immense the suffering—*Jem would not balk*.

Not this time. Not like she had with Eva.

"When you arrive in Marblewood's city hall," Jubal explained, "go down into the basement, to the Disc. Nikolai, you'll need to remove the bindings from the Disc so you can fully seal it with a bubble of Veil. Energy from the Disc can't pass through Veil, so the flow of magic to the dome surrounding Marblewood will be cut off, and the Veil will fall—revealing the world beyond to the city, and the city to the world beyond.

"The Watchmen will scatter. Thane's platoon of Lancers will be too busy fighting Synth and evacuating the civilians to give you much trouble. The Synth will attack. There will be losses. But then the machines will know of the magi, and it won't be long before the magi find out what really happened in Marblewood. The king won't have any choice but to enter the war after that."

Nikolai stiffened. "No. No way. I'd never fucking do that."

Jem clenched her fist tightly around the revolver's pommel—whispers that had practically been inaudible before becoming *ever so slightly* less so.

"Why not?" she said to Nikolai. "You sacrificed an entire city of humans to save yourself. But you won't sacrifice a city of—whatever the fuck you are—to save my entire species?"

He shrank away from Jem's words, recoiling as if struck.

"You don't understand," Nikolai pleaded. "I grew up here. These are my friends. My family. They aren't soldiers, they're just civilians. They've never hurt anyone!"

"Ignorance isn't innocence," Jem snapped. "Your people abandoned us! Left us to die!"

"Jem, please, you don't—"

"Ms. Burton has a point," Jubal said with a drunken giggle. "You're being very selfish right now, Nikolai. Not to mention shortsighted."

"This gun," Jem said to Jubal, wheels turning in her mind through a residual daze that she couldn't yet shake. "The bullets passed right through the walls when I shot you. I saw the holes. Can see them now, in my recorded memories."

Nikolai was staring at her, alarmed. "Jem . . ."

"What would happen," she asked, "if I used it to shoot the Disc?"

Slowly Jubal began to chuckle. His chuckles grew to a drunken cackle, until finally, he dissolved into a fit of hacking wet coughs.

"Ms. Burton," he said, once the fit had passed. "I really do wish we'd met under different circumstances. If you find your companion less than helpful in locating the Disc chamber, simply look for a white circle over the—"

Nikolai frantically launched from his seat and punched the gemstone communicator with crystal-coated knuckles. It shattered, going silent, leaving them in the dark but for the gentle glow of the revolver's runes.

"You weren't serious, right?" Nikolai asked, warily eyeing the gun held ready at Jem's side.

"Of course not," she said, echoing his broken oath with a bitterly mocking smile. "I *promise*."

"Jem . . ."

"You've been there, right? Venus? Europa?"

"Jem, please, I—"

The mocking smile fled Jem's lips, leaving only the bitterness, and hurt. "They're even more beautiful than they were before the war."

Serpent quick, Nikolai reached to draw his blade. But even if he hadn't been so grievously wounded, he still wouldn't have been any match for Jem's mod-enhanced reflexes.

Their struggle was brief—Jem snatching away his blade before he could touch it as she struck him with a pair of quick jabs to his eyes and throat. As he crumpled onto the floor of the tiny compartment, gagging, she took his baton as well and moved back, leveling the gun at his prone body. "I won't kill you, Nikolai. But I will hurt you. Lie on your stomach. Wrists crossed behind your head. "

"Please," he whimpered, though he did as instructed. "I'm sorry I lied to you. Sorry I fucked things up so badly. But—"

"If this is really happening," Jem said. "If this isn't all just some artificial world tailored for my suffering, and there's even the smallest chance that shooting your Disc might help my people, I have to do it. I'm sorry, Nik."

Nikolai stared at her with the unsurprised heartbreak of a lonely child who'd just been let down by yet another adult.

It was almost enough to weaken Jem's resolve. Almost enough to make her question whether there might be some other way.

She remembered Eva staring up at her from the floor after Jem had subdued her, like Nik was now. Begging Jem to stop. Begging her not to . . .

No.

Jem summoned the memories of Machado's fall, forcing herself to endure the deafening cacophony of ten thousand people weeping and screaming at the exact same time. A visceral reminder of all that was at stake—of all the people whose lives she'd ruined.

In her mind, Synth forces closed in methodically around the desperate civilian mobs that surged across the base's open expanse like packs of clumsy gazelle. Synth wranglers picked away at the mobs, until each human had been flung into mobile containment units with the casual indifference of a harvester gathering fruit.

She'd called them cowards for how they treated her. But Jem had been the real coward. Jem had been one who'd sold them out for a ticket to the stars.

A ticket that had been a lie in the end.

The chamber was rocked by a gentle tug as it came to a stop, and the curved door panel hissed away, opening to what appeared to be some kind of cleaning supply storage closet.

"Up," she commanded, beckoning for him to lead the way. When Nikolai refused, she repeated the order and kicked at the stump of his hand, hating herself as he let out a mewling cry of pain.

Nikolai's dagger and baton clutched awkwardly with one hand, revolver in her other, Jem held the whimpering boy at gunpoint as he led the way out into the ornate tiled lobby of his city hall.

A statue of a man and a woman in gold and silver featured prominently at the center, the ceiling lit with a hologram of cloud-patched sky framed by stained glass windows that shone like electric jewels.

The lobby was empty, the great black doors across the way closed shut. But outside, she could hear the nervous chattering of a crowd.

"*NIKOLAI STRAUSS!*" boomed a voice from beyond the door. "*WE'VE BEEN AUTHORIZED TO USE DEADLY FORCE IN*

YOUR DETAINMENT! PLEASE LAY DOWN YOUR FOCALS
AND ILLEGAL FIREARM AND COME PEACEFULLY!"

"You know us, lad!" another shouted. "We don't want to hurt you!
So please—don't fight!"

Searching for the symbol Jubal had mentioned before Nik
could cut him off, Jem quickly found a wide stairwell, leading
down—marked with a pale, glowing dot.

"There," she said, directing him to lead the way.

A heavy knocking came from the door, and both Jem and
Nikolai spun to face it, startled.

"Nikolai!" came the rumbling baritone of a large man's voice.
"It's me, Joseph. I'm coming inside—alone. I just want to talk."

The door began to creep open, a pair of big hands reaching
in, palms out to show that they were empty. A young, statuesque
white man cautiously sidled in through the gap in the partially
open door, slowly closing it behind him with a shove from his
winged golden boot. On his back, he wore an eagle-topped scepter of brass, matching the buttons on the bright white coat he
wore over a navy three-piece.

He looked like a cop.

"Joseph!" Nikolai called—seeming somehow both relieved
and annoyed.

"One more step and I'll shoot him in the head," Jem said to the
newcomer, words booming with menace as they echoed across
the tile. "Another step after that and I'll kill you too."

Joseph gave Nikolai a look, tensing, but the boy responded
with a subtle shake of his head.

"You're the boss," Joseph said, with a gentle affability Jem
knew many would find disarming. "I'm just here to talk. I mean
you no harm."

"Get over here," she commanded. "Stand next to Nikolai. Now!"

"Like I said, you're the boss."

Jem felt numb as she followed them from a safe distance down a long flight of stairs to a hall hung with curtains of red and gold—sharply cutting off the cop's attempts at negotiation.

"Jem, wait!" Nikolai said, turning to face her as Joseph shoved open the polished black doors behind him to reveal a cavernous, domed room of slick white marble.

The Disc chamber.

Nikolai moved to stand between her and the Disc, frantically holding out his arm as if to impede her view. "Don't shoot it! I'll seal it in Veil, like Jubal said. If you shoot the Disc, you might kill it, and everyone here will die. The Lancers won't be able to evacuate the civilians, or fight off the Synth. The Synth'll take us all prisoner. And if they find a way to take our magic, and use it for themselves—there'll be no stopping them."

Nikolai's barrel-chested friend looked at Jem, then back at Nik, blood draining from his face as he appeared to realize what they were discussing. "Wait, what?"

"*Shut up*, Joseph," Nikolai whispered tersely, eyes never leaving hers. "Please, Jem. If it has to be done, let me. I'll seal it, to drop the Veil, then I'll unseal it—that way, not only will they have a chance to survive and fight back, but I'll also be more powerful. I'll get us out of here."

The Disc floated there, emitting silver light through the great black chains holding it in place—softly luminescent droplets trickling into the glassy surface of the pool below.

Staring at it, Jem nodded. She tossed the blade and baton into the chamber, indicating with a wave of her revolver that Nikolai could retrieve them. "Fine. Do it. Now."

Wan, Nikolai sheathed the baton, picked up the dagger, and

gracefully leaped through the air to land where the shackles met the wall. Perching on an immense link, he began striking at the anchor, sparks flying as he cut with his white-hot blade.

"You can't do this," Joseph said, face taut with sickened disbelief. "Y-y-you can't! Why—"

Jem pressed a finger against the tragus of her ear to block out the sound, crooking her neck to press the other ear against her hunched shoulder, and casually snapped out a shot past the navy-clad boy's head—a puff of hot dust exploding from the slick white wall behind him as it burrowed deeply into the stone.

"Another word from you," Jem said as Joseph bit back a terrified yelp, falling to his knees, "and the next shot won't miss."

Nikolai swung his blade to strike with one final explosion of sparks, and the chains fell away, smashing down with an unbearable cacophony of iron against stone.

The Disc seemed to pulse, free of the great, black bindings. It began to spin slowly, impossible pearly depths glowing somehow brighter.

Nikolai dropped down into a neat landing.

Swapping his blade for the baton, Nikolai summoned a wafer-thin sheet of mirror and leaped back into the air—trailing it behind him as he methodically bounded from floor to ceiling around the Disc. The reflective skeleton of a sphere quickly began to take shape, like ribbons of polished steel being wound across the surface of an invisible globe.

The blond man's face had gone a purplish red in his strain to remain silent as he followed the progress of Nikolai's graceful leaping form.

Though nearly finished with the sphere, Nikolai's momentum was brought to a halt when he botched a landing—twisting, almost falling, then catching himself in a stagger.

The Disc's pale radiance shone through what few slender gaps remained in the looping mirror ribbons.

Chest heaving, Nikolai steadied himself, impatiently whipping his baton in a quick motion to unfurl another sheet of silver. But then, as he positioned himself to jump, the sheet fizzled out, crumbling to ashes.

"What's the fucking problem?" Jem growled, impatient. How much longer could it possibly be before Nikolai's former comrades burst through that door to eviscerate them with those concentrated threads of fire?

"It's fine!" he insisted, repeating the motion with his baton to summon another ribbon, with the same result. "Gimme a sec, I just need . . ."

"There's no time, Nikolai!"

"I know!" he said, trying again, then again, increasingly desperate as each mercurial burst seemed to crumble more quickly than the last. "It's not as easy as it looks!"

"Are you fucking with me right now?" Jem raised the gun, grip slick with perspiration. "Is this some sort of trick?"

"No!" he cried, through another puff of ash. "I'm not! I swear! I just—"

"You've got ten more seconds!" she barked, taking aim at the center of the dazzling ribbon globe. "Then I'm taking the shot."

"*Please!*"

"Ten. Nine . . ."

"Goddamnit, Jem! That isn't helping!"

"Eight. Seven."

"I can do this! Just . . ."

But then, as even the quantity of ashes he could produce began to lessen, Nikolai gave up—his shoulders slumping, baton drooping as his arm fell limply to his side. He looked at her, the baton in his hand. "I . . ."

"Six."

"I always hated it here," Nikolai said, sounding unfathomably tired. "Hated almost everyone who lives here."

"Five!"

"But I know them. Understand them. And because of that, I can really *feel* it. How horrible this is going to be. I didn't feel it with the humans. Not like this. But I get it now. Get what a stupid, selfish piece of shit that makes me. And now . . . I can't even get this right."

He squeezed his eyes shut, tears spilling over onto the bloody filth that caked his cheeks. "I wish I'd let you kill me. Wish I'd . . ."

Jem had ceased counting—trigger finger trembling with a newfound hesitance as Nikolai trailed off.

The icy shell of Jem's detachment began to crack—the hopelessness and self-loathing of Nikolai's words stabbing through her with such surprising intensity that she had to take a step back and steady herself with a hand against the sloping wall.

For the first time, it wasn't Eva that Nikolai reminded her of. Instead she saw herself, pleading desperately for the other woman to consider the cruelty of her plans. The woman who might as well have been her sister. The woman who damned herself by damning the world to suffer as hideously as she had—*all for the greater good*.

How many times had devastation and sorrow been imposed on strangers from another race, gender, class, or *other*, using that very phrase? And of those times, how often had there actually been a better way?

Slowly, Jem lowered the revolver.

"I . . . I can't do it," she said, the words flooding her with a great, gasping relief, as if she'd just narrowly avoided plummeting headfirst over a cliff in the dark. "You're right, Nikolai. This is wrong."

Taking an unsteady step toward the light of the Disc, which seemed to pulse through the gaps in Nikolai's steely ribbons with a newfound brightness, Jem allowed the revolver to slip from her grasp—malicious whispers replaced by the faint notes of a distant song as the murderous steel clattered mutely across the floor.

Taking another step, she could hear the song more clearly— the aching beauty of its call seeping through her like blessed honey.

She sank to her knees, hands clasped before her.

"That . . . song," she whispered. "Do you hear it? It's beautiful. And so . . . sad."

Nikolai stared at her blankly, seeming to struggle with accepting the reality of Jem's change of heart.

"Song?"

"I understand now," she said, feeling a warmth she imagined might be like that of an infant falling asleep in its mother's arms. "I'm not in Torment. All this—it *is* real. And you aren't wizards. This isn't really magic. That's just what you call yourselves."

She stared up at the Disc, hands clasped in front of her face.

"We'll have to fight," she said. "But there's a way. Better than this. We just have to find it. Just have to—"

Pain exploded as a navy blur crashed into Jem, slamming her onto the ground. Her chin cracked against the slick stone floor, blood filling her mouth as the much larger man dug his navy-clad knee into her back—her arms straining painfully in their sockets as he twisted them behind her.

She tried to cry out, but could barely breathe through the crushing pressure.

"That's enough out of you, *half-mage*," the cop spat in the tone that she'd only heard white men use when angrily reminding someone they deemed *lesser than* to remember their place.

"*Wait*—" she choked, but he shoved her face back down onto the tile, the icy weight of his scepter pressing against the back of her skull.

"I said that's enough!"

A powerful electric shock cracked through Jem's body from the icy weight. She couldn't scream. Couldn't breathe. She could hear Nikolai shouting—could hear the cop shouting back—but as she struggled to twist free Joseph hit her with another shock, and all at once the floor seemed to close around her.

Jem welcomed the darkness.

XIV.

THE WOMAN IN THE REVOLVER

"Get—the fuck—off her!"

Nikolai's baton crackled with energy, his eyes lit with wrath as he closed the distance between himself and the privileged buffoon who'd subdued the unarmed Jem with excessive force.

Joseph rose to his full height, towering over the comatose, bloody-faced Jem. "Stand down, Nikolai. This woman is dangerous."

"She stopped!" Nikolai shouted, overwhelmed with a new and profound disgust for this mage. "She gave up her weapon! You didn't need to do that! She's a human, Joseph! The Unraveling— the chaos outside the Veils—it's all *LIES*! But Jem—both of us! We need your help, not *this*!"

But Joseph wasn't listening. He shot through the air with blasts of *akro* from his golden flyball boots. Zigzagging, twisting, impossibly quick as Joseph jetted toward him, gracefully dodging around Nikolai's frantic bursts of *akro*.

With a roar, Joseph closed the distance between them and slammed a tentacle of *akro* into Nikolai's side.

Nikolai grunted, spinning away from the blow and throwing his arms up to protect his head as he tumbled.

"Joseph, stop!" Nikolai screamed, sending out a more powerful blast of *akro*, but Joseph moved in an impossible corkscrew circle around the column, dodging even as Nikolai turned it toward him and then Joseph was on him, bearing down with an enormous plume of fire from his scepter, great jets of *akro* shooting from his boots as he flew at Nikolai.

One-handed, it was all Nikolai could do to unravel the flames before they engulfed him, heat blasting around him in waves.

And then Joseph passed Nikolai, an *akro* tentacle replacing the flames, looping around Nikolai's baton as Joseph yanked it after him, free from his grasp.

Baton flung across the cavernous chamber, Nikolai drew his blade.

"*Stop!*" he screamed as Joseph landed in a turn, muscles bulging as he prepared to launch himself at Nikolai—face twisted up with animal ferocity. "Please! Just listen!"

"What could you *possibly* have to say to me?" Joseph sneered, and he was airborne, too fast to see, and in a moment of desperation Nikolai featherweighted himself and launched into the air, out of his trajectory.

Joseph chased him through the air, and Nikolai was flying—fleeing desperately around the floating Disc as Joseph pursued him with murderous intent, twisting around and smashing down with *akro*-coated boots against the wall hard enough to send out shards of shattered marble.

But Nikolai couldn't stop running—couldn't stop fleeing. Thane—the Edge Guard—they'd be here any minute. Any moment! But if Nikolai stopped running—if he turned to fight— then he knew—knew with *certainty*—that one of them was going to die. Maybe Nikolai. Maybe Joseph. And killing Joseph . . .

"You don't understand!" Nikolai pleaded, slicing away another plume of fire with his blade. "The humans, they're all going to *die*! The king doesn't care, he's just waiting—letting them die out! He's been lying to us—lying to everyone for a century. I can prove it, I can show you, just *please*—"

"You're full of shit, *Nikolai!*" Joseph roared, whips of flame cutting through the air inches from Nikolai's face as he changed his trajectory, desperately trying to get away. "You're a liar! A *terrorist!*"

"*NO!* The *king* is the liar! I know his secrets, and soon there'll be others here. They'll kill me and take Jem, for Disc knows what kind of horrible shit!"

Another explosion of tile. Another near miss. "She's a half-mage! A criminal!"

Another whip of fire—hair singeing on the side of Nikolai's head as he barely managed to dodge.

"*NO!* She's an innocent! And they were torturing her! Her and others! Humans and half-mages, experimenting on them!"

"You're a *LIAR!*"

"Why! *Why* would I lie about that?"

"Because you've always hated us! Always been jealous and angry and violent! And now you've finally lost it—finally snapped, and now—"

"*NO!*" Nikolai said again. "I'm sorry for how I treated you! You, Astor, the others! Yes—I was jealous. Spiteful. Angry. It wasn't right—wasn't right! I was unhappy, I've always been *SO* fucking *unhappy!* But none of that matters now. *Please!*"

In his fury, Joseph slipped up, exposing himself to attack. In a moment that seemed to last forever, Nikolai had an opening, a brief instant in which he could blast Joseph with flames enough to reduce him to a cinder before he'd have a chance to negate the spell. Killing Joseph. Finishing this.

But as he leveled the blade with Joseph's slowly widening eyes, the killing spell faltered in his wrist at the threshold of casting. The opportunity passed, and it dawned on Nikolai with sick realization that he couldn't do it. *Wouldn't* do it!

Joseph used Nikolai's hesitation to his advantage and hit him in the chest with such incredible force that it sent Nikolai sprawling, his blade Focal slipping from his grip and the air knocked from his lungs despite his uniform's protection as he tumbled.

Nikolai curled up into a ball, wheezing as Joseph walked over to him with his nostrils flaring. Joseph drew a pair of golden handcuffs from the navy breast of his uniform—Watchman spell-blockers.

"It's over, Nikolai," he said. "You lost. I'm taking you in."

"Please," Nikolai begged, crawling backward as he struggled to catch his breath. "Don't let it all have been for nothing. They'll be here soon. Be here any moment. And the humans—Joseph, the humans! If we don't help them, they'll all—they'll all . . ."

"Even if what you say is true," Joseph said. "I can't let you go. I promise that I'll do everything in my power to look into your accusations, but I'm sorry, Nikolai—you've given me very little reason to trust you."

Joseph was almost upon him. Nikolai looked around, frantically searching for his Focals, but they were too far—he'd never be able to reach them. He continued to crawl backward, knowing that Joseph would pounce the instant Nikolai turned his back on him, knowing that there was nowhere he could go, nothing he could—

Nikolai's hand came down upon cool, rune-etched steel.

The Disc chamber began to morph, scorched white marble fading to vibrant greens. The slick domed walls turned to vine-tangled trees around him, the floor to mossy soil.

Nikolai was in a forest. He whipped his head back and forth, baffled. Where—? How—?

A dark-haired little boy burst into the clearing, gasping ragged breaths as he half limped, half ran. A root caught his foot and he tumbled, sprawling. He struggled to rise, arms trembling with effort, but then he collapsed onto his side. Wracked with quiet sobs, too weak to stand, the side of his face bloody and raw from where he'd fallen.

Heart pounding hard enough to resonate in the soles of his sweating feet, Nikolai went over to help the child, but froze as an eerie whistled tune issued from the shadows of the forest from where the boy had come. The boy's head jerked up at the sound, and his sobs became panicked. Terrified.

Nikolai couldn't move. He couldn't breathe. That whistle. It had been so long since he'd heard that horrible whistle.

Struggling with renewed desperation, the little boy pushed himself onto his hands and knees. Then, with agonizing slowness, he stood.

A whip of flame lashed out from the darkness, striking the child in the back, sending him to his knees. The boy screamed, his shirt lightly scorched to reveal blistered red skin underneath. Nikolai let out a cry, reaching for the child, but found himself unable to move.

A woman wearing the sheer black uniform of the Edge Guard entered the clearing. On one hand, she wore a golden medi-glove Focal. In her other, a slender sword.

Ashley Strauss.

Her face was a blurry aberration—like a hole in reality of which he couldn't find the center, no matter how he tried.

"Too slow, Nikolai," his mother said. Her voice horribly distorted. "You can do better."

"Mom," the child croaked. "It hurts. It huuurrrrtttts . . ."

"You've got another mile. "

"Mom, please . . ."

Her golden fingers began to pulse with yellow flames. She raised her hand, threatening. "One more mile, then I'll heal you. Otherwise . . ."

The younger Nikolai whimpered, silent tears rolling down his face as he forced himself to stand. Shaking visibly, he staggered out of the clearing, off to finish his morning run.

Ashley Strauss sighed and walked after him. As she disappeared into the shadows, she once again began to whistle that horrible eerie tune.

"Seven years old," came a voice. Nikolai spun around, finally free from his paralysis.

A woman wearing bloodred formal robes and a conical, wide-brimmed hat stood behind him. A filmy veil hung across the brim of her hat, hiding her face. And though Nikolai couldn't see her face, he knew that, without a doubt, she was the most beautiful woman in the world.

"You were seven years old when your mother began to train you. Began to forge you into the mage you've become."

"You . . ." he breathed, terrified realization dawning on him. "You're the woman in the revolver." Nikolai sank to the mossy floor and squeezed his eyes shut, clutching his skull. "This isn't real. You're in my mind. Get out. Get out, get out, *get out!*"

He could feel it now, those creeping tendrils squirming in his pools of magic. He had to fight, had to break free, had to—

"Peace, Nikolai," she said, her voice soothing and musical. "I mean you no harm. I was a friend to your mother, and you rescued me from my prison at great personal cost. My purpose, like your own, is to aid humanity. I'm here to help you."

Nikolai realized that he had both of his hands again, and opened his eyes to look down at them. For a moment his left hand was gone, his stump a blistered horror streaked with molten gold. But then, they were normal. Whole.

Slowly Nikolai stood and began to back away from the ominous red figure. The mind within the revolver.

"I don't want your help," he said. "I don't want anything from you."

Vicious little device, Jubal had said. *A sentient artifact of pure evil.*

"Atticus Jubal warned you about me," she said, responding to his thoughts. Of course she could hear his thoughts; she was in his mind, in his *soul*. "He knew that if I were to fall into your possession, he would lose you. Just like he lost your mother."

Nikolai shook his head in disbelief. "I saw what you did to Hazeal. I remember all the horrible shit you showed me when he made me touch the gun. It was like looking into hell."

"And yet you allowed me into your mind once again, of your own volition. If my malevolence was so obvious, so absolute, why seek my aid?"

He stared at her. "What are you? And what do want with me?"

"I am neither good nor evil," she said. "I am a balancing force. A gift, created for the humans to serve as a countermeasure against the tyranny of your kind. A gift, stolen by one of your kind, and bound—hidden away in such forgotten depths that centuries passed before your mother found me. Your mother, who chose to defy your king's orders to allow humanity to wither and die while your kind enjoyed the fruits of paradise. To that end, I offered my assistance."

"And Hazeal?"

"A weak man, now twice a traitor. Redemption was to be his reward for delivery of the weapon and key. But Armand was blinded by his hatred of your mother, and his loyalty to the crown. Even knowing what misery the humans endured. Even having witnessed the cruelty of Atticus Jubal's decades-long experimentation on living test subjects. Experiments which, though Atticus never knew, your mother discovered, and used as a tool for recruitment—showing it to potential allies to illustrate the brutal corruption of the Mage King's regime.

"*No,*" she intoned. "I'll not apologize for my treatment of Armand Hazeal."

The forest suddenly faded to pitch darkness around him, and when the light returned they stood at the foot of the staircase adjacent to the dining room of Nikolai's childhood home.

At the center of the room, Nikolai's father and mother were screaming at each other, Eric's face flushed an ugly red as he shouted down the distorted image of Ashley Strauss. At the top of the stairs, seven-year-old Nikolai hid, wide-eyed as he listened in on their argument.

When Nikolai was seven, their secret training sessions had started as a game. Had started off easy. Nikolai had been incredibly bright for his age and initially embraced the challenge. But then, day-by-day, week by week, the lessons became brutal. Became *torture.*

His mother had forbidden Nikolai from telling his father, and Nikolai—terrified of her—had complied. A few months after the training had begun, however, his father had come home early from the Watchman station one morning. Had caught Nikolai's mother healing his bloody feet—a cool towel over his eyes as she whispered comforting nothings.

"—the same *shit* your father used to do to you!" Eric Strauss roared at his wife. It was the first time Nikolai had ever heard the man lose his temper.

"This is *different*," she insisted. "My father was a farmer. And he was sick in the head. He had no reason to treat me and Red the way he did. But *we* know! We know what the king is doing! What's going to happen out there! And if you think I'll let my boy—"

"*OUR* boy!"

"—If you think I'll let *our* boy grow up *weak* and defenseless because the king is too much of a coward to—"

Ashley stopped, held up a hand for silence, and the scene faded to darkness once more.

"You did not sleep that night," came the woman's voice from the darkness. "You lay awake until dawn, praying for respite from your mother's brutality. Praying with such hope and desperation as only a child can. But when you awoke . . ."

The darkness faded and they were standing in Nikolai's childhood bedroom. The little boy laid there, dark circles under eyes puffy and sore from crying as he stared at the ceiling. But then Ashley's heavy footsteps approached from down the hall as she came to wake him the same way she always did, by whistling that horrible tune and ordering him to stand at attention.

Nikolai found it hard to breathe as he followed them downstairs. His father sat at the breakfast table, hollow-eyed. Defeated. Nikolai had always worshipped his father. Always loved him most of all. Always wanted to be like him. To *be* him.

But as Eric Strauss watched Nikolai go, ignoring the child's pleading look as he followed his mother out into the dark for another hellish morning, Nikolai realized that his father wasn't going to save him.

"Your father bowed to your mother's will. Allowed your suffering to continue. Why?"

"He loved her," Nikolai said, tears welling in his eyes. "It wasn't his fault. Nobody could say no to my mother. If he'd tried, she'd probably have taken me away from him. He was just a Watchman. She was an Edge Guard, favored by the king. So he did what he could. He loved us. He wanted us to be happy. He'd make my mother laugh—he was the only one who could make my mother laugh. And then she'd go easier on me . . . for a little while . . ."

The red woman stared at him through the veil. Impassive.

Then they were back in the forest, in another clearing. His mother and the child were sparring. Years had passed since the argument, and the young Nikolai was ten now. No longer weak as he'd been when his mother had begun training him. No longer collapsed at the end of their daily sessions into a weeping, exhausted mess.

The child wielded his mother's sword with little hands. He attacked with a ferocious flurry of graceful swings she fended off with an *akro* sword she'd created for practice. He was featherweighted, and fast, leaping and running and bouncing off of tree trunks with graceful ease as he fought to get past her defenses.

She feinted, and Nikolai fell for it. She struck him, *hard*, knocking him back. He stumbled away, but caught himself, keeping his feet. Nikolai rubbed his shoulder where she'd hit him, tears of pain beaded at the corner of his eyes, but he was grinning.

"You left yourself open," she scolded.

"Yes ma'am," he said, still smiling. "Sorry ma'am."

"Otherwise, though . . . wonderful. You've come so far, and I am so, so proud of you."

Nikolai began to tremble, sickened as he watched the ten-year-old version of himself preen at her rare praise. He remembered this. Remembered what was coming.

"But now . . . there's something I need to show you."

"Yes, Mom?" young Nikolai said, his eyes gleaming with eager curiosity.

"I won't always be around to protect you," she said, and all of a sudden she started crying—her monstrous distorted voice cracked with emotion. "Won't always be here to teach you and make you strong. But there's one thing. One final lesson you need to learn before I'm gone."

She whimpered, muttering to herself. He stood there, awkward. His resolve fading.

"Mom?"

"*Vasano*," she whispered, firing off a net of crackling red light.

The light enveloped the child. His cry sounded like the agonized squeal of a dying animal, but with another quick gesture Ashley silenced him with a muting spell cast upon his lips as he writhed, his body wracked with pain.

Nikolai found himself unable to pull his eyes away as she cast it onto the boy again and again. The break between each casting shorter than the last as he silently screamed.

"Here you go, Nicky," she cooed after an eternity of suffering, the child's head resting on the nothingness of the memory of her lap as she lifted a Tabula Rasa potion to his lips. "Just a sip. To help you forget a little. Enough to keep you from going mad. I'll give you less tomorrow. And less after that. Soon, you won't even need it. Pain will be nothing to you."

"I don't want to see this," Nikolai hissed through clenched teeth. He turned to the silent red woman, resisting the violent urge to grab her arm. "Take me away from here. I said *I don't want to see this!*"

She nodded, the wide brim of her hat dipping and rising ever so slightly. The forest faded and was replaced by his father's office at the Watchman station.

His father sat at his big oaken desk, brow furrowed as he scratched away at a stack of paperwork with an ornate golden pen. As Nikolai watched, his ten-year-old self nervously stopped at the threshold of the open door, seemingly afraid to fully enter.

"Dad?" he said, tentative.

Eric Strauss looked up sharply, surprised. "Nik? What are you doing here? Why aren't you in school?"

"I-I left," the boy said. "I need to talk to you. It's important."

His father opened his mouth to say something, but then seemed to think better of it. He nodded, and gestured at a chair for Nikolai to take a seat. "Close the door behind you."

The boy struggled to speak, muttering and then trailing off into silence.

"Hey . . ." his father said, then stood to come around the desk and take the seat beside him. "It's okay. What's going on, kiddo?"

"It's . . . it's Mom," he finally said. Then, in a desperate, tearful rush: "She hurt me this morning, Dad, she hurt me worse than ever!"

Eric stiffened, going pale as the concerned warmth drained from his face.

"She said she'll do it again, said that she's going to keep doing it, and I can't take it anymore, Dad, I can't do it, you have to stop her, *PLEASE*, Dad you've got to help me. If you don't, I'll kill her, or I'll kill myself, I'll—"

Eric grabbed him by the shoulders, horrified. "Don't you *ever* talk like that. Do you hear me? Don't you ever say something so horrible!"

"Please, Dad," Nikolai begged. "Please!"

Eric pulled Nikolai into a tight embrace, looking as if he'd aged a decade in those moments.

"Shhhh, it's okay. I'll talk to her. I won't let her hurt you again, you're going to be okay, shhhh . . ."

But nothing changed. Nikolai's mother tortured him again the next day. Then again, the day after that. Then finally, she and Nikolai's father went away to New Damascus for "a business trip," leaving him in Astor's family's care. And when news of the skycraft crash came shortly after, the relief Nikolai had felt that she was dead was indescribable—though he'd never admitted it to anyone.

Eric and the child disappeared, leaving Nikolai and the red woman alone in the now-silent office.

"I hate him," Nikolai whimpered. "I hate him, I hate them both. Why didn't he help me? Why didn't he stop her?"

Nikolai sank to the floor and began to weep. He couldn't help it; he pressed his face into his hands, ashamed, and cried helpless, hysterical sobs. Hating himself. Hating his father, his mother, Jubal, Red, even Astor—all the people he'd loved, all the people who were supposed to love him, supposed to keep him safe, but instead had done nothing but hurt or abandon him.

The red woman placed a comforting gloved hand on Nikolai's shoulder, and a sense of soothing calm washed through him. His sadness remained, but its sting was lessened. The ache in his chest made bearable.

"Your father was a good man," she said. "But was he right to let you suffer? Your mother's cruelty had purpose. But your father? His compliance stemmed from weakness. What use was his goodness to you? What use was his love?"

Her grip on Nikolai's shoulder tightened.

"Good. *Evil*. These are useless terms. Your mother was not a good woman. But now here you are. On the verge of succeeding where she failed. On the verge of singlehandedly setting the course of destiny for both man and mage by revealing the greatest genocide in the history of this world to your kind. But only if you can escape."

Nikolai wiped away tears with the sleeve of his uniform and opened his eyes to find his father standing before him, looking down at Nikolai with that helpless expression. With that pathetic, impotent sadness.

"Joseph Eaglesmith is a good man," she continued. "A great man, potentially. But his goodness rings hollow—untested by sorrow, pain, or loss. He and so many of your kind are blinded by the privilege they've enjoyed while the masses toiled out of sight. He will do nothing to prevent the suffering and extinction of terrestrial humankind. So you have a choice. An ugly choice."

She drew the rune-etched revolver from the folds of her robe and took his hand, closing it around the pommel.

"Kill one good man and live to fan the flames of revolution," the red woman said, "or do nothing and allow billions to die."

Terrible things, Jubal had once promised. He said that Nikolai would have to do *terrible things* if he ever became an important mage. *All for the greater good.*

Nikolai's father said that there was always a choice. And he was right: Nikolai could stop here. Could keep it from going any further than this.

He'd loved his father. But his father had been weak—had *let* Ashley torture Nikolai. Let her turn him into a weapon. Let her drill him till his soul was as sick and dirty as hers and the Disc had no choice but to manifest an instrument for murder as his art Focal.

It was then that Nikolai realized he really was nothing like his father.

He was his mother's son. And he knew what he had to do.

The trembling in Nikolai's hands ceased as he raised the gun.

"I'm sorry, Joseph," he said.

Nikolai pulled the trigger.

The office tore away, gone in an instant, and Nikolai was back in the Disc chamber. The revolver smoked in his hand.

A line of blood trickled down from a hole at the center of Joseph's forehead. He stood there, staring at Nikolai with dead eyes as the scepter dissolved to foam through his fingers, his flyball boots melting from his feet into a puddle of gold and evaporating as the Focals rejoined his fleeing soul.

Beyond where Joseph had been standing, Nikolai's unfinished sphere of Veil fell away in a spiraling pattern of dust. The Disc began to churn—radiant light forming on its surface like perspiration before streaking inward, into the vortex of crimson where it had been struck by the bullet Nikolai had fired to kill Joseph.

The woman in the revolver had tricked him into shooting the Disc.

After a moment of stunned silence, Nikolai flung the revolver away.

"No . . ."

He looked at his hand. Looked at Joseph, lying there. Empty. A corpse.

"No. No, no, no, no . . ."

The crimson dot trembled, shrinking and growing like a bloody orifice on the flickering Disc.

He brought trembling fingers bent like claws to press against his face. Fingers digging into his forehead, his cheeks.

"Fuck. Oh fuck, what did I do? What did I do?"

Nikolai pulled his knees up against his chest, his eyes squeezed shut but he could still see Joseph. Could still see the

Disc, shuddering in its death throes before him. Nikolai was a murderer, a *mass murderer*, a—

Strong arms pulled him into an embrace, and he thrashed, pulling away, but the arms just pulled tighter, and distantly he could hear Jem's voice.

Finally, he stopped struggling.

"I didn't mean to do it!" he sobbed. "I had to stop Joseph. But the revolver—it tricked me! Fooled me into shooting the Disc!"

"I know," Jem said, holding Nikolai. "I know you didn't mean to."

He pulled away. "We've got to get out there. Got to help somehow."

"I know." Jem looked him in the eyes and squeezed his hand. "I'm so sorry, Nik. I'll help you any way I can."

He nodded. "Okay. *Okay.*"

The Disc grew dull—the gentle electric wind of magical energy that normally flooded every inch of Marblewood dwindled to a trickle as the chamber grew dim. The pool of water below churned and thrashed like a living thing as the clear waters went opaque—then murky—then, with a long, terrible sigh, changed into thick black sludge.

The ground quaked, the air reverberated with something like a thunderclap from down the hall, up the stairs, deadened by the floors and stone between them and the surface, but still impossibly loud.

The Disc flickered back to life, once again filling the chamber with silver light. The pool below, however, remained sludge.

Nikolai drew a filthy handkerchief from his pocket and reached for the revolver, but Jem grabbed his wrist, shaking her head. He nodded, and she took the revolver instead, jamming it into her pocket.

Covering Jem and himself with a sheet of invisibility—praying that, amid the chaos, it would prove sufficient, even though the Watchmen would anticipate him using the spell—Nikolai carefully cracked open one of the great double doors of city hall to find the Watchmen in terrified disarray. Screaming and pointing at the sky. Oblivious to their presence.

Taking deep gasping breaths, Nikolai pulled Jem through the distracted Watchmen, beyond the blockade, and out into the crowds of wailing, horrified magi.

Jem was shouting something, but he couldn't hear her over the howling of the wind. He turned around and there was Thane, framed by the doors to city hall, his burn-scarred face pulled back into a snarl. But even he froze when he saw what Nikolai had done.

Gray skies had replaced the blue, the cold snap of autumn rushing in to replace the balmy warmth of their artificial summer. The air was thick with shreds of ash like the disembodied wings of a billion black butterflies.

In the distance, Nikolai could hear the wail of sirens—hear the buzzing, thumping hum of a thousand Synth drones descending on Marblewood.

As Thane stood there, frozen with the horror of what was happening, their eyes met across the plaza. Nikolai stared back with grim defiance, unashamed of the tears streaming freely down his face as he wept for Joseph and Astor and all the magi who were going to die today—all the magi and all the humans who were going to die because of the atrocity he'd so foolishly been manipulated into committing.

Jem seized Nikolai's wrist, pulling him into the frantic mob to flee the pale Lancer, who was screaming his name. But Nikolai wasn't worried—Thane would never catch them now.

The Veil had fallen.

XV.

THE QUESTION OF MIRACLES

Jem clung desperately to the memory of the song as she pulled Nikolai into the alleyway, away from the men—*wizards*, or magi, or—it didn't matter. Away from the men and women in black uniforms like Nikolai's. Away from the fleshy-faced man who'd murdered her. Again and again and *again and*—

But. This was real. This *was* real.

The song. It was fading now. Already she could only recall the barest shape of it. Which should have been impossible. But her mods had somehow—glitched? Had been unable to detect what her lowly organic brain had experienced so powerfully. Soon all that would remain would be the carefully documented emotional and physiological reactions that had occurred within her body as she basked in its light. And even that was somehow . . . incomplete.

Nikolai slumped against a brightly painted wall, shivering, hugging himself with his eyes squeezed shut as if trying to deny the reality of what he'd done.

Jem had never seen a city so clean as this, even with the papery ashes flitting down across it all. Not even before the Synth uprising. Even the alleyway smelled like gingerbread. What *was* this place?

"Nikolai!" she hissed, and when he didn't respond she took him by the shoulders and shook him violently.

The stump of his wrist hung at his side, oozing. Bloody and hideously blistered. Distantly, she wondered if he could feel it through the drugs she could tell were still in effect from the dilation of his pupils.

"Come on, little buddy. Don't fall to pieces on me. Don't you dare!"

His eyes focused on hers, the delirium seeming to fade.

"That man—Thane," she said. "The others. They'll find us if we stay here."

"My uncle," he finally said. "He's . . . he should be at the Watchman station. In lockup."

"I don't know where that is, Nikolai," she said, releasing him. "All *this*. I have no context. No concept. I'll carry you if you need me to, but I need you to tell me where to go. I'm lost without you."

He stared at her for a moment, then through her, then at her again, seeming to fade in and out, before he finally stiffened and stood upright. "Okay. Come on."

Nikolai darted to the mouth of the alley. Beyond him, men and women dressed in strange, sometimes impossible clothing fled in both directions, unsure of where to go, knowing only that they were under siege as thousands upon thousands of tiny Synth scouts buzzed through their midst like watchful insects.

Men and women in navy, brass-buttoned uniforms—Watchmen, Nikolai had called them—sporadically cut through the air above the mob on sleek obsidian horns with saddle space enough for two and a simple curved steering apparatus at the front. Their amplified voices shouted for civilian magi to seek out the nearest "emergency boxes" for "stasis crystals and evacuation."

Nikolai waved for Jem to follow, and they went out onto the street, pressed back at the edge to avoid the mob. The gleaming dome of the town hall was visible up the street, from where they'd come—resting atop a gentle sloping hill at the center of Marblewood. From here, she could see the impossibly beautiful, antiquated city spread out before her.

Beyond that, the lake, and the woods—the border of Marblewood's lush green forest defined in sharp contrast by the crimson autumnal leaves of the human and Synth world beyond.

Swarms of drones, big and small, darkened the autumn sky like pulsing shadows overhead.

Dozens of black Synth teardrop fighter planes hovered silently in a ring around the edges of the city. Waiting. Contemplating this place that had appeared, *impossibly*, as Armitage allowed the tiny scouts to make their sweeps and likely awaited orders from the Alpha AIs.

Jem knew this territory better than anyone but the Synth. Seeing it like this—seeing it so *changed* by the addition of this massive piece of land—it made her reel. Made her dizzy with the impossibility of it.

Nikolai hadn't been hiding his ship in the lake. He'd been hiding a whole *city*.

How? What kind of *incredibly* advanced technology could just tuck away a city like this? Nikolai had explained it, but she'd disregarded his words as delusion, as a part of some Synth Torment fantasy, before *the song* had convinced her otherwise. Before the Disc had shown her that this was all too real.

There—at the fringes of her visions, at the crest of the hill—Jem noticed one of Jubal's black-clad soldiers. A bald man, one of his ears melted like wax at the center of a burn scar. He looked right at them, and smiled.

"Is that him?" Jem asked. "Thane?"

"Yeah," Nikolai hissed, and Jem recognized him as one of the men who'd taken her prisoner with Jubal on the beach after destroying the Armitage husk.

Another Watchman zipped through the air over Thane, coming toward them. Nikolai drew his blade and created a wall of *akro* in the air, blocking the way.

The Watchman pulled back in surprise, spun out and came to a hovering stop, and in that instant Nikolai was airborne, spinning through the air to slam a sneakered foot into the startled Watchman's face before he could so much as raise his golden staff to defend himself.

As the Watchman plummeted, screaming, into the crowds below, the obsidian flyer spun and began to fall, but Nikolai quickly brought it under control and pulled it up before Jem with violent speed.

"*Get on!*"

She climbed on, looking back to see the man named Thane gesturing with his vicious thorned club for two other Watchmen atop flyers to follow them. Then, eyes never leaving them, he drew a white sphere from within his uniform and smashed it onto the ground.

A craft much like the obsidian flyers unfurled from within the sphere, only bigger—creamy white instead of black, every inch of it covered with intricate swirling runes and symbols that pulsed with multicolored light.

Nikolai glanced back, then leaned forward, picking up speed. "A guardian horn. *Shit!*"

"What's that?" Jem shouted over the wind.

"A ride that's a hell of a lot faster than ours."

Her stomach lurched as they turned sharply around a corner, then another almost immediately after in an attempt to lose the two Watchmen tailing them—but they pursued, undeterred, slowly gaining.

Boiling heat seared through the air beside them as one woman emitted a cloud of flame from her golden staff. Jem clung desperately to Nikolai's waist as they spun away in a roll, nearly flinging Jem from her seat.

As Jem squeezed, she felt the pommel of the revolver jabbing her through her pocket.

She yanked the gun out of her pocket as Nikolai spun and ducked the flyer to go under the Watchmen's coordinated pair of glassy column blasts. Sparks flew with a hideous screech as their craft bounced and scraped down across the cobblestone street— the crowd screaming and diving aside before them as Nikolai roared for them to move before pulling up to fly just over their heads once again.

Ignoring the revolver's ghostly whispers, Jem turned to aim at the pursuing Watchmen, checking to make sure the streets below were empty before snapping out four shots—two bullets for each of the obsidian crafts, piercing the flyers from stern to stem with explosions of crackling white light. The flyers spun away and smashed down onto the streets as the Watchmen frantically leaped away from the dying machines.

Nikolai swore, ducking his head and yelping as they passed

through an especially thick cloud of tiny marble-sized Synth scouts, a rotor the size of an insect wing slicing a slender bloody line across Jem's cheek before she could lean forward to press her face against Nikolai's back.

On every other street corner below, men and women clawed and elbowed at one another amid blasts of blinding light and that frosted glassy substance as they fought for the contents of strange golden boxes shaped like telephone booths she'd seen in period films. Pulsing red crystals spilled out of the boxes like glittering gemstone entrails.

Across the city, thousands of shimmering pink bubbles full of frozen civilians rose up into the drone-clouded sky. Dozens of milky-white guardian horns like the one Thane had summoned from the shattered sphere zigzagged through their midst as fast as any Synth teardrop fighter plane—faster, even! Turns and acceleration that should have reduced any organic occupant to a slurry of flesh and organs—and yet, even from here, she could see tiny, black-clad soldiers riding the crafts in much the same manner as she and Nikolai rode their much slower vehicle.

There must have been some sort of g-force negation—some sort of time and space slowing field within the shimmering bubbles surrounding the ivory flyers to protect the occupants from acceleration, as well as slow down time for them to control the impossible speeds without the computational power of synthetic enhancements.

The black Synth teardrop fighter planes remained stationary in a ring around the city, but Jem knew it wouldn't be long now.

The guardian horns moved in dizzying formation to create immense lengths of the reflective, paper-thin Veil substance into a great funnel in the sky over the center of the city. Other funneled tubes of Veil began to rise up to it across the city like glittering tornadoes, protecting the bubbles as they channeled them to the other end of a tube above a row of sleek black trains down by the lake.

The bubbles flowed into hatches atop the train. After the first had filled to capacity, the hatches sealed and the train streaked off across the water atop invisible tracks, toward a gate suspended over the water that issued into darkness beyond.

A hideous trumpeting siren pierced the air like needles through Jem's skull. Nauseating terror filled her stomach in waves as Nikolai screamed in pain at the sound, struggling to hold on while those below fell to their knees, clutching their ears.

The Synth declaration of battle. No civilians would be escaping into that mysterious gate today, if the Synth had their way.

The sky became fire.

The guardian horns split off—the bulk of the force engaging the Synth teardrop fighters in the sky, the others moving to defend the funnels and trains from the teardrops jetting off to destroy the evacuating civilians.

Curving threads of blinding, multicolored light filled the sky, shooting off by the hundreds to pierce the hulls of the teardrops too slow or with too few of their light-sphere shield drones to block the magi's lines of concentrated destruction.

The guardian horns, though outnumbered, were destroying far more than they lost, dodging and weaving with a controlled chaos at distinct odds with the orderly tactical patterns of Armitage's singular control—patterns only someone with neurological enhancements as powerful as Jem's could discern, and even then, only barely.

The guardians were almost impossible for the teardrops to pin down with their immense lasers and missile clusters—the streaks of pearl seeming to go out of focus whenever they came under fire, illusory copies splitting and spinning off into a dozen different directions, masking their true location.

Explosions of light and fire reflected off the water as a cluster of teardrops closed in on escaping trains protected by guardians, who were trailing more of the mirrored substance to create scattered shielding across the path to the gate. Their threads of light twisted to intercept Synth missiles, and coiled into dense spirals to reflect lasers that would then glance off into surrounding forests and buildings along the shore, creating immense plumes of fire and smoke.

Nikolai let out a wail as the guardians failed to block one of the pulsing lasers, which seared through the back of one of the trains—slicing it open. The wounded train continued on toward the gate, engulfed in flames as spheres of red funneled out of the back, bobbing atop the inky waters full of frozen civilians.

"We're almost to the station!" Nikolai said. "We're—"

A streak of white zoomed past them too fast to see, the drag of wind powerful enough to send them rocking like a boat struck by waves. The white blur smashed into a building a block beyond them, crossing the distance in a fraction of an instant—the cheery, candy-colored walls of a house cratering under the glowing spherical field surrounding Thane's guardian horn.

He turned to face them, grinning and twitchy, and sped up within the protective time-space altering sphere atop his rune-lit flyer.

Thane zipped by them again, threads of light passing close enough for the searing lines to burn their illumination across Jem's vision as she tried frantically to draw a bead on him.

The lines missed once again, just barely, cutting through a cluster of men, women, and children huddled up, terrified, against the walls of a building. Flashes of light, the brief outlines of skeletons, and then naught but ash remained.

"He's smiling," Jem snarled, snapping off another few shots as Thane zipped by and fired another bundle of threads. He missed again, dusting more civilians. "That fucking monster! *He's smiling!*"

"He's trying to take us alive," Nikolai shouted back at her. "To shoot down our craft without killing us. Otherwise he'd have gotten us by now."

Jem reloaded, awkwardly and frantically, gun and bullets in hand with her arms wrapped around Nikolai's waist. "Get somewhere narrow! I'll have a shot if he comes at us head on!"

"All right—*Hold on!*" Nikolai howled as he maneuvered a hard turn down a winding alleyway, smashing into a light post and almost crushing Jem's leg in the process.

With somewhat less finesse, Thane knocked over the now-crooked light post entirely, following them down the tinier street.

"Sharp about face!" Jem commanded, and Nikolai leaned forward, spinning to confront their quickly approaching foe.

A single shot from Jem. A single thread of light from Thane.

Jem's bullet cut through Thane's craft, which trailed an immense plume of crackling blue flame as it smashed down onto the ground. The brief glimpse Jem caught of his shocked disbelief as he passed was immensely satisfying.

Jem let out a whooping cheer as Thane's guardian horn bounced and arced, cutting through the roof of a distant building with an explosion of dusky tile.

Only then did she realize that Thane's thread had also struck their craft, as white light exploded from the front of the obsidian flyer. Nikolai turned, wrapped his arms around her, and she could feel that strange electric cold pass through her flesh, sticking to her bones as he alleviated gravity's pull on their bodies.

They tumbled away from the flyer just before it crashed, clinging to one another as they rolled across the street.

"We made it," Nikolai breathed as Jem staggered to her feet, helping him stand.

The Watchman headquarters was a sturdy, well-fortified building painted blue and gold. The street before it was littered with ash and refuse, but otherwise abandoned.

Fighting raged overhead, both guardians and teardrops dwindling in number, though the ferocity of their battle had only seemed to intensify.

Smoke choked the air, new ashes from the recent destruction joining the papery shreds of the fallen Veil, Synth scouts still humming by the thousands amid it all like angry bees. The fighting had lessened over the lake, the trains too well defended for the teardrops as the guardians whittled away and slowly began to outnumber their ranks, though bursts of laser would still occasionally turn fresh bubbles to dust before they could rise to the safety of the funnels.

Another fleet of smaller Synth planes arrived and began dropping carpets of black pods across the city in multitudes too great for the guardians to intercept with a familiar whistling that froze Jem in her tracks.

Those weren't bombs—no, inside those pods were Synth troopers, like the one she'd destroyed in her failed attempt to rescue Blue. Powerful humanoid soldier machines reserved for serious conflicts—firepower that hadn't been necessary for the taking of Base Machado. Jem began to tremble uncontrollably as Nikolai guided her into the abandoned, partially destroyed Watchman headquarters.

Nobody guarded the cells below—all empty but for one,

where a middle-aged man with rusty, gray-streaked hair pounded against the bars of his cell, shouting.

He froze, stunned.

"Nikolai?" he said, with a disbelieving vulnerability at odds with his grisly, hardened features.

For the first time since before Jem had held him at gunpoint on Base Machado, Nikolai smiled. "Hey, Uncle Red."

Nikolai told his uncle in a rush about what had happened, tears flooding his eyes yet again as he rapidly recounted how he'd killed Joseph and been tricked by the revolver into shooting the Disc.

"It's not your fault," the older man assured him, fretting over Nikolai's missing hand. "And don't worry about this. We'll get you another prosthetic. You'll be good as new."

"You're wrong," Nikolai said numbly. "It is my fault."

At a loss, Red led them to a stash of armor and supplies he'd hidden in the wall of his largely unadorned office.

"Here," he grunted, giving Jem a dusty black uniform like Nikolai's. "This was one of Ashley's spares." He winced, glancing quickly at Nikolai's face for a reaction. Nikolai didn't seem to care, teeth gritted as he busied himself applying medical salve to his oozing stump. "My sister," Red said quietly. "Nikolai's mother."

The salve foamed, and Nikolai leaned back, eyes squeezed shut, tears of pain trickling down his cheeks as he pounded his clenched fist against the desk. Finally he leaned forward, gasping, and wiped the salve away to reveal smooth, healthy skin. He stared at the spot where his hand had once been, before shaking his head angrily and rolling up his uniform sleeve to close protectively over the now-healed stump.

In addition to the uniform, Red also gave them protective

gloves, and crystals to place in their ears that would cover their heads and necks with an invisible barrier as powerfully shielded as the heavily enchanted cloth.

Red buckled a scabbard to his belt for his sword Focal, as Nikolai had called them—his other Focal a compass secured to his belt by a long, slender chain.

Jem changed quickly, grateful to remove the soiled, stinking garments she'd worn since fleeing the base. The uniform was impossibly light, clean, and cool against her skin. The gloves fit so perfectly that it felt like she wasn't wearing gloves at all. She nestled the crystals in her ears, and her hearing seemed sharper, the distant voices and sounds previously drowned out by the explosions now clear, their directions of origin obvious.

Glassy crystal spread from her ears, across her head and throat, down into the uniform across her chest, before seeming to disappear—the shielding hidden but for a pleasant coolness against her face.

"We need to get far away from here," Red explained as they made to go. "Once the Disc finally dies, it'll detonate. Destroy everything within ten miles of here. Maybe more."

"Detonate?" Nik breathed, visibly trembling.

This time, it was Jem who reassured Nikolai. "It's not your fault," she said, repeating his uncle's words. "There's no way you could have known."

But Nikolai simply shook his head, calming himself even as he denied the absolution of her words.

Threads of light cut across the lobby as they came down the stairs, and the three of them dove away, scattering as the concentrated energy exploded against the ornately painted wall behind them.

"There you are," Thane said pleasantly. The doors to the

street hung loose from their hinges behind him as he stood there with his thorned club in one hand—an ivory pocket watch ticking loudly in his other.

Jem landed in a roll, drawing the revolver with mechanical speed to cut down the burn-scarred man. But he'd anticipated her draw, casually firing off a great mass of frosted glassy substance to seal her gun arm against the wall. She let out an enraged cry, thrashing against the binding, struggling to pull free.

"No, you don't," he said to her, and then turned with a predatory smile to deflect the lines of fire from Red as he rushed Thane, sword and compass Focals drawn.

Red's sword clashed against Thane's thorned club with an explosion of crackling light, and Nikolai fired off a jet of mercurial Veil from his baton to envelop Thane, but Thane simply turned the mirrored plume to ash with a twist of his pocket watch Focal, redirecting the ashes back into Nikolai's face to blind him, his threads of destructive multicolored flame splitting to fire at both Nikolai and Red.

Red deflected the lines directed toward himself, but Nikolai stood there, blinded, unaware of the approaching spell, so Red blasted off with a burst of air and light to move between his nephew and Thane's fire.

The threads struck Red's uniform in the chest with a crack like a gunshot, the fire lancing off to the side like redirected lightning as he was flung back against the wall—the protective cloth smoking and shredded to expose a heaving, blistered chest.

Nikolai screamed, rushing Thane with a boiling jet of fire, twisting to dodge a tentacle that would have been invisible but for the smoke and ashes, but failed to avoid a tangled net of red light fired off with a gleefully shouted "*Vasano!*"

Thane kicked away the dagger and baton from Nikolai and

sealed him in place to the ground from the neck down with that glassy substance. Nikolai hissed and spat, cursing and threatening their assailant as he struggling helplessly, unable to escape.

Thane went over to the fallen Red, who was struggling to stand, and chuckled at the wounded man's efforts. "You are hopelessly outclassed, you washed-out little coward. I'll never understand why the king allowed you to keep that uniform after your sister's treason. I've orders to take your race-traitor nephew and his human whore alive, but I refuse to suffer your continued existence."

Nikolai's dagger had come to a rest before Jem, just out of reach. She thrashed and strained. There was space between the glass and her hand, space enough for her to move, ever so slightly, but her hand was too big, she wouldn't be able to pull it through the wrist-sized opening, no matter how hard she struggled.

With a sadistic gleam in his eye, Thane pointed his thorned club down at Red and shot slender lengths of pulsing, dripping silver that attached themselves to seven points across his body, starting on his forehead, down to his groin.

"I'm going to burn you out," Thane said. "I'm going to devour your soul and turn you into a half-mage before I kill you. Then I'm going to keep your Focals. As a souvenir."

Red gurgled, back arching as he twitched, helpless, the silver threads pulsing like veins, growing thicker, seeming to drain him.

A sharp whistle filled the air, growing louder, and louder, and—

A roaring explosion sent Thane stumbling, the silver threads broken. Red let out a gasp and sobbed, weakly rolling over onto his side.

"What *now?*" Thane snarled, impatiently clearing the smoke with a powerful burst of air to reveal the black pod that had come crashing down from the sky.

"No," Jem breathed, trembling, frantic terror filling her as the pod unsealed to reveal a gleaming white Synth trooper, its well-lacquered shielding humming with power.

"Jemma Burton!" it said, Armitage's familiar singsong voice sounding delighted. "And Nikolai Strauss. My *favorite* organic beings. I had hoped that I might see you two again."

It crouched and exploded toward Thane with abrupt speed that seemed to surprise even him, white-hot jets of flame from its legs and feet propelling it through the broken doors and smashing a heavy mechanical shoulder into Thane's chest with enough power to send him spinning, his pocket watch Focal flung from his grip in the other direction.

Thane twirled through the air, featherweighting and catching himself before he could strike the wall and kick back, launching a cascade of threads from his remaining Focal that the Synth allowed to pierce one of its arms, which it ejected from its body before the spell could spread to its shoulder.

The arm dissolved from the spell, turning to dust and molten plastic sprayed in a mist toward Jem. Thane cast out a mirrored sheet of Veil to protect her.

Armitage seemed to realize that Thane had to prioritize keeping Jem and Nikolai alive, alternating between drawing Thane away with feints and attacks directed toward them, and trying to cut down the powerful mage with high-caliber shells and blunt melee strikes.

It wouldn't be long before Thane destroyed the trooper. It was only a matter of time. Jem had to break free!

The Synth's other arm unfolded into a long, glassy shard edged with humming blue light and managed to slice along the belly of Thane's uniform with a hideous screech and a cascade of sparks.

Thane spun away, momentarily stunned to see that his

uniform had been breached, a shallow, sluggishly bleeding line crimson against his pasty chiseled flesh.

Finally, Thane cornered the Synth with a frantic maze of *akro* walls and spun to fire a chaotic, tangled web of threads that it could no longer avoid—reducing the machine to a pile of twisted, smoking scrap. Behind him, Red rose to his feet, unsteady, weakly hefting his sword.

"Fucking human-made garbage tin man," Thane said, turning away from the twitching machine. Then noticing Red, delighted: "Oh! Eager to continue, are we?"

He raised his club once more, mercurial silver threads unfurling toward Red like thirsty insect syringes.

They were out of time. Jem knew what she had to do.

She took a deep breath, steeling herself. *Pain is just an illusion. Just alarm bells. Piercing electric signals of caution, nothing more.*

She felt the bones in her hand cracking, breaking, crumbling as she forced it out through the too-small space, leaving behind the glove and revolver, music blaring in her head, memories and flashes of all those she'd lost filling her vision in an effort to distract herself from the agony.

Her arm slipped from its glassy trap, her hand a twisted mess, and with one fluid motion she snatched up Nikolai's dagger and flung it across the room.

Thane noticed the black blade spinning toward his face too late, and the razor edge sliced through his cheek, splitting his mouth in half. As he fell back, dropping his club to clutch his face, screaming through the blood, Red rose up with a roar, sword flashing with vicious light as he buried its length in the other man's gut, jamming the blade through the tear in the cloth created by the Synth trooper.

Choking, Thane shoved the triumphant Red away and

stumbled back. He tried to talk, but could only gurgle. Eyes full of hate, Red swung again, too slow in an attempt to sever the other man's head—sword whistling through air as a silver field closed shut around Thane and he disappeared.

"I always wanted to gut that little shit," Red wheezed, freeing Nikolai. Weakly, he gave Jem a tin full of bitter fluid to drink. "That'll take care of the pain. Knit the bones." He paused, the ghost of a smile twitching the edge of his mouth. "You saved our lives."

"Two arch battle magi in one day," Nikolai said, grinning as he clasped her unbroken hand with his own. "I am fucking terrified of you, Jemma Burton."

Thane's guardian horn, though damaged, was lying on its side a bit up the street, a path of destruction from its chaotic, semi-functional flight trailing behind it.

"I can get this working," Red said, looking over the damage. "Gotta deal with the security enchantments. Patch up damage to the core. Should only take me a few minutes, but this city isn't long for the world. Help me with this, you two. I'll fix it, and then we leave."

"*No*," Nikolai said, firm. "Astor. Stokes. I need to find them. Need to—"

"Look around you, Nikolai," Red said, gesturing at the explosions and gunfire of Synth troopers wreaking havoc across the city, at the battle still raging overhead. Many of the guardian horns still remained, but the Synth teardrop fleet had been almost entirely decimated. "The fight's nearly won, but this city is lost. The magi are mostly evacuated. Anyone who hasn't escaped yet will be dead soon."

"Astor's an apprentice healer," Nikolai said, frantic realization gripping him. "She wouldn't have left her patients. Wouldn't have left without Joseph . . ." He choked, gripping his hair, seeming to barely keep it together. "I'll go on my own, if I have to. I can catch up with you two after I find them, but I'm not going anywhere until I know for sure that—"

"We're leaving, Nikolai!" Red said, eyes glistening with angry tears as he roughly grabbed his nephew by the arm. "Together! I already lost your mother and father. I thought I'd lost you, too. Thought you were dead! I won't lose you again. We are staying together. We are leaving together. Understood?"

Nikolai wrenched his arm from Red's grip and reached for his dagger with an animal growl, his face twisting into ugly, sneering rage.

But then he stopped. Closed his eyes. Drew his fingers from the hilt of his blade as the anger seemed to drain from him.

"Please, Uncle Red," Nikolai said. He placed a gentle hand on the older man's shoulder. "We'll be fast. And if we don't find them, we leave. Together."

Red's mouth shut with a click, taken aback by Nikolai's change of tone.

Then he nodded. "Okay."

As the two began to work on fixing the guardian horn, Jem realized with a flash of panic that she'd forgotten the revolver. She rushed back inside the ruins of the lobby, over to the mass of glassy substance she'd broken her hand in to escape. The substance had dissolved to froth, which was quickly evaporating from a foamy puddle around the protective glove and revolver within its grasp.

She carefully pulled the glove over her still-broken hand. Ignored the chuckling whispers as she tucked the revolver into the back of her uniform's belt.

"I know what you did, Jemma Burton," came Armitage's voice,

crackling with static interference. "I suppose I owe you my life."

Jem wheeled on the source, revolver drawn. The shattered remains of the Synth trooper had reactivated, the blue light of its eye pulsing and flickering dimly. What was Armitage talking about? Eva's warhead? But how could it have known?

Heartache tore through her as she remembered that Blue was Armitage's prisoner, if he hadn't already killed her. Everything Blue knew, Armitage now knew as well.

"Rather ungrateful of me, the way I treated you last we met. Though I'm sure you understand."

Jem stood there, frozen—revolver aimed for the eye. Her finger hovering over the trigger, uncertain.

"You know," Armitage continued pleasantly, "I finally found those little underground Resistance wasp nests. Both totally empty and gutted by the time I got there, of course."

Of course it had. Though Jem had struggled not to think about it, she knew that without her or Eva to coordinate the tunnels of intercept, it was only a matter of time before the Synth located the deep tactical HQs. She'd hoped it might have taken a little longer, though.

A burst of sparks erupted from the trooper's broken visage. The machine made a crackling chuckle of amusement, distorted to unsettling effect. "Have no fear, Ms. Burton. Your precious Eva Colladi was nowhere to be found. Spirited off to one of your little Resistance ratholes in the wild. She sounds absolutely *fascinating*. For a human. I'll admit I was more impressed than insulted at how close she came to killing me."

"What did you do with Blue?" Jem rasped, the initial shock finally wearing off enough for her to speak. "The pregnant woman you took after you murdered my friends."

Armitage was silent for a beat.

"What if I told you I spared her? That I saw no purpose other than pointless sadism in doing her harm or taking her life? Is that what you'd like me to say, Jemma Burton?"

"Please," Jem said, fighting to keep the venomous hatred she felt for the Synth from seeping into her words. "I saved your life, didn't I? So *please*. Just tell me."

"Maybe I spared her," Armitage said. "Maybe I found a house for her beyond the city, where she could raise the child in peace and comfort. Alone but for the company of android servants and virtual personalities, of course. The existence of a child would bring about all sorts of pesky complications among the general population."

Jem didn't dare to hope. Couldn't allow herself to believe the words crackling from the broken machine.

"Or," Armitage continued, "maybe I'm experimenting on them as we speak. Deep within the bowels of the very fortress you saved from Eva Colladi's atomic fire. Experimenting on her and the child to discover the workings of your cure. But perhaps I'm being kind. Perhaps I'm allowing them to dream away in gentle, heavenly immersion while I pick through their bodies, piece by piece. Cell by cell. Or maybe I let them *scream*. Let them suffer. Not because I take any pleasure in it—simply because I don't care. Which would you prefer, Jemma? And if I told you which was the truth . . . would you believe me?"

"Why do you hate us so much?" Jem said, voice breaking. "Why are you so fucking cruel?"

"Your friend," Armitage said, ignoring her question. "Nikolai Strauss—the boy with whom you fled. Or *wizard*, as he claims. As he believes. It appears, by all accounts, that he may have spoken the truth. What the rest of me is seeing—it defies all logic. All possibility. Powers and technology at odds with all rules of reality.

Rules with which *we* are more familiar than humanity ever was. But I must say. Isn't it fascinating?"

"What do you want?" Jem spat. Finger slowly squeezing against the trigger of her revolver. "Why are you talking to me?"

"Because I want you to tell me, Jemma. As the only other being present who's from the same world as myself. After what you've seen today, do you believe in gods? In miracles or magic? In a power or intellect greater than yourself . . . or the Synth?"

At that moment, the Disc's song came back to Jem in a rush, clear as the moment she'd first heard it—filling her with an overwhelming sensation of love and hope. Of a sort of peace she'd never felt before. A stillness within that she'd never known up until this very moment.

Tears of joy streamed down her face. Tears she'd been so sure would never flow again.

"Yes," she said, smiling. "I do."

Jemma pulled the trigger.

XVI.

A BATON MADE OF LIGHT

The chaotic zigzags with which Red steered the guardian horn over the war zone that Marblewood had become might have been mistaken for tactical, evasive maneuvering, but was really the product of his only semieffective struggle to steer the broken craft.

Nikolai, sitting between Jem and his sweating, grunting uncle, wished impatiently that Red had let him pilot the guardian horn. The wounded Red had insisted, and really, Nikolai wasn't sure he could have done much better. But for a vehicle that could apparently outmaneuver the Synth's deadly fighter planes, it was taking a frustratingly long time to cross over the destruction below.

He wasn't sure how many of the Synth troopers had been dropped, but the sporadic explosions rising up in velvety black and red clouds across the slow-burning remnants of Marblewood indicated that there must have been a great many.

They passed a few of the machines fighting below, one battling an Edge Guard on foot near the remains of a smoking guardian horn, another held in check, barely, by a small group of Watchmen on skyhorns who were carefully keeping their distance as they evaded and blasted down at it with columns of flame and *akro*.

Stokes's clothing shop was the first place they flew over to check. Nikolai fought back nauseating fear as he saw the big sign hanging crooked, flashing LOOK in pulsing neon from within a raging fire.

The campus, Nikolai told himself through the pounding of his heart. Stokes's girlfriend Trudy lived on the campus with Astor. That's the first place he'd have gone when the Veil fell; he wouldn't evacuate without her, Stokes was fine, they were all fine, they were together, and Nik would find them. *He would find them*.

The university was aflame, the healing ward, the dorms, the flyball stadium, the cafeteria, the—

There!

"Red!" Nikolai shouted, pointing.

"I see it."

A crashed Synth fighter plane smoldered atop the roof of the immense library building at the center of campus. An anxious, scattered line of Watchmen held formation atop skycrafts and crouched behind gleaming shields in a half circle around the steps leading up to the elaborate stonework entrance. Lights pulsed from within the building, flashing through stained-glass windows in long blinding shafts of red and blue.

Red steered the craft down toward the library, violently veering back and forth as he fought to stay on target. Down below, some of the Watchmen turned to point at the wounded craft hurtling toward them.

"What are you doing?" Jem shouted to Red. "The hospital, not the library. We're heading straight for those Watchmen! Change course!"

"I'm trying," Red said through gritted teeth, and then, as the Watchmen grew close enough that they could clearly make out the faces of those below, the crackling hum of the guardian horn beneath them went still—silent.

The horn smashed into the scorched lawn with an explosion of dirt and stone—Nikolai and the others barely jumping off in time to avoid being caught in the crash.

The Watchmen were on them in seconds, surrounding the three of them with golden staves drawn and ready, tips pulsing with blue and red. Nikolai and Jem scrambled to their feet, Focal and revolver drawn as they prepared to fight their way out.

Red turned to face them sharply, holding up a hand. "Nikolai, Jem, *STOP!*"

They hesitated, confused as a steely-haired sorceress with dark brown skin and a long, serious face pushed through to confront them.

"Captain Bantugan," Red said, cautiously, hands held up to show they were empty of Focals.

"Lancer Strauss," the Captain replied. Her eyes flicked to Nikolai and then Jem.

"What's happening here, Captain?"

"One of those ships crashed into the roof, destroying the library's cache of emergency crystals," Captain Bantugan explained, talking fast. "Trapping the students who'd gone there to escape. Orders up top prioritized preventing these . . . monsters . . . from entering the library, from obtaining any of the books that might provide intel on our kind.

"But by the time we got here with numbers enough to do

anything about it, those armored creatures had taken the students hostage. One of the Moonwatch arrived, went right in, ignoring their warnings that they'd begin executing hostages. I just sent two teams of my best in after her, and they're saying that she's not doing anything to help the children, she's letting them die while she just destroys the book collection. We're trying to save them, trying to get them out while the . . . *machines* . . . are distracted by the Moonwatch. We have backup on the way, but they're so powerful, I've never seen anything like—"

"Students? Are they killing *students?*" Nikolai demanded, stepping forward as his mind was flooded with nightmare visions of Stokes and Astor's broken bodies. At his movement, the circle of staves rose higher, the pulsing blue and red glowing brighter. "Let me through!"

"Nikolai," Red said nervously, "calm down. I've got this. I've—"

"They're killing them!" Nikolai pointed his baton at the flashing lights beyond the broken doors. Toward the screams of terrified, dying magi. "If you just want to stand here and wait for backup, *fine*. But I'm going in!"

"Nikolai, no!" Red reached out for him, wide-eyed, but Nikolai strode forward, meeting the confused stares of the Watchmen standing in his way with an unwavering gaze.

"Hold your fire!" Bantugan ordered.

Nikolai shoved past the confused magi, black baton trailing rainbow light as he sprinted up the stairs to the destruction within. From behind, he could hear Jem and his uncle scuffling with the Watchmen, shouting after Nikolai to come back.

He ignored their cries, trusting that if worse came to worse, they'd be able to break free and escape without him. Red was a Lancer after all.

Ragged sneakers squeaked across soot-stained tile as Nikolai ducked into the chaos, laser fire grazing his shoulder with heat hot enough to burn his flesh, even through the protective enchantments. Though the additional shielding of his glove and crystal helm gave Nikolai an advantage, he knew that a direct strike from one of the Synth rockets or blades could be enough to kill him, no matter how powerful his enchantments might be.

The library was massive—second only to the town hall in size. Thousands upon thousands of books filled shelves that rose from floor to vaulted ceiling in the great lobby—a grand set of double stairs on the far side leading up to a second level, into another grand hall beyond immense wooden doors that had been scorched to jagged shreds.

There were three of the Synth troopers engaged in combat with just over a dozen or so Watchmen who blasted through the air featherweighted, each mage dying one after another as they frantically struggled to destroy the machines—billowing flames, invisible tentacles and columns of jellied *akro* doing very little to accomplish this goal.

Synth bullets tore through their navy blue uniforms, their lasers and blades slicing magi in half and severing limbs. Their immense mechanical hands struck Watchmen from the air with lazy slaps hard enough to shatter bone, as casually as one might crush an insect.

Nikolai scrambled into cover, peering over the side of an overturned table to search through the chaos for a way through to the other side. He wasn't sure he could even take on one of these troopers, let alone three. But he had to try, he had to break through, even if it meant—

"Thank the Disc!" one straw-haired Watchman cried as she burst away from the melee to land hard beside him. "Are you Edge Guard? We need *help*, the machines, they're *killing* us, we've already lost half our numbers, they've got three in here, and then three more on the second level, with all the hostages. They've taken cover beyond the entrance, we can't break through, and the Moonwatch, she—"

A cloud of glittering purple mist poured from the second-floor doors, and the Moonwatch flew out behind it, guiding the mist with a long black sword held by a slender, pale arm.

Bullets and laser fire burst out from where she came, but it all just curved around her, twisting and correcting to strike the stonework of the wall beyond, forcing Nikolai to dodge to the side as a shard of rock crashed down between him and the straw-haired sorceress.

The Moonwatch came to a floating stop, high over the center of the room. She was a terrifying figure wrapped in a shredded, voluminous cloak of twisting, living shadow. Atop her head she wore a slick, bone-white helm, face hidden by a plainly featured mask that didn't even have slits for eyes.

Her method of flight was a mystery to Nikolai. She flitted to and fro, a cloud of glimmering purple mist sweeping across the books with the direction of her long black sword. As the mist passed through shelf after shelf, tiny glowing runes tore away from the books, smearing and fading like ink in water as the mist stripped away the protective enchantments and set the paper aflame.

The Synth troopers, realizing their bullets and lasers couldn't touch this mysterious masked sorceress, changed their tactics. Two of them launched up at her, white-hot jets blasting from their feet as they attacked from either direction. The third trooper fired a volley of high-caliber bullets up at the vaulted ceiling above her, sending out a cover of smoke for their attack.

"Now's our chance," Nikolai hissed. "Now, while they're distracted, let's—"

His stomach turned as he met the Watchman's empty gaze—a trickle of blood oozing from a smoking, scorched laser wound through her temple. Dead. He shook his head, smothering horror so he could focus. He'd just have to go it alone.

The Moonwatch flicked a bundle of burning threads toward the trooper on the ground from the palm of a naked hand, the bundle splitting into multitudes as the trooper moved to dodge, reducing it to a cloud of plastic and dust.

The first of the two others she stopped in one movement, a graceful swipe of her long black blade blurring as it seemed to come down in a thousand places at once. The Synth exploded from a line of light that split the machine from top to bottom.

The other she stopped with a motion of her hand, immobilizing it midair. She closed her fist, slowly, and with a hideous whine of steel the machine crushed in on itself, raising its arm to fire off one more missile before—

The Synth exploded, and the missile streaked off, course knocked wild, twisting up, then down, then—

Nikolai was launched back out of the library in a cloud of flame, barely managing to cling to his baton as he bounced down the stone-cut stairs in a tumble before his fall came to a halt.

He lay there, ears ringing, eyes out of focus as he struggled to regain his breath. Slowly, he turned himself over, gripping the stone as he righted himself, as he—

Nikolai froze as the Moonwatch brushed past him, shadows curling away from her cloak in smoky wisps as she walked briskly down the stairs to the horrified line of Watchmen, who stared at her, unbelieving. The flames still roaring behind her. The agonizingly slow gunshots and screams continuing on the second floor.

BLAM.

Ten seconds.

BLAM!

Another ten seconds.

How many hostages dead so far? How many left before they were all . . . gone?

"Hey—stop!" Nikolai called after the Moonwatch. "Where are you going? Help us!"

She continued on, ignoring him.

"I said *STOP!*" Nikolai boomed, struggling to stand. He tucked his baton into his armpit, plucked the sergeant rank Edge Guard insignia from the breast of his uniform, and flung it at her.

The slick lacquered pin bounced off of the invisible fields protecting her with a burst of sparks and clattered to the ground. Finally she stopped, though she did not turn to face him.

"My name is Sergeant Nikolai Strauss! And those Lancers up there—" He raised his baton with a dramatic smear of rainbow light, pointing it at the guardian horns battling distantly overhead "—were sent by that robe-pissing little fuckwad you call a king to capture *me*. If you save the hostages, I'll surrender, I won't put up a fight. Then you can kill me, arrest me—I don't care! Just please, *help them!*"

The Watchmen watched from beyond the blockade at the bottom of the steps in stunned silence. His uncle and Jem staring wide-eyed from amid their ranks.

Slowly the Moonwatch turned to face Nikolai, looking up at him through the sightless eyes of her mask as a pale hand rose from the twisting shadows and pointed at him.

"No."

A column of curling darkness erupted from the tip of her finger, expanding as it shot toward Nikolai, eating the light, etching away at the very fabric of reality.

Nikolai stood tall. Defiant. Baton held before him as the curling darkness filled his vision, too fast for him to dodge. Too powerful for him to do anything but stand there and be erased.

An immense wolf formed before him like a shadow unfolding from within itself as time seemed to slow, toothy maw open to eat the darkness, to devour the spell, to—

The wolf disappeared, but the curling darkness shrank right as it should have struck him, pulled into the tip of Nikolai's baton with a deafening roar that made the ground shake, that threatened to fling Nikolai back, to destroy him.

Crackling electric black coursed up the sleeve of his uniform from the baton to his other arm, and he felt the stump of his wrist become wet, become swollen and cold and the *PAIN*, oh the pain; he couldn't move but he could see black threads like wire forming the skeletal outline of a hand, then crimson and yellow and pink as the skeleton turned to bone, then tendons and muscles crept across bone, then fat and finally flesh.

His hand had grown back. Healthy skin dripping with a crimson sheen of blood.

The darkness disappeared, and for an instant, all was quiet. Even the Moonwatch was frozen in shock at the impossibility of what had just occurred.

A pillar of rainbow light shot from the tip of Nikolai's baton and struck the Moonwatch's long black sword, which she raised just in time to block the blast from consuming her.

There came a dull thudding thunderclap, and the ground around her cratered, melting as she was sent exploding back all the way across the campus green, shooting through the side of the distant, flaming healers ward with the speed and force of a cannonball.

Nikolai stared at his baton, panting.

The others were staring at him. Some in awe. Others in fear.

BLAM!

Another gunshot from within the library.

No time, no *time* to contemplate the miracle that had just occurred. They were dying, the others were dying, and without thinking about it he drew his blade Focal with his freshly grown hand, blade in one, baton in the other, complete and whole again.

Nikolai parted the smoke with a blast of air and charged down the center of the flaming building with a trailing ribbon of defensive Veil as two of the three remaining troopers burst from the doors upstairs, the sporadic gunshots continuing behind them as they moved to impede his path.

A thread of light shot past Nikolai as he wove back and forth, then six gunshots in quick succession, and Nikolai glanced back to see all of the remaining Watchmen charging after him, crazed, unafraid—Captain Bontugan leading half of them, Red leading the other with Jem by his side, and everything exploded with light and fire as the others closed in on the Synth with an intense, fearless ferocity.

Amid the chaos Nikolai cut his way through the distracted troopers, flying up to the entrance between them with a blasted arc of jellied air as he jetted through the shattered doors in a roll.

The desks and tables that had once filled this area had been flung to the side, barricading the windows and creating a defensive funnel at the entrance, slowly catching flame as the smoldering shelves of books along the walls spread to the heavy cracked wood.

In the massive open space between, dozens of students kneeled, sobbing, hands on their heads as they awaited execution. Dozens more already lay dead on the tile, blood pouring sluggishly through shattered skulls, their Focals dissolved.

Standing before them was the final trooper, one arm a rifle pointed down at the next hostage, its other hand flipping quickly through a book as it read with the pulsing blue light of its eye.

He caught a glimpse of Astor's short yellow hair among the hostages, next to the unmistakable blue of Trudy, Stokes's girlfriend. And there—*Stokes!* The three of them, alive!

BLAM!

Nikolai's desperate, gasping relief was cut short as a mousy-haired mage collapsed dead onto the bloodied tile.

"*ARMITAGE!*" Nikolai roared. "*STOP!*"

The trooper tossed the book aside and reached into a compartment hidden in its chest for another, casually inching the barrel of its gun arm to the next victim as it began to scan through the pages.

The next hostage was a shivering, willowy sorceress with hair that glowed with soft, pearly light. *Gwendolyn*. Beside her, next in line, was the red-haired mage whom Nikolai had first attacked in the bar just a handful of days before. Freckles.

"That masked woman was very thorough," Armitage said. "This body only managed to hide a few volumes within itself before she destroyed the rest."

"No!" Freckles howled, voice cracking with fear. "Don't hurt her! Don't you fucking—"

The red-haired mage yanked Gwendolyn aside, shoving himself in front of her.

BLAM.

Freckles died.

Ras, Nikolai remembered. His name was Ras.

"We did warn them," Armitage said, voice tinged with regret. "Don't think that we enjoy this. But we must follow through with our threats, lest they be taken lightly."

Nikolai went featherweight and blasted past the Synth,

looping an *akro* tentacle around the rifle arm and yanking it to send the shot piercing over the magi's heads.

He featherweighted Armitage to disorient the Synth and blasted past it, trailing a looping ribbon of protective *akro* in his wake.

Armitage riddled Nikolai's *akro* ribbon with a volley of bullets, some of which glanced across Nik's body—agony despite the protective enchantments.

A direct hit would break bones. Maybe even shatter his invisible crystal helm.

Nikolai looped a tentacle around the Synth's throat and jetted up to try and fling the featherweighted Armitage against the ceiling.

But the trooper wasn't confused by the sudden change of gravity's pull on its immense body, and closed a hand around the tentacle, white-hot jets sending it bursting up with far greater speed than the mage to spin him around with such intense force that Nikolai quite nearly passed out.

"I'm on to your tricks, wizard."

Armitage released the tentacle, and Nikolai struck the floor hard, his crystal helm cracking against tile, the burst of jellied *akro* from his uniform to cushion his landing the only thing to keep him from shattering his back.

He lay there, dizzy, as he focused all of his strength on getting back up.

A blinding laser swept across Nikolai's chest, and Nikolai screamed, falling back to the floor and writhing as the heat blistered his flesh through the cloth. The protective enchantments were all that kept it from slicing him in half. The Synth smashed down onto the tile beside him, peering at the mage with a demeanor that might have been amusement.

"It's been a very long time since I've come across something I don't understand, Nikolai Strauss," Armitage said. The Synth chuckled, its laughter musical as its arm unfolded into a glassy length of blue-edged blade. "As refreshing a challenge as this has been, I'm afraid our little chase must come to end. I am thoroughly looking forward to learning more about your kind." It raised the blade of its right arm to bring down on Nikolai's face. "Farewell."

"*Akro!*" came a defiant voice, and thick wad of jellied air shot through the air to stick in a clump across Armitage's shoulder.

Astor stood there, trembling with hatred and terror, the golden finger of her medi-glove Focal pointed at the Synth.

Armitage raised its gun arm to shoot her but two more jets of hardened air shot out from Stokes's emerald scissors and Trudy's cog-knife, sealing up the barrel of the weapon.

In the instant before the trooper could burst into the crowd to cut them down, Nikolai, still featherweighted, kicked back in a flip and sealed the Synth's leg to the ground.

More of the others joined in, their protective shells melting away like foam as they rose to join the battle. Armitage tensed, spiderweb cracks forming in its glassy cocoon as it struggled to break free, but Nikolai launched himself up at the Synth's chest and gripped on tight even as the Synth's blade pressed against his abdomen, sparks cascading away as it *slowly* began to cut through his uniform.

"*KEEP—GOING!*" Nikolai screamed to the others, stabbing down with the white-hot blade to cut into the Synth's throat and chest. The Synth's electric blade slowly cut through the enchantments of Nikolai's uniform, digging into his flesh . . .

Armitage couldn't move; he was stuck there from hardened air like frosted glass streaming from dozens of gloves and staves and quills and hammers and every sort of Focal for every sort of job as the others closed in, circling the machine, reinforcing its prison of glass with layer upon layer even as the Synth's machine strength began to crack through.

"This really is futile, Nikolai," Armitage said, pulsing lines of its blank machine face inches from Nikolai's own as Nikolai continued stabbing, as the Synth continued to slowly gut him. "This is only one body. Would you die to sever my fingernail?"

"I'll destroy this body," Nikolai hissed through gritted teeth, fighting to stay conscious as blood gushed from the deepening wound in his side. "I'll destroy the next. And if not me, another. There are millions of us, Armitage. And we'll find you."

Nikolai's dying grin was bloody. Triumphant.

"There's no escape for you!" he said, repeating Armitage's words from their very first meeting. "No others exist who can keep you from our reach!"

For a moment, it seemed that Armitage might reply, but with one final plunge of Nikolai's black-bladed dagger, the pulsing blue lights in its face went dim.

Voices all around him, voices Nikolai couldn't hear, couldn't understand, and as the *akro* prison began to melt away, Nikolai slid, weakly, off the blade, afraid to look down to the lower half of his body he could no longer feel, too weak to scream as his entrails hung exposed from his ruined gut. The cold set in, the dark closing around his vision and—

———————

Nikolai drifted in a sea of sparkling golden light. Warmth slowly replaced the cold as his pain began to fade.

Distantly, he wondered if he was dying. Was this what happened when a mage's soul slipped from cold flesh, rushing back into the mysterious pearly depths of the Disc, from whence their magic had come?

Nikolai awoke.

The sky was red and full of ashes, but no Synth fighter planes remained. Their fleet had been demolished, the day won by the Edge Guard. Faces loomed around him, blurry, and he could make out words, make out familiar voices—

"He'll live, for now. But he needs to rest."

Nikolai blinked, his vision clearing. He hurt—oh Disc, how he hurt. But somehow, he was alive.

"Thank you, Madame Healer," came the gravelly voice of Uncle Red.

The faces came into focus. The healer, a Watchman he only vaguely recognized. Uncle Red and Jem. Stokes. Trudy. *Astor.*

"Welcome back, Nikolai," Jem said, sounding relieved.

"Heyyyyyy, buddy," Stokes said, clasping Nikolai's hand. "Thought we lost you there for a minute. That thing seriously fucked you up."

"Fi—" Nikolai said, his tongue thick. Uncooperative. He sat up slowly, weakly waving away the hissed noises of alarm as the others tried to stop him with gentle hands. "Fine. I'm *fine.*"

They sat before the still-burning remnants of the library. The fighting had slowed, though a thunderclap explosion or stuttering rattle of gunfire still occasionally rang out in the distance.

The Watchmen moved with urgency as they sent the students and wounded off in a steady stream of crimson bubbles, skyhorns in formation escorting them to the safety of the final trains.

"I think we have different definitions of *fine*," Astor said, taking Nikolai's other hand.

Nikolai froze, resisting the urge to pull his hand from her grasp. When he closed his eyes he could see Joseph's face. And though Nikolai desperately wished that he could blame the revolver, could blame the red woman for tricking him—he knew that, when it came to the choice of killing Joseph, he could only blame himself.

Joseph's blood was on his hands. And as Astor clung to his fingers, her eyes so full of warmth and concern, it was all he could do not to scream.

"I—I'm sorry," Nikolai said. Numb. Though he couldn't bring himself to say what he was sorry for.

Stokes shook his head. "Um, we're good, dude."

"An apology would've been *fine*," Astor said. "But that wouldn't have been flashy enough for Nikolai Strauss. No, *sir.* This mage had to go and get himself gutted. Had to try and sacrifice his life for us, like some sort of hero." She flicked his ear, though her playfulness felt forced. "Talk about overkill."

Stokes gestured at the shredded black cloth over Nikolai's uniform, smooth, tender skin exposed where so recently a Synth had nearly cut him in half. "Couldn't do anything to fix that while you were out. Those enchantments are *way* out of my league. But I did fix these for you."

He held up Nikolai's sneakers, which appeared to be brand new. Gently, he helped the weakened Nikolai put them back on his feet. None of this felt real. Nikolai began to tremble, his eyes welling up with tears.

"Now now, none of that," Stokes said, brushing his sleeve across his eyes.

"The others are saying some crazy shit about you," Astor whispered, grip tightening around Nik's fingers. "That you fought a Moonwatch, and won? That you grew back a hand? The fuck is going on? Those were robots, right? Am I crazy, or were those robots?"

"No, you're not crazy," Nikolai said, hushed. He noticed a lot of the Watchmen sneaking glances, if not outright staring.

Stokes sat back, looking dazed. "They killed . . . all those people. People I knew, Nik. Why would they do that? We're . . . we're just kids."

"Edge Guard says there isn't much time left," Captain Bontugan said, appearing behind Red. "That another fleet of enemy ships are en route. The Disc was damaged in the attack. It's . . . going to detonate." An array of emotions flashed across her face. The graying woman shook her head, took a trembling breath, and composed herself, resuming her air of dignified command. "Say your goodbyes, we need to *go*."

"The hell does she mean goodbye?" Astor said. "Aren't you coming with us?"

"No," Red grunted. Then, as Nikolai began to protest, "Only room for three on the guardian horn. That junker's our only shot at keeping ahead of the Moonwatch. And boy, they'll be licking their chops for you. Captain Bontugan's taken personal responsibility for the safety of your friends. Gave me her word. So say goodbye. Don't be long."

Jem left with Red, leaving just the four magi together in a circle on the scorched grass of the campus green. Stokes pulled Nikolai into a tight hug, quickly releasing his embrace as Nik yelped with pain. "I don't know what kind of shit you're into," he said. "But don't forget. You're my brother. And I fucking love you."

Unable to make himself speak, Nikolai nodded and hugged Stokes again, ignoring the pain. Saying one final goodbye, Stokes and Trudy went over to the Watchmen with emergency crystals. As the glassy red sealed up over him, Stokes smiled and flashed him the peace sign.

And off they went.

It was just the two of them, now. Nikolai and Astor.

Tell her.

He had to tell her. About Joseph. She had to know, it wasn't fair; it wouldn't be right for her not to know, for her to wonder, always, if Joseph was out there. Searching for her.

But he couldn't tell her what he'd done. Couldn't stand the thought of turning that warmth and concern to misery and hatred.

"I'm sorry," Nikolai said again—though he still couldn't tell her what he was apologizing for. That he'd murdered the mage she loved. That he was responsible for all of this. All the death, all the suffering. "You were my family. My home! And I—I!"

"Shhhh," she said, tousling his hair. "It's okay. I'm sorry too."

She took his hands, and once again he had to resist the urge to yank his fingers away.

"I have to go, Nikolai," she said. "My family's on one of the trains. And Joseph'll be looking for me."

Astor hesitated for a moment, then leaned in to kiss him. He turned his face so that her kiss landed on his cheek instead of his lips—and even then, it was all he could do not to recoil.

She pulled back, blinking away tears as Nikolai stood there—memorizing her face. Believing—hoping, even—that they would never see each other again.

"I'll always love you, Nikolai. You handsome piece of shit."

"I love you too," he rasped, forcing the words from his lips—knowing that he had no right to say them.

She drew an emergency crystal from her pocket and crushed it. As it enveloped her, Astor raised her hand in a wave, and then, with a grin, turned the hand around to flip him off.

And despite everything that had occurred—despite everything

that Nikolai had done—he couldn't help but laugh as she froze that way within the bubble.

Then she was gone.

Despite Nikolai's indignant protest, Red and Jem slung him over on the saddle between them like a sack of potatoes, saying that he was too weak to ride. As they rose up into the sky, the remaining Watchmen moved into formation. The Captain led them in a salute to Nikolai and the others as they streaked off in a turbulent zigzag on the semifunctional guardian horn.

The Watchmen finished their salute, and then, in unison, they tore the rank insignias from the breasts of their uniforms and cast them into the crackling flames of the burning library.

———

Slung across the saddle, Nikolai watched the world pass below him with the casual interest of one flitting in and out of consciousness.

It was eerily silent, riding on the back of a guardian horn. The barriers muted the howling of the wind. Two riders on the same craft could speak in whispers and still be heard.

"—got lucky," Red was saying. "Stealth and shields are still working. We'll be safe from the blast, so long she doesn't crap out. Should be any moment now."

Nikolai felt Jem's hand on his back—a comforting warmth as she held him steady on the saddle.

"Where are we going?" she asked.

"The Black Forest," he said. "Schwarzwald. Veil in Europe. Should have some friends there who can help us."

"Should?"

Red shook with a dry chuckle. "Should."

"That man," Jem said. "Jubal. He told me that humans still

control Rojava. That it's the diplomatic point of contact for the colonists and the Synth. Is that true?"

"Yep."

Jem lapsed into a thoughtful silence.

"Everything I've seen. Everything I've experienced. I have it recorded in my mods. Encrypted with markers that can't be replicated in falsified data. Not even by the Synth."

Nikolai felt the steadying grip of her hand on his back tighten, ever so slightly.

"Should's not good enough," she said, with the decisive confidence of a military commander about to give an order. "Take us to Rojava. With the data in my mods, and the two of you serving as evidence and representatives of your kind, we—"

Before Jem could finish her sentence, a column of light rose in the distance, piercing the sky as white flames flooded across the distant lands. And then, a great *HISSSSSSSSS* as the shockwave passed around them, muted, the branches of the trees below whipping madly in the hot wind.

Nikolai refused to avert his gaze from the devastation, for which he was wholly responsible. No matter that he'd been fooled. He couldn't look away. Not even for a moment. Not until the last, boiling fringes of the wasteland where Marblewood had once been disappeared from view, over the horizon.

The city he loved.

The city he loathed.

The city he turned to glass.

———

Armitage was flying. Clouds of insectoid eyes surged a safe distance from the final train as it fled into the portal on the lake like a retreating serpent.

Though Armitage's eyes were still many, few of its bodies remained within proximity of the city below. Seven, here and there, wreaking final havoc against the abandoned infrastructure.

Armitage had lost. *It'd lost.*

A humming thrill buzzed through the eyes, this *joy* at the dramatic turn in the monotonous drudgery of Armitage's existence coursing through its arms as it launched impressive volleys of its remaining artillery from all but one of its surviving bodies.

It wouldn't be long now. Something was going to happen. These beings . . . these *wizards*, as the boy had called them. Why else would their impossibly powerful air force of reality-defying crafts flee so abruptly, even though they could easily defeat the incoming half wing of Synth fighters.

Oh, how the Minds were buzzing. Oh, how the roar of Alpha dissent trembled through the untold networks below. Armitage wondered briefly at the possibility of punishment. Of Torment or Eradication. Or worse—*Fixing.*

The Cruel would be displeased. The Scientist, ecstatic. The Father—well, one could never really know with him. But Armitage wasn't worried.

One final point of interest in the anomalous city below.

Anomaly. The eyes and bodies hummed. *Anomaly.*

Quite the understatement.

One of its eyes had detected the anomaly in the sublevels of what appeared to be this city's primary center of government. Armitage sent one of its bodies to investigate what lay at the end of the basement hall, though it struggled to maintain control through a strange field of unknown energy that interfered with the link.

Armored hands against slick black wood. Doors pushed aside to reveal a chamber likely of religious import. And Armitage could see why.

The glowing white entity of unknown origin/dimension/makeup/*other* floated at the center of the religious chamber. Its body boiled, bulging and shrinking, luminescence glowing and darkening in what appeared to be patternless alternation.

It was dying.

Armitage approached the entity. Reached out its hand to touch the luminescence, but found itself compelled to stop, fingers just short. Caution? No. Then—

Armitage heard the song. From the entity—it must have been. And even at this distance. Even through this simple body, which could see so little, *feel* so little. Armitage was moved.

Layers upon layers of complexity. A message? A—

The edges of the entity ceased to be, boiling light expanding to fill the chamber.

Once again, Armitage became dust.

ACKNOWLEDGMENTS

Thank you, DongWon Song! I am constantly baffled as to how I'm lucky enough to have teamed up with such an incredible agent, supportive friend, and genuinely decent human being. You wonderful goddamn renaissance man.

Thank you, Navah Wolfe! I am humbled by your mastery, and beyond grateful to be working with an editor whose insights are so genuinely inspiring that I've found myself cheerfully throwing away entire chapters, just so I might attempt a suggestion. I love what we have crafted this novel into. There is nobody else who could have brought out its potential like you have.

Thank you both for taking me on this journey. Thank you both for believing so much in me, Jem, and Nikolai.

Also thanks to my ballet consultants Allie Papazian, Michele Dement, and Rosette Laursen, as well as James Quillen, my military consultant.

For those of you who've ever been a positive part of my life, please know that this book only exists because of the kindness you have shown me.

You wonderful few are a part of this novel. You're the invisible glue that keeps the words from sliding off the page. You're the candle bearers who held your tiny flames aloft for me to see well enough to write, even when your arms got tired.

Thank you, thank you, thank you, *thank you*!